Two Weeks' Notice

Revivalist Series

Book Two

Rachel Caine

Allison & Busby Limited
13 Charlotte Mews
London W1T 4EJ
www.allisonandbusby.com

First published in Great Britain by Allison & Busby in 2012.

A CIP catalogue record for this book is available from
the British Library.

10 9 8 7 6 5 4 3 2 1

ISBN 978-0-7490-1232-8

Typeset in 11.5/16.25 pt Sabon by
Allison & Busby Ltd.

The paper used for this Allison & Busby publication
has been produced from trees that have been legally sourced
from well-managed and credibly certified forests.

Printed and bound by
CPI Group (UK) Ltd, Croydon, CR0 4YY

To my dear friend, and superhero,
Rosemary Clement-Moore. Just because.

CHAPTER ONE

It was a perfect day for a funeral. Overcast, cool, no rain; sweaters, not coats. The wind was light and fresh, and although fall had arrived (as much as it ever did, in California) the grass remained a bright jewel green.

From a purely objective perspective, it couldn't have been better . . . though, in truth, Bryn Davis, funeral director, didn't much care for the cemetery itself. This was a modern-style interment facility, so instead of picturesque Gothic headstones or marble sculptures there were long expanses of lawn, spreading trees, and gently rolling hills – the impression of undisturbed nature, but oh so carefully created. Except for the recessed vases, some holding bright bouquets of flowers, it might have been a golf course. She wouldn't have been at all surprised to see a cart roll over the hill and someone line up a difficult five-iron shot past the tent that covered the mourners and casket.

But then, she didn't have to like this place, really; that was the family's burden. She just had to give the impression of calm dignity as she stood with her hands folded. Until the ceremony was finished, her job was on hold – Mr Raines' remains had been processed and prepped, dressed and finished; the coffin had been sealed and carefully polished (nothing worse than seeing sweaty fingerprints on the shiny surface); flowers and memorial handbooks had been delivered and arranged; hearses and limousines had been freshly washed, stocked with tissues, and neatly parked. The actual graveside ceremony was Bryn's downtime; it was her opportunity to run through the checklist in her head, over and over, to be sure she hadn't dropped any details.

Next to her, Joe Fideli, her second in command, leaned closer. 'Red alert. Mistress at your four o'clock,' he whispered, and she glanced in that direction without moving her head. He was, of course, absolutely right. The widow, dressed formally in black, sat ramrod-stiff in the front row beside the coffin, but they'd already been warned that she wasn't the only woman in Mr Raines' somewhat colorful life.

His mistress had gone with mourning color, at least. She'd chosen a Little Black Dress, more appropriate for clubbing than a funeral, and paired with heels that were too stiletto for the grass on which she was walking. Those shoes resulted in more of a stagger than a controlled stride. Lots of leg on display, and glossy, overdone hair.

She was headed for the funeral like a torpedo for a stationary ship, and Bryn could well imagine the spectacular bang that would make.

'Let's avoid the drama,' Bryn whispered back, and Joe nodded. He was a big man, but he was light and quick, and besides, all eyes were on the priest. Joe faded back in slow, almost imperceptible movements, and put himself in the path of the other woman.

The priest finished his message and the prayer began. Most bent their heads, including Bryn, but she continued to watch through her lashes just in case. That was how she saw the mistress try to continue to move forward, and Joe smoothly block her, put a gentle hand on her shoulder, and bend to whisper something to her.

She burst into tears, which was a bit remarkable. She seemed to be the only one who was actually sorry to see the old man go; the dry-eyed wife certainly had never displayed a speck of feeling in all the time Bryn had spoken with her, and wasn't showing any now. Neither were the children, both in their teens, who looked bored. At least they weren't texting.

The prayer finished, the priest walked to offer his (probably unneeded) comfort to the wife and kids, and right on cue, the soft music that Bryn had arranged for began to play, signaling the end of the public gathering; she'd cautioned the cemetery employees that she wouldn't tolerate any jumping of the gun, and she was pleased to see that they were still hanging well back, pretending to be gardeners until the time came for the actual burial. There was another tent erected across the way. She knew they were pressed on their schedule to get the next funeral ready, and she was sympathetic to their need to get things moving, but still. She was a great believer in respect.

Joe had engaged the mistress in tearful conversation, and was walking her away from the graveside. The woman might have been planning a dramatic flinging-herself-over-the-coffin moment, or at the very least, a shrieking catfight with the more legally bereaved. Mrs Raines was already heading for the limousine that would take her home; the mistress was too far away now for any effective dramatics. Deprived of any other possible entertainment, the assembled mourners – not that Mr Raines had many – were scattering fast.

Bryn caught up with Mrs Raines and offered her last condolences, which the widow accepted with a distant, frosty confidence. She was already basking in the soft, warm glow of being a rich woman of means, motive and opportunity.

Poor man. His mistress, for all her tears, probably wouldn't mourn him much longer than it took to pawn whatever he'd bought her. Bryn's mind wandered off into lurid pulp magazine plots of poisoning, evil widows, sinister mistresses, eager-to-inherit children, but truthfully, she had no reason to suspect any foul play. It was just something to do to pass the time, standing in the cool wind, watching the living depart and leave the place to the dead.

She didn't except herself from that description. In truth, Bryn was just as dead as Mr Raines. She just wore it a whole lot better.

Bryn finally nodded to the cemetery staffers, who with quick, efficient movements stripped off the flower covering on the casket, and began the less-than-photogenic process of the actual burial. They dropped the sides of the tent for the mechanics of it. A third uniformed worker began folding up the chairs and picking up fallen programs from the AstroTurf that had been laid down around the tent. While she was watching that happen, Joe Fideli came back across the carefully manicured lawn. There was still something a little intimidating about him, no matter how much tailoring might have gone into his very nice suit; maybe it was the shaved head, or the way he moved, but he had a hell of a lot of presence.

Made a pretty good funeral director, though. And an even better bodyguard.

'Thanks for that,' she said to Joe, and he nodded.

'She looked like she was powering up for a full-on drama explosion,' he said. 'So. That's lunch, then.'

The death business, Bryn thought, was so strange. It was all about emotion and pain and stage management, and then suddenly . . . lunch. 'You know,' she said as she and Joe walked toward the Davis Funeral Home sedans, 'it occurs to me that what we do is pretty much like being wedding planners . . . just with a much unhappier ending.'

He smiled. 'Oh, I don't know. Depends on the wedding,' he said. 'I've seen some that might have been better off as funerals. You think people are capable of mayhem here, you should see what they get up to with a little champagne under their belts.'

Joe had a unique perspective on mayhem, Bryn thought; he might work for her as a funeral director, and he was a good one, but that was hardly his main vocation . . . she'd never met anyone who was quite so comfortable with violence. And considering she herself had been in the army, that was saying something. She strongly suspected he had a background in special forces – Rangers, SEALs, something secretive and highly trained. For all that, he was a nice guy. Just very, very deadly.

And he was her very own private security. She knew, in fact, that he was armed with at least one weapon, possibly two; he usually doubled up when they went out in public, mostly because she hadn't been able to find a side arm that was easily concealable under her tailored jackets. He'd made her drill on the procedures of what to do in the event that he ever had to go for those concealed weapons: one, get behind him; two, be ready when he pitched her the second gun. Three, fall back to cover while he laid down fire.

Most funeral directors, Bryn thought, never needed to think about those kinds of contingency plans. Lucky them.

Her watch alarm went off with a tiny vibration, just at the time Joe checked his cell phone and said, 'Time for meds, boss.'

'I know,' she said. It came out a little sharp, and she shot him an apologetic glance. 'Sorry. I don't think I'll ever stop hating the needles.'

'More than the alternative?'

That didn't deserve an answer. 'I thought Manny was working on some kind of pill form.'

'You know Manny,' Joe shrugged.

'Well, not really. Do you?'

He snorted and let that one go, because the fact was, she had a point. None of them really knew her chemist, Manny Glickman, and since her life depended on the man to a great extent these days, that bothered Bryn more than she liked to admit.

'Anyway,' Joe said. 'No arguments. Time for the booster.'

'I thought I was the boss.'

'You are,' he agreed. 'You sign the checks and everything. Don't mean that you can make me ignore the schedule, since that's definitely part of what you pay me for, right?'

Right. It wasn't that Bryn necessarily *needed* a reminder for this, but having one made her feel less . . . vulnerable. In oh so many ways. 'Meds,' she agreed. 'As soon as we get back to the office.'

For answer, he slid a syringe out of his coat pocket, held it up, and said, 'No need to wait. We can take care of this in the car.'

Bryn glanced around. Nobody was watching them. 'Easier out in the open,' she said, and unbuttoned and removed her suit jacket. Under it, she wore a light blue silk top, sleeveless – the better for shot access, unfortunately. She took a deep breath and presented her shoulder to him, and Joe uncapped the syringe, plunged it home with a quick flick of his hand, and pressed the plunger, fast.

The contents spread into her system in a slow, steady burn that traveled through muscle, entered her bloodstream, and suddenly bolted like fiery acid through her entire body. She was familiar with pain, intimately; fortunately, so was Joe, and he put a supporting hand under her elbow in case her knees gave way. They didn't this time, but it was a close thing. The fire began to cool, and she kept the scream locked down, pressed tight into a faint moan.

'So,' Joe said, in a neutral tone, 'any better?'

She took a couple of deep breaths before even trying

to answer. 'If you mean does it still feel like I'm being flayed, the answer is yes,' she said, but by the time she finished saying it, the pain had rolled through her and vanished, except for a few last whispers haunting her joints. 'Maybe a little less painful than last week's formula, but this one has a worse aftertaste.' She wanted to scrub it off her tongue with a wire brush. Manny changed the formula about once a week, trying to fine-tune and improve it, but that didn't mean it was a joy to experience. Especially when she had to endure it every day.

'Don't suppose that aftertaste would be, say, chocolate?'

'More like bleach and sewage,' she said, and couldn't help the gag reflex. He held on to her until this, too, passed, and silently handed over a tin of Altoids mints. She chewed two of them, and the relief of getting that awful taste out of her mouth was worth the intense peppermint burn. 'Wow, that was *not* pretty.' She pulled her jacket on again as Joe stepped back, assessing her with a professional kind of analysis that made her feel less like a woman and more like a machine in need of maintenance. 'I'm fine.'

'Okay,' he said. 'Manny said to watch out for tremors and signs of decomp. He's still working out the kinks on the combo formula. This one should suppress the Protocols better, but there may be some side effects. Could also burn off faster. Hard to know.'

Bryn had long ago accepted that her status in this world was going to be lab rat, but that didn't make it any easier to take pronouncements like that. 'So I should watch out for tremors first, or decomp?'

'Both,' Joe said. 'But stay calm while you're doing it.'

Yeah, that was her life. *Keep calm, and watch for decomposition.* She got a shot, every day; they were still trying out new formulas to counter different nasty things built into the nanites that rushed through her bloodstream, acting as her life-support system and keeping her . . . well, if not alive, then a very convincing copy. She never knew what the day's shot would bring. Every day was a new surprise, and most of them were unpleasant.

Her cell buzzed for attention, and she checked the screen. 'We should be getting back,' she said.

'Uh-huh. Trouble?' She sent Joe a long look, eyebrows raised. 'Never mind. Stupid question.'

Joe took the driver position; she wasn't allowed in the front, or to sit directly behind him. On his insistence, she always sat in the sweet spot where she would – theoretically – be the safest in the event of a gunfight. Bryn thought it was bullshit, because in the event of a gunfight, she could hold her own, and besides, she was relatively damage-resistant. Thanks to the nanites, the curse that kept on giving.

She'd never intended this to be her life. She'd just

taken a job, a regular job as a funeral director, and discovered her boss was reviving the dead for profit in the basement. That had ended badly for her, with a plastic bag over her head and a one-way retirement.

Except that Joe and his boss Patrick McCallister had brought her back to find out what had happened, and now she was stuck here, taking shots to stay on her eternal treadmill between life and death.

Because getting off that treadmill meant having to die all over again, and not nearly as neatly and quickly.

It meant rotting alive.

While Joe drove back to Davis Funeral Home – once Fairview Mortuary, but recently renamed since she'd taken it over – Bryn checked her emails.

'Crap,' she sighed. Joe sent her a look in the rear-view mirror. 'My mom's emailing. She wants to know if I've heard anything from Annalie.' Her sister's disappearance hadn't caused too much of a stir yet . . . Mom was accustomed to Annie taking off for weeks at a time, gadding about on sailboats or backpacking trips or affairs with boyfriends that never quite worked out. So she was just casually asking right now, with a tiny flavor of concern.

But that would change, soon, and the problem was that Bryn *did* know what had happened to Annie. She just couldn't tell her family.

Joe nodded. 'Does she still think Annie's on vacation?'

'Yeah. But I can't keep this up much longer. It's been

too long, and sending Mom the occasional text from Annie's phone number isn't cutting it anymore. She's going to want to see her daughter. Soon.'

Not that Bryn could do anything about it. Annie was missing. Waiting for information was the worst part . . . and while she waited, there wasn't anything else she could do except test out new shots, hope for some new intel, and hope for the best. Wait for the government, who now solely owned the raw formula of the drug Returné that Manny worked from, to decide what to do with her, and all the others addicted to this drug. She'd signed papers. Papers that meant, essentially, that she was trading cooperation with them – ill-defined as that was – for continued life. Apparently, the pursuit of life, liberty and happiness wasn't guaranteed after you'd actually *died*.

She met Joe's gaze in the mirror for a second before he focused back on driving. 'If we find her, do you think this formula will work for Annie?' Because her sister, like her, was dead in every way that didn't show. Dead, and addicted to the drug that had Revived her.

'We can give it a try,' he said. 'But she's been on the Pharmadene formula for a long time now, with all the Protocols activated. We'd have to detox her, and frankly, Manny hasn't had enough test subjects to know if there are some people who might be resistant to the new mix. But try to be patient, okay?'

She wasn't patient at all, and he knew that. But first

they had to *find* Annie, then worry about the detox period, so patience was all she had right now. Patience, and running the business of caring for the dead.

Her cell phone rang before she could tell Joe what she thought about being patient. When she thumbed it on and answered, 'Davis Funeral Home, Bryn Davis speaking,' she knew she sounded less than her usual soothing self, so she added, in a deliberately warmed-up voice, 'How may I assist you?'

'Funny you should ask that. I have a job for you,' said the voice on the other end. A familiar one – brisk, female, businesslike. The caller ID was blank. 'Assuming you're not in the middle of some corpse you can't put aside.'

'Hello, Riley Block,' Bryn said aloud, for Joe's benefit. She saw his eyebrows rise a little as he glanced in the rear-view mirror at her. 'How goes the FBI's dirty work?'

'Tolerably well,' Riley said, with just a cool trace of amusement. 'How goes the death business?'

'Never a dull moment,' Bryn said. 'What do you want?'

'I'll be at your office in thirty minutes, we can discuss it then.' Meaning, of course, that Riley Block, professional paranoid, wasn't going to talk about it over the airwaves.

'Fine,' Bryn said, and hung up. She liked Riley, despite all the reasons she shouldn't; the FBI agent had started out working undercover in the funeral home, and had almost gotten her killed, but hell, half her friends had that last particular honor. Not to mention at least one relative.

'So,' Joe said. 'Riley. Great. Are we going to her, or is she coming to us?'

'She's coming to us.'

'Want me to shoot her, or bake her cookies?'

'I'll let you know,' Bryn sighed. She felt tired and achy, but that was a side effect of the shot. It was a little more painful this week than last. She wished that Manny would finalize his formula once and for all; she was tired of not knowing how she'd feel, what the side effects would be. They seemed to be getting worse, not better. And that was worrying. It wasn't as if this process had been tested and FDA approved. 'Jesus, I'm in a bad mood. Tell me something good, Joe.'

'Well, the profits are up, I think the sun's coming out tomorrow, and your six-month anniversary as boss of this flaky outfit is coming up. I'm thinking I'll get you some flowers.'

She shuddered. 'Please. Don't.' Flowers were one thing they both saw way too much in this business, and besides, he knew perfectly well that the six-month anniversary also tokened something else, something grim: the anniversary of her death.

The anniversary of her *murder*.

Bryn had been Revived for information, and hadn't

been able to offer much in exchange for her daily infusions of life-support nanites. She'd been lucky to survive at all, she knew that; every extra day of her life – such as it was – had to be looked on as a gift.

But that didn't mean she had to celebrate it, either.

Joe was quiet for a while, navigating the turns, and finally said, in a totally different voice, 'Bryn. Don't do that.'

'Do what?'

'Drift,' he said. 'It's a long way back to shore when you do that. And I'm not sure you're that good a swimmer yet.'

Maybe not, she thought. But one thing was sure: she had plenty of lifeguards.

She shook her head, and went back to checking her email.

Chapter Two

Davis Funeral Home had some of the nicest hillside real estate outside of San Diego . . . which made it expensive to maintain, but restful and lovely, and as Joe Fideli took the turn up the drive, past the bus stop where Bryn had once had to wait for her transportation, Bryn looked up to enjoy the view. Down the hill was the winding road, leading down toward the spill of pastel houses toward the sparkling bay. Today, the ocean was a dull lead-gray, and the colors were muted, but it was still breathtaking.

The funeral home itself had been built in the twenties, solidly art deco lines and beautiful gardens. It really was gorgeous in its own right, and she still got a mingled thrill and jolt of alarm seeing her own last name on the sign. The old Fairview Mortuary sign had been original to the building, but she'd tried to match the style as best she could. She felt a certain kinship with the old place . . . after all, she'd come into it a new, eager employee, and died on day one. Like her, the building was a bit of a Frankenstein monster, repaired and brought back to life.

There were two cars parked in the VISITOR spaces. Joe dropped her off at the door and went off to park, and she put her phone away, straightened her jacket, and walked into the lobby.

No Riley Block yet, but there was a whole crowd of people waiting in the chairs near Lucy, the office administrator's, desk. Lucy was utterly warm and professional, with years of experience in the business; nothing much rattled her.

So when Bryn caught sight of the tight expression on Lucy's perfectly made-up face, she had plenty of warning for what was to come.

She hadn't even shut the front door before one of the people who'd been sitting shot to his feet and charged at her, red in the face. 'You *bitch*!'

That was a mistake. Bryn wasn't inclined to let people grab her; she slipped sideways, evading his attempt to seize her arm, and heard Lucy take in a deep, startled breath. Options presented themselves in fast flashes – she could drop him in three moves, even as big as he was; she could get out the door and let Fideli take care of it, which would be efficient and not too kind to the attacker; she could have Lucy call the cops, because as angry as this man was, they might well need them.

But she rejected all that, in rapid succession. There were people watching, and she couldn't afford to look weak or out of control – or less than understanding. She needed to handle it, quickly and quietly. So instead of decking him, Bryn stepped closer, grabbed his arm just above the elbow, at the nerve cluster, and squeezed. The man – over six feet, and built like he worked out – hadn't expected that burst of pain, and it threw him off balance . . . especially when she took his hand in hers and shook it firmly, while still maintaining that painful grip on his arm. 'Sir,' she said, quietly. 'I understand you must be very upset, but this isn't the place to discuss things. Please, come with me.'

She'd taken the wind out of his sails. Her office was only a few steps away, and she ushered him in, shut the door, and let go of his arm at the same time. He rubbed it reflexively as he scowled at her. 'Please,' she said. 'Sit down. Can I get you anything?'

He was still struggling to figure out what had just happened – not the brightest bulb in the box, she saw, but there was no doubting his anger. 'You can give me back fifty thousand dollars,' he shot back. 'Right now. Or I go to the cops, you greedy bitch!'

That made her pause, just for a few seconds, but she got it together and sat down on the sofa at the far end of the office. He glared at her resentfully; she mutely gestured to the couch facing her on the opposite side of the low coffee table. After a few agitated seconds of pacing, he finally took a seat, leaned forward, and continued glaring as if he intended to do it all day.

'Let's start over,' Bryn said. 'I'm Bryn Davis. I don't believe we've met, sir.'

'Don't give me that crap,' he snapped. 'Where's Fairview?'

'He's deceased, sir,' she said. 'I inherited the funeral home about six months ago. He was my uncle.' Thankfully, that wasn't true; she didn't think there was enough mind-bleach in the world to imagine Lincoln Fairview polluting her family tree. It had been a cover to allow her to continue to operate the funeral home. Fiction, pure and simple. 'And I still don't know your name.'

'Tanner. George Tanner,' he said, through gritted teeth. 'My brother David came here to bury his wife Margaret.'

'I see,' Bryn said, in her calmest, quietest voice. 'How long ago was this?'

'About a year ago, I guess, I don't know. I was out of the country. Just got back and found out that my brother paid this rip-off artist Fairview fifty thousand dollars for a funeral! You can't tell me that's legit. No way.'

It wasn't. Bryn recognized the Tanner name; he was right, David Tanner had been a Fairview customer, but the fifty grand hadn't been to simply bury his wife in style. Most of that had been blackmail money. Fairview's racket had been simple, but effective – revive the dead with Returné, the drug stolen from

Pharmadene Pharmaceuticals' top-secret trials, then charge exorbitant rates for each additional shot to keep the deceased 'alive' . . . as alive as Bryn was now. At thirty-five hundred a week for the shots, Tanner had hung in there quite a while before running out of resources. But eventually, he'd gone broke, just like the other unfortunates . . . and his wife had gone back to her natural state – dead.

Not before gruesomely decomposing. But she couldn't tell Mr Tanner any of this.

Bryn cleared her throat and said, 'Have you spoken to your brother about this?'

'David's dead,' George Tanner said. 'Blew his brains out months ago. And I can promise you, I didn't have him sent here.'

'I'm sorry for your loss,' she said, still calm. She couldn't afford to get angry, not now. 'Sir, there were some accounting improprieties that happened under Mr Fairview's administration, there's no denying that fact. I can certainly refund you thirty-five thousand dollars right now. Will that do?'

This was, sadly, not her first angry-relative rodeo. She'd been cleaning up after Fairview's messes for six long months, and she'd learned fast – offering *all* the money back made people even more suspicious. But offering to return *most* of it and keeping a reasonable fee seemed to mollify them, weirdly enough. They felt that was more honest.

And just like that, it worked again, because George Tanner frowned at her for a moment, then blinked. 'Thirty-five thousand back?'

'Yes sir. If there are expenses greater than fifteen thousand owed for her burial I will happily take that cost. Is that acceptable to you? I can write you a check right now.'

He hadn't expected that. He'd come prepared to do hand-to-hand combat, and instead she was offering him cash money. After a long moment, he said, 'Okay. But don't think I'm forgetting about this. You're a bunch of crooks, you people.'

'These accounting issues are exactly why I changed the name and hired new staff. Sir, I must apologize for all that you and your family suffered, and I completely understand your anger and frustration. Please accept my personal apologies.' She kept on with it, talking softly and calmly until she could see the tension had gone out of him.

Then she wrote him a check and sent him on his way.

So much for turning a profit, she thought, as she shook his hand; Joe Fideli was standing, apparently at ease, not far from her door in the hallway. He sent her a questioning look, and she shook her head to stand him down as Mr Tanner left the building.

'Lucy let me know you had a hot one,' Fideli said. 'Figured you might need a hand, but I see you're doing fine.'

'Not so fine for our financial health,' Bryn said, 'but it had to be done. Fairview not only robbed his family blind, his brother probably committed suicide over it.'

It wasn't the first time. When Fairview's victims stopped coming up with the money, Fairview had stopped giving the shots; it took a horrifying toll. Bryn had been forced to help one of those victims out of her agony, and it haunted her every night in her dreams. She hated to think how many family members had been given that same awful choice.

Fideli said nothing to that, just nodded; he was a good man, but all this was business to him. He wasn't one of the Revived; he didn't face the same terrifying dissolution she did if (when) the shots failed her. 'So,' he said. 'Just to make your day more fun, Riley's waiting outside.'

'What about the other family that was waiting?'

'I'm on it. They're looking over brochures right now. Want me to show her in?'

Not really, Bryn thought, but she nodded. There was no avoiding it, after all. Fideli nodded back and left, and in a few seconds he was holding the door open for FBI Agent Riley Block. She'd changed her hair to a looser, more tousled style around her sharp face; with Riley's English-rose coloring, it suited her, made her look less severe.

'You're not wearing a patch,' Bryn said, and indicated the guest side of the sofa. 'I assume your eye's better?'

'Much,' Riley said. 'Only a few scars from our

last little outing together, thanks for asking.' She sat back and crossed her legs, looking casual and fiercely competent in her blocky pantsuit. 'I'm back on active duty again. I see you're looking well.'

Oh, aren't we cordial today? Bryn thought. She gave Riley a calm professional smile that revealed nothing of how betrayed she still felt; Riley had come to work at Fairview Mortuary under false pretenses, spying on her, working against her, and she'd almost succeeded in destroying Bryn's life, such as it was.

Just the job, Riley would have said. And she'd be right, that was the maddening thing.

'So, what exactly do you want, Riley?'

Riley smiled back, just as professionally. 'I thought the script called for offering me some kind of refreshment before you dive in.'

'We're not on a script.'

'I'd love some coffee.'

'And there are plenty of Starbucks stores in town. Just get to it.'

Riley considered her for a few seconds, and said, 'You've changed.'

Bryn couldn't keep a hollow laugh from escaping. 'You think? All things considered?'

'Not the physical changes from the nanites,' Riley said. 'You used to be less . . . bitter.'

'You mean back in the days when I was still in a state of shock and fighting for my life? I've had time to reflect. And I've taken control. If that seems bitter to you, well, I'll try to contain my grief. Why are you stalling?'

'I'm not.' Riley shrugged. 'I'm assessing, that's all. To see if you still seem capable of carrying out what I'm going to ask you to do. "Bitter" sometimes means "tough".' She studied Bryn with her head cocked to the side for a long moment. 'And sometimes it just means fragile. I can't really afford fragile.'

'Are you giving me a job or not?'

'That's the deal you made with me,' Riley said. 'And Uncle Sam. You work for us, doing anything we need you to do. So yes. I have a job for you.' She reached in the briefcase she'd rested at her feet and unsnapped it to withdraw a thick folder. 'Sign the paper clipped to the front before you break the seals.'

It was a contractor agreement in wordy legalese, and what it boiled down to was that Bryn was not an employee of the FBI, nor bound by its codes of conduct, but that by breaking the file seals she accepted the penalties for violating secrecy. The penalties weren't specific. She assumed they included death. Everything in her life did, these days.

Bryn signed, pulled the form off, and handed it to Riley, who filed it back in her briefcase. Then Bryn broke the seals and opened the folder. There was only one page in it, and it was short. She read for a moment, then looked up at the other woman and said, 'You're kidding, right?'

'We generally don't kid at this stage of the process, after the paperwork.'

'You want me to work with *Pharmadene*?' The company still featured in her nightmares in a starring role . . . especially the clean, white room where they'd left her to rot. The whole idea of going back there made her guts knot up. 'Are you kidding me?'

'It's not the company you knew,' Riley said. 'You never have to see the lab area again. Just meet with the CEO in his office. He's one of ours.'

'Ours? What, are we a team now?'

'One of the FBI's agents,' Riley clarified without a flicker. 'He's in the process of dismantling the company and disposing of the assets, shutting down production lines. More of an accountant than a field agent, really. He's discovered something in the books that needs some investigation – large payments made to an outside firm that don't make any sense with how they're coded.'

'Don't you have people to ask questions? I thought that came with the shield and ID card and was, you know, kind of your whole purpose.'

'There are reasons we can't approach these people. You're not FBI, and you're . . . uniquely suited to the task.'

As in, if this organization got suspicious and decided to put a bullet in her head, it wouldn't matter; she'd wake up. Lovely. Bryn flipped pages, not finding anything that made the deal more palatable, and said, 'Can I refuse?'

That met with silence. She looked up and found

Riley watching her with an indefinable chill in her expression. 'I'd really rather you didn't,' Riley said. 'The consequences would be difficult.'

'For you, or for me?'

'Both.'

'You don't control my meds, not anymore,' Bryn said. 'I don't need Pharmadene, and I don't need you.' It was bravado. Manny was supplying her daily shots, but he lacked the resources to stockpile the nanites; he took the allotments from Pharmadene and modified them, created his own variations. She still needed them, and Riley knew it.

But she was nice enough to ignore that part. 'You *do* need Manny Glickman, your little tinkerer,' Riley said. 'Like it or not, he's a point of vulnerability, and if we have to cut you off from him, we will.'

That was unexpected, and sent a cold rush of alarm through Bryn's body. 'You wouldn't. Manny's one of yours.'

'Manny is *ex*-FBI, and frankly he needs meds and professional care, we both know that. But I'm not threatening him. I'm just saying that there are ways we can prevent you from reaching him, and if that happens for long, you know what the consequences would be.'

Bryn knew, all too well. She'd felt it before, in that white room at Pharmadene . . . the exhaustion setting in, the bruising and discoloration when she slept, the damp skin, the *dissolution* . . . it hadn't gone so far she couldn't come back, but it stalked her, always, just a step behind. Death in real, waiting form.

Consequences. 'You're a real bitch, Riley.'

Riley shrugged. 'Yes or no, Bryn? All I'm asking you to do is meet with one person at Pharmadene, then do a little fact-finding investigation and report back. It isn't that complicated. Or that dangerous.'

Bryn closed the folder. 'Fine.' She didn't bother to point out how little choice she had; Riley knew all that. 'If you threaten Manny again—'

'I didn't,' Riley said. 'And I wouldn't. I like Manny, and I respect him. But you know that all I need to do is warn him he's in danger, and next thing you know he's moved and left no forwarding address, and you're roadkill. I'm serious, Bryn. He's a failure point for you. You need to be careful how much faith you put in him.'

That almost was an expression of . . . concern. Which seemed very strange, coming from Agent Block. Bryn nodded, and felt the tension in her neck relax, just a little. She crossed to her desk and locked up the file as Riley gathered her briefcase.

'So,' she said. 'I guess I'll get on script after all. Coffee, Riley?'

Riley smiled, and seemed relieved. 'Thought you'd never ask.'

* * *

When she told her boyfriend, it didn't go well.

'Have you gone completely off the ledge?' Patrick McCallister asked. He didn't yell it, didn't even sound angry, but there was a tension in his shoulders that warned Bryn he was very unhappy. 'You can't do this for them, Bryn. It's blackmail – oh, come on, dog, that's the third time you've watered the same spot. Move on.'

He was talking to Mr French, her bulldog, whose leash he held; Mr French's start-and-stop progress was worse today than usual, and whatever scent he was trying to eradicate by peeing on it was clearly pretty stubborn. Mr French ignored McCallister, nosed the grass, let out an explosive sneeze, and peed *again* on the same spot. Then he licked his chops, circled the perimeter, and must have decided he'd done his job, because he trotted on. For a few steps, anyway, before snuffling the bark of the next tree.

It was, Bryn reflected, a real test of a good boyfriend that he'd come out in the rain and put up with this. She was carrying the umbrella as the evening shower pattered down; Mr French didn't much care, but he would later, when she had to towel him off to take him into Patrick's huge, fancy house. No, mansion.

McCallister gave her a straight-on look, and she read the worry in it. He was a good-looking man, although not drop-dead gorgeous . . . it was more subtle than that with him. He was usually guarded, but not now, and not with her; she could see his concern, and all that went with it.

Bryn took hold of his right hand – he was holding Mr French's leash with his left – and leaned forward to brush her lips over his cheek. 'Blackmail or not, it's not worth it to test their patience just now,' she said. 'Riley was right. Manny's fragile, and he'd bolt at a real scare. Think about where that would leave us.'

She realized, when he cast her another look, and a devastating smile, that she'd said *us* and not just *me*. Not that McCallister shared her . . . condition, but he was invested in her safety, both financially and personally. Without McCallister, she'd be dead several times over . . . but that was also true of Joe Fideli, and even Riley Block. The difference was that when she got near McCallister, her whole body came alive and warm. She wasn't quite prepared to call it love, at least not out loud. They'd started out as adversaries, then allies, then . . . something else.

And now he was walking her dog. In the rain. And worrying about her. She wasn't sure what it meant, long term, but it felt so, so good to have him here.

'Manny's fine,' he said. 'And he's tougher than he seems, trust me. He can't be stampeded quite that easily, though they'd like to believe it. They've already tried scaring him off a few times.'

'They did?'

'Sure,' he said. 'Manny was expecting it. The government would very much like to have total and utter control of the drug, but he's not about to part with his own formulas.'

'They've got Pharmadene's. They don't need his, do they?'

'They want it all, of course, but their biggest problem is that Pharmadene encrypted the formula and all the developmental records, and the FBI scientists aren't having much success at cracking it. They've got a refrigerated warehouse of the stuff to try to backwards engineer, but it's getting used up fast. They need Manny's formulas, and he's not sharing.'

'I'm surprised he doesn't trade it to them and run.' Manny Glickman was a bone-deep paranoid, but he still held some residual loyalty to the FBI who'd trained him; if he was going to give up the formula to anyone, it'd be Riley Block and her team.

'He's not that keen on them right now.'

'I'm just worried that he could get spooked and leave us.'

'He's already moved three times in six months,' McCallister said. 'But he always lets me know where he touches down. Don't worry about him. I'm busy worrying about *you*. You don't have to play in the FBI's snakepit, you know. You don't really owe them.'

'I know,' she said, and squeezed his hand. It was a nice sentiment, for all that it was completely unrealistic. She took in a deep breath; the air was cool and heavy with moisture, and it tasted clean and sweet. They paused beneath another tree as Mr French investigated the area, then finally decided to do his solid-waste business. Raindrops splashed heavily on the umbrella she held over the two of them, and Bryn leaned in closer. McCallister freed his hand and put his arm around her shoulders to pull her closer. They were much of a height, and she could feel the solid muscle of his body beneath the clothes; it woke all kinds of things inside her – hunger, pleasure, memories, longings. *Living* things. In his presence, at these times, she could forget, a little. 'Will you promise to keep an eye on me, though?'

'I thought you'd never ask,' he said. He let go of her as Mr French finished up, and fished in his pocket for the plastic bag, which he snapped open with a flourish of his wrist and handed to her.

'Really?' she said. 'I thought *you* were walking him.'

'I am doing the manly part of holding the leash,' he said. 'But he's your dog, and I have to draw the line somewhere. This seems like a good place.'

She grinned, kissed him on the lips, and bent to clean up after her dog, who chose that precise moment to shake himself, shedding mud and rain like a sprinkler. Lovely. 'I don't know why I put up with either one of you,' she told Mr French, severely, as she scooped the poop. 'It's *way* too much trouble.'

'Obviously, because we're adorable,' McCallister said, on behalf of Mr French, who barked sharply to support the statement. Or maybe just to indicate his desire to get in out of the rain.

Bryn disposed of the bag in the first bin they passed on the way back to the house, and then stopped to look back. 'Pat?'

'Yes?'

'Since when are there garbage cans on the lawn?' If you could call the enormous, sprawling, carefully manicured parkland around the McCallister estate something so prosaic as a lawn.

'They're for the gardeners,' he said. 'Don't worry, I didn't have them put in just for you.'

'Liar,' she said.

'If it makes you feel better, garbage day is Thursday. You can roll all the bins to the curb.'

That summed up why she liked him so much, she decided: when he was relaxed, and the armor was off him, he was oddly unaffected by all . . . this. The sumptuous multimillion-dollar estate. Most people of his particular social status probably wouldn't have known what day the garbage was taken out any more than they could locate the laundry room – but Patrick McCallister was one of the most practical people she'd ever met. It helped that he didn't actually *own* this place; his family had left everything in a trust, and his income was relatively modest, given the lush surroundings. He was more like a caretaker than the lord of the manor – or at least, that was how he felt about it; the odd thing was that he was *happier* that way. *Too much money makes people callous*, he'd told her once. *I don't want to take that chance. I've seen what can happen.*

They walked in companionable silence, Mr French tugging at the lead, and stopped in the mud room to make themselves, and the dog, fit for entry into the house. He didn't like it, but the simple, physical effort of toweling him off was kind of bracing.

So was the kiss McCallister gave her, warm and sweet, before they went into the more formal areas. McCallister headed towards the library, which was his favorite evening spot; Bryn was following when Liam came down the stairs with a telephone in his hand.

Liam insisted he wasn't a butler, but Bryn couldn't help but think of him that way. He was silver-haired, dignified, and even though he didn't wear butler-ish clothes, he definitely had the manners. And the grace. She'd felt clumsy and glaringly out of her league when she'd first come here, but he'd never made her feel anything but welcome.

Tonight, he gave her a smile and said, 'I have a phone call for you from someone who doesn't wish to give a name. Do you want me to decline?'

That call could have been from anyone, but Bryn had a sudden, painful conviction – irrational as it was – that it would be her sister Annalie. The metallic taste of adrenaline filled her mouth. No one had seen or heard of Annie, or her kidnapper Mercer, for more than a month; there were no reports coming in through Pat McCallister's contacts, or through Joe Fideli's.

They'd simply dropped out of sight.

She needed to know that Annie was all right, so without a word, she held out her hand, and Liam put the phone into it, then walked away to give her privacy. She headed off in a different direction, Mr French at her heels, and said, 'Hello?' Her voice shook a little, more from eagerness than fear. *Annie, please let it be you. Please.* She'd let her sister down in a huge and awful way; she'd allowed Annalie to come into her life knowing things were dangerous. She'd done it because, in the aftermath of her death and Revival, she'd been feeling so alone, so vulnerable. It was Annie who'd paid the price for that.

Annie too had joined the ranks of the Revived, against her will. And she now depended on Mercer – the original creator of the drug – and his slimy henchman Freddy for daily shots to keep her alive.

Please, Annie, help me find you.

It wasn't her. In fact, it was a voice Bryn didn't recognize at all. 'Bryn Davis?' A man's voice, medium register, not much of an accent she could detect.

'Yes.'

'I-I'm sorry for calling out of the blue, but I was given your name by a friend. A Pharmadene employee. Like me. Her name is Chandra.'

She turned her back to the doorway, unconsciously

shielding the phone from any accidental eavesdropping by Liam or Patrick. 'I'm listening.'

'My friend said you run a kind of . . . counseling service. Support group.' The man pulled in a deep breath, then let it out again. 'For those of us who are, you know . . . addicts.'

'You mean, you need your hit every day, or you get very sick?'

'Yes.'

'Uh-huh.' There was a desk in the corner of the room, largely ornamental, but it held some writing paper and a pen, and Bryn quickly jotted down the number on the caller ID and said, 'Do you want to meet somewhere and talk things over?'

'Yes.' He sounded relieved. 'Yes, I need to talk. Please.'

'Anyplace you feel comfortable that you can get to tomorrow?'

He named a coffee shop she knew, and she wrote it down. 'I'll be reading a book,' he said. 'Stephen Hawking, *A Brief History of Time*.'

'What's your first name?'

'Carl,' he said. 'Carl—'

'I don't need your last name, Carl, that's fine. How about 10 a.m.?'

'Fine. Thanks. I just need – I need to deal with this, and I haven't been doing a real good job lately. It's my family. My wife. It just seems . . .'

'Overwhelming,' she said. 'I know. It gets better when

you talk to someone else who can really understand.'

Carl was one of those the government had saved, and kept saving, every day that they provided him with a shot. He probably had the same question Bryn did: how long would that last? *Not long,* Bryn thought. She wouldn't tell him that, but she knew the ruthless truth: the government didn't need these people, other than a key few; they were just excess baggage, and sooner or later, they'd get dumped as the stockpiled supplies of Returné dried up.

These were victims, *innocent* victims – Pharmadene employees who'd been designated as mission-critical. They'd been 'converted' – corporate-speak for killed, then Revived. And now the government was stuck with a bunch of people they couldn't allow to run around loose and unsupervised, because of their undead status . . . but there were too many to simply, conveniently, disappear.

Bryn didn't fool herself into thinking there was any genuine moral or ethical dilemma involved. Just expedience, risk, and reward.

Word was starting to get out, and Carl wasn't the first Pharmadene employee to cold-call, looking for answers. Bryn didn't know how many Revived there were out there under the government's control, and Riley Block wasn't going to tell her . . . but this, in a small way, was making a difference.

Though absolutely *nobody* wanted her to do it. Particularly not Pat McCallister. He thought there were risks – and he was right. She just couldn't *not* do it . . . she felt responsible, somehow, to all these luckless bastards who had (like her) never asked for this sinister gift of pseudo-life, who had lives and families and who had to live a lie now.

Her lies, at least, were less personal.

She finished the call and hung up, and turned to find – no surprise – that Pat was standing there silently watching her. She shook her head. 'Don't start.'

'I won't,' he said, but she could tell by the stillness in him that he wanted to. 'Come on. Dinner. Liam won't be happy if you let his beef Wellington get cold.'

It was so odd that she lived in a house where *beef Wellington* was what was for dinner. And it wasn't even that exceptional.

'I need to change,' she said, and kissed him quickly on the way out the door. 'Be down in a minute.'

Her room still didn't feel like *hers*, exactly, although all her stuff was here, or as much as she'd wanted to bring with her . . . she hadn't wanted the old, cheap pressboard dresser, the second-hand couch or bed, but she'd brought the old armchair she'd always preferred, and her pictures, mementoes, books, music and movies were all neatly ordered on shelves. The room had come with a television, a vast, flat-screen thing that probably also made coffee, as high-tech as it was, but she was a little scared of it. It had its own curtains to conceal it, so as not to upset the soothing autumnal glory of the furniture and fabrics; they wouldn't have been out of place a hundred years ago, in this very house.

Her clothes were not great, but they were better than they had been, mainly because she had some grasp now of how to dress for her job. She'd come straight out of the military to her first funeral home job, and wearing a uniform hadn't prepared her for the challenge of buying suits. She'd gotten some advice from Lucy, the funeral home's formidable administrator, who'd surely trained with some kind of fashion-related Zen Master.

Bryn stripped off her doggy-mudded jeans and shirt and put on what was casual evening dress here in the mansion – a dress, which was a little sexy, like a first date at an upscale restaurant. She added a necklace that she'd been given by her mom, years ago, and then picked up the nice watch that Annie had given her as her 'first job' present.

I wish—

Bryn stopped the thought, held the watch in her hand for a moment, and then put it on with sure, quick snaps of her fingers.

I'll find you, she promised the absent ghost of her sister. *I will. I swear.*

But she had nowhere to look, and nothing to go on. If her sister was still out there, still alive, still *waiting*, Bryn was letting her down with every moment she didn't find her. Worse, she was letting down her whole family, who didn't even know Annie was in trouble.

After a deep breath, Bryn went downstairs for a dinner for which she had, suddenly, very little appetite.

CHAPTER THREE

Bryn had never liked mornings, but she'd usually been an early riser anyway – life in the army did that to you, accustomed you to being out of bed before dawn whether you wanted it or not. She woke in the predawn light, comfortable and warm, with Mr French snuggled against her legs on top of the covers. His chin was on her hip, and he was snoring like a little old man, and twitching as he dreamed. The room was cool, dim, and soothing, but for a moment it felt . . . *wrong*. Early mornings sometimes brought her doubts out of the depths and up to breach the surface. *What am I doing here? I don't belong here, in this house.*

Her apartment – cheap and crappy as it had been – had been her own space, but she'd started worrying not about her own safety there, but that of her neighbors. Innocent people, families, who had no knowledge of the kind of knife-edge on which she lived. She'd woken up with every noise, every car engine, wondering if the government was coming to make her disappear, or worse, if someone else had decided to grab her, experiment on her . . . the paranoia (justified or not) had driven her half-nuts.

Patrick McCallister had made the offer to give her a room at his mansion – a protected space, safe, controlled, where she endangered no one who didn't know the score. She hadn't been able to bring herself to take that last step with him yet, and they weren't lovers, but she knew she could trust him. And she knew that she *wanted* to be with him.

But in the mornings, she still wondered whether she'd sacrificed her independence for security.

Then again, she thought, and yawned, *the apartment complex didn't set out a full breakfast, and have coffee going by the time I got up.* Which Liam did, every morning. He was an even earlier riser than she was, and he seemed to feel that it was his sacred duty to be sure she had fuel before starting her day. *Screw independence. Who doesn't get used to that?*

She didn't, apparently. She still felt like a guest here; regardless of what Patrick did, or what Liam would excuse, she didn't feel that she could roll out of bed in her bathrobe and shuffle down to breakfast. No, she had to get up, shower, fix her hair, do her make-up, dress, and *then* go down. And she was self-conscious about it. Every day, she had the argument with herself about moving out, finding her own space, but every day, the larger part of her wanted to stay.

And truthfully, it was because of Patrick. They hadn't slept together, but they'd had some fantastic everything-but skin sessions; she didn't feel like either of them were reluctant to take the next step, but she did feel that they were both . . . cautious. And careful not to push. He was waiting on her, and she was waiting on him, and that made for an interestingly frustrating relationship because, fairly soon, one of them was just going to seize the moment.

She couldn't help but think about that. A lot. And she imagined that he did, too.

Down, girl. Time to get up and focus. She had a meeting at Pharmadene today, which she dreaded. And she had to meet with Carl, the Returné-addicted Pharmadene employee, and try to give him a little help and perspective. If she liked his vibe, she'd invite him to the evening group meetings they had once a week . . . a support group, but even though they jokingly called it Dead Persons Anonymous, it was more about reaffirming their humanity than talking about the inevitable. If he was ready for it, it might be a place for him to turn to release that inner stress and panic that had been building up. The others claimed it helped.

Bryn just liked being reassured that she wasn't the only one facing this weird, uncertain future.

Bryn moved Mr French off her (he grunted, snuffled, and rolled over without waking up) and turned the lights on. Getting ready was mechanical routine, and she didn't do a lot of thinking while that was going on . . . brain on idle until the checklist was done. Make-up slowed her down a little, because she was still relearning the tricks she'd ignored as a teen and never mastered in the military, but she was ready for breakfast in a record thirty-five minutes, even so.

Downstairs, Liam was laying out the chafing dishes in the small dining room. He had all her favorites ready – bacon, low-cholesterol eggs, bagels with cream cheese, orange juice, and best of all, free-flowing coffee. She didn't know what Liam made his coffee with, but it had to be magical sparkles and crack beans, because it was the most delicious stuff she'd ever tasted. She was on her third cup when he sat down with his own breakfast.

'Nice to see you this morning,' he said, and took a sip. He liked his coffee black, and she'd never seen him eat anything at breakfast except the occasional soft-boiled egg. Although he never wore what she would have described as butler clothes, he was definitely well dressed at all times. Even now, he was rocking a petting-soft sweater vest that matched his steel-blue eyes and graying hair. 'Is there anything else you need this morning?'

'No, and if I do, I'll get it,' she replied, and flashed him a smile. 'I know where the kitchen is.'

'Horrors,' he said dryly. 'Next you'll be wanting to do your own laundry.'

'I already do my own laundry.'

'Appalling.'

'Good.'

Liam tapped delicately at the shell of his egg and removed the pieces. 'May I ask what your schedule is today?'

'Only if I can ask yours.'

'Then let me phrase it another way: do you expect to be home for dinner at seven?'

'As far as I know,' she said. 'I'll call if I have to change plans.'

'That would be helpful. You *are* being careful, are you not?' Liam knew everything about her current not-dead status; Patrick had seen to that, on the excuse that Liam knew everything anyway that went on under this roof. She still wasn't entirely comfortable with that, but the horses were well out of the barn on that one.

'I'm taking my medicine on time,' she said, 'thanks, Mom. And I promise not to pet stray dogs or talk to strangers with candy, too.'

Liam sent her a quelling look for that particular snarkiness. 'I mean it sincerely,' he said. 'I sometimes worry you don't take enough care of yourself.'

'I do nothing *but* take care of myself,' she sighed. 'And if I ever forget, I'm sure you'll call to remind me, Mother Hen.'

'Eat your breakfast,' he said, and smiled. 'I'm only looking after the McCallister Trust's investments.'

The McCallister Trust had bought the old Fairview Mortuary and repaired it after the fire, and in effect, she worked for him as the trust's administrator . . . which was a head-spinning turnabout, when she took the time to analyze it. The trust also paid for Manny's research on Returné that kept her shots coming without relying on the government supplies, so in pretty much every sense, Liam held her life in his hands.

And made her breakfast. It was all very emotionally confusing.

'Liam,' she said, and licked a bit of jam off her fingers, 'why do you do all . . . this? I mean, you're the trust administrator. You're not *actually* the butler here. If anything, Patrick works for *you*.'

'I enjoy routines,' he said. 'My father worked in this house, and I've been on staff since I was fifteen years old. The fact that the late Mr McCallister decided to entrust me with the family's assets instead of his son does not require me to stop doing a job at which I'm actually quite expert.' He was quiet for a moment, then met her eyes squarely. 'This is Patrick's birthright. His father was cruel to him. It doesn't mean that I need to continue that cycle.'

'I didn't mean—'

'I know,' he said. 'I do it because I wish to do it. And that's all there is to say.'

It might have led to an awkward silence, but Liam, after a brief pause, asked Bryn what she thought about replanting the gardens, and she was grateful for a change of subject – so grateful, she even got enthusiastic about bromeliads. After her meal, Bryn walked Mr French, then headed for work.

On the drive, she called ahead to the office. 'Lucy? Hey, girl. I don't have any appointments, do I?'

'Clear schedule this morning,' Lucy said. 'You've got that afternoon thing at Pharmadene.'

'Then I'll be in the office after lunch.'

'*Please* tell me you are off to some romantic rendezvous with hot Mr Pat.'

'It's not a romantic rendezvous,' Bryn said.

'Then tell me you're not picking up a dead person, because it is way too early for that.'

Bryn laughed. 'See you soon, Luce.'

'You know Joe's gonna ask me where you are this morning.'

'Yes,' she said. 'I know. Good luck with that.'

'Boss! Don't you hang me out to dry!'

'Tell them I had to meet with a vendor off site and I'll be in after lunch.'

There was a short silence, and then Lucy said, all traces of humor gone, 'And will I be lying to him?'

'You know, I think I'm having a bad influence on you,' Bryn said, and cut the connection. Lucy didn't try to call back, thankfully, and Bryn felt only a little guilty.

What Lucy didn't know would ensure that Joe didn't decide to helpfully drop in on her meeting this morning with Carl, who was probably nervous enough to bolt if he *imagined* he saw anyone watching him.

Coffee Jack's was doing – as usual – brisk business; Doorman Dave saw her parking and got up from his table to swing the door open and hold it. 'Top of the morning!' he told her with absolutely insane cheer, and gave her a sunny smile. Doorman Dave didn't work for the shop; he was an elderly African-American man who was just here every morning, with a giant cup of coffee and nothing to do. This was his hobby, meeting people, chatting, and . . . opening doors. He'd been doing it for years.

'Morning, Dave,' she said, and gave him as optimistic a smile as she could. 'So, anybody new this morning?'

'Ah, you know, couple of dozen walk-in-and-outs.' He gave her a surprisingly sharp look. 'Are you here to meet the nervous fella?'

'Dave. You know I come here all the time, I'm a regular.'

'Yeah, but you never asked if there's anybody new.' He nodded inside. 'Back table, in the corner. He's drinking unleaded. That's probably wise, since he's jumpy as a cat in a dog factory.'

Bryn glanced at the coffee in Dave's big hand. 'You need a refill?'

'Could do with one,' he said, and his smile, if possible,

got even brighter. 'You spoil me, Bryn.' Dave greeted hundreds of people every day, but he remembered every single name. It was amazing, really.

'I'll order you one up,' she said. 'Thanks, Dave.'

He winked at her and let the door fall shut behind her. She ordered herself a cappuccino and Dave's regular poison, chatted for a second with the counter staff (necessary at Coffee Jack's, which was the most chatty place she'd ever visited) before looking around for Carl.

Just as Dave had said, there was a pale, nervous man in a suit sitting in the back table in the corner, next to the noticeboard. He was watching her, and took a quick swig of his cup and stood as she came over. 'Carl?' she asked. He nodded, and she slid into the seat opposite his. 'Good to meet you.'

He nodded and sat down himself. He had the look; Bryn would have recognized it even if she hadn't had the heads-up from Doorman Dave. There was a certain haunted expression in the eyes that she still saw traces of in her own mirror. If Dave still worked at Pharmadene, he was likely one of those lower-level employees who'd gotten his death-and-rebirth courtesy of a corporate memo. Bryn's murder and Revival hadn't been pleasant, but at least there had been a *point* . . . unlike these poor bastards, who'd just worked in the wrong cubicle, for the wrong company. And now, like her, were saddled with an addiction that was as onerous as it was terrifying.

'I heard about you from Chandra in the research labs,' he said. 'She said you're . . . like us. But you don't work for the company.'

'That's right,' Bryn said. She tried the cappuccino, and as usual, it was amazing. 'I was what you might call a lab rat. I got the shots before anyone at Pharmadene did.'

'So you understand . . .' Carl hesitated, shifted his coffee around without drinking it, and finally burst out with it. 'The government brought in counselors, you know. We're supposed to talk to them. But I don't . . . I don't trust them. Any of them. I want to get out of this, and get my family out of it. Get free.'

'I don't blame you,' Bryn said. 'But it isn't that simple. You *can* get free of Pharmadene, at least to a certain extent, and if you want I can help you do that, but this isn't a situation that gets any better. It's maintenance. Scenery can change, but every day, the shots have to happen, for ever. Once you reconcile yourself to that, you can start to deal with it.'

'But I don't *want* to reconcile to it. I want it to stop. There has to be a way—'

'There isn't,' she said flatly. 'Look, I went through this, Carl, and I'm *still* dependent on the government program to some extent. I've consulted experts. I've done everything I can to make this go away, but it doesn't. There isn't a cure. There's just . . . living, day to day. And I'm sorry, but you need to accept that before you get yourself into trouble. If there aren't con artists preying on your desperation yet, it's only a matter of time before one figures out there's an opportunity. You need to be pragmatic about this if you want to survive.'

'I haven't told my wife,' he said, and looked down. 'I don't know how to even start doing that. How did you . . . ?'

'I'm not married,' she said. 'And I can't tell you what to do, Carl, but you can't hide this from her. She needs to understand why you can't go on vacation for a weekend, or miss a day at the office, or . . . whatever the situation might be. *Not* telling her is only going to get harder. The counselors at Pharmadene have training for this . . . take your wife in with you, sit down with them, and talk it all out. She'll have to sign the government agreements, and accept being monitored twenty-four seven – not that she isn't already. She'll be shocked, and angry, and betrayed that you lied to her for this long, but it's better if you do it in a situation where others can support what you're saying . . .' Her cell phone buzzed for attention, and Bryn pulled it from her pocket and checked it. 'Sorry. Hang on a minute.' She recognized the caller ID.

Bryn walked over to a quiet space, and took the call. 'Mrs Renfer?'

'Bryn?' The relief in the woman's voice was as tragic as it was obvious. 'Bryn, I *know* you told me not to call all the time, but this is important. I think . . . my husband knows something. I cut my hand yesterday, a bad one, and he knows it healed up.'

Same song, second verse. 'Lynnette, you haven't told him? Why not? Didn't we talk about that in the group?'

'Yes, but . . . but I just can't, I can't tell him the truth yet. What if I tell him . . . something else?'

'Like what?'

'I'm . . . a . . . a fast healer?' It was funny, but the desperate panic in Lynnette's voice wasn't. Bryn was just about out of patience with the woman; there had been at least ten of these calls now, and a whole lot of meetings, and Lynnette was stubbornly stuck in place, unwilling to move forward. Maybe having her husband actually see something that tipped the scales was a good thing, ultimately. It took away any chance of Lynnette avoiding the crash.

'You know that's nonsense,' Bryn said. 'Just tell him. Take him to Pharmadene and educate him. Please.'

She hung up on Lynnette's standard Reasons Why That Can't Happen, and went back to Carl, who was still staring into his no-doubt-gone-cold coffee as if it held the answers. 'Was that, ah, one of us?' he asked.

'Yes,' she said. 'Not everybody deals with it well. Carl, I'm not kidding, it's very important that you not stay where you are right now, emotionally. It's not a good place. Your family can help you, and you need to read them in on this as soon as you can, okay? Promise me you will.'

He nodded, but it was more of a mechanical action than agreement. 'What about the shots?' he asked. 'I hear you have someone else you get them from instead of the government. Should I do that? I mean, if there's a choice, I'd rather not have the FBI looking down my throat, you know?'

'I know,' Bryn said. 'But the fact is, my guy can't manufacture enough to support everyone who needs the drug, and the other option I know about is worse than the FBI, trust me.'

Carl laughed, a little hollowly. 'What's worse than being owned by the government?'

'Being owned by a madman who wrings you dry,' she said. 'Don't go looking for that, Carl. This is early days. Things will change, and maybe they'll get better, but for now, play it safe. And get your wife into this. I mean it.' When he stayed silent, Bryn said, 'Do you have kids?'

'Two,' he said. 'A nine-year-old boy and a six-year-old girl.'

Her heart broke a little – not just for him, but selfishly, on her own account. She'd wanted children, but in that vague, rosy-future sort of way that she'd assumed would eventually come into focus when she'd met the right person.

She'd met the right person, she thought. But there was no future of babies. Not for her.

Bryn smiled and said, 'Pictures?'

He looked startled at that, but of course he had them, snapshots on his phone at least. He passed it over, and she paged through the photos. 'Wow,' she said. 'Great-looking kids. What are their names?'

'Robert and Josie,' he said. 'What am I supposed to tell *them*? They're going to grow up, and my wife is going to get older, and I'm going to just . . . be *this*. Every day, the same. I don't get older. I don't change. I just . . . exist.'

'Some people pay good money for that,' Bryn said. She was going for a joke, but he didn't smile, not even a little.

'We're never going to change,' he said. 'Until we rot away. How do I *explain that*?'

There it was, naked and panicked in his eyes, the same feeling Bryn faced, and pushed down, at least once a day. As far as she knew, they all felt it, the same shadow stalking them, relentless and dark.

She reached out and touched his hand, and felt him flinch. 'I don't know,' she said. 'We're all making this up, Carl, every day. But you have to start with your wife. It's your only real choice.'

She talked to him a little more, but it was just noise, really; he wasn't hearing her, and she had to resign herself to the fact that Carl, like Lynnette, just wasn't ready yet. He'd get there. He'd have to.

Easy for you to say, part of her mocked. *You don't have to explain things to your kids*. Except that she forced that out of her mind too, every day . . . that she'd never have kids to explain it to, never hold her own baby, never see her child grow up. That had been taken from her, along with her life, in the basement of Fairview Mortuary, and she'd never get it back. The nanites coursing through her bloodstream could keep her walking, talking, doing almost everything the living could do . . . but not that.

The door was closed.

Carl walked out ten minutes later, and she sat for a while, sipping the last of her drink and feeling a little comforted by the busy, self-absorbed bustle of those around her. Like Carl, she felt like a ghost, an alien, a fake. *And they come to me for help*, she thought. *As if I had any idea what I was doing.*

Her phone rang. Oh God, it was Lynnette, again. Damn. Bryn felt a bright, sudden burst of fury, and answered. 'Mrs Renfer, I mean it, you need to stop calling—'

A scream exploded out of the phone, wordless and full of horror, and Bryn almost dropped it. 'Lynnette?' She stood up, shoving the table back as she did so; her almost-empty cup tipped over and spilled milky fluid. 'Lynnette! What's going on?'

It was chaos on the other end of the phone, screaming, shouting – a man's voice – Lynnette, begging *don't, don't, don't* . . .

And then an ear-shattering blast of sound.

Lynnette's screaming stopped.

Bryn stood very still, unable to breath. She could still hear the man's hoarse, half-sobbed curses.

And the sound of children crying.

And then two more quick blasts.

Only the man's sobbing now.

And then one more blast.

And silence.

Bryn numbly hung up the call, stared at the phone a moment, then dialed Patrick McCallister's number. He answered on the second ring.

'Lynnette Renfer,' she said. 'Meet me at her house. Pat? I think it's bad.'

He didn't ask. He just said, 'I'm on my way.'

Bryn made it to Lynnette's small suburban home on the northern outskirts of San Diego in ten minutes, but she didn't remember the drive at all; all she could hear was the sound of the crying, the shots, the silence. When she pulled in at the curb she saw that Patrick McCallister had arrived ahead of her, in a nondescript dark sedan.

There was another car already there – like Patrick's, it was a dark sedan, and it had a government plate on the back. Bryn wasn't too surprised to see the front door open, and Riley Block step out. 'You'd better come inside,' she said to them. 'This isn't a discussion we should have in front of the neighbors.'

'Police?' Patrick asked as they crossed the threshold.

'Called off,' Riley said. Up close, Bryn could see the lines of stress around her eyes, her mouth, although she was doing a good job of holding her poker face. 'It's just us chickens. Come on. She's going to wake up soon, and I'll need some help.'

Riley had brought along another FBI agent Bryn didn't know, but he was clearly read in on Pharmadene or he wouldn't be here. He looked up and nodded as they entered the Renfer's living room, and Riley went to talk with him quietly in a corner.

Bryn didn't want to look, didn't want to *see*, but she forced herself to do it. Two small bodies lay near the sofa. Lynnette was dead on the blood-soaked cushions, the phone still clutched in her hand.

The husband, unrecognizable, lay with the shotgun fallen next to him. The place smelled like fresh, hot blood, loosened bowels, gunpowder, and – obscenely – fresh cinnamon.

'He saw her cut herself and heal,' Bryn said. 'Last night. She told me. I kept telling her she had to bring him in – I told her that.' She felt . . . well, she didn't particularly feel anything, at the moment. Just revulsion, with an edge of horror that only sliced when she looked at the bodies straight on. So she focused on the walls. Safe enough, until she saw the big, framed formal portrait photo. Lynnette and her husband, sitting with hands clasped. The two little girls in their laps.

A simple, adorable family, glowing with happiness.

The breath went out of her in a rush, and she felt her knees start to give. Patrick's hand was right there when she needed it, bracing her elbow, giving her an anchor to cling to as the world began to drift dizzily away.

'I was on the phone with her,' Bryn said softly. 'When this happened. She was begging him not to . . . why? Why would he do this?'

She thought it was a rhetorical question, but Riley answered it. 'He wrote a note on his laptop, time stamped about thirty minutes ago. According to him, this was the only way. He thought some kind of demon had taken over his wife,' Riley said. 'He didn't want it to get into him and his girls. He was so scared he thought death was better.'

For a long moment, nobody spoke, and then Patrick said, 'She's going to come around soon. It shouldn't be here, looking at her kids.'

Bryn moved in to help, but she was politely, but firmly, pushed back. Riley and the nameless FBI agent picked Lynnette up by the shoulders and feet and carried her off to another room – the bedroom, hopefully.

'You shouldn't be here,' Pat said, and Bryn looked up at him, startled. 'You should go. The FBI can handle this.'

'No,' she said. 'Pat, I was *talking to her*. And he killed her. He killed himself. He killed their *kids*.'

'And there was nothing you could have done to stop it,' he said, and took her in his arms. She hadn't even known she was shaking until she felt the warmth of his body against hers, and his hand cupping the back of her head. She squeezed her eyes shut and buried her face in the soft material of his suit jacket. 'Lynnette was supposed to tell him, but she didn't. You tried to help her, Bryn. Some people – some people just won't listen.'

She nodded, and after that precious moment of letting herself feel safe, she pushed back. She didn't feel like crying, oddly enough; there were no tears in her, not for this. Just . . . silence. And a heavy feeling of inevitability.

'She's going to come back any minute now,' Bryn said. He was watching her with a complicated mixture of worry and exasperation.

'You don't have to be the one to tell her they're gone,' he said. 'Let Riley.'

'It's not that,' she said. 'It's just that Riley doesn't understand how it feels to wake up . . . like this. It's not the same.'

She walked into the bedroom, and Pat didn't try to stop her, even though she could tell he was tempted. Riley was sitting on the side of the bed, sponging blood from Lynnette's face with a damp cloth; her eyes looked darker now, and the lines around her mouth deeper. The other agent had backed away to lean against the wall next to a dresser. A clumsy papier mâché plaque behind him had two sets of small handprints, with names doodled on them in awkwardly shaped letters. That hurt so much that Bryn felt short of breath.

She waited with Riley as the seconds ticked by, and suddenly, Lynnette's bloody body convulsed, thrashed, and she took in a breath so deep it seemed to suck all the oxygen out of the room.

And then she shrieked.

It was a familiar scream; Bryn heard it in her head every day, that waking nightmare sound they all gave out when they woke from death. Like the cry of a newborn, but filled with horror none of them could explain, after the fact.

It faded, and Lynnette opened her eyes. Riley put the cloth aside. There was still a wound in Lynnette's head, but it was closing fast now, and Bryn could almost see the silvery flash of the nanites weaving together tissue and bone.

Lynnette said, 'Ted? Where's Teddy?'

Bryn said, 'He's in the other room, Lynn.' She kept her voice low, warm, soothing. 'Give it time. Try to stay calm.'

'Teddy had a gun,' Lynnette said. 'Is he okay? Is everything okay?' She reached out and grabbed Bryn's hand with sudden strength. 'Please tell me everything's okay. I promise, I'll talk to him, I'll tell him everything . . .'

It was too late for that, and Bryn suddenly, horribly wanted to blurt that out. She was angry, she realized. Angry with Lynnette for bungling this, and angry at Teddy for descending into this hellish cauldron of lunacy. Maybe he'd been onto something about the demon possession, because she wanted so badly to lash out at those who couldn't defend themselves.

She fought back those cruel impulses, but it was tough, really tough, and she had to clear her throat before she said, 'Lynn, just take a deep breath. Please. Just let the nanites work. You'll be all right in a few minutes. Stay still. Riley's going to give you a shot now to help you.'

Riley already had the syringe laying out on the bed, uncapped, and now she picked it up and administered the dose of Returné with an expert flick of her wrist. It took only a second.

Then she picked up a second syringe and injected Lynnette with that, too. Lynnette's eyelashes fluttered, her eyes rolled up to show the whites, and she stopped breathing.

Dead . . . again.

Riley nodded to her subordinate. 'Get her stripped and in the shower. I'll get some clothes for her. We have about ten minutes before she comes around again, and I want her clean, dressed, and in the car by then.'

'What the *hell* are you doing?' Bryn blurted. The other agent pushed her out of the way, scooped Lynnette up, and took her into the bathroom. 'Riley!'

'She can't stay here,' Riley said. 'She's going back to Pharmadene, where she can get treatment she needs.'

'And the bodies? You called off the cops, didn't you?'

'This will all be handled, Bryn. Now, you both need to go. I don't have to tell you that this is a national security matter, do I?'

'You can't just cover this up and make her disappear—!'

'I can,' Riley interrupted her, 'and I have. This entire neighborhood is being evacuated right now for a gas leak. In twenty minutes, this house is going to blow sky-high. The only casualties will be the Renfer family.'

There was a moment of silence, and then Patrick said, from the doorway, 'You mean, including Lynnette. Right, Agent Block?' He had that flat, cold look in his eyes Bryn knew meant trouble. 'She's an inconvenient survivor, and you can't depend on her to keep her mouth shut. What's her future – quick decapitation? Fast-burning furnace? Or just let her decompose in the white room so you can chart her process?'

If he was planning to ruffle her calm, he was disappointed. 'She goes back to Pharmadene,' Riley said, without much emotion. 'And you're right, she can't leave there again; she's too high a risk. If she decides she wants to end her drug regimen, or chooses another method of . . . termination, that is entirely her choice; it's one we give all the addicts. Frankly, if it was me in this situation, I wouldn't want to go on.' She looked up then, but not at Pat – at Bryn, who felt a chill ladder up her spine. 'Would you?'

Bryn didn't reply, but she knew if she'd been forced

to do so, she'd have had to confess that dying, however horrible, might have been better than living the rest of an immortal life with the burden of this on her conscience.

The shower cut off in the bathroom. Riley went to the closet and combed through clothes (how do you choose an outfit for a time like this, Bryn wondered?) and handed underwear, pants and shirt off to her colleague. 'You should leave,' Riley said to the rest of them. 'The clock's ticking. You should be able to go without any questions being asked, but if you're stopped at the cordon give them my name.'

Bryn said, 'You can't just—'

'Can't just *what*?' Riley snapped, and for a moment her shell of calm cracked through to white, furious rage. 'Can't clean up this mess? That's all I do, Bryn, it's my fucking *job*. Day after day. Night after night. I see the wreckage that Pharmadene left us with, and I get to sweep up the broken glass. So either get out of the way, or grab a broom.' She paused for a second, shut her eyes, and then looked at Pat. 'McCallister, get her the hell out of here. Now.'

He stood still for so long that Bryn was convinced he'd do *something*, stop what was happening, *try*, but instead when he did move, he only crossed to Bryn and took her hand. 'We need to go,' he said. 'There's nothing we can do.'

'We can't let them just abduct her—'

'Bryn, we're on thin ice as it is. You can't fight this.

Listen – *listen to me*!' She was trying to pull free of him, and get to Lynnette, and he grabbed her by the shoulders and shook her. Hard. 'You exist on the government's sufferance, and that can end any time they want. Don't fight them on this. *Don't.* There's nothing we can do for her!'

'There should be!' she snapped, and broke free of him . . . but then didn't know which way to go. Toward Lynnette, whose limp body, clothed now, was being carried out by the male agent . . . or to cold-cock Riley Block, just for the hell of it.

In the end, the choice was taken from her, simply because the FBI didn't stick around for it. In the next breath Lynnette was out of the room, and Riley was a step behind, and it was just her and Patrick standing there, with Lynnette's blood staining the bedspread in the outline of her head.

And he was, as always, right. She didn't have the power to fight the FBI on this, and Lynnette probably wouldn't thank her for doing it. Still, she gulped in a few breaths, and said, 'It isn't right. What they're doing.'

'No,' Patrick said. 'And we can discuss that all you want. But right now, we need to leave. Now.'

She knew that, but looking around the house she felt a moment of disorientation, of utter *loss*. 'Just a minute,' she said, and went to the plaster cast of the childrens' handprints on the wall. She took it, cast another look around the room, and had no idea what else there was. A whole life – *four* lives – had been lost, and all she could think to grab was this one thing.

She didn't have the heart to look anymore, certainly not at the bodies cooling in the other room. In the end, she just walked out. She knew Patrick was worried about her, but she didn't feel upset. She'd shut down. She just felt . . . distant now. Resigned, and oddly, at peace.

She got in her car, put the plaque in the passenger seat, and leaned out the window to say, 'I'm going to work. See you tonight.'

'Bryn—'

She rolled up the window on whatever he was going to say, and drove away.

It wasn't until she was in her office, holding the plaque in one hand and looking at the walls as she tried to figure out where it should go, that the walled-off parts of her crashed in like a tsunami, and she had just enough time to put the thing down before she collapsed against the solid bulk of her desk.

She was still crying when her phone rang. It was Lucy's ringtone. Bryn gulped in air, wiped her eyes, and tried to clear her throat before she answered. Better to keep it short. 'Yes?'

'You wanted me to remind you about that vendor appointment this afternoon,' Lucy said. 'Dang, you've got a lot of off sites all of a sudden, what's that about?

Oh, and don't forget you've got Mr Chen's interment tomorrow at eleven. In case your meeting runs long today.'

'Thanks.'

Even keeping it brief didn't help, because after a second's pause, Lucy said, in a totally different, concerned tone, 'Honey, are you okay?'

'Fine.' Bryn hung up, because she definitely couldn't talk about any of this, not with Lucy, not with *anyone*. She didn't need to be sobbing on the floor right now; it wasn't helping the dead Renfers, or Lynnette, and it wasn't helping her. Lucy rang back, but Bryn ignored it, went into the private washroom attached to her office, and ran cold water over her hands and face. Her make-up needed significant repairs. Doing that steadied her, focused her, and by the time she stepped out and locked up her office door, she felt almost herself again.

Almost.

She turned and almost mowed Lucy down as the woman strode forward down the hall. She flinched. Lucy didn't. 'I *know* you didn't just hang up on me just because I asked if you were okay.' The other woman peered at Bryn closely, and despite all the make-up repairs, Bryn felt suddenly very exposed and fragile. 'You're not okay. What happened?'

'I . . . lost someone,' Bryn said. 'Someone I was trying to help. That's all. It was just . . . hard.' Even that much was tough to say without choking on the words, letting the memories flow out and overtake her. 'I'm fine, Lucy. Thanks.'

'Okay, then,' Lucy said, but she was still frowning just a little. 'You sure there's nothing I can do for you?'

'Just tell Joe that I'm off to Pharmadene. I need him to stay here and cover the shop.'

'He doesn't like letting you go off by yourself. If I didn't know better, I'd say he was kind of obsessed with you.'

That was . . . funny, in a strange sort of way. 'Trust me, he's really not,' Bryn said. 'His wife would kill both of us.'

'Seen *that* happen. Hell, I think Mr Chen might have, too, him dying on top of that hooker and all.'

Bryn dredged up a smile for her, from some unknown storage compartment deep inside. 'Joe's got the address where I'm going. I'll probably have my cell off during the meeting.'

'You be careful,' Lucy said. 'And if you don't mind me saying so, stop off and have yourself a drink after. You look like you need one.'

Boy, was *that* true.

Chapter Four

Pharmadene's building was more like a corporate reservation – acres of land, mind-bogglingly expensive on the outskirts of San Diego, all surrounded by both an obvious fence and (Bryn was sure) more high-tech methods of security that were invisible to the naked eye. She had talked herself into feeling confident, at the beginning of the drive, but as she rolled up toward the guarded iron gates (much thicker and more imposing the last time she'd been here), she realized that she was trembling – fine little vibrations throughout her muscles, but most noticeably in her hands.

Her body was sensibly telling her to run like hell. It, at least, hadn't forgotten what it felt like to rot. Bryn took a swallow of lukewarm water from a bottle to combat the sensation, and had her ID out and ready as she came to a stop at the guard station. The man on station there looked at her with professionally cold eyes, checked her ID, and checked the handheld tablet he was holding for confirmation. Then he had her press her finger to a scanner, for print recognition, before handing over a parking pass.

'Go straight until you see the sign for visitor parking,' he said. 'Turn right, take only the space number that matches this pass. Leave the paper on the dashboard and proceed directly to the security desk inside the building. Don't make any stops along the way. You'll be monitored.'

He wasn't kidding around, and neither was she; she followed the directions exactly, even down to making sure that she took the shortest possible path from her car to the glass-and-steel doorway. There, trapped between that door and another of bullet-resistant glass inches thick, she had to scan her fingerprint again before a cool female voice said, 'Please proceed directly to the security station. Welcome back, Ms Davis.'

Bryn shuddered hard at the creepy fact that this place *knew her*.

Inside was a vast atrium, designed to awe those who stepped within; the central bank of elevators rose up at least twenty floors, and sunlight flooded down through the thick paned glass on top to glitter coldly from even more steel. The security station was made of that same burnished metal, about as comfortable as a morgue table . . . of which she had some experience.

Behind the chest-high desk stood no less than four people, but three of them were stationed well back from the one who smiled professionally at Bryn, accepted her ID, and passed over a badge. It was marked as ESCORTED VISITOR. 'You'll need to stay close to your escort, ma'am,' he told her. 'If you get too far away—'

'I know,' she said. 'Condition Red. Alarms go off. I get tasered.'

'Something like that,' he said, without much concern. 'Ms Harris will take you upstairs.'

Ms Harris was one of the other three behind the counter, a black woman with a military-short haircut and the posture of someone who'd spent hours standing for inspection. She had a handgun, a taser, pepper spray, handcuffs, and a number of other things that Bryn couldn't identify at a glance. Ms Harris was not chatty. Bryn said hello, Harris nodded, and that was the extent of their entire personal conversation all the way up to the twentieth floor. She couldn't help but imagine Lynnette taking this same journey, but going down, down into the basement levels where all the labs were.

Down was where the white room was located, where (in the bad old days) Pharmadene had watched Returné victims decompose and recorded every single moment of it. Bryn was on those recordings. She hadn't gotten far enough to be sluiced down the drains, but far enough that the memory made her shudder, no matter how much she blocked it out.

Was Lynnette in the white room? Or would she choose some other way to go?

The doors opened on more glass, more steel, and expensively abstract art. All of the people sitting at desks looked busy, and as glossy as the surroundings. Harris marched her directly down the hallway, past closed doors, to one with yet another security scanner. Harris handled that on Bryn's behalf. Beyond lay a sea of pale carpeting, more art, tamper-resistant windows, and a desk and some waiting areas.

Ms Harris shut the door behind her. Bryn walked across the rug to the man sitting behind the desk. She was trembling even more now. The last time she'd been in the executive offices of Pharmadene, she'd been meeting with a VP who'd been shooting for this very CEO position . . . and it hadn't ended well for her. Bryn had spent the next few days locked in that white room, dying. As Lynnette might be now.

Not something she could put out of her mind, or convince her body it wouldn't happen again. Something in her was shrieking in a raw, half-mad voice to *get out of here*.

The assistant at the desk – younger than she would have expected – looked up from typing on his keyboard and checked her badge. 'Ms Davis,' he said. 'Please take a seat. Mr Zaragosa will be with you in a moment. Coffee?'

Bryn had a sudden flashback to her own meeting with Carl this morning, the taste of coffee, the sound of Lynnette screaming, and said, tightly, 'No, thank you.' She wasn't eating or drinking anything in this place.

Her palms were sweating. Holding a cup would only show off the unsteadiness of her hands, anyway, and she didn't need the distraction.

He nodded, picked up the phone, and spoke into it quietly. After he'd hung up he went back to the keyboard, and the white noise of key clicks was a subdued, even soundtrack as Bryn sat down in one of the modern, uncomfortable chairs. There was an old issue of the company newsletter on the table – three months old, probably the only one produced after the fall of the previous administration. Curiously, the magazine didn't mention how most of the employees had been callously murdered and Revived by their bosses, but it did have perky, happyspeak articles about how much the company cared. Corporate values. What a crock of shit.

She was glad she hadn't accepted anything to drink. Even with her stomach empty, the articles made her nauseated.

The interior office door opened with a sudden rush of air, and Bryn forced herself to wait a beat, then replace the reading material neatly before she got to her feet to greet the oncoming Chief Executive Officer of Pharmadene.

'Raymond Zaragosa,' he said, extending his hand. She took it, feeling a little off balance now, because he wasn't what she'd expected. 'Steve, hold my calls, would you? Ms Davis, please come in. Thanks for making the trip. I'm sure this was the last place you'd like to be today, given the history.'

He was on target, of course, but as she followed him into the inner sanctum, she found herself considering Zaragosa himself, not her potentially dire situation. He wasn't corporate poster-boy material, for one thing: graying hair, yes, but not recently cut; his suit looked nice enough, but he hadn't bothered with tailoring. Added to that, he had a stern, lived-in face with lots of character lines. No nonsense.

'Have a seat,' he said. 'Sorry about the modern-art furniture. I hate this stuff, but it comes with the office, and I'm not wasting taxpayer money on redecorating just because I think it's uncomfortable.' He didn't indicate the chair in front of his desk, but instead one at the round meeting table in the corner, decorated with a speakerphone and piles of folders. 'First of all – and let's just get this out of the way – I know coming back here must have been traumatic. If there had been any other way to ensure secure transfer of information, I wouldn't have dragged you back to this place. I know what happened to you here.' There was compassion in his expression, and it seemed genuine.

Bryn tried to smile as she said, 'Thank you, but I'm fine.' The second that his gaze lingered on her let her know he recognized the lie, but was prepared to ignore it. 'Let's just get down to business, if you don't mind.' She thought about asking about Lynnette, but the fact was, he wouldn't have any personal information. Not about that. They'd keep him away from the disagreeable part of the Pharmadene equations.

And besides, he was already talking. 'First of all, I'm FBI, and yes, I'm fully qualified as a field agent, but my focus is on white-collar crime,' he said. 'Forensic accounting. That's why they brought me in here to try to autopsy the Pharmadene books while I administer the shutdown process. Most of what I found is totally above board; like all major corporations, they had to have yearly audits from reputable vendors. But what happened this past year was completely out of the ordinary. I'm sure the plan was that by the time the audit requirement came around, they'd control a large enough chunk of the *important people*' – given finger quotes – 'that they wouldn't be at any risk of discovery. All that should have come to a stop when Irene Harte and her contingent of corporate rebels was taken out, but the thing is, some of these suspicious financial activities haven't stopped, and I'm hitting a stone wall. If I take it through official channels, my fear is that word will leak out before we can really nail down what's going on. So. You're our . . . black ops team, I suppose. For lack of a better term.'

'You know that it's a condition of my continued freedom to do whatever work the FBI wants me to do,' Bryn said. 'It's not as if I really have a choice.'

'I know about your agreement. And I also know that Pharmadene continues to dispense, out of the refrigerated stockpiles, a limited quantity of Returné to selected individuals. You're one of them.'

And, in fact, she wasn't using her store directly; she gave it to Manny Glickman, who tinkered with the formula, stripping out all of the 'extras' that Pharmadene's genetic engineering had put into it. Those extras would have allowed Pharmadene's in-the-know executives – those that had survived, anyway – to control her in a real and immediate way, and it was something she never wanted to experience again. Certainly the government knew of the built-in Protocols by now. She could never take that chance.

But she merely said, 'Yes.'

Zaragosa shook his head. 'I know this sucks, Ms Davis, and I wish there was a better answer for it, but please understand – I believe that the people receiving these payments are probably involved in the illegal manufacture and sale of Returné. Neither of us wants to see that continue. It's a drug that has no real upside, not for anyone.'

'What about the cancer cure it was intended to be?'

'We're working it back to that, but the revival drug itself . . . we'll never manufacture it again. It's just too dangerous. The formula has been wiped completely from servers, backups, everywhere.'

She really doubted that, although Zaragosa probably believed it. No way was the government going to just *delete* that information; there were secret backups, secret labs probably even now working on the formulas. Dangerous things didn't get incinerated, they got archived. Like smallpox. Just in case.

'What do you have so far on tracing the payments?' she asked. Zaragosa pulled out a folder from the stack and thumbed through it, then handed it over to her with one page pulled out to the front. It looked like a flow chart, but it was incredibly complex – the payments went to a shell company, split, flowed a dozen directions, all of which bounced to other accounts, all around the world. 'You do realize that my skills aren't exactly accounting-related, don't you?'

For answer, he produced another, handwritten sheet of paper. She somehow had no doubt that he'd written it himself. On it was an address in Los Angeles, and the short message: CAN'T PUT THIS ON RECORD. WE ARE BEING MONITORED 24/7, EVERYWHERE.

She glanced up at his face, and saw the intensity there. He wasn't kidding. He didn't trust his own people.

'As you can see,' Zaragosa said, 'all I can tell you is that although the payments *look* legitimate, they are definitely suspicious just from the care that's been taken to reroute and conceal them. I would start with the apparent front company, if I was you. But please, be careful. I can't guarantee that this won't be dangerous.'

He meant that, she could tell; she nodded, closed the folder, and tucked it under her arm. 'I understand,' Bryn said. She stood up and offered her hand. 'I'll call you when I have something.'

'My card,' Zaragosa said, and reached over to pull one from a stack – except the one he pulled out had writing on the back, she could feel that without even turning it over. She nodded, tapped it once, and slid it into her jacket pocket. 'Call any time.'

'Am I free to go now?'

'Of course. Steve will walk you out. I'm sorry I can't go myself, but I'm scheduled for a conference call in just a few moments. My thanks for being so understanding of our dilemma.'

She nodded, and the assistant's arrival at the door derailed any possible reply she might have come up with. There was a lot going on here, and a lot she couldn't understand . . . but she trusted Zaragosa, maybe unreasonably so. If what he had scribbled out was true, there was a grave problem within Pharmadene – a crippling problem for the FBI that they probably didn't even trust their own technical people to investigate. There were cameras everywhere in this building, and it wasn't hard, if you were inside the system, to keep track of everyone's computer activity, read messages, monitor digital phone calls. There was no privacy, especially if they had people bugged at home, too.

Pharmadene had always had oppressive, intrusive security, but it ought to have been turned off by now, or at least under the FBI's control.

That it wasn't was a sign that things were still very, very dangerous.

So of course, they throw me right in the middle of it, Bryn thought. The temptation to read what he'd put on the back of his card was very, very strong, but she didn't dare. High-definition cameras were everywhere. She'd be sharing the contents of the note with anyone who cared to look.

McCallister wasn't going to be any happier about all this intrigue than she was. That was somehow a little heartening.

Steve was about as chatty as Ms Harris had been. He had a nicer suit than his boss, and there was something about his subtle, expensive aftershave that irritated Bryn; he seemed more like Old Guard than New FBI. She wanted out of the elevator, out of the building, out of the clinging slime of Pharmadene, but she had to patiently wait out the long drop to the ground floor, sign out, turn in her badge, fingerprint out, get in her car, fingerprint out again at the gate before she finally achieved some kind of freedom. Nobody searched the folder during her exit interview, which she found curious until she saw the stamp on the outside. It had Zaragosa's personal signature on it, and it said EYES ONLY, with her name listed.

She drove off of the Pharmadene campus and five miles along the winding road until she felt it was safe, and then turned off into a large park and made sure to pull into the shade of a big, spreading tree. The place was mostly deserted. She opened the windows, turned off the engine, and first checked the folder over very, very carefully – not the contents, but the structure of the paper.

That was how she found the device, tiny as it was, embedded in the thick folder itself. It was certainly a tracker; it might do more than that, too – she couldn't take the chance. She separated the contents of the file from the folder, then looked through each page, holding it up to the light for any telltale shadows. All she found were standard watermarks.

Bryn took the folder to the nearest recycling station and added it to a bin destined for shredding. *Then* she turned his business card over and read the back of it.

It read, *Do not trust Riley Block.*

The address he'd written out longhand she kept in her pocket, along with the business card – which she also checked for a tracker – and the rest of the paperwork would go into her safe at the office until she had time later to study the thick, dense information.

If they're listening in right now, she thought, *it'll be silent as the grave.*

It was only a little funny, once she considered it.

'You are *absolutely* not going alone,' Pat said, beating Joe Fideli to the punch by about one second.

They were sitting in Joe Fideli's workshop, located behind his house. It was 9 p.m., post-dinner; Kylie, Joe's wife, had seemed happy to have them as guests, though Bryn guessed she'd never be completely comfortable with Joe bringing his work home with him. For Bryn, it had been a delightfully relaxing experience, being back in a house that featured well-worn, comfortable furniture, chaos, and noisy children. Mr French loved it, and she knew that leaving him to play fetch with the Fideli children would be good for everyone.

As nice as the dinner was, there was a great deal of relief being in the soundproofed, security-hardened workshop, too. For one thing, Joe had fine single malt Scotch stockpiled here. Cask-conditioned sixteen-year-old Laphroaig. It lingered like sunlight in her veins, though the nanites in her bloodstream took care of any intoxication pretty fast, which sucked.

Together, the three of them had gone through her meeting with Zaragosa, the written notes, and the official paperwork.

And the two men were united in their opposition to her running the FBI's errands.

'You're seriously trying to tell me what I can and can't do?' she asked Patrick, watching his face with full concentration. 'Because I'm pretty sure you can't, Pat. And neither can you, Joe.'

'Okay,' Joe immediately said, holding up both hands in surrender. 'No arguments from me, you can do whatever you want. But I think what Pat meant was that it isn't smart for you to go without backup. Right, Pat?'

Pat was staring her down, a frown deepening between his brows. 'Maybe.' She reached over for the Scotch and poured him another dram. 'You could be walking into another meeting with Jonathan Mercer; he's got his fingers in everywhere. And we all know how splendidly that's gone so far.'

He wasn't pulling punches, but he wasn't wrong, either; her first face-to-face with Mercer, one of the two inventors of Returné and an all-around madman, had resulted in a gunfight. Her second had gotten Joe Fideli put into the hospital with a punctured lung.

Her third time hadn't been the charm. She'd gotten her brains mashed with a frying pan, at the hands of her own sister, while Mercer laughed. That sort of thing wasn't necessarily fatal to her anymore, but it was damn sure one of the memories she could have done without.

'Neither one of you are quite as durable as I am,' Bryn said. 'And if it *is* Mercer, it's better if I get him myself without putting more people I care about at risk. It's bad enough he's got Annie. I can't let you two go walking in there to end up the same way. He'd love to recruit the two of *you* to his army of the walking dead, with all your ninja combat skills.'

'I'm not a ninja,' Pat said.

'Speak for yourself, man.' That earned Joe a poisonously angry glance from Pat, and he toasted the two of them, drained his glass, and stood up. 'Right. You two work this out between you and let me know when I'm needed. I'm going back to wash dishes before my wife kicks me out to sleep here. Feel free to not mess with anything. And lock up when you leave.'

'Good night,' Bryn said as he left, and then looked at Pat, eyebrows raised. 'I didn't think he trusted anybody enough to leave them here with all his toys.'

For answer, Pat pointed to the corners of the room, and Bryn saw the discreet glinting eyes of cameras. 'He trusts us,' he said, 'but that doesn't mean he won't rewind the video. Just in case.'

'Trust, but verify?'

'Exactly.'

Joe had good reason to have such good security on his workshop – *workshop* being a euphemism for something between a well-stocked panic room and an arsenal that would give the ATF nightmares, if they had any inkling it existed. Joe Fideli had a past with some branch of the military, but he'd been working on his own for a long time, and that work involved serious and varied weaponry . . . neatly stored on racks, hung on boards, and packed in crates. The gleam of black metal and the smell of gun oil permeated the place. Bryn had asked him, straight out, if he was a mercenary; Joe had replied, without even a flicker of concern, that he was a military contractor. Which was, probably, a yes.

And in this, he had a lot in common with Pat McCallister – who'd also moved in the same circles in the military, and afterward. Bryn still didn't have a good inventory of his skills, except that they were wide, varied, and expert. He was probably checked out on all the weapons stored around here, for instance; she knew he was a deadly good shot, and had good hand-to-hand combat experience. More than that, though, he had *contacts*. Lots of them. Enough to solve problems that guns wouldn't.

Pat's smile faded back into seriousness, and he leaned forward, hands clasped between his knees. 'Bryn, you *cannot* go into this alone. I'm serious about this. It isn't safe.'

She mirrored his posture, just as intent, and said, 'I'm serious when I say that as much as I appreciate your . . . concern, I can take care of myself. And I *will*. Clear?' The hiccup of a pause before she said the word *concern* was telling, and she knew it. The warmth didn't leave him, but it banked itself back to a low simmer, and Pat leaned back in the chair, watching her with suddenly guarded eyes.

'Are we back to this?' he asked. 'All of a sudden it's just that I'm *concerned*? Are we just friends now?'

She didn't want to have this discussion, not now, not here – not with the video evidence of it left behind on Joe Fideli's cameras. She and Joe were tight, and he was trustworthy, but this was deeply personal business.

'I don't know,' she said, very evenly, although what was going on inside her was full of sharp edges and sudden drops. 'Aren't we?'

Pat shook his head, not to answer her but just to indicate he was done with the conversation. She set her unfinished glass of Scotch aside and stood up. 'I'll meet you back at the house,' she said. 'We can talk there.'

He wanted to push it, she could tell, but he was just as private as she was about their relationship, whatever it was. 'I'll be up late.' He meant, *don't go to bed without talking to me*. She didn't acknowledge that at all, just offered him a cool kiss on the cheek and left without another word.

Outside, the night air felt damp and cool, heavy with mist. She went into Joe's house through the back door – keypad lock, to which she had a code – and found Joe and Kylie in the kitchen, finishing up the dishes. Without a word, Kylie handed her a towel, and she helped wipe down the damp china and put it away.

'So,' Joe said. 'That was a short conversation.'

'Yeah.'

'Something you need to share?'

'I didn't know this was an AA meeting, Joe.'

Kylie shot her husband a warning look. She was exactly the kind of woman Bryn would have expected to attract Joe, actually. Lovely, strong, intelligent and sensitive. She reached over with a soapy hand and picked up the half-full wine glass sitting by the sink, which she finished off. 'Cheers,' she said. 'It's not, so ignore my nosy-old-lady husband. Thanks for coming over. The kids love seeing you, and Mr French.'

'Mostly Mr French,' Bryn said, but she smiled anyway. Right on cue, her bulldog wandered into the kitchen, panting. He flopped down next to Bryn's feet, clearly exhausted, and gave her a piteous, long-suffering groan, complete with puppy dog eyes. 'I think he's ready to go.' She wiped the last plate and put it away.

Kylie dried her hands and hugged Bryn close, kissed her cheek, and whispered, 'Be careful.'

'I will,' Bryn whispered back, then let go and hugged Joe, too. He didn't bother warning her, and there was no cheek-smooching from him. It was like hugging a block of concrete. It always surprised her how densely muscled he was; he carried himself so casually that it was easy to miss. 'See you tomorrow.'

'I'll wear my best gun,' he said, without a trace of irony.

Mr French groaned again, heaved himself back to his feet, and followed her out to the car, where he jumped up on the passenger seat, turned around three times, and flopped down with a sigh that said, more clearly than anything, how run out he was. He didn't even beg for the window to be down. By the time she'd driven to the end of the block and made the first turn out of Joe's neighborhood, her dog was completely, utterly asleep. And snoring like a little old man.

Bryn rested one hand on his warm, short fur. He woke up long enough to twist around and give her fingers a sleepy lick, then fell right back to sleep. 'Everything's all right, dog,' she told him. He snored. 'We're going to be okay. I promise.'

She wasn't talking to the dog, of course, not really. Apart from being asleep, Mr French had total faith in her ability to make everything right. In his doggy universe, that was her job – to make him happy and safe, to keep the food and water coming, and to toss the ball.

Simple.

There were times Bryn ached to have that simplicity for herself, though she knew full well she'd hate it if it came. Life was never simple, and it wasn't meant to be.

She took the long way home. She stopped at the beach to walk on the sand, shoes off, breathing in the mist and listening to the timeless, steady hiss of the surf. She wasn't alone out here, but she could pretend she was; that was what all the other shadowy figures – sometimes entwined – were doing, pretending they were invisible, locked in their own private universe. Nobody bothered her, or even spoke to her, and after ten minutes she was chilled to the bone but only a little soothed.

The drive home was uneventful until her phone rang. Bryn hit the hands-free button on her steering wheel and said, 'I'm on my way,' because she knew it would be Pat, checking on her slow progress.

But the voice that came out of the speaker's wasn't Pat's. It was her sister Annalie's. 'Bryn?'

Bryn steered hastily to the curb, put the car in park, and said, 'Annie? Annie, where are you?'

'Bryn, I need you to come get me, please come get me . . .' She sounded desperately scared and lost. 'I need to see Mom, I need to get home . . .' In a much softer voice, her sister said, 'I don't know what's happening to me.'

'Sweetie, where are you?'

'I-I don't know. I think I'm dying, please come get me . . .' Annie was crying, Bryn realized with a wrench; she sounded disoriented. 'A boat, I think I'm on a boat. I can't get out, I need help. Please—' Annie sucked in a sudden breath that sounded almost like a scream, it was so drenched with alarm, and then there was a soft click and the call died.

'No,' Bryn whispered, and fumbled for her phone in her purse. 'No, no, no, Annie, no . . .' She checked the number: CALL BLOCKED. She dialed Pat McCallister's number. Her mind was clear, cold, and running very, very fast. When he picked up, she said, 'I need you to pull my cell phone records and trace the call I got right before this. It was Annie, Pat. Annie called me. She said she thought she was on a boat.'

He was silent for maybe a second, and then said, 'I'll have the intel ready before you get here.' She didn't doubt for a moment that he would have someone, somewhere, who owed him enough of a favor to make it happen.

'Pat—' The line was already dead. He hadn't said goodbye.

Mr French, who'd been woken up by the sudden stop and the emotion radiating out of her, whined in concern and licked her arm. She leaned over and hugged him, and said, 'We're going to find her, baby. We're going to find my sister.'

He barked, as if he agreed, and settled down in the seat as she put the car in gear and headed home with absolute disregard for speed limits. *God, if he's decided she's of no further value to him . . .* Mercer was not a nice man. If he'd decided that Annie wasn't useful, he'd dump her like a bad date. In Annie's case, that meant no more shots, and no more shots of Returné meant a slow, agonizing, and gruesome death. She could already be far along the path.

He's luring you, the cooler part of her brain warned her. *That wasn't just Annie being resourceful and getting her hands on a cell phone. He wanted her to call. He wants you to go rushing in to save her.*

Maybe. But honestly, Bryn couldn't see how else to play it. Annalie was her sister, and she'd been innocent in all this, a victim. There was no way Bryn could play it safe if there was even the remotest chance that Annie could be rescued and out of Mercer's hands.

She also knew what Pat was going to say. She just didn't want to hear it.

CHAPTER FIVE

The first words McCallister said to her, as she and Mr French rushed inside the mansion's big entry hall, was 'This way.'

'Do you have the information?' Bryn asked, dumping everything but her phone next to the door.

'Yes. Come with me.' He'd taken off his suit jacket and tie, and his pale-blue shirt was wrinkled, the first two buttons loosened – he looked unexpectedly vulnerable to her, somehow. She was so used to seeing him completely *together*. As she followed him, he said, 'Bryn, you have to expect that this may be—'

'A trap,' she said, well aware of the tension in her voice. 'I know. Just help me find her, Pat. I *need* to find her. Please, don't tell me the dangers, just . . . *help*.'

He said, 'I will,' in a soft, flat voice, and closed the door behind her. She hadn't paid attention to where they were going, but in the sudden rush of stillness, she realized that they were in Patrick's personal office . . . a place she'd rarely gone, simply because the door was always shut, whether he was inside or not. It was a warm, book-lined room of dark woods and maroon fabrics, with soft gold light fixtures that lit but didn't dazzle. The desk was massive and heavily carved, and the chairs matched. It was all very masculine and Victorian, except for the gleaming, ultra-modern laptop sitting on the tooled leather desk top.

Pat lifted his gaze to hers and said, 'Info's on the laptop screen. I printed a copy for you to take. But make no mistake, Bryn; I might be willing to accept letting you go alone on Pharmadene's black flag op, but not on this. No way in hell. So I'm coming too. I'm not entertaining any arguments. If you tell me no, I'll just take another car and beat you there.'

'I wasn't planning on trying to shut you out,' Bryn replied. 'I'm scared. I'm scared for Annie.'

'And I'm scared for *you*. You're too desperate to find her, and that's a liability. Slow and careful. That's how we're going to find her, and how we're going to get her back safely, without losing anyone else. Agreed?'

'Agreed,' she said, but her heart wasn't in it. 'Do you think he ordered her to make that call?' Jonathan Mercer's moral compass – if he'd ever had one in the first place – had shattered into a million sharp pieces when he'd helped create Returné. What was left was something Bryn didn't really understand at all. Mercer was capable of anything – of luring them in to be killed, most obviously, but he was utterly unpredictable. He might just be screwing with her to entertain himself. Even if he let Annie go . . . if Annie was still under his control, she'd be a perfect Trojan Horse.

Or maybe, just *maybe*, her sister had somehow won her freedom and needed, desperately, to find safety.

Pat sank down in the desk chair, holding both her hands in his. 'I think if Mercer wants to have a chat with you, he'd think using Annie to arrange it was just good business,' he said. 'So until we find out differently, we have to assume that he knew she was calling, at the very least. It wouldn't be safe to do anything else.'

She looked past him at the screen. It had a cell phone number on it, but he quickly crushed her hopes by saying, 'The number's not useful in itself; it's a throwaway. But I have the cell's last GPS location. It's been switched off, but you were right. It was at a marina, right here.' He brought up a map, and pointed. 'It's not exactly the Yacht Club. The place is a favorite for drug smugglers. If we go, we go in armed and ready.'

'*If* we go?'

'Mercer—'

'Pat, Mercer didn't set this up. If he had, he'd have at least had her give the location to feed me, wouldn't he?' Even as she said it, it had a hollow ring and she knew it. She wanted to believe that Annie had gotten free of him, that she could be saved. Could be *fixed*.

And at the same time, she knew that was bullshit, but she couldn't let it go.

Pat, however, was going to make her do it. 'Knowing we could grab the number off your records and get the GPS coordinates? No. He gives you more credit than you give him, Bryn.' He leaned forward, capturing and holding her gaze in his intense stare. 'I *will not* let you throw yourself away on this. We'll play the game, but we'll play it safely. You don't go charging in, are we understood? Say yes and mean it, or I zip-tie you and leave you here while Joe and I go on our own.'

'You *wouldn't.*'

'You think not?'

She couldn't actually swear that he wouldn't; McCallister could be coolly ruthless when he needed to be, and he might think that he *did* need to be right now, with her. 'I could probably get those zip-ties off. I mean, skin and bones do grow back on me.'

A smile shadowed his lips, but didn't show itself plainly. 'Probably,' he said. 'But it'd slow you down.'

'So does a bag over the head.'

The smile, never really present, disappeared completely. Pat's grip on her hands tightened, then deliberately loosened. 'I will never, *never* do that to you,' he said. 'You believe me?'

She did believe him, and always had – from the moment she'd first seen him on her second birth, she'd somehow believed in his essential goodness. And on impulse, she leaned forward and kissed him – caught him by surprise, for once, and for a second his lips were soft, yielding under hers before pressing forward, parting, meeting hers with equal amounts of need and longing. His tongue stroked gently over her mouth, and there was a buried wildness in her that broke free when she allowed it entrance. His body was tense against hers, and his hands traveled slowly down her sides, curved inward, cupped her hips, and pulled her tighter against him. She had no idea what drew him to her with such constant and consistent force, but it was always there, that buried attraction that only required a moment's slip of control to surface. It was wildly sexy, but more than the pure attraction of him, there was a kind of beautiful strength to Patrick that she couldn't begin to define.

Why he wanted *her* was such a mystery to her, but there was no question in her mind, no question at all, how much she wanted *him*. She wanted to blot out the world with the red race of pulses and bodies, the damp solace of kisses and sweat and hot, mind-wiping sex. She needed to feel *alive*, with Pat, *now*.

But she couldn't. Because of Annie.

So she sucked in a deep, angry breath, and backed away.

McCallister reached for her, but when he saw the look on her face he let his hands fall back to his knees. He pulled in a deep breath, dropped his head against the cushion of the chair, eyes going narrow. 'I still mean it about the zip-ties.' He *almost* succeeded in making it sound as if nothing had happened between them. Almost. But there was color in his face, and his lips were damp, and she couldn't stop focusing on them.

On the shining light in his eyes.

'I know,' she said. 'And I want to . . . continue this. But if she's out there, if Annie's out there and loose, we need to find her before Mercer can. Please.'

It had been unfair of her to do that to him, but he only nodded and said, 'Then we go in five minutes.'

He meant five minutes to tell Liam where they were going, put on body armor (Bryn didn't need it to survive, but she did admit that *not* being shot was still preferable), and arm up with what Patrick kept on the premises – almost as complete a selection as Joe Fideli did in his workroom. Patrick and Joe had been friends a long time, and there was no doubt that part of what had built that foundation was how similar their backgrounds were – if they'd served together, they'd never spoken of it, but Bryn wouldn't have been surprised.

Joe almost certainly provided his armory.

It was five minutes on the dot when she met him downstairs. He was holding a shotgun, and sliding a handgun into the holster he wore.

'Are you sure that's enough?' she asked, as she checked her own sidearm. He handed her extra clips for her belt pouch, and after ensuring the magazine was ready and there was a bullet in the chamber, she safetied the weapon and put it away. 'Remember who we're dealing with.'

'I'm well aware,' Pat said. 'But your sister's in the middle of it, and as much as he probably deserves it, we can't take the risk of killing Mercer. So pick your shots. Joe's our backup. He'll have the heavier stuff.'

She hadn't seen him call Joe, but it didn't surprise her that he'd managed to fit the call in while her back was turned. As she watched, Pat readied a small bag with more extra clips, shotgun shells, and three sealed preloaded syringes. 'You said that Annie didn't sound so great. She'll need boosters, if so.'

'Manny's formula?'

'No,' he said. 'Pharmadene standard's all we can spare. We don't have enough of Manny's to use for anyone but you.'

He strapped on his own bulletproof vest with smooth, competent, almost instinctive motions, and Bryn was suddenly struck by the fact that he was the at-risk one in this equation. She could take a bullet. So could Annie. So could Fast Freddy, Mercer's slimy little thug, equally Revived.

But not Patrick McCallister. He was still alive, and vulnerable. 'Pat, you don't have to do this with me. I can go alone and just check it out. I promise, I won't do anything stupid.'

He glanced up at her and smiled – a real smile, one that lit his eyes, crinkled the skin next to his mouth, and made her shiver somewhere deep. 'I'm not that fragile,' he said. 'Trust me. And I need the practice.'

She sincerely doubted that last part. Pat looked about as comfortable with weapons as anyone she'd ever seen; his movements with them were precise, careful, and had the grace of incredible familiarity. He'd never told her *exactly* what his military experience had been, but it must have been far, far more intense than her own. And the fact that he'd survived it without too many visible scars told her that he was either seriously good at it, or lucky, or both.

It was a very good combination, if so, because right now, she could use some serious luck.

And so could Annie.

Pat was right about the area of the marina . . . it was murky, industrial, poorly lit, and in a part of town where the police traveled in numbers when they came at all. As she braked the dark sedan into a spot as far from the wan security lights as possible, another vehicle coasted in to a stop beside her – a big pickup truck, in the same basic, lightless black. She knew it by sight: Joe Fideli's vehicle. It wasn't a surprise when he stepped out, dressed for battle in dark-gray urban camo, with a black watch cap over his shaved head. As Pat had promised, Joe held the heavy arms – an FN P90, or a lookalike. The military had classified it as a PDW, a personal defense weapon, but it was capable of some fearsome offense, and was probably highly illegal to carry around in the wild.

That was the weapon she could see, but she had every confidence that Joe had a selection at his fingertips. He was the kind of Boy Scout who came prepared.

Joe leaned against the bed of his truck as she and Pat got out of the sedan. 'Fancy meeting you here,' he said. 'Going for a midnight sail?'

'Nobody goes for a midnight sail out of this marina unless their passenger is a hundred pounds of coke,' Pat said. 'Thanks for coming out.'

Joe shrugged. 'You know. Five hundred channels on TV, nothing's on. What's the op?'

'Annie called me,' Bryn said. 'She may be out here somewhere.'

Joe looked toward the marina, and the bobbing shadows of ill-kept boats. His eyebrows rose, just a little. 'Somewhere,' he repeated. 'So, very specific intel, then – that's always just so great. We got a plan, or is that just as poorly defined as our objective?'

'It's loosey-goosey,' Pat said. 'But we haven't got much of a choice. If she *is* out there, she's in trouble and she needs help. Joe, I need you to stay put and watch our backs.'

'Right. I'll be lurking here, by the transformer. Pat, what channel are you on?'

'Three,' Pat said, and reached up to touch a control on his earpiece. 'Test.'

'Got ya.'

'I don't get one?' Bryn asked. The two men exchanged a look.

'You don't leave my sight,' Pat said. 'So you don't need one.'

'Are you *kidding*? There must be a hundred boats here. If we stick together we'll never get through this in time!'

'Not negotiable,' Pat said. 'Are you coming?' He was already walking away.

Bryn looked to Joe for some kind of support, but he just shrugged. 'He's the boss tonight. Sorry.'

She had to take long strides to catch up, since Pat didn't slow, but by the time she'd caught up to him she'd calmed down. He was right, of course. This wasn't an area where either of them needed to be poking around alone. It wasn't just the risk of Mercer and Fast Freddy getting the drop on them – there were plenty of paranoid, well-armed gun enthusiasts out here protecting drug-related investments. She didn't see anyone, but she could sense the danger; the shadows were constantly shifting as the boats rose and fell on the waves, and the constant creaks and groans of wood whited out other telltale noises. It was calm in the bay, but never silent.

Pat said, 'We start on the right and work our way left. Don't board any boats without signaling me first.'

She nodded and took a deep breath. She smelled rotting wood, the low-level stench of the still water, a sharp, foreign tang of oil and metal. She had good night vision, but she saw no one moving.

Certainly no sign of Annie at all.

She tried to redial, but got nothing except a recorded message from a robotic operator telling her that the mobile customer she had dialed was unavailable. The phone was switched off, or (just as likely) tossed overboard . . . if Annie had been caught, that would have been the most logical thing to do. *And then they would have raised anchor and gotten the hell out of here, not waited around for us.* Unless, as Pat assumed, it was a trap. Her gut was telling her that this was bad, and turning worse with every passing moment.

But damn her gut. What it boiled down to was that she could not, under any circumstances, let a chance to get Annie back slip away. Not without a fight.

The docks were as slimy and ill-maintained as she'd expected, but Bryn had worn thick, gripping boots, and she had no trouble with her footing as they methodically examined the boats. Most were fast, light craft without a cabin; there were only two moored at the first dock that had any chance of holding Annie in concealment, and Bryn slipped aboard each of them and searched. Empty.

The second dock didn't hold anything of interest, either, but the third was clustered with larger fishing boats (probably not used for fish, these days; she imagined they were prime smuggling vessels). She and Pat were very quietly debating which to choose when he held up a hand for silence, and turned his head slightly to the side.

She mouthed the name *Joe?*, and he shook his head, gestured sharply, and headed back toward where they'd parked.

Bryn had an urge to yell, but she was sensible enough to know it was *not* a good idea, not here. Besides, the speed with which he was moving was telling.

When he was off the dock and onto the dirty gravel beyond, he broke into a full run, and she had to work to keep up for the sprint . . . but it didn't last long. Pat skidded to a stop, and drew his sidearm at the same time. *Not* the shotgun, which was in a canvas holster on his back. He had a steady aim almost before his feet stopped sliding.

Bryn pulled her gun as well, though she had no idea what she'd be aiming for . . .

Until she saw Joe Fideli, on his knees, hands laced on his bare, bloodied head.

With his P90 pointed at his skull.

Fast Freddy Watson, former embalmer for Fairview Mortuary, stood there with his finger on the trigger. He bared his teeth at Bryn. It was his version of a winning smile, and she supposed if she hadn't been acquainted with him it would have had a charming quality to it. He was a good-looking man, but there was something base and rotten behind the candy coating. Something truly awful that the nanites had enabled to be even worse, somehow. Whatever shreds of decency he'd ever had were long, long gone.

'Hello, friends,' he said, and pressed the P90's blunt barrel to Joe's head. 'Drop 'em if you want Daddy here to see his kids again—'

Bryn let her weapon fall.

It hadn't hit the ground before Patrick took the shot. No hesitation at all. The bullet hit Freddy in the exact center of his pale forehead. Freddy stumbled back, and his finger spasmed on the trigger once before it fell out of his hand to hit the gravel. The round went wild, spanging off the metal of the nearby transformer casing and disappearing off into the night.

Joe pitched forward onto the gravel and rolled. 'Jesus *Christ*, Pat!' he yelped, and got to his feet as he wiped blood from his eyes. 'Little warning next time?'

'He'd have killed you the second I disarmed,' Pat said. He sounded steady. He *looked* steady. 'It was the best chance I had to save your life. The odds were bad either way. And since when do *you* get sucker-punched?'

'Since I met you.' Joe bent down and picked up the P90.

He was in the act of putting the sling back over his neck when Annie's voice said, softly, 'Bryn?'

She spun around, reaching blindly for the gun at her side, but that was instinct, and the weapon was still lying on the gravel at her feet. No time to get it, and when she saw her sister, the gun was the last thing on her mind.

Annie was dying. Worse than that. She was dead, dead and rotting and *still standing*. Bryn froze, unable to move, unable to *think*. She just stared, drenched in a cold, drowning horror. Annie's eyes were cloudy, her face gray and wet, her hair in matted, thin clumps. There was something so wrong in the way her skin hung loose over her muscles.

The wind shifted, and the smell of death made Bryn choke.

'Bryn,' Pat said softly. 'Don't move. Stay where you are.'

She didn't think she *could* move. There was something gut-deep wrong, seeing her little sister like this – sweet, vibrant, laughing Annie. This was nightmare Annie, bathed in stark moonlight and black shadows. Something no one who loved her should ever, ever see.

'Annie,' Pat said, and came a step closer. 'Annie, we can help you. Where's Mercer?' He didn't bother to ask *is he here?* because Fast Freddy went nowhere without his master. Mercer was here, somewhere. Watching.

She didn't seem to hear him for a long moment. Bryn knew, with sickening certainty, how slowly Annie's brain would be processing things – how hard it would be to put together concepts and understand questions. Decomposing like this was like being lost in the dark, fumbling for a doorknob on a door that might not even exist.

'Here,' she finally said. It came out a bare thread of sound. 'He's here . . .'

Regardless, Mercer didn't show himself. Pat continued his slow, steady progress to Annie, and Bryn didn't understand why he was going so slowly, so carefully . . . until she saw what Annie was holding in her hand.

It was a grenade.

'Supposed to . . .' Annie froze up again, then slowly stuttered on. 'Drop it. Next to you.'

Pat reached out and squeezed Annie's hand tightly closed, then took away the grenade. 'The pin's out,' he said.

'Does she have it?'

'Do *you* want to search her?' Pat asked. 'Joe, your throwing arm's better than mine. Go.'

'Bad idea, man. We're going to wake up the neighbors.'

'I'm pretty sure shooting Fast Freddy already rang the alarm clock.'

Joe carefully took command of the grenade, and ran to the docks, as far as he could get toward the ocean. Then he shouted, 'Fire in the hole!' and threw the explosive as far as he could out into the water. It hit, sank, and a second later, erupted in a geyser of smoke and shrapnel.

Someone from a nearby boat fired on him.

Joe dropped and rolled, bringing up the P90; he returned fire, and Pat joined him, concentrating on the boat where the muzzle flash had appeared.

Bryn dashed past him to take Annie's arm.

'I was supposed . . . to . . . do something.' Annie frowned, or at least that was what Bryn thought she was trying to do. 'Drop it. I was supposed to drop it when he was close.'

He. Mercer hadn't set this up to get Bryn. He'd set it up to kill *Pat McCallister*. To rob her of her support and make her alone and vulnerable. Bonus points – he'd almost gotten Joe as well. The grenade probably wouldn't have killed her, but it would have destroyed them.

'Pat!' Bryn said sharply. 'Pat, we need to go, *now*!' Whatever else Mercer had in his bag of tricks, they didn't need to stick around for the full show.

Pat nodded and poured a white-hot stream of bullets into the boat, allowing Joe to get to his feet and make it to cover, then zigzag his way back. Other boats were showing activity now; there were people in several of the larger boats, and Bryn was sure they were all armed to the teeth.

Joe made it back and said, 'That was fun. Next time, you get to throw the grenades while people shoot at you.' He was panting, and favoring one side; Bryn saw a hole in his flak vest. He'd taken a round, but as soon as she noticed it he was shaking his head. 'I'm okay. The guy got in a lucky first shot, but the vest took the round. I'm just bruised.'

'I need to do something,' Annie said, with that same

deliberate pace, and an edge of panic in her voice. 'Something . . . it's important . . .'

'Hush, baby, it's okay, it's going to be okay,' Bryn said. She wanted to hug her sister but she couldn't, not when she was . . . like this. Fragile and rotten and falling to pieces. *Dear God, please help us, help . . .* 'We have to get her out of here, Pat!'

'I know,' he said. 'Joe. Truck bed.'

Joe nodded and slammed down the gate, then jumped up on the raised surface. He crouched to present a smaller target, but the truth was the gunfire had died down. Whoever was out there couldn't see the parking lot well, if at all, and they were more interested in taking their boats (and cargo) out of danger. One by one, the engines were starting up, revving noisily.

Pat took Annie by the waist and lifted her straight up. Joe took her in his arms and crab-walked back, laying her down flat once her legs were in. 'Bryn,' Joe said. 'Better ride with her. Watch out, she may forget where she is and try to get out.' He swung over the side and into the truck through the open window, a move he'd obviously practiced. 'Meet you back at your house,' he said to Pat, who nodded. 'Watch your ass, man. I mean it.'

'Pat!' Bryn called, as Joe started the engine. 'I need the syringes!'

He unhooked the canvas bag from his belt hook and tossed it to her just as Joe put the truck in reverse.

Bryn braced herself against the wheel well and unzipped the case. There were three preloaded shots. She uncapped the first with her teeth as she ripped Annie's sleeve open one-handed, and then drove the needle home into the graying, slippery flesh. *Don't think about it*, she told herself grimly. Annie was watching her with haunting, clouded eyes. She looked afraid. 'It's okay,' she told her sister. 'It'll make you better again. It's okay, Annie. You're safe now. We've got you.'

'Have to do something,' Annie said again. She shut her eyes. 'Have to.'

Bryn dropped the empty syringe and repeated the process with a second, then after a moment added the third shot. It'd make her very sick, most likely, but there was no telling how long Annie had been missing shots. Days, certainly. Or Mercer was giving her haphazard treatments, just enough to keep her ambulatory, trapped in a living hell. It was hard to tell, and Annie certainly couldn't make much sense right now.

Bryn smoothed the damp, limp hair back from her sister's face and held onto her as the truck bounced and swerved around corners. The cool night air masked the smell of decomposition, which was a blessing; Bryn turned her face toward the rushing wind and breathed deeply. Annie didn't move, didn't speak, but by the time the truck began to slow down and head toward the McCallister estate, she seemed to be looking better. That might have been wishful thinking, but the alternatives were grim. There were, Bryn knew, limits to what the nanites could do, and there was no real proof of how long the drug could continue to do their work. Everything failed, eventually. What if Annie was just unlucky? Developed a sudden resistance to the therapy? What if she just . . . wore out?

Don't think that way, Bryn told herself. *Face what's in front of you.*

What was in front of her was that she had her sister back. Maybe Returné-addicted, maybe fragile, maybe not the same person she'd been . . . but *back*. Surviving.

Annie whimpered a little. The repair process hurt, Bryn knew that; her nerves were coming back online. That would get worse; as the nervous system was reconnected properly, it would feel like burning alive, at least for a few moments. She knew all the steps, the stages, the pain.

She wished it was possible to spare Annie, but the only way to get through something like this was to keep going. There weren't any shortcuts.

'It's okay,' she kept whispering to Annie, and holding her trembling hand. 'It'll be okay.'

And then they were parked in front of the McCallister mansion, and Annie opened her eyes and said, 'I know. I'm safe with you.'

And Bryn's heart broke, just a little bit more, because Annie wasn't safe anywhere anymore. She knew, better than anyone, that the drugs would have made Annie susceptible to all kinds of orders, made her capable of terrible things that the regular woman never would have considered. Mercer had invoked Protocols on Annie, and there was no telling how much she'd been compromised.

But just for now, at least, she was too weak to do much damage.

For now.

Annie stayed oddly passive as she healed up.

Bryn stayed with her, helped her shakily undress (those clothes would have to be incinerated), and helped her scrub down in the big claw foot tub in the guest room next to Bryn's. This one was called the Harvest Room, and it was decorated in muted autumnal colors, with reds and greens and yellows. Soothing and rich, as all the rooms in this ancestral pile of stone were. Annie didn't even notice. She ran the shower for nearly an hour, until her skin was once again pink and clear and healthy. Her hair was thinner, but that would take time to replace. At least she'd had plenty to work with in the first place.

Bryn dressed her in a pale-pink robe, gown and slippers, and tucked her into bed before asking Liam for some clear soup. He had it up to them in minutes, as if he had been waiting for the call. Annie didn't speak, didn't make a sound, but she obediently spooned up the chicken broth, and her hand only trembled a little.

Her eyes were clear now, but very distant.

'Sweetie?' Bryn said, and took the empty bowl and spoon to put aside. She put a hand on her sister's forehead. 'Hey. Do you feel okay now?'

'Fine,' Annie said. Her voice, like the frozen stare, was dim and far away. 'Thanks for coming for me. I was . . . I was afraid.'

'Of course you were,' Bryn whispered, and smoothed the rich brown curls. 'I'm so sorry, baby. I'm so sorry you got caught up in this. It's my fault. I should have made you turn around and go home first thing, I should never have let you stay with me, not even for a minute. But I wanted you here. I wanted to feel . . . *alive*. You helped me to do that. It was selfish, and I am *so sorry*.'

Annie's gaze moved to focus on her, and her sister raised a pale hand to touch Bryn's face. 'Not your fault,' she said. 'I shouldn't have fallen for it. But he was so *cute*.'

She must have meant Fast Freddy. Annalie had been on her way to the airport, headed home, when she'd disappeared; nobody had been able to pinpoint how that had happened, but now Bryn understood. Somewhere along the way, maybe even at the airport, her sister had run into Fast Freddy, and he'd sweet-talked her into a drink before her flight. Or something more intimate; there were hotels you could get to without even leaving the terminal. But instead of getting a free margarita, or a cheerfully sexual good time, Annie had gotten something else entirely.

Because Freddy liked killing women. He was good at it. And Mercer would have allowed that to happen, then administered the shots to bring Annie back, simply because she was someone he could use against Bryn.

Leverage.

I'm not going to cry, Bryn ordered herself fiercely. *I can't.* Her sister needed her strength, not her self-pity. She could let that out later, in private, where only the dog could hear and sympathize, but now she had to be the older sister, and *hold it together*.

'You're going to be fine now, I promise,' Bryn said. 'You're safe. Freddy's not coming near you again. Neither of them are.' She swallowed hard. 'Annie, I'm sorry to have to do this, but I need you to listen. I'm invoking Condition Sapphire.'

Annie's gaze snapped to hers, suddenly and intensely unnerving. That wasn't Annie looking at her. That was the nanites, waiting for a command.

'Cancel all previously invoked Protocols,' Bryn said. 'Confirm Condition Sapphire.' These were Pharmadene codes, built for military operation; Mercer had developed them, and he would have used them on Annie. He'd tried to use them on Bryn, before Patrick had helped her find Manny Glickman and develop the blocking agents.

'Confirmed,' Annie's voice said, but again, it wasn't Annie at all. There was a cool, mechanical tone to it. 'Protocols canceled.'

And then the shine in her sister's eyes faded, and it was just Annie, shivering. Bryn adjusted the blanket around her. 'It's okay,' she told her. 'You're okay now.'

Annie, for the first time, seemed to take an interest in where she was. 'This is . . . where is it? Not your apartment.' She almost laughed, but it was more of a rasping sound. 'I've been to your apartment. It's not this fancy.'

'No. I don't have that place anymore. I gave it up.'

'Why?'

'Well . . .' Bryn gestured around vaguely. 'This was kind of . . . available. And it's safer. And nicer.'

'Huh,' Annie said. She blinked. 'It's *his* house, isn't it?'

'Patrick's. Yes.'

'Rich?'

'His family is. I don't know that he's personally dripping with it.'

Annie smiled a little. It was newborn and fragile, that expression, but at least it was an attempt. 'Wow. Who knew *you'd* be the one to snag a billionaire? And I was really trying. I read books about it. I was thinking about going on one of those reality shows.'

'He's *not* a billionaire,' Bryn insisted, and felt her cheeks heating up. 'And you need to rest. Your body's exhausted from the repairs. I'd give you something to help you sleep, but it doesn't really work; the nanites burn it off fast.'

'Nanites,' Annie said. 'There are times when I think this is all just a crazy drug trip, you know that, don't you? We're talking about *tiny little machines*. In *my blood*.' She was definitely much better, but she seemed drowsy. Exhausted. Maybe that was a good thing.

'I know it's crazy.' Bryn kissed her forehead. She smelled like Annie now – clean, scrubbed, flowery as spring. But there was still something wintery in her expression, as if she'd never really let go of the fear again. 'Please, try to sleep. I'll check on you in the morning. I'll be right next door.'

'Okay.' Annie kissed her when Bryn leaned down, then turned on her side. 'Bryn?'

'Yeah, sweetie?'

'Thank you,' Annie whispered, drugged by exhaustion. 'Thank you for coming to get me.'

Bryn pulled the heavy tapestry coverlet up and over her, turned out the lamp, and left her bathed in the dim glow of the night light. She didn't want to leave her, but Bryn was exhausted herself, and full of a sharp, cutting tangle of emotion. She needed to talk, and she couldn't with Annie.

She locked Annie's door from the outside. Just in case. And then she changed out of her battle gear and into a soft pair of pajamas, a thick robe, and then took Annie's soup bowl and spoon downstairs to Liam.

He was in the kitchen, tidying up – there was never a spot, a crumb or a thing out of place in this temple of culinary arts. He took the empties from her and rinsed them, then added them to the dishwasher racks. 'You look tired,' he said. 'I assume that Annie's all right?'

'Better,' Bryn said. She wouldn't go so far as to say *all right*, not without a full hearing of what Annie had been through. 'Thanks. She needed something to eat.'

'Quite all right. If she's hungry later, there are some pre-made things in the refrigerator you can heat up, or you can ring me.' Liam finished wiping down the sink and folded the rag before putting it in the laundry basket beneath the counter. 'Are you in search of cocoa?'

'I could murder one,' she admitted. 'Would you mind? I know you're probably off duty.'

'I live here too,' Liam said, and sent her a sharp, kind smile as he got out four cups, cocoa, sugar, milk and marshmallows. 'And I make myself snacks from time to time. I expect we'll have company as soon as they smell things heating.'

He was right about that. As he mixed and stirred the cocoa in a copper-bottom pot, Pat and Joe came in and took seats at the round kitchen table. Joe had a neatly applied bandage on the side of his head.

'I forgot to ask,' Bryn said. 'Joe, how are you?'

'Flesh wound,' he said. 'But Fast Freddy got me with a Taser from behind. My own fault. I should have known that little fucker is sneaky.'

She pointed at the bandage. 'That's from a Taser?'

'Nope, that's from the gratuitous boot to the head

after the Taser. Your friend Freddy's a real piece of work.' Joe popped his jaw, and winced. 'Should have sawed his damn head off when we had the chance.'

'There were other problems at the time,' Pat said. 'How's Annie?'

'The shots are working. She seems better. Just tired. I'm letting her sleep.' She cleared her throat. 'I canceled the Protocols. And just in case, I locked her door.'

He nodded, gaze lingering on her as if trying to tell, without asking, how *she* was. For her part, she wondered about him. He'd taken an awful risk, dropping Freddy like that with Joe's life at stake. Even Joe had been rattled, and he didn't spook easily.

Ice water in his veins. When Patrick had spotted the grenade, he hadn't hit the deck, he'd calmly, methodically taken it away.

There were times when Bryn would swear Patrick, rather than her, was part machine. He could just . . . switch things off. She envied that, a little.

Looking at him now, as he accepted his hot cup of cocoa, he just seemed like a normal guy. His five-o-clock shadow was pronounced, and he looked tired, but not the same ice-cold professional who'd done the things he'd done tonight. When that switch was off, it was *off*.

He looked like a man who badly needed human contact, just now. And when he saw her watching him, he smiled. There was warmth in that, and understanding.

If we were alone . . . but they weren't. All too often, really, they weren't.

Liam joined them with his own drink. 'So,' he said. 'I gather tonight was productive? And, from Mr Fideli's bandage, eventful?'

'You could say that. Pat almost shot me in the head,' Joe said, with remarkable cheer. 'Mmm, good cocoa.'

'"Almost" doesn't count,' Pat said. 'I told you, he was going to drop you if I didn't drop him first.'

'Yeah, and I'm still partially deaf in that ear from the round he popped off on the way down. Next time, just give me a signal first, okay? I'd like to get a last prayer sent up.'

'I thought working with me, you'd be fully paid up on that account at all times.'

'Point,' Joe said, and toasted him. 'You know what would make this so much better? Alcohol.'

'Irish whiskey, coming up,' Liam said, and rose to get it. He came back and poured a shot into each of their cups, including his own. 'To surviving. May it happen every day.'

'Every day,' Joe said, and clinked china with Liam. Pat and Bryn echoed him, although Bryn's had a strong taste of irony to it. Joe sipped, and winced. 'Damn, I think I cracked another rib.' He held out the cocoa. 'Medic?'

Liam added a second shot.

'Aren't you driving home?' Bryn asked, and saw Joe and Pat exchange a lightning-fast glance.

'Nah, thought I'd stick here tonight. No sense in waking up Kylie. I already let her know I'd probably be out.' He sounded casual, and if she hadn't caught the look that had passed between the two men, she'd have thought it was legitimate. 'Besides, staying here at the Millionaire Home for Wayward Orphans ain't exactly stressful.'

Something was up. Bryn drained her cocoa, and the warm flush of the alcohol only stayed in her system for a few minutes before it faded, carried off by those industrious little nightmare machines. 'I'm going to check on Annie,' she said. 'Good night. Thanks for the cocoa, Liam.'

He nodded to her with another of those warm, gentle smiles. 'I'm glad you found her safe.'

As she pushed her chair back, Patrick rose as well. He took both their cups to the sink and rinsed them, then put them in the dishwasher. Liam watched him with, Bryn thought, a certain amount of alarm, as if he hated seeing anyone else touching things in his kitchen. Which was probably the case. 'I'm off too,' Pat said, and Joe raised a hand in lazy farewell.

'Usual time for breakfast?' Liam asked.

'I'll be off early tomorrow. I'll catch some coffee on the way in the morning, don't get up.'

'But it's the most important meal of the day!' Joe called after him, and then, to Liam, 'Listen, if you want to make me breakfast, I'm damn sure going to let you . . .'

His voice faded behind her as she followed Patrick through the dimly lit rooms. One of the estate's many dogs – a greyhound – watched them from the comfort of his bed in the corner of the gorgeous sitting room but didn't get up; they were all more Liam's pets than Pat's, or Bryn's.

She wasn't planning on catching up with Patrick, but she found herself moving faster, nevertheless, and by the time he was at the top of the stairs to the second floor, she was beside him, step for step.

Patrick stopped. 'You're checking on Annie?' His voice was neutral, and she couldn't read his face at all.

'I should,' she said.

'Good night, then.'

'Yes, good night,' Bryn said, and watched him walk away. He didn't glance back, just opened his bedroom door and closed it with a firm *click*. She went to Annie's room and checked her door; still locked. Bryn turned the key in the lock, slid it open a crack, and peeked inside.

Annie was asleep in a tangled mound of covers and a storm of disordered brown hair. She looked so young, this way, and so thin that it made Bryn's heart ache.

But she was breathing steady, and she looked ... alive.

And she was safe. Safe, finally.

Bryn shut the door again, turned the key, and leaned her forehead against the heavy wood. It smelled of lemon polish, a comforting, normal thing, and for a few seconds she didn't move at all.

Then she pushed away and looked down the hall.

Patrick McCallister was standing in the darkened doorway of his room, looking back at her. His black shirt was unbuttoned halfway, as if he'd stopped in the middle of the task, and he looked deliciously, warmly rumpled. Like someone awakened from a vivid, sensual dream.

'She's all right,' Bryn said. 'Sleeping.'

'I suppose we all should be,' he said, again. But he didn't go in. He just kept watching her.

She walked to her door, passed it, and kept moving toward him.

He stepped back to let her inside, and for the first second they just . . . looked at each other. Then Bryn reached over, swung the door shut firmly, and said, 'You look tired.'

'Aren't you?'

'Yes.' She pulled in a deep breath. 'And no. Not particularly. I thought maybe we could . . . continue what we started earlier tonight. In your office.'

He didn't speak, but the incendiary look in his eyes answered for him. She reached out and drew her fingers gently down the exposed skin of his chest until she hit cloth and button, and began to undo the rest.

It was as if she'd unlatched a cage, and the tiger leaped out. Her reactions were by no means slow – faster, if anything, with the addition of the helpful nanites – but she wasn't prepared when he lunged forward and pushed her against the door, then put his hands on either side of her head. He got kissing-close . . . but their lips didn't meet. 'I want this,' he said, and there was a rich, focused intensity in the words that made her shiver. 'I want this very, very badly, Bryn. So don't start this if you don't. Just tell me no, and I'll back off. You can go. And everything can be as it was yesterday.'

It was as much a warning as an invitation, she thought. And there was definitely something different about him now; Patrick was such a careful, controlled man, and seeing him trembling on the edge of letting go was like standing in front of an oncoming hurricane.

It was exhilarating and frightening.

'I need to know something first,' she said. 'Don't you care?'

'Care about what?' He took in a deep breath, as if he was savoring the smell of her skin.

'About me being *dead*.' There, she'd said it, and it surprised him, but only a little.

And it didn't drive him away as she'd expected it would.

'You're not dead, Bryn.'

'I'm not alive, either. I'm . . . stuck.'

'Oh, you're alive,' he said. 'Your heart beats. Your skin's warm. You feel things.' For proof of that, he touched a fingertip to the notch of her breastbone and traced the hard outline of it, the hollows around it. 'In no way do I think of you as dead.'

'I need a shot to stay this way.'

'And I need to eat, and drink, and sleep. Even then, every day I come a little closer to the end of my life. And you don't. Which of us is dying, exactly?'

'You saw me,' she said. 'You saw me with a bag over my head. I was *dead*. How can you—'

He put that single finger over her lips, stilling them. 'That's not what I remember,' he said. 'I remember you turning on the water.' She blinked, because that made no sense, no matter how she ran it through her head; her confusion must have shown, because he smiled. 'When you woke up in the room at Pharmadene, and I left you there to think about things, what did you do?'

'I—'

'You went to the bathroom and turned on the tap, and put a cup in place to catch the drops. You timed the drops to pulse beats. You made a water clock so you could keep track of the time,' he said. 'It was brilliant. You'd been murdered. Revived. I'd just told you I might let you rot. And *that's* what you did. You took control of your own existence in the only way you could.'

'I *really* don't understand why that's a turn-on, Patrick.'

'I like women who take control,' he said, and his lips came close again, but didn't touch. 'I also like women who know when to give it up. Do you trust me?'

Did she? Did she *really*? Suddenly, there were so many sensations and emotions in her body that she couldn't sort anything out. It was all just . . . overwhelming.

'Say something,' he said. It came out as a bare, raw whisper.

'Yes,' she said. Just that.

It was more than enough.

He kissed her with so much force behind it she felt a burning instant of panic, but then the hurricane hit, blowing through her defenses and barriers, and she met him at least halfway. His hands yanked the hem of her knit shirt up and fitted around the bare skin of her waist, and *oh*, the burning brand of them, she felt as if they'd left scorch marks. She finished loosening his shirt, but he was too busy to strip it away – busy pulling hers up, baring the black satin of her bra cups. She didn't want to stop touching him, not for an instant, but she had to lift her arms. The soft knit was a cool counterpoint as it slid away, and then his big hands circled her wrists and held her arms pinned above her head as his lips came back to hers. She let out a trembling breath that was lost in the heat of his mouth, and the silky invasion of his tongue as it teased hers.

When he let her arms go again, he did it slowly, sliding his fingers all the way down the smooth, taut skin to her shoulders. As she reached for him again, he put his hands around her waist, pulled her forward, and spun her around with dizzying speed to face the door. She gasped and slapped both hands flat on the surface, about to push off, but he was close against her, heat like a bonfire at her back. Those suddenly gentle fingers traveled up her arms again, and he whispered in her ear, 'Now do you trust me?'

In that flickering second, she wasn't sure. He was so strong, so fast, so . . . decisive. Like he'd been out there at the marina, facing Fast Freddy and calculating the odds of killing his best friend. *Could* a person who could do that be trusted, really?

'No,' she said, and felt him go intensely still for a second before she said, 'but I want to trust you. So help me.'

He sighed, breath stirring the hair on the back of her neck; it made her shiver in delicious dread. 'I'll work on it,' he promised, and settled a sensual, warm kiss where the gooseflesh had formed. She felt a faint pressure on the bra catch, and then it loosened; the straps slid off her shoulders and down her arms. 'Do you want me to stop?'

God, no. A thousand times no – her whole body shrieked in protest at the idea. 'Would you? If I said yes?' His fingers stroked down her back, and that was *not* helping her keep focused on words.

She almost missed the very soft answer. 'With a great deal of effort. Of course.'

Bryn pulled in a shaking breath. There was something so . . . revealing about that answer, on all levels. It spoke to the depths of what he was feeling, and to the man he was.

And more importantly, she believed him.

She licked her lips and tasted the memory of his kiss. 'Do you want me to stay like this?'

'For now.' His whisper this time was dark, deep, and as silky as the touch of his skin on hers. She moved her head to the side as his mouth touched her neck – a lick, and gentle suction, then moving up. She made an inarticulate sound as he sucked her earlobe, teeth clicking on the gold stud earring, and then his warm tongue traced the outer curve of her ear and left her shuddering with bizarre pleasure. She'd *never* liked that, but somehow, the way he did it . . .

And then his hands moved up her sides, and he reached under her loosened bra to cup her breasts. When his fingers crossed the aching surface of her nipples, she felt them swell under his touch, every slow caress harder, more demanding, just trembling on the edge of pain but tipping into pleasure.

She *wanted* him, with a feverish, vivid intensity that shocked her. She hadn't ever wanted anything so badly. It frightened her, and delighted her at the same time.

He was expert at stripping more than her defenses. Her belt went next, and then her pants. He kept her panties on, for the moment, but they were hardly a barrier to the relentless progress of his hands, and as they slid beneath the elastic she arched against his chest in a silent explosion of pleasure. The contrast of the hard, cool wood against her bared breasts, his heat at her back, those clever hands exploring her boundaries drove the breath out of her in hot waves. Not quite an orgasm, not yet, but he was toying with her, reading her frequency.

Patrick might be out of control, she thought in a rare lucid moment, but he was also more *in* control than she could have imagined. He was also deeply aroused, she could feel that in the pressure of his body against hers, and she teased him with hers, encouraging him without words spoken to go further, deeper, harder.

It seemed to take hours before he finally let her panties slip away. His pants and underwear followed, and she'd almost forgotten how to interpret words when he put his lips to her ear and whispered, 'Tell me you want this, Bryn.'

'God,' she said, and rested her cheek against the cooling wood of the door. She was shaking all over, flying apart with need. 'Yes. Please. I do.'

He slipped inside her with a sudden, breathtaking thrust, pressing her against the solid surface, and she let out a low cry of pure, animal pleasure.

And then more, and more, and more, until the world shattered around them in a white-hot fury.

Chapter Six

Somehow, they found the bed afterward – a giant Victorian thing, tall and forbidding, but full of luxurious layers of sheets and blankets that felt soothing and soft against Bryn's hypersensitive skin. She rolled on her side and stared at him; McCallister, like her, looked flushed, and his skin glistened with sweat. There was a vagueness in his eyes that she couldn't recall ever seeing before. It looked like peace. For this moment, at least, he wasn't on guard.

'I'm sorry,' he said, which startled her into a blink. 'I'm usually . . . not that—'

'Don't tell me that,' she said, and smiled. 'Because it was fantastic.'

'In that case, forget what I said. I am *always* like that.' But he was looking at her with a trace of . . . something odd. 'I imagined the first time to be slow and romantic, face-to-face. Not out of control and up against my bedroom door.'

'Something in you wanted it that way. And trust me, something in me wanted it, too. I think we've been thinking about this for *way* too long.' Bryn reached out and traced a slow, lazy pattern on his chest. 'You might have noticed that.'

'I might have.' He took her hand and kissed the back of it, and the softness of his lips made her ache inside, again. Impossible that she could want more just now, but . . . there it was.

'I hope—' She bit her lip on a sudden, strange impulse to laugh, and felt color pinking her cheeks. 'I hope that wasn't as loud outside the room as it seemed like it was in here.'

'You're worried about your sister?'

Annie. God, she hadn't thought of Annie at all, honestly, and that was mortifying. 'I was thinking about Liam. Wouldn't want to scandalize him.'

'A little scandal would do him a world of good,' Patrick said. 'And don't worry, he wouldn't have heard unless he was just outside. I'm sure he'd be polite enough to walk away, in that case. Or at least be discreet about it.'

'Thank God. Uh . . . does he have to be discreet often?'

Patrick's warm, slow smile sparked more heat. 'Not as often as all that. Are we into the confessions portion of the evening?'

'Depends on how much you have to confess. Judging

from how well that just went, I'm guessing it might be a long story.'

He didn't affirm or deny it, just kept smiling. She gave him an irritated shove on the shoulder, but that got her nothing except her wrist captured in his hand . . . and then he pulled her closer, and said, 'If you don't mind me saying so, you seemed like a woman who hadn't been properly satisfied in a long time. From the . . . intensity.'

Had she been blushing before? Because it felt like a bonfire in her face now. 'Well, you know. It's been a while.'

'And if I had to guess, I'd say you've not had very good experiences. Which is a real pity, because you deserve them.' He kissed her, slow and warm and languorous, and she was torn between the hot magic of his mouth and the teasing sensation of her hard nipples brushing against his chest. And his hand, leaving her wrist to slide slowly down her waist and hip. 'So. In the morning, are we just friends?'

She pulled back, staring at him. 'Why would you say that?'

'Because I don't know. I don't know if you want this to be . . . something else, or just the pleasant thing it is. You live here, Bryn. I don't want you uncomfortable. Or feeling you owe me anything.'

'You've just given me the best orgasms of my life,' she said. 'I *do* owe you.'

'I think that was more of an in-kind trade, not a gift.'

'Do *you* want it to be . . . something else?'

He regarded her with a sudden, sharp focus. 'The first day I met you I thought you were complicated and dangerous. No matter how far I go with you, it seems there's more to find. So yes. I'd like it to be more, but I can't be the only one to think so or this won't work. It'll end badly.' He said that with so much conviction she was sure it had ended badly for him before. 'I'm not rushing you. Tonight is . . . tonight. And tomorrow you can be my platonic friend, friends with benefits, or my lover, but they're very different things.'

'*Friends with benefits?* Somehow, I never pegged you as one of those guys.'

'I'm just saying that if you don't want any emotional commitments, I'm not sure I can totally oblige you, but I'd try very, very hard.' He looked wickedly watchful, and she didn't miss the double entendre, or the direction his hand had taken from her hip, stroking gently at the curve. 'Would you like me to try?'

'Maybe, if you're going to try very *hard*,' she said, and closed her eyes on a sigh as his hand moved down. 'Oh. *Oh*.'

He did a great deal more than try, and if this was what being friends with benefits meant, she decided that she could settle for it, gladly, at least for a while. There was something dark and unromantic about the whole thing, but the benefits were . . . amazing.

After, though . . . after the second time, which was so different in tone from the first, but no less breathtaking, she lay curled in his arms, filled to bursting with a kind of peace she'd never really felt before. Her mind was still and quiet – no regrets, no criticisms, no apologies. There was just a simple comfort to it, a trust she couldn't quite wrap her head around because she had never expected to feel this, not for Patrick, not for *anyone*.

Especially not after she'd *died*.

She dropped off to a childlike, trusting sleep, and the last conscious thought she had was *he is just not the kind of man you sleep with and stay just friends*.

Bryn had no idea how long it was between when she'd slid off to sleep, relaxed and comfortable, and when she woke, but it was a sharp, focused sort of waking – not just the normal thing of rousing when a strange bed-partner moves, but a tense, tingling sense of purely instinctive alarm.

It was because of the *way* she'd felt Patrick react. It wasn't a slow, sleepy gesture, it was something that spoke of alerts and danger, and though he didn't stir again, she knew he was completely awake and alert.

And so was she.

There was a crack of dim light coming through the door. The windows showed no signs of dawn; it was, according to the digital clock on the nightstand, just about four in the morning.

Bryn heard a very faint creak of wood, and felt Patrick's hand press lightly in warning, and then move slowly off her skin without stirring the covers. His breathing remained deep and regular, and she had to force herself to try to mimic it. *Something's wrong, something's very wrong here* . . . they both felt it.

And then it was too late to try to think, or plan. She only had time to act.

A light blazed on right in Bryn's face, halogen-bright, and she sensed the attacker lunging at her. Something sharp flashed in the light. Bryn didn't stop to think, just lunged forward, blocked what was coming down at them, then met the attacker's rush with one of her own. The flashlight went flying in a spiraling arc that showed color, wood, a confusing whirl of shadows . . .

She grabbed the intruder more by luck than skill, and held both his arms away from her body as she used her momentum to drive him backward into a waist-high heavy table. She expected it to be Fast Freddy Watson, her nightmare bogeyman, or possibly worse, Jonathan Mercer . . .

But it wasn't a *him* at all. The cry was feminine, and in the moonlight Bryn saw a long, sharp kitchen knife fall to the carpet. There was bright blood staining the first inch. From down the hall she heard dogs sounding alarms, led by Mr French's deep, ferocious barks, and ten seconds later, as she fought to hold on, the door of the room banged back and the lights went on.

Bryn was grappling with her sister.

Annie struggled wildly, screaming now; her hair

whipped around her distorted face as she tried to break Bryn's grip. She didn't look . . . sane.

No, no, no . . . this was what they'd feared, what she'd dreaded, but Annie had seemed so much better. And she'd responded to the Protocol cancellations . . .

'Out of the way!' shouted a voice from behind – Joe Fideli, still fully dressed, who instantly grabbed hold as Bryn let go and backed away. He easily held Annalie and forced her down on the floor, where he put a knee on her chest to pin her as he administered a shot. It took only a few seconds, and then she went out, still as a . . .

Still as a corpse.

He'd killed her. Anesthesia for the Revived.

Joe didn't look up. 'Get dressed, Bryn.'

She realized, with a burst of shock, that she'd been fighting naked and hadn't even realized it. She found her shirt and pants and dragged them on without bothering with underthings, and then, belatedly, realized that there was one participant absent from the drama going on in the room.

Patrick was still in bed. He was alive, and he was breathing, but he had his left hand clamped tightly over his slashed right arm.

The bedding was a mess of fresh blood.

'Pat!' Training kicked in, and Bryn forced herself to slow down, push feelings aside. 'Did she get the artery?'

'Yes,' he said. 'Look after her. I'm fine.'

Not with that much blood outside his body, he

wasn't. Bryn grabbed up her belt from where it lay by the door and wrapped it around his arm above the wound, then yanked it as tight as possible before twisting it even tighter. 'We need an ambulance,' she told Joe, who nodded and rose to his feet to pull out his cell phone. 'What the hell happened?'

'What Pat thought might happen,' Joe said. 'Your sister's under Protocol. Mercer didn't lose her; he sent her like a guided missile to kill you, or Pat, or both. Until we detox her with Manny's new formula we can't break her Protocol conditioning, so I have to keep her out for a while, but we needed to be sure.'

Bryn remembered what it felt like to have her will taken away; it was one of the hidden military applications of Returné. That *undocumented feature* – that was what it was called, in bureaucracy-speak – was one of the first things that McCallister had asked Manny to change in the formula he'd developed independently . . . and the most difficult.

It wasn't that Annie felt right about trying to kill them – she just had no choice. She was a passenger in her own head, with no will of her own, until they could break the Protocol. *Which I thought I'd done.* It had been stupid. She'd fallen into the trap of her own wishful thinking.

But she couldn't worry about Annie just now, not with Pat's skin fading to a pale, shocky color under the olive tone. He looked calm, but there were stress lines around his eyes and mouth.

'I'd love to put on some pants,' he said. 'If you don't mind. Joe—'

'I'll do it,' Bryn interrupted. She helped him dress without another word, and Joe kept watching Annie's limp body as if his life depended on it. He was keeping his observations strictly to himself, which was very un-Joe-like.

'Hey,' she said, and put a hand gently on Pat's face as he lay very still on the bed. He had his eyes shut, but he opened them and focused on her. 'Don't think I missed the fact that she was going for me first, and you got in the way.'

'I've been thinking,' he said, just as if the segue made sense, 'that I don't want to just be friends with benefits.' It was possible he'd lost enough blood that he'd forgotten Joe was standing in the room, unable to *not* hear this. Bryn tried not to glance in that direction, but her cheeks burned a little. 'I hope that's all right with you.'

'Yes,' she said, and swallowed hard. 'I've been thinking the same thing.'

'Good,' he whispered, and closed his eyes again. 'Very good.'

Joe cleared his throat as his cell phone dinged for attention. Text message. 'Ambulance is on the way,' Joe said, and pocketed his cell phone. 'Damn. It's way too early for this kind of excitement.'

Bryn wasn't sure which kind he meant, exactly, but it didn't seem a prudent time to ask.

Chapter Seven

Patrick's slice to the interior aspect of his forearm needed stitches to close the brachial artery, and then more to match up severed muscle and flesh. It wasn't good, but it wasn't nearly as bad as Bryn had feared. It was, for one thing, his left side and not – as Joe had laconically remarked – his main trigger hand. 'Can't shoot for shit in his left anyway,' Joe had observed. 'If a barn's attacking us, he might get a solid hit.'

Bryn could tell by Pat's eyes that he was still doped when they rolled him out in his official release wheelchair, but only mildly, and the first thing he said was to Joe, not to her. 'Is she still out?' Meaning Annie. He'd given the ER doctors a bullshit story about a kitchen accident, which they'd probably not believed but had accepted nonetheless.

'Like a hammered ox,' Joe said, as Patrick got out

of the wheelchair and walked toward the sedan parked in the covered area. Bryn tried not to hover. He'd had a unit of fresh blood, but even so, he still seemed pale to her. 'I let her wake up and put her on a slow drip of the new formula, but it's going to take time. The Pharmadene standard is pretty strong stuff, and it's not easy to erase a Protocol, you know that.'

'You left her with Liam?'

'He's armed, warned, and she's strapped down.' Joe paused in the act of opening the car door and said, 'I'm sorry, man. I should have gotten Liam to spell me when I hit the toilet, but she'd been so quiet all night I didn't think she'd move. I was gone maybe two minutes, tops. Don't know how she beat the door. My fault.'

'Mine, not yours,' Pat said. 'I expected her to go for Bryn first, and Bryn *always* locks her door from the inside. I thought we'd have time to intercept. And I needed to let her try to act, so we'd be able to verify what he'd done to her.' He sent her a half-apologetic glance. 'I was hoping I was wrong, but I thought you'd need proof to convince you that I was right.'

'Well, I think you've got it,' she said. 'And how do *you* know I always lock my door?' Bryn always did, even in the mansion – the habit of growing up in a large family, and living in an apartment complex where theft was a common occurrence.

He didn't answer that, other than with a slight smile.

'Oh, and by the way, no worries about me busting in on you,' Joe said with an insane amount of cheer. 'Didn't see a thing.'

Pat sighed and put his head back against the seat, eyes closed. 'You're not going to forget it, are you, Joe?'

'Which part? The two of you naked, in bed? Bryn going hand-to-hand, naked? Because it's fairly memorable, my friend.'

'Pervert,' Bryn said. 'I'm going to tell your wife.'

'She'd be shocked if I *didn't* remember. And then she'd check me into the hospital.'

Bryn smiled, but her mind wasn't on the banter; it was on her sister. Annalie had been lost for months, and come back . . . brainwashed wasn't the correct word, but neither was *wrong*, because she'd simply lost control of her body to the program. *It can be fixed*, Bryn told herself. *It can all be okay.* But she didn't know that for certain. She'd seen Annie when Mercer had first taken her, and even then, she'd looked . . . damaged. Desperate. Almost destroyed.

Six months later, how much of the original Annie was still there to be saved? *I'm so sorry. I never should have gotten you involved in this.* She'd regretted it, every day, but regret wasn't helpful.

Nothing was helpful right now. She just had to wait and see how Annie came out of it. And Pat was right – she'd have to keep her guard up, regardless. She couldn't trust her own sister anymore. Protocol instructions were wicked difficult to countermand when raised to their highest levels like this.

It was now already almost eight o'clock in the morning, and as Joe drove them back to the McCallister estate, she held Pat's free hand without even considering that she was doing so until they were almost home. It felt . . . right. Comfortable. After last night, they couldn't reset the clock, couldn't take that giant step backwards, even if she wanted to – which she didn't.

Whatever was ahead, she'd keep moving. Maybe it would end badly, or just end, period, but one thing was certain: the ride was bound to be . . . extraordinary. And bumpy. It was insane that she'd finally reached that breathless, intense space with Patrick, and had the world crash on them almost immediately, but she had the sense that any relationship with McCallister was going to be driven hard by adrenaline.

Maybe he might say the same about her.

Bryn checked her calendar on her phone, and sighed. 'I have the job for Pharmadene this morning,' she said. 'Don't give me that look, Patrick, it's fact-finding. It's not dangerous, it's just fact-finding. All the file asked me to do was go in, meet with the owner, and ask some questions about invoices. It's nothing. It's white-collar crime, at worst.'

'Sure,' he said. 'That's why they're sending the woman who can come back from the dead. Because it's not dangerous. You're not going without backup, and I'm not in shape to help.'

Joe held up a hand. 'Yeah, backup, that'd be me. No bullshit, Bryn. I'm not going in with you, but you're going in wired for sound and vision, and I won't be far.'

'Wait a minute. Aren't I *your* boss?'

'Sure, in a certain time and place. This ain't it. The good news is, probably no big deal for me to run a wire up your bra anymore, now that I've seen you naked.'

She glared at him, and he gave her a slow, delighted smile that she couldn't, finally, help but return. Especially when he gave her that wink.

Liam wasn't waiting by the door, as he usually was; Bryn walked up the stairs behind Patrick, mainly to be sure he didn't pass out, as Joe passed them taking three steps to their one. By the time they'd reached the second floor, he'd already checked with Liam, and stepped out of Annie's room to give a silent thumbs-up.

'I need to check her,' Bryn said. 'I know she's fine, but . . . I need to do that.'

Patrick nodded, as if he understood. He probably did. She squeezed his hand a little and stepped into her sister's bedroom. Annie wasn't on the bed, as she'd expected, or at least not on the big, king-sized Victorian four-poster; she was, instead, strapped to a hospital-style gurney with thick Velcro restraints at her ankles and wrists, plus longer straps over her chest, waist and upper thighs.

She looked as calm and peaceful as her own memorial statue. 'God,' she whispered. 'Is she all right?'

Liam was sitting in an armchair a few feet away, with a handgun on the marble table beside him. From the looks of it, he had it cocked and ready. He put down his book and said, 'She's resting quietly. Don't worry. She's fine.'

'Is she—' Bryn bit her lip. 'Is she breathing?' Because neither dead nor alive really applied in this particular case.

'Yes, very slowly. She's in a medically induced coma while we administer the new doses.' Sure enough, there was an IV on the stand next to her, leading straight into her arm. 'She'll be all right, I think. But it may take some time, you should clearly understand that.'

Annalie had been through hell itself for six months. *All right* was a dream Bryn didn't even try to imagine. She settled for *breathing*, for now. She smoothed her sister's hair and kissed her pale forehead gently, then bent to whisper in her ear. 'It's okay,' she said. 'Annie, listen to me: it's okay. I know you couldn't help what you tried to do. I know Mercer did this to you, and I promise, you're never going to be this helpless again. You're going to wake up in control of yourself, and nobody will ever be able to make you do something like this again.' She felt a blinding impulse to cry, and forced it back as she blinked back the tears. 'I love you to bits, you know that? I hope you do.'

Bryn pressed another kiss to her cool cheek, and took a deep breath as she straightened. Liam was watching, and didn't look away, or pretend to misunderstand her distress. 'It's possible she can hear you,' he said. 'I hope that's so. She's in need of all the comfort she can get, I think. I've been reading to her, just in case.'

'Watch her,' Bryn said. 'And . . . watch over her, too. I'll be back soon.'

He nodded. 'No harm will come to her. Just be sure none comes to you either. She needs you, Bryn, probably now more than ever.'

'I'll be watching her back,' Joe said from the door. He held up a tiny device. 'If you want to get this done, time to get dressed, boss.'

She nodded and followed him into her bedroom.

The daily shot came first, of course, even before she changed clothes. She waited out the grim side effects, trying to decide if it was better this time, or worse; she couldn't tell. It just felt awful, again. Then . . . gone. *Another twenty-four hours of borrowed time,* she thought. *I'm a life addict.*

Patrick would say that they all were, but, just now, she didn't feel in the mood for that slightly disingenuous platitude.

Dressing was a bit of a problem. If it came down to a choice between a business suit and heels, or black cargo pants and ass-kicking boots, Bryn greatly preferred cargo pants – they were enough like her old uniform fatigues that she didn't feel like she was wearing some sort of antique, clumsy costume. In dangerous situations – or potentially dangerous ones – she liked to play it safe.

Today, though, she was on Pharmadene's payroll, and hence the FBI's, and there was a dress code for these kinds of things. So she put on a skirt that was fuller than she would normally wear, and stretchy, so that she could run and kick if necessary. She matched it with mid-heeled pumps, a conservative powder-blue blouse, and a jacket that *almost* concealed the bulge of the sidearm she wore under it, at the small of her back.

Because there was no way she was going in without some kind of weaponry.

'I thought that camera thing went in my bra,' she said to Joe, who waited patiently, back turned, while she finished adjusting her clothes. 'Okay, I'm decent.'

'I was just messing with you,' he said, and pinned a piece of jewelry to her jacket – a floral pin, something she wouldn't have chosen for herself but at least it matched. And in the center was the tiny device she'd seen earlier in his hand. 'High-def camera and audio receiver, state of the CIA art that I got from a friend of a friend, you know how it goes. It's got a limited range, and it's a little hinky in tunnels and such, but this is as safe as it gets. What's your panic word?'

'Um . . . magenta.'

'Love me some *Rocky Horror Picture Show*,' he

said, 'and that's good, not something you're likely to say by accident. If I hear *magenta*, I'm at your side in less than two minutes.'

'Guns blazing?'

'Let's try to avoid that. I hear the cops frown on turning downtown San Diego into Dodge City.' He stuck a tiny little receiver in her ear, and put his hands on her shoulders and stared into her face for a second. 'Good to go?'

'Five by five,' she said.

'I won't be following,' he said. 'You won't see me. But I'll be around. Good luck.'

She nodded, and bent down to pat Mr French, who was sitting at her feet, watching all these preparations with a puzzled expression. He stood up, wagging his tail. 'Sorry, pup,' she said. 'You can't go this time. Work now.'

He understood something out of that, because he gave her a sad look, turned three times, and plumped himself down on the floor with a depressed expression on his pushed-in face. Then he sneezed.

She was letting everybody down today.

Joe tapped his watch, and she nodded.

Time to go.

She walked out to the cars with him – her sedan was in place, and he'd traded out the truck for something that might have come straight off the rental lot, as nondescript as possible. She didn't expect it, but Patrick was outside, too, leaning against one of the tall fluted porch columns. 'Seeing me off?' she asked. 'You ought to be resting. You lost a lot of blood.'

'I'll rest soon. Bryn, be careful.'

'Always.'

He stepped closer to her and lowered his voice. 'The FBI wouldn't send you if it wasn't something they know is bloody dangerous.'

Bryn shrugged. 'It could be just another bureaucratic miscommunication. Riley was told to find an operative; she tapped me because she didn't know what the operation was, and she didn't know its danger level. Agent Zaragosa didn't tell her. He just told me, and it turned out to be sort of . . . vanilla.' Privately, she thought Zaragosa simply had wanted to get a look at her, and to warn her that even the FBI themselves were under surveillance.

'Zaragosa may be playing an accountant, but he's not a pushover. Do *not* get in over your head. He won't fish you out of the deep end.'

'I'm fine, Pat. Joe's got eyes on me. He'll back me. And we both know I don't have much choice. If the FBI decides I'm not cooperative for any reason, they can pull me back into Pharmadene and I'll just . . . vanish.' *In that white room, where troubles get washed clean away.* 'I need to do this to keep them off our backs for a while longer.'

They both knew that the government wouldn't keep

the current state of affairs going long; they'd made promises to the former Pharmadene employees they'd saved, the ones addicted to Returné, but what promises had the government ever made that didn't eventually get broken? This was all locked under tight Top Secret, and if a hundred people or so had to disappear, it could be managed. Efficiently and quietly. Wouldn't be the first time.

The only guarantee Bryn really had was Patrick. He wouldn't flinch from doing whatever was necessary to ensure her continued survival, she trusted that.

She trusted *him*.

It wasn't the time to say anything, or even for a kiss, so she just smiled at him and said, 'See you in a couple of hours. I'll bring back Chinese.'

'I knew you delivered.'

That earned him a kiss, just a quick one. She got into her car, started it up, and watched him in the rear view as she drove away. He didn't wave, but he was still right there, staring after her, until her car made the turn to the road.

'Feeling kind of alone now,' she said. 'Testing, testing . . . I hope this damn thing works, Joe.'

'Working fine,' Joe's tinny voice said in her ear. 'Feel free to sing along with the radio if that makes you feel better.'

'Trust me, it wouldn't make *you* feel better.' She tried humming, though, until he winced. 'See? I have a tin ear.'

'Ouch. Too bad for me, I don't,' he said. 'Okay, radio silence from me unless you say the panic word, but I'm monitoring and recording. Starting . . . now. Say your name, date and time.'

'Bryn Davis, September 9th, oh nine fifty.'

'Joe Fideli, monitoring. Okay, we're good to go. See you soon.'

'Copy that.'

The nav system had been programmed to her destination from Zaragosa's information, and it led her straight there without any unnecessary complications. She kept an eye out for Joe's nondescript wheels, but saw nothing, just as he'd promised. For all she knew, he'd beat her to the area and parked somewhere out of sight. The street address was a low-rent office building sandwiched between a donut shop that emanated the aroma of stale sugar and worse coffee, and a dollar store that looked as if it might be going out of business. It was a bad sign for the economy, Bryn thought, if the damn dollar store couldn't stay afloat.

There was a tenant list on the aged felt sign in the lobby; only a few names were listed on it. Most were bail bondsmen clustered on the bottom floor of an almost entirely empty building. Her eyes rested on the last listing for the top of the building: GRAYDON INDUSTRIAL WASTE SERVICES. It was on the eighth floor. There was probably a reason for the mass upper-floor tenant exodus, which Bryn found as she pressed the button for the elevator. When it opened, the floor of it was about two feet below ground level, and made an alarming grinding noise.

She took the stairs.

Those weren't much safer, mainly because the lights were dim (or out) on the stairwells, it had been clearly used as a toilet from time to time by passing drunks, and there may have been a dead animal somewhere. She tried holding her breath as she jogged up, and after that became impossible, drawing in shallow gasps. By the time she arrived at the door to the eighth floor, her lungs were aching, and so were her calf muscles. *Right*, she thought. *More jogging, less lounging.* She stepped out into the hallway – also dimly lit, but blessedly urine-free – and took a second to compose herself again. Her breathing smoothed out, and she took long, confident strides past shut doors until she saw one in the middle that had a glow bleeding out from under it. There was no sign on the door, but the number was the same as had been listed on the sign below.

She knocked, then tried to turn the knob. It opened.

Inside was a standard, cheap reception area with thin, stained carpet and the dead skeleton of a potted plant leaning against the corner. Two plastic chairs, the kind sold at the dollar store neighbor, most likely. The receptionist's empty station had a high counter and thick glass that looked bullet-resistant. From the dust on the desk, it wasn't too likely anyone had been answering the phones in a while.

There was an interior door. Locked. Bryn tried the polite thing first, knocking and calling out in her most inoffensive voice. No response. She pulled out her cell and tried the phones, which rang on the other side of the glass and went to voicemail.

Enough Ms Nice Lady, she thought, and hoped her shoes were up to it.

Her kick landed squarely where she aimed it, and the cheap lock shattered like glass, throwing the door open and back with a boom. That didn't draw any more attention than her knocking or phone-ringing. Not a good sign.

She stepped into the hallway beyond it. Right or left? It looked like there were offices in both directions. No sound of anyone at home. She listened, turning her head each way, and when she directed her attention right, she got a hit.

Not a sound. A smell. Just a bare hint of it, ripe and rotten.

God, no. Not again. She had a flashback of walking into a rich woman's house on the hill, and hearing the storming buzz of flies, stepping over the march of ants, seeing the moving, rotting *thing* on the bed.

Sack up, she told herself. *You've seen it before.* She had. She wasn't frightened of the dead, and decomp didn't shock her. What had shocked her back in that house had been seeing the spectral ghost of her own future, of being dead and still living, still *knowing* as her body fell apart around her.

But that wasn't the case here.

She found the staff of Graydon Industrial Waste Services gathered in the break room, if it could be dignified by that name – there was a cheap old TV in the corner with a broken antennae, and a coffee maker still grimly reheating a carafe of days-old undrinkable sludge. There were also seven bodies, each wrapped neatly in plastic tarps and secured with duct tape, envelope folds at the ends. It smelled chokingly vile. They'd been dead a while, no doubt about that. The blood that had been spilled on the walls and floor was long dried to a bitter brown.

Bryn said, hand over her nose, 'You getting this, Joe?'

'Copy,' he said. He sounded grim. 'Get out. I'm calling the cavalry.'

'Not yet,' she said. 'I'm checking the offices. They died for something.' She had a briefcase with her and opened it to remove and don a pair of disposable gloves. She hadn't touched the break room doorknob; it had been cracked open already, so there'd been no need. She retraced her steps to the left and began opening doors. The first was an office. There was no nameplate, no pictures, nothing personal . . . just a desk, a dead computer monitor with no PC attached, some junk in the drawers, and a few emptied-out file drawers. She checked around. Nothing hidden.

The next was another office – again, stripped bare.

The third door led to a file room with ten cabinets. She checked the drawers. Empty, again. A small safe was built into the floor, but it had been cracked too.

The next door was a bathroom. The killers must have used it for clean-up; she saw drips of dried blood on the sides of the sink, and a pale stain on the porcelain. The trash can was overflowing. She forced herself to search anyway.

That was how she found the thumb drive.

It was a small silver thing, wrapped in a clean paper towel and shoved down the side. It wouldn't have wound up here by accident, not wrapped that way. It spoke of panic, and fear, and a last-ditch effort to hide something.

She was, in effect, holding someone's last testament in her hand.

Bryn said, 'Joe?'

'Yeah, I see what it is. Come out, Bryn. We need to get the cops in this.'

She had no pockets in this suit, which hadn't annoyed her until now; the briefcase she had with her was her only purse. She propped it on the sink and started to open it, but one of the combination locks had spun, and the left side stubbornly refused to open. *Screw it*. She took the thumb drive and stuffed it into her bra.

'One more door to go,' she said, and went out and down the hall.

She knew the second that she opened it that something

was wrong; it just *felt* wrong. In one sense it was the same as the others – emptied-out desk, missing computer, no personal effects.

But there was a square, dark shape sitting on the desk, just a dim outline in the flickering fluorescents.

It had a blinking red light that sped up as she stared.

'Get out!' Joe's voice exploded in her ear, and her own instincts screamed it a half-second later.

She was out the door and in the hall when the bomb went off with a violence that threw her ten feet, limp as a rag doll. Fire rolled overhead, and the fact that she'd fallen flat was all that saved her from the ball bearing anti-personnel shrapnel that shredded the walls at waist level. It was a wrath-of-God explosion, shaking the building, blowing out glass, shattering walls, and she was buried in a fall of brick and drywall.

No time for a damage assessment of her body; she clawed her way free of the debris and saw that there was a murderously hot wall of burning rubble behind her, and a mound of burning debris that totally blocked the way to the reception room.

'I think we've got a magenta situation here,' Bryn said, and had the wild impulse to laugh. Shock. She had blood in her mouth, and spat it out in a vivid red rush; something broken inside, but that would heal. She got up, but her legs wouldn't hold. Something broken there, too. She crawled, instead, heading for the far end where the fire wasn't yet taking hold. The smoke – black, thick, terrifying – billowed out and up. In seconds it had formed a thick layer over her head, and the stench of plastics melting made her retch up more blood as she crawled. *Keep going*, she told herself. *You've had worse.*

Not really. *Magenta, magenta, magenta* . . . She was back in Iraq, with her supply convoy under heavy attack. *IED, we hit an IED, the truck rolled* . . . she'd survived that, survived with only minor injuries. She could survive this.

Hell, she couldn't die . . .

No, she could. She could *burn*.

The fire terrified her, and the fear forced her to keep crawling even as the nanites rushed to the injuries and began the cattle-prod pain of repair. Joe was two minutes out, he'd said so, he might be even closer . . .

He can't get to you, said a cold little logical voice. *You have to get out by yourself. Now, before it's too late.* The smoke was lowering, thickening to the consistency of black water. She'd drown in it, pass out, and then the fire . . . she might be alive and aware for that part of it. The nanites would struggle to keep her going, even while she was burning.

'Bryn! Talk to me, tell me what you want to do!'

There was a white-hot snap of agony somewhere deep in her back, and she jerked and convulsed with it. When it subsided two breaths later, she felt pins and needles stabbing into her skin, and then she felt her legs moving.

Whatever had gone wrong in her spine, it was gone now.

'Bryn, I'm coming up!'

'No,' she said raggedly. 'No, you can't. Stay down there, Joe. You can't help.' She scrambled up to her hands and knees. Her legs weren't working *well*, but they moved, and she moved drunkenly toward the end of the hallway. Even then, the air felt thick and toxic, the smoke swirling as heavy as fabric around her face.

The break room was the last door. She slammed the entrance open and braced herself for the smell, but the stench of the fire had overwhelmed everything else. The plastic-wrapped bodies still lay in an orderly row, but the coffee pot had given up its struggle; electricity had shorted out. Fires burned at the outlets. This room would go up in minutes, and there was no safety here.

There was a window with daylight beyond it. A route of escape.

But it was barred on the outside.

Bryn screamed in fury. She grabbed a chair from one of the tables pushed against the wall; it was heavier than the cheap plastic ones melting right now in the reception area, and she swung it hard into the glass. The window shattered halfway down, and two more hits disintegrated the rest of the panes . . . but the sudden breeze sucked into the room made her realize she'd just screwed herself, hard.

The fire roared into the open room, sucked in by the

rush of oxygen, and it leaped from carpet to walls to ceiling, licking everything as it went. Plastic-wrapped bodies began to smoke and sizzle.

There was no quick-release on the bars outside. They were fastened in hard. She wrapped her bloody hand around one and tugged. No leverage.

'Bryn!' she heard Joe's voice in her earpiece, and it sounded taut with stress. 'You have to get those bars off. It's your only way out.'

'I'm not the fucking Bionic Woman!' she yelled back. 'How do I do that?'

'Find a lever!'

Lever. *God.* What the hell was she supposed to use? Something metal, something strong . . .

The chair. It had metal legs. She battered it in panic against the wall and floor until the plastic split, and one of the legs fell free with a rattle. Her lungs were burning, and her eyes; she coughed, gasped, and choked on a mouthful of rancid black air. The bonfire clawed at her back; *no*, that was just the heat, the heat.

She smelled meat cooking, but that was the dead people, not her, not yet.

She threaded the metal between the side of the window and the bars, and threw all her weight into it.

The leg bent. Not the bars.

Goddammit!

'Fuck it. Get down!' Joe shouted in her ear, and she did, pressing her face flat to the floor.

Gunfire slammed into the outside of the building, a continuous rattle of firepower, and when it stopped she scrambled up and took hold of the bars. He'd concentrated his fire into the brick on two corners of the window – beautiful and precision aiming, and the bars were loosened. She pulled and yanked and twisted, and they swung suddenly free. The whole grate came loose from the building and fell in a spiral down to clang and bounce on the street below. The air was being sucked in through the window, and as Bryn climbed up onto the sill she realized that it was a straight drop. No fire escape. Nothing to break her fall. Just the merciless, remorseless concrete.

'Oh God,' Joe said in her ear. 'Bryn, don't, don't do that, Christ—'

She didn't have a choice. The fabric on the back of her jacket was burning now, and she could feel her skin starting to sizzle.

I'm not burning to death.

The jump was a vivid, conscious decision, and as she stepped off she felt a sudden, absurd regret that she'd worn a skirt as it blew up around her waist. The last sensation she had was of panic, of the wind pulling through her hair and clothes, and then . . .

The landing, she supposed. But that, at least, she didn't feel. Everything just went from hyper-bright and chaotic to . . . black.

When she *did* feel something again, it was, of course, total bloody agony.

She tried not to shriek. Someone was holding her hand. She couldn't see – *blind, oh God, I'm blind* – and then dim shapes began to ghost through the dark.

She made out Joe Fideli's face as he loomed over her. He had a hand over her mouth. 'Easy,' he said softly. 'Easy, kid. I've got you. Had to move you. Cops are already here, so is the fire department. Couldn't let you be found where you landed. You're healing. I know it hurts, but you can't scream, understand? You can't attract attention.'

She understood that, but it was a lot harder to control. She stopped trying to claw Joe's hand free and instead pressed her broken fingers over his straight ones to keep the gag in place.

And she let the scream burn itself out against his muffling palm.

'Jesus,' he whispered, clearly shaken. 'Okay. Okay, relax, relax, let it go . . .' His other hand stroked her hair. He didn't say anything else. When she felt steady enough she nodded, and he raised his hand, cautiously.

'Bones healing,' she whispered. 'Help me.'

'Uh . . . how?'

'Pull them in line.'

'*Fuck*. Okay. Here, bite down on this.' He shoved something between her teeth – leather, it felt like. She bit down hard, knowing what was coming, and felt him pull and twist her right leg. It was like dipping it into boiling lava, but the pain, while extreme, was brief enough. She hardly screamed at all. He did the left, then palpated up her body to find the rest of the damage. She had a broken pelvis, but that was clean enough. Her left arm needed resetting for the compound fracture. He straightened out her back for the spinal injury.

Then, last, her fingers, one sharp, star-bright snap at a time.

She passed out sometime before that, thankfully; when she came to, the pain was an ebbing burn, and everything felt straight, though weak. She spat out the leather strap – his belt – and concentrated on breathing in and out. If she had lung damage from the smoke, the nanites were thorough in cleaning it away.

In another twenty minutes, more or less, she felt human again – especially after the booster shot Joe gave her. Even the side effect rush didn't seem so bad, comparatively.

'That,' Joe said in a hushed voice, 'may be the most disturbing fucking thing I have ever done, and that's saying something. Bryn? You still with me?'

'I'm okay,' she said. That was a lie, but not as much of one as it would have been earlier. 'I can walk. We need to get out of here.'

'I can clean the blood, but your clothes are pretty much totaled,' he said. 'You look like you've been in the fire. It'll get noticed.'

'Should have worn my cargo pants.'

'Probably,' he said. 'Turn your skirt and jacket inside out. It'll do for a quick walk to your car.'

'Had to leave my briefcase,' Bryn said. 'Goddammit, the FBI files were in there. I dropped it somewhere during the explosion.'

'Then it's toasted into little bitty pieces. You're covered.' He helped her take off her jacket and flip it to the relatively undamaged lining side; it looked weird, but not as strange as the smoke-damaged, fire-roasted fabric. She did the skirt by herself. It was almost presentable. Her shoes were weirdly misshapen around her feet, but they'd do. 'I'm walking you to the car. Just hang on to me and don't slow down.'

'Wait.' She reached inside her bra, and found the silver thumb drive; it looked undamaged. 'Take this, just in case we get separated.'

He nodded and put it into a zippered pouch. The hunter's checked vest he was wearing concealed Kevlar – his version of street legal flak gear. 'You good to drive?'

She laughed, but there wasn't much humor in it. 'Sure,' she said. 'Thirty minutes ago I was a leaking bag of broken bones, and now I'm good to drive. Nothing odd about that, is there?' The problem with living as a Returné addict wasn't so much coming to terms with surviving as it was coping with the *wrongness* of it. Something inside just wouldn't accept the terms on which she lived . . . and especially at times like these, when she was so frankly and nakedly *not human*. But therapy could wait, of course. She'd need mountains of it, in the end, but right now she needed to take the first step, then the next. Get in the car. Drive home. Collapse into Patrick's arms and try, for a moment, to forget.

Find out what was on the thumb drive that seven people – eight, if she counted herself – had just died for. It had something to do with Pharmadene, something the FBI undoubtedly suspected and had kept from her. She didn't *think* they'd known about the dead people, or the trap, but she couldn't be sure.

She couldn't trust anyone, except Joe and Patrick and Liam.

Certainly not Riley Block, or Zaragosa, who'd warned her about Riley in the first place.

Good to go, she told herself again. It was an order, and she followed it all the way home.

CHAPTER EIGHT

The explosion was breaking news, but the FBI spokespeople were out in front of it, in a joint appearance with the local police. The official explanation was something crime related, Bryn didn't pay much attention. It was all bullshit, and from the tense look on the agents' faces, they were aware of that, even if they had no idea *why* it was bullshit.

Riley Block had the very same tense expression when she showed up at the gates of the McCallister estate, one hour after Bryn and Joe rolled in. Bryn was in the kitchen with Patrick and Liam when the FBI-issue sedan pulled up, and Riley got out to show herself to the camera. She didn't speak, but then, she didn't need to. They all recognized her face.

'Patrick?' Liam asked, standing next to the security controls. 'If you'd like me to send her away—'

'She won't stay away,' Patrick said. 'Let her in. I want to know what the hell is going on, and she's the only one who might be able to tell us.'

'Don't tell her we recovered anything,' Bryn said. She felt . . . good. It was such a bizarre fact of her unlife, that she could jump to her death from eight stories up, and feel fine a couple of hours and a hot bath later. 'Everything but that.'

He nodded. 'I'll let you do the talking, since I'm still a little off.' Of course he was. She wasn't the only casualty of the morning – just the only one who'd come back from it so quickly. 'Go on, Liam. Let her in.'

Liam didn't seem pleased with the ruling, but he hit the control and activated the speaker to say, 'Please drive to the front, Agent Block.'

'Thank you,' she said, and got back in her car. Well. She was in a polite mood, that was something, at least.

Liam turned the screen off and gathered up the coffee cups she and Patrick had been using. 'I'll bring a light lunch,' he said. 'Enough for the three of you.'

Joe wasn't there; he'd stopped off to hand back the thumb drive, then headed home to see his family and get to the funeral home to cover for Bryn. Patrick shook his head. 'Never mind lunch. Go watch Annie. I still don't trust her to stay put, even sedated and restrained.'

Liam looked disapproving, and before he left he set out a tray of chilled finger-food sandwiches – cheese, cucumber, roast beef. 'I'll get the door and send Riley back here.'

'All right, Mom,' Patrick said. Liam gave him a downright dour look.

'I believe your friend is having a bad influence on you. *Sir.*'

'Don't "sir" me, Liam, or I'll dock your pay.'

'*I* write the checks, if you recall. *Sir.*'

'Game, set, match.' Patrick's moment of levity passed, and so did Liam's. 'Careful up there.'

'Careful in *here*,' Liam said, and included Bryn in that as well; he'd taken her ruined clothing away, without commenting on the blood, smoke and fire damage, but the looks he gave her were worried and reproachful. 'Ring if you need me.'

'I think I can handle Riley Block,' Patrick said.

'One-handed, sir?'

That evoked a smile, a thin one, that showed no lack of confidence. Liam nodded and disappeared from the doorway. He was back a moment later, ushered in Riley, and left again.

Riley was, in fact, *not* in a polite mood, at least not by the time she arrived in the kitchen. She looked very official, Bryn thought; she was wearing a navy-blue suit with a gray blouse that practically shouted FEDERAL AGENT. The only thing missing was the visible shiny badge. She stared at the two of them for a moment, then yanked a chair out from the table and sat down without an invitation. 'Don't even fucking *try* to tell me you weren't there,' she said, leveling a finger at Bryn. 'What the hell happened? I have seven dead bodies, Bryn! And we're damn lucky there aren't more. And I know good and well that this has something to do with Pharmadene.'

'If it had been anybody else but me, you would have had eight bodies,' Bryn said. She shoved the plate of sandwiches toward her. 'Lunch?'

Riley's glare was hot enough to toast the bread. 'What. Happened?'

'How do you know it's related to Pharmadene?'

'Because I was doing a little digging of my own when the word came in,' Riley said. 'Graydon is a contractor doing janitorial work for the company. Your turn.'

'I did just as Zaragosa asked. I put on a nice suit and went there to ask questions. When I got there, the place was locked up tight.'

'And you what, broke in?'

Bryn shrugged and ate a finger sandwich. The cucumber was delicious. 'Well,' she said, chewing, 'it was that or wait around for someone to show up. I kicked in a door. It wasn't like I stormed the place with a machine gun.'

'And then?'

'And then I searched. I found seven bodies neatly wrapped up in plastic tarps, bound with duct tape. From the smell, they'd been dead for days.'

'Where?'

'Break room.'

'Where, by some weird coincidence, the police found *bullet holes* around a grate that had fallen off?'

'I'm getting to that.' Bryn laid it out, one step at a time – the search, the bomb, Joe Fideli's bullet-related assistance in her escape. The jump. That made Riley flinch a little, imagining the subsequent fall and damage, which Bryn made sure to describe in detail. Through it all, Patrick sat in silence, studying Riley with unsettling intensity.

When she finished, there was a short silence before Riley said, 'So you came away from that with nothing.'

No way in hell was she handing Riley the thumb drive. 'Not only did I not find anything, I had to leave my briefcase behind when I spotted the bomb. So if you find any traces of that . . .'

That earned her a shake of Riley's head. 'Not much chance,' she said. 'The place was an inferno. The only reason we know how many dead there was is the floor collapsed in that room before the bodies were completely incinerated. We'll be weeks figuring anything else out. Dammit.' Riley's short fingernails drummed the tabletop, and she reached for a sandwich and bit into it, almost as if she didn't realize she was taking up the offer of food. 'We needed someone *alive*. Or at least some records to examine.'

'The place had been sanitized. I'm no professional at

that kind of thing, but the computers were missing, and the file drawers emptied.'

'No DVDs? Backups?'

'Nothing like that,' Bryn said. It wasn't *quite* a lie. She still didn't know what, if anything, was on the thumb drive. 'What exactly was Graydon into? I'm assuming someone doesn't go black ops on a company that just cleans toilets, even if they clean them for Pharmadene.'

'I asked Zaragosa that question. He tells me that on the books, they look like a legitimate company.'

'I didn't even see a broom in the place, but I suppose theoretically they could have been storing all their cleaning supplies in a warehouse somewhere, and these were just the main offices. But there were a *lot* of file cabinets for a simple waste management company. And we keep coming back to the question: why wipe out seven people who do nothing but empty the trash?'

'Access?' Riley said. 'Pharmadene always had tight security, even before the invention of Returné.'

This time, finally, Patrick entered the fray. 'First, I used to be in charge of security at Pharmadene, and I wouldn't have authorized the murder of seven people, whatever the situation. Also, those people died recently, not under the old administration, bad as it was. They were killed *after* the company went under FBI control. Even so, one thing's certain. Whatever happened, odds are it had to do with Returné.' He spoke with authority. He'd left Pharmadene in the debacle that had led to the demise of Irene Harte and the old administration, and if anybody knew what the company had been involved with then, he did. For all their insidious dealings, Patrick had tried to keep the security department clean, or at least as clean as possible given the circumstances, until the circumstances had changed violently for the worse.

Then, like any sensible person, he'd – what was the phrase? – *left to pursue other opportunities.*

'Zaragosa already audited inventory records and accounted for every single vial of the drug still in existence. I just ordered random testing to be sure the vials hadn't been tampered with or switched, but I don't think these people were being used to smuggle it out. They wouldn't have had access to the storage areas.'

'Then they were doing something else, but as to what it was . . . ?' Bryn shrugged and ate another sandwich. She had no idea how she could be this hungry after something so traumatic, but her stomach was cheerfully ignoring any PTSD. 'I'll be honest, this was damn thorough and paranoid work. The killers are ghosts, and so are your Graydon people. If you want my advice, just let it go. Maybe they were just what they appeared to be: janitors.'

'Janitors don't usually end up being killed and gift-wrapped, but I take your point,' Riley said. 'If you came away with nothing, we're at a dead end.'

'Good. Job's over. Bryn is finished working for you,' Patrick said.

Riley studied him for a long moment. There was doubt in those dark eyes, and calculation, and she finally inclined her head an unwilling inch. 'Done for now,' she said. 'Don't think I won't be looking into this further, and if I find out you're holding anything back . . .'

Patrick said, in a deadly quiet voice, 'You should go now, Agent Block. My welcome's wearing thin.' He stood up, and even with one arm in a sling, he looked utterly dangerous. Riley got up, and she didn't turn her back on him. He, on the other hand, walked past her, opened the kitchen door, and held it for her. 'Go.'

The FBI agent left without another word. After exchanging a silent look with her, Patrick followed her – seeing she left without any side trips, Bryn assumed. She sat back in her chair, feeling an indefinable sensation of loss; she'd originally liked Riley on some level, when Riley had been acting undercover at Fairview Mortuary. Being at odds with her now was just one more way she was cut off from the world of the normal people. *Who can't jump from an eight-story building, on fire, and eat sandwiches afterward.*

Well, in that particular case, at least, being a drug-addicted dead person was proving to be an advantage.

Bryn ate another sandwich before Patrick returned, not so much out of hunger as a restless kind of boredom. He turned on the security camera array built into the far wall of the kitchen and watched Riley drive to the gates and leave before he poured a pint glass of beer and brought it to the table.

Then he slid it across to her. 'Congratulations,' he said. She took the glass and drank. 'You successfully lied to her. I'm fairly sure that's not been done often.'

She slid the drink back, and he sipped and claimed one of the rapidly diminishing supplies of sandwiches. 'I don't know what's on the thumb drive yet. It's hard for anyone to spot a lie if you aren't telling one. We should find out what this thing tells us, Pat.' She started to get up, but he shook his head and tugged her down into her chair again.

'After lunch,' he said. 'Unless you can't finish the beer.'

She smiled, took the pint, and chugged it. 'Heresy,' she said, and slapped the glass down. 'I'm army. We *always* finish the beer.'

The thumb drive was encrypted, which to Bryn's mind didn't seem to be normal procedure for a janitorial company. Patrick was a lot of things, but apparently he wasn't a superspy encryption expert, and he ejected it from the laptop within a minute or two.

'Couldn't we—?'

'Mess with it?' he finished for her dryly. 'Encrypted files are nothing you can pick with a paper clip. We need an expert or we risk triggering some kind of countermeasure that wipes the device clean. Or my laptop.'

'Worried you don't have your porn backed up?'

'Would I do that?'

'The porn?'

Patrick raised his eyebrows. 'Not backing it up. I *am* a careful man.'

'So what do careful men do at times like these when you have encrypted files hidden by murder victims?'

The moment of humor was over, instantly, and he said, 'Call someone who's even more careful. And paranoid.' He reached for his cell phone and dialed, ignoring her silent question *who?* And then sighed after a few seconds. 'Authentication Bravo Ten Seven. Call me back.' He hung up.

The question of *who* was moot. 'You called Manny Glickman.' Manny was . . . well, a bit indescribable, Bryn thought. He was brilliant, no doubt of that, but he was also scared of his own shadow. Not without reason. Manny was ex-FBI, and he'd had bad experiences that had left him with significant psychological . . . issues. But if you wanted a man to solve a puzzle, particularly a scientific one, he was the one to consult. Like the altered nanite formula running through her veins and keeping her alive.

If you could reach him.

'He's developed a new habit,' Patrick said. 'You call an Internet number and read out the code he assigned to you. Then he calls back from an encrypted number. If he feels like it.'

'I didn't think Manny could get any weirder. Can't you just talk to Pansy?' Pansy Taylor was Manny's girlfriend, lab assistant, and psychological prop, and she was the one who kept Manny from drowning in the deep end of the crazy pool.

'I would, but Manny had some kind of scare, and he's cut off the cell phones again. So this is the only way to get to him until she goes behind his back and activates them again.'

The wait wasn't actually very long – two or three minutes, at most, until Patrick's cell phone rang back. He hit the speakerphone button and said, 'McCallister.'

'Glickman,' said the clipped voice on the other end. 'Am I on speaker?'

'Just with me and Bryn.'

'I'm still uncomfortable.'

'Deal with it. I guarantee you, it's safe. I have a job for you – it's an encrypted thumb drive and I need a jailbreak on the files. Can I courier it to the lab?'

'No,' Manny said. 'Send it to this address . . .' Bryn grabbed a pen and paper and wrote it down. 'That's a mail drop. I'll pick it up from there.'

'I need it soon, Manny.'

'I run a first-in, first-out system, you know that. And I have about half a dozen jobs ahead of you today.'

'Double pay.'

Manny was silent for a moment, and then there was a rustle as if someone else picked up the phone. 'Hey,

Patrick, it's Pansy. What did you say? Something about double pay?'

'Yes.'

'Congratulations, you just jumped the queue. No, Manny, don't even start; if you want to keep the shelves stocked, sometimes we have to make adjustments. Bryn?'

'Right here.'

'Mark out that address. This is the direct one.' Pansy read it out, and Bryn blinked in surprise.

'You're in San Diego now?'

'Been here for about a week,' Pansy said. 'Come on over. We'll do lunch and I'll take a look at your encryption problem. Manny's taught me a thing or two, and I wasn't too shabby with that stuff to start.'

Bryn smiled as Manny started swearing in the background about compromised security, and Pansy sighed. 'Come soon,' Pansy said. 'Or I swear to God I'll shoot him and hide the body.'

Patrick hung up and said, 'Do you feel up to it?'

'Seeing Manny? I've had worse today.'

He handed her the thumb drive, but didn't let go of it when she pulled. 'You're firewalled and full of adrenaline right now,' he said. 'I know you probably don't know it, or feel it, but what happened is inside you, and it's going to come out. Get back here as soon as you can.'

She shook her head. 'I'll take this to them, and then

I need to go in to work, Patrick. And I'm fine. Really.'

He said, 'I know you think so. When you need me, I'm here.' He let go of the thumb drive, and she leaned over to kiss him, just a quick, soft brush of lips. For some reason, she didn't want to go further with it, not now. She needed to *move*.

In fact, she practically jogged upstairs, taking the steps two at a time, and paused in the doorway of Annalie's room to look inside. Liam was sitting in the armchair, reading a leather-bound book; his handgun was sitting on the table beside him, as was a glass of wine. He adjusted his reading glasses down and looked at Bryn over the top of them.

'She's still quiet,' he said. 'She woke for a moment, but didn't fight the restraints. I believe she's improving. We'll know better tomorrow when she finishes the treatment course.'

Bryn nodded. 'I'm going out,' she said. 'To Manny Glickman. I'll be back after work.'

'You're going to work?'

'Why, shouldn't I?'

'I should think the reasons would be obvious.'

And of course, he was right. Annie; the early morning panic of Patrick's injury; the events at Graydon. It had been a very full twenty-four hours already. Calling in sick would have been more than logical.

But it wasn't only that; she sensed it in him, as she had in Patrick: concern. She supposed she ought to be pleased they were so worried, but they were assuming she had some residual trauma from the day, and she didn't.

She felt great, actually. The nanites had done their work, flesh and bones were strong and knitted, and there was no trace at all of the damage she'd sustained.

Nothing to be traumatized about.

Bryn changed into a business suit and higher heels, fixed her hair and make-up, and was out of the door in record time. She descended the stairs faster than usual and found that she'd left her sedan conveniently parked just around the curve – she didn't remember parking at all, somehow, or driving home. Opening the door of the sedan, she smelled smoke, and a faint, rusty tang of blood. *Hers*. There was an old sweatshirt discarded on the back seat, and she used it to wipe down the seat. It came away smeared and dirty, and for a second something in her wobbled unsteadily, until she forced it to stand still.

Then she got in the car and drove away, windows open to clear the smell out.

Manny's new laboratory was located across town; as usual, he'd chosen a warehouse, but this one looked new and very secure indeed. The chain link was ten feet high around the property, and there were dozens of security cameras; the whole area was posted against trespassing, a legal nicety that meant it'd be much easier to shoot intruders, or arrest them. She found the one entrance, pushed the red button, and stayed still for the security cameras until the gates rumbled open. A sign she passed said PLEASE TUNE RADIO TO AM CHANNEL 720. She pushed buttons until she got the frequency, and heard a cool, professional voice saying, 'This property is strictly monitored for security purposes. Do not deviate from the approved route or police will be immediately notified. Have your identification ready to present at the next station. No weapons of any kind may be brought into the facility. Be prepared to undergo standard security sweeps of your person and any belongings you may bring with—'

The voice cut off, and Pansy's cheerful voice said, 'Hey, Bryn? Keep coming straight. You'll see a metal garage door ahead, it'll come up for you. Park inside. Oh, and get out with your hands raised, okay? Follow the signs.'

That would have seemed strange anywhere else but here, Bryn thought. The broadcast returned to the droning, severe voice telling her that all security measures were strictly enforced to the limit of the law.

She took that to mean *death*.

As the door slammed down (faster than was strictly comfortable) behind her car, Bryn parked in the warehouse and slowly exited the vehicle, hands up. There was an eye-in-the-sky camera on the ceiling. The downstairs was one big, empty room that could have easily held twenty or thirty large trucks. It was spotlessly clean, and mercilessly bright from rows and rows of overhead lights.

Bryn stared up at the camera and waited until the automated voice said, 'Please lower your arms. You are now cleared to proceed to the elevator. Place your palm flat on the scanner for access.'

The elevator was in a thick concrete block about fifty feet away, and there was a separate, shiny built-in scanner on the wall big enough to accommodate a palm twice her size. She watched the light skim down on the other side of the glass, and a tone sounded from the speakers as the doors opened. She stepped in and looked for buttons. There were none. It was a nondescript metal box without any controls at all, but when the doors slid closed, it moved smoothly upward.

It opened on a plain concrete room with a door at the far end. It had no handle, no lock, and no visible hinges, and Bryn waited, tapping her heel impatiently, until it swung open.

'Hey,' Pansy Taylor said, and gave her a huge, delighted smile that lit up her round face. She'd changed her hair a bit, and it swung longer around her shoulders; she was trying out new eyeshadow, too, but other than that, same woman Bryn remembered. Fondly. 'Get your ass inside before Manny hits some kind of countermeasure button and kills us all.'

'When are you going to admit he's not boyfriend material?' Bryn asked her. Pansy winked and let the door swing closed with a boom behind her as she entered.

'When he stops being amazing. The crazy is just part of the attraction . . . come on, this way.'

The layout of this warehouse lab was eerily similar to the one she'd been in before, and it had been hours from here. Manny had a network of locations, most funded by his mostly-not-legitimate clients around the world, and he regularly hopped between them. In emergencies, he could pack up the contents of this place in crates kept in constant readiness, and be out in a few hours. She'd seen it happen.

There was no sign of Manny around the rows of machinery, the testing tables, or in the clustered array of computers. No sign of him anywhere, in fact.

Until she heard his voice overhead, and looked up to see him on a railing above. 'Did you check her ID?' Manny asked Pansy. He had a rifle in one hand, held casually, but you never knew with him.

'I don't need her ID, we both know her.'

'Check it anyway.'

Pansy rolled her eyes and held out her hand; Bryn pulled her wallet out of her purse, and Pansy gave it a glance before handing it back. 'Bryn Davis,' she said. 'Which you know, so please put the gun away and go back to what you were doing, sweetheart.'

He hesitated for a long moment, then said, 'How are the side effects of the latest batch?' Manny, even foreshortened by the distance, was a big man, burly, with a truly impressive explosion of curly dark hair and eyes that had a Rasputin-quality crazy to them, at the worst of times. This wasn't, luckily, one of them. It was more a garden-variety paranoid schizophrenic.

'It hurts,' she said. 'I don't know that it's better or worse. Thanks.'

'For what?'

'For doing what you're doing. Refining the drug.'

He shrugged. 'I get paid.' With that, he turned and walked away down the metal gantry, and disappeared in a network of pipes beyond. Going to his man-cave, she assumed; she'd never seen it, but she was sure he had one, and it was probably booby-trapped six ways from Sunday.

'He's charming today,' Bryn said, and turned to Pansy. 'So you're doing the work?'

'On this one, yes.' Pansy held out her hand, and Bryn gave her the thumb drive. 'Where did you get it?' She led the way to the area where the computers were located – big, custom-built machines for the most part, but a couple of separate laptops that were running on their own.

'You heard about the explosion and fire today across town?'

'It's all over the news. Seven dead.'

'Eight,' Bryn said, and pointed to herself. 'But I got better, more or less. The other seven had been dead for days, and the whole place sanitized of data except for this.'

Pansy disconnected one of the laptops from its moorings. 'In that case, let's take some basic precautions. This is a burner laptop – basic system plus de-encryption programs, no data kept on it. It's not connected to the network, and there's no enabled Wi-Fi. If there's any kind of malware on here, no harm done.' She slotted the thumb drive in place in the USB slot and waited for the disk image to appear on the screen. When it did, she opened it and studied the apparently random file names, then brought up a new screen of programs. She chose one, and started it running. 'Let's try this first. The pattern looks a little familiar.'

'I thought it'd be more difficult, somehow.'

'It depends on who encrypted it, and why. Obviously, the point of coding something is to make sure that nobody unauthorized can read it, but it's no good if there's no key. You just need the right formula. Most people don't create their own encryption, they buy it. Low, medium, Cadillac plan.'

'Is this the Cadillac plan?'

'Nope. You said seven people are dead, so I don't think they were paranoid enough, which means they weren't on their encryption, either . . . ahhhh.' Pansy made a pleased sound when the computer gave a little chime. 'First file decrypted. Here we go.'

She brought up the file. It was tagged with a number, not text, and she double-clicked it. It turned out to be a video file, and Bryn stayed very still as it played out. The sound was low, but it didn't matter. It was loud and familiar, inside her head.

She slowly sat down in the nearest chair.

They were both silent for a long, long second, and then Pansy, gone very pale, said, 'What the hell is this?'

'Dangerous,' Bryn said. She felt . . . numb. And terrified, suddenly. 'Very, very dangerous.'

The second file decrypted. It, too, was a number, and Pansy hesitated, then double-clicked.

Like the first file, it was surveillance video, shot from the exact same angle as the first images. Two men in the plain coveralls of janitors rolled a gurney into view. On it, struggling against the restraints, was a man in his fifties, wearing some kind of jumpsuit.

Bryn knew him. 'That's Jason Drake. Former Pharmadene. VP of marketing, hooked on Returné in the last days of the push to get everyone aboard. He was having problems coping with the change. He was in my . . . group.'

'Your group?'

'Support group, kind of. It's informal, people drop in and out a couple of times a month. He hasn't been around since . . .' She thought back. 'Jesus, two months ago. I haven't heard from him, either, but he said he was going to focus on work. I assumed he'd come to terms with things. He'd signed up for the counseling the FBI was offering.'

She'd seen the first video, so she knew what was coming and didn't flinch in surprise, only in horror. Jason was awake, fighting to get free, asking the same questions she would have been asking. *What are you doing? What do you want?* There was a horrible edge of panic and dread in his voice, as if he knew all too well what was going to happen.

The two uniformed men ignored him. One went to the wall just at the edge of the camera's view and hit some buttons on a control panel, and a low rumble sounded. It was hard to see details on the video, but Bryn could see a gauge light up, and an indicator begin to climb.

The second man pulled out a silenced semi-automatic pistol and put three bullets straight into Jason's forehead. It killed him, of course. Temporarily. Bryn held still for that part. She knew how it felt, dying from a head wound. It wasn't so painful. *Stay dead, Jason. Just stay dead.*

But of course he wouldn't. Fifteen minutes or so, and he'd be back.

It took ten for the gauge on the wall to rise far enough that the man operating the controls nodded, and then he and his companion unstrapped Jason's limp form, hit another button, and a small, square door opened in the wall. A metal drawer slid out from it, and the two men dumped Jason sloppily on it, then pushed it into the square opening.

Before it closed, fire began to roar inside as the incinerator started its work.

Bryn took in a deep breath as the first screams began. Through a small glass window, she could see Jason thrashing and fighting his death.

Pansy stopped the video with a single, fast punch of the space bar and sat back, still staring at the screen. She said, 'It goes on as long as the last one.'

It took twelve minutes for one of the Revived to die in that incinerator, then. Five minutes of screaming that grew softer and softer, and then seven minutes of . . . noise. Random and desperate *noise*, until finally the body just couldn't hold itself together enough to fight.

Bryn had no idea if the brain was conscious through all that, or if, mercifully, awareness was the first thing that was burned away. She hoped so.

'How many files?' she asked.

Pansy couldn't tear herself away from the still image on the screen for a long few seconds, and then she minimized it and checked. Another soft *ding* reported a file decrypted. 'Three,' she whispered. 'If they're all like this . . .'

'At least three of the Revived have been murdered,' Bryn said. 'By fire.'

Chapter Nine

Bryn was shaking as she got back in her car, with an unencrypted copy of the thumb drive tucked in her purse . . . she felt cold, icy cold, even though the air was still warm and moist. As she drove toward Davis Funeral Home, she couldn't seem to get warm even with the heater blasting on full. Her skin felt cool, pallid, and damp.

Of course you're feeling bad, she told herself. *It's horrible. What's on the video is horrible.*

But she couldn't help the feeling that it wasn't *just* the idea of the death of those three people – it was more. It was something shifting inside her, tectonic plates moving, friction-building energy that had to release somewhere, somehow.

Bad things. Very bad things. Pharmadene employees were disappearing.

She knew where three of them had ended up.

Her nerves seemed all on edge now, the bright edges of things as sharp as blades. She had to fight not to flinch when someone blew a car horn at a light; she had an unreasoning, trembling impulse to get out, find whoever had done it, and beat him – or her – to a bloody pulp. *Stop. Stop pushing me.*

A sudden, tuneless noise startled her into hitting the brakes with a screech, almost causing the car behind to rear-end her. It was her phone. Had it always been that loud? That *annoying*?

'What?' she snapped as she hit the hands-free call button on the steering wheel. 'What is it?'

'Bryn? It's me.' Patrick. She sucked in a deep breath and tried to slow down her racing heartbeat. 'I just wanted to be sure you're okay.'

'Oh. I'm . . . I'm fine,' she said. She wasn't, and she was starting to realize that, but she didn't want to let Patrick know. 'On my way to the office.'

'Did Manny help?'

'Not really, but at least he didn't shoot me. Pansy did the work.'

'You got the files decrypted. And . . . ?'

'We can talk later,' she said. She *really* didn't have the stomach for talking about this, not now. 'I've got to go, Patrick.' She hung up on him without waiting for another word. She knew he could sense how off balance she was just now, and she didn't want his sympathy, or his concern. She wanted to fight back to the place she'd been when she'd left the estate: strong. Energized. *Ready*.

Three dead. Three. And one she knew, had laughed and talked with. She felt responsible for him, somehow; he'd come to her for help in adjusting to his new unlife, and she'd let him drift away, somehow, into the hands of his killers.

A horn blasted behind her, and she realized that she'd been sitting at a green light, staring blankly at it for long seconds. She hit the gas and drove too fast the rest of the way to the funeral home, parked crookedly, and had to take a moment to breathe in deep, ragged breaths before she got out and went in.

The subdued smell of flowers hit her first; it was more pronounced today because someone had sent those damned day lilies for the main viewing room, and the sweet, musty scent made her throat tighten. The waiting room was empty for the moment, and Lucy looked up from her chair behind the reception desk to smile. 'Well hello, Bryn. I thought you were taking the day.'

'Sorry I'm late, my appointment ran long this morning. Anything I should be on top of?' This was good. Lucy was calm, professional, unemotional; dealing with her was always steadying.

'You had a couple of vendor calls, I put it all in the folder on your desk.'

'Where is everyone?'

'Joe's out with the Chen burial. Ms Kleiman is meeting with some new clients down the hall.

Bryn smiled, just a little. 'Isn't she Gertie yet?'

'Not yet,' Lucy said. 'That woman's going to be Ms Kleiman until she gets that stick out of her butt.' Gertie Kleiman was an older woman, newly hired, and she didn't seem to have an informal bone in her body – which was fine most of the time, especially since Lucy steered the elderly clients in her direction by design. 'And I can't be on any first-name basis with a woman who calls me *that colored girl up front*.'

'She *said that*?'

'On the phone. Not to me, I just heard it.'

Bryn sighed. 'I'll talk to her. Sorry, Lucy.'

'Not the first time I've run into it,' Lucy shrugged. 'Oh, and William's working downstairs, he's pretty busy.' William was their new, very competent embalmer; all of them could, and had, pitched in, but William had a nearly flawless touch with it. He was the best Bryn had ever seen, with the exception of Riley Block.

'New intakes?'

Lucy's voice dropped lower, just in case anyone strolled in. 'Married couple sent over from Scripps Mercy. Car accident. The son's coming over this afternoon; I had Mr Fideli down for him, but if you want to take it . . . ?'

'Yes, that's fine, I'll meet him. What time?'

'Four.'

'Thanks, Lucy, you're amazing. I'm sorry about Kleiman. Tell her I want to see her before my four o'clock.'

'Okay. But don't be *too* tough on her. I just want her to call me by my name, not my skin,' Lucy said. The phone rang, but this time it didn't startle Bryn quite so much; the funeral home's lines were all muted to the lowest possible setting, and the most soothing ringtone choice. Lucy turned to attend to that, and Bryn walked down the hall. She'd been hoping today would be a routine kind of thing, but already she had sensitivity training to deal with. The four o'clock would be raw and emotional, and that probably hadn't been a good decision, either, but she needed to work.

Work kept her from thinking too much about herself. The folder on her desk had a summary sheet on the top: schedule for the rest of the week, including a conference call tomorrow morning; phone messages from Bates Casket and one of the embalming suppliers; contracts to be signed. Bryn took care of those first and put them in her OUT box, followed up on phone messages, and then kept herself busy searching her laptop for emails to and from Jason Drake, formerly of Pharmadene, formerly Revived. The last one she had was dated over a month ago, and in contrast to the warmer tone of previous emails, that one was a simple notice that he wouldn't be able to attend her meetings anymore, and was seeking counseling services inside the company. On reflection, it didn't sound like him –but then, she could have been (and probably was) coloring things with her own interpretation, given what she'd discovered.

Bryn toyed with a pen, thinking, and suddenly realized something important. *Jason was on Pharmadene shots.* That meant he had to check in daily to get them. Unlike her own shots, re-manufactured by Manny Glickman, the Pharmadene doses were administered in syringes that were fingerprint-locked to the technicians authorized to give them. Jason couldn't have stockpiled any and self-injected.

More than that, the Pharmadene shots were regulated so strictly that if Jason hadn't shown up for a shot, it would have triggered a red flag at the FBI.

Riley. Riley Block must have known about this – or, at least, known three of her Pharmadene addicts were missing. *Son of a bitch.* Zaragosa had been right not to trust her. She hadn't mentioned it, hadn't asked for help about it. Hadn't given Bryn any indication at all there was something going on out of the ordinary – it had taken the Pharmadene CEO to do that.

Bryn picked up the phone, dialed part of Riley's number, then slowly put the receiver back in the cradle. If Riley didn't want her to know, there had to be a reason for it – one that Bryn wouldn't agree with, either. Zaragosa had warned her not to trust her.

An ice-cold chill swept over her, and she stared blindly at her computer screen. *What if they've had an order to end the project?* That would, in fact, explain everything. The contractors, hired to abduct and destroy Returné addicts. Maybe Zaragosa didn't know. Maybe Riley herself didn't know. But sooner or later, Bryn had fully expected the government to tire of the expensive job of hiding the truth; this was a neat way to end their problems. Neat for everyone but those going into the incinerator, anyway – especially in a budget-cutting economy.

She couldn't trust Riley, or Zaragosa, or anyone with government ties. They had to know these three had disappeared, and if there had been an investigation, surely they would have involved Patrick, at least.

Would Patrick have told you?

Yes. Yes, he would have. Bryn had no doubts about that.

Unless he was protecting you, or thinks he is.

God, this was a circular cycle of paranoia – She could implicate everyone, and no one, but the only real proof she had was seven dead people at Graydon, and video of three Revived – like her – burned alive.

Bryn took the thumb drive out of her purse and stared at it for a moment, then slotted it into a USB port. Maybe watching it again, blocking out the horror, she'd gather some little detail, some hint to follow. Tonight, she'd find out if Patrick knew anything.

Tomorrow, she'd go after Riley Block and find out what *she* knew about it. If it was the government cutting their very substantial losses, then they'd have a fight on their hands. A public and bloody one – the very last thing they wanted. If word of Returné hit the streets, things would go insane. Everyone would want Revival – for themselves, for a loved one. And that was a cycle that never, *could* never, stop, and would destroy governments, crush economies, and lead to chaos like nothing she could imagine. People were genetically selfish, and they were panicky. A bad combination when something like this was dangled in front of them, like a life preserver to the sinking ship of their mortality.

Bryn didn't want to see that happen, and in truth she'd try her best to keep Pharmadene's dirty secrets, but the threat was significant enough to force the government's budget-cutting madmen off their backs.

Hopefully.

She lost track of time, staring at the video files; even with the sounds muted, the images made her feel trapped, mired in a nightmare. The calm efficiency of the killers was chilling; it said they'd done this, or things like it, so much that it was just another day on the job. That utter lack of empathy reminded her of soldiers at concentration camps, and Rwandan butchers chopping up innocents. The human race, alive or Revived, was a terrifying thing.

Bryn flinched when she heard a knock at the door, and slammed the laptop shut on the video. She hastily put it away, pressed her sweating hands on the desk for a moment, and tried to still her racing heart. Wasn't entirely successful. 'Come in,' she said.

It was Gertrude Kleiman. She was a tall woman,

with pale hair going imperceptibly gray; she wore it in a teased style that reminded Bryn strongly of her mother's prom picture from high school. Not a warm person, but a competent one, and she dressed better than Bryn did – old money, the break room gossip said. Not that Bryn listened, much. 'You wanted to see me, Miss Davis?'

'Please, have a seat,' Bryn said. She'd never had to give anybody a dressing-down, outside of her time in the military, and she figured it probably wouldn't be wise to approach it the same way. 'Would you like a glass of water?'

'No, thank you.' Kleiman – even Bryn couldn't really call her *Gertie* – sat down primly on the edge of the chair, knees together and at just the correct angle. Not a wrinkle in her expertly tailored suit. She had dark-blue eyes and a very direct gaze. 'Ms Kleiman, I had a report that you've been referring to our office administrator in a less than appropriate way.'

'Meaning?' Kleiman said without even a blink.

'I believe the phrase was *that colored girl up front*.'

Now Kleiman blinked, as if that wasn't at all what she was expecting. 'Excuse me? I don't understand the problem.'

'The problem is that she'd like you to refer to her by name, not by her skin color. She's also not a girl; she's older than I am. I realize that the phrase used to be appropriate years ago, but—'

'I was trying to be *polite*!' Kleiman said, and if anything, looked more rigid and cold. 'If you'd like me to say what I really think, I think that . . . that *woman* is taking great advantage of you. She's hardly qualified to run something as complex as a business like this . . .'

'Actually,' Bryn said, 'I'm fairly certain I don't want to know what you really think, and neither does Lucy. Lucy works for me, not you, and I'm the final judge of her performance in the job, as I am of yours, and it's *your* job performance we're discussing, not Lucy's. So consider this a warning. If you use inappropriate terms toward *any* of my staff again, the next time we talk about this will be the last.'

'This is ridiculous! What I said was not in any way offensive!'

'In your opinion,' Bryn said. 'And the point of something being offensive is that it was offensive to *someone else*. We're done now. Thank you.'

It was a clear dismissal, and Kleiman took it that way. She also slammed the door on the way out, which was damned difficult, since the doors were on hydraulics to make sure they didn't make a lot of noise. Impressive. Bryn sighed and called Lucy's desk phone. 'Incoming,' she told her. 'Kleiman's on fire. Let me know if she comes after you.'

'She comes for me, she'd better be wearing asbestos,' Lucy said. 'Nope, she just passed me by and went to her office.'

'If you have any problems . . .'

'Come to you, yes, boss. Your four o'clock's not here yet. I'll ring you when he comes in.'

'Thanks.'

Bryn looked at the clock, stretched, and decided she was too restless to sit still for twenty minutes. She stood, put on her white lab coat from the closet, and took the backstairs down to the preparation area.

William Nguyen looked up as she came through the frosted-glass door and gave her a big, warm smile. 'Hey,' he said. 'Busy day, eh?' He nodded down at the body lying on the table in front of him.

It was gruesomely damaged, but from the part of the face that hadn't been mangled, the man was in his fifties, with short-cropped graying hair. There was another body on the second table, covered with a clean white sheet.

'Are these the accident victims?'

'Yeah, it was a nasty one – rear-ended by a drunk driver at a stop light, pushed their car into a dump truck. The drunk must have been going about a hundred; the car looked like it already went through the cube crusher. This is Mr Lindell. I'm just doing gross examination right now. I'll email you the general outline of what it'll take, but if the son wants open casket this is going to be a pretty intricate job.'

'Thanks,' Bryn said. 'Just let me know as soon as you can. Hey, William . . .'

'Yeah?' He didn't look up from his close analysis of Mr Lindell's cheekbone. 'Damn, this is all splintered in here. Gonna be tough to find good anchor material for the reconstruction.'

'Have you had any problems with Gertrude Kleiman?'

'Nope,' he said. 'Except she won't talk to me.'

'Excuse me?'

'Never says a word. Even when she comes down here, she hands me paperwork, or picks it up, and leaves. If I say hello, she just ignores me. I don't know, I just figured she was shy.'

'Huh,' Bryn said, which was about as neutral as she could make it. 'Okay. Thanks.'

'For what?' He still didn't take his attention from the dead man in front of him, gently palpating torn tissues.

'Just thanks.' *For being cheerfully oblivious*, she thought. But the idea that Kleiman was rude to him, too, made her burn. 'See you later.'

'Yeah, see ya.' He finger-waved her off, and she went back upstairs, wondering exactly what to do about Gertrude now.

She didn't have much time to think it over, because as soon as she'd hung her coat back on the rack in the closet, Lucy paged her to let her know her four o'clock had arrived. Bryn checked herself in the mirror – habit – and went out to greet him.

He was a tall young man, and he looked athletic, but when she spotted him sitting in the chairs he looked . . . unstrung, like a discarded puppet. He looked up vaguely when she stopped in front of him and said, 'Mr Lindell?' in her gentlest voice. 'I'm Bryn Davis. Why don't we go into my office.'

'Are my mom and dad here?' he asked, still seated. 'Can I see them?'

'Please, come with me,' she said, and the persuasive, understanding tone worked, got him up and moving with her. As she shut the door, he looked around her office with blank incomprehension, and she guided him to one of the two small sofas, with the table in the middle. She'd learned her lessons from the old owner Lincoln Fairview well; there were tissues in a wooden box on the table, and a trash can tucked discreetly just where a visitor would expect. All her materials were ready – pens, forms, iPad with photographs of options. She sat young Mr Lindell down, fetched him hot coffee when he indicated he might drink some, and otherwise just listened as he talked for a while. He didn't, thankfully, return to his request to see his parents; that was something she wanted to avoid, at all costs.

'They said at the hospital it was instantaneous,' Mr Lindell said. 'That they never even knew.'

It most likely *wasn't* true, but Bryn wouldn't have said so. Not to him, not at a time like this. 'I know it was very quick,' she said. 'I'm so sorry, Mr Lindell.'

'Eric,' he corrected softly. 'I'm Eric. I want . . . I want to be sure I do this right, but I don't know how.

I've never . . . I've never even been to a funeral before. When my grandfather died I was a freshman in college, I couldn't get back in time for the services . . .' He seemed very pale, and much younger than Bryn had initially thought. 'What happens now? What do I do?'

'Do you have any other family members who want to be involved?' Bryn asked. She felt sorry for him, for the vacant suffering in his face. He was maybe twenty, she realized – much younger than her, in every way. She'd gone into the army and seen death and brutality; the worst this man had seen might have been a drunken fist fight at a frat party.

Eric shook his head. 'My sister's off in Thailand on some kind of hiking trip. I can't even reach her. It's just me.' He suddenly took in a gasp of air and said, 'I need help. I can't do this, I can't.'

It was like a cry, and Bryn reached out and took his hand in hers. Instinct. It stilled some of her own pain that still boiled inside. 'I know,' she said. 'And I'll help you through this.'

It was the best part, she thought, of doing this job – seeing the relief in the eyes of those who sat in this couch, knowing they weren't going through it alone.

In the end, she undercharged him for the funeral, because it just . . . hurt to do anything else.

The work *did* help, Bryn discovered when Eric Lindell finally left, paperwork in a folder for him to keep. It had been a long session, almost two hours, and the funeral home was quiet when she walked him out to his car. He seemed calmer now, and steadier, and as he was opening the car door his cell phone rang.

His sister, calling from Thailand. Bryn watched him from the indoor window as he talked, and cried, and finally drove away.

Suddenly, she wanted to be back at the McCallister estate, with Patrick. *Life is short.* She was reminded of that every single day, here. *I need to decide what to do about Kleiman*, she thought. It was a thorny sort of administrative case – William hadn't made a complaint, and Kleiman had taken the reprimand for Lucy's complaint without too much grandstanding. Hard to dismiss her without incurring some kind of lawsuit, given the facts in hand.

Maybe she'll quit, Bryn thought. That would be a nice solution for everyone – voluntary departure. *And maybe pigs will fly. You don't ever get off that easily, do you?*

No. No, she didn't.

It was the work of a moment to pack up the laptop and thumb drive, then another five to check the doors and windows of the building and set the alarm before exiting. She was locking up when her cell phone sounded off, and she juggled it along with the keys. 'Hello?'

'Bryn? Hi, this is Carl. I was . . . I was checking in to see when you were planning on having that support group meeting. I'd really like to be there, if possible.'

Crap. She hadn't thought about the support group at all for days. 'I don't know, Carl, let me make some calls and see if I can set something up. Have you spoken with your wife yet?'

'I . . . no. Not yet. Maybe if you would go with me to talk to her – I mean, having someone else there would be good, wouldn't it?'

Only for Carl. His wife would probably find it intimidating and terrifying, given the situation. But that depended on her, and him. 'I'll call you back,' she promised. 'Are you having any other issues right now?'

'I can't sleep,' he said. 'At all. I try, but I just lay there and think – I can't shut my brain off. It's like the nanites are making me do it. Did you ever feel like that? That they're making you do things you don't want to do?'

That was alarming, she thought, and leaned against the pillar. 'Like what specifically?'

'I don't know. Turn the car one direction instead of another. Think about . . . doing bad things.' He sounded positively strange now. 'Nobody tested this stuff. They tested it on *us*. How do we know it's not changing us, not making us dangerous? Do you know? Does anybody?'

All of a sudden, Carl sounded like the darkest voices of her id coming out of the depths, and it was spooky. She'd wondered these things herself, from time to time; it was easy to fall into despair in this situation, and imagine every random thing that happened as a symptom of a non-existent disease. The deadly thing was that if Carl convinced himself he *wasn't* in control, what would he do? What *couldn't* he do?

'Are you thinking about hurting yourself? Hurting someone else?' She was *not* qualified for this, she thought in a sudden, angry fit of despair; no one had trained her, given her a diploma in how to manage dead peoples' fears. Not even her own.

His hesitation made her nervous, but then he said, 'No, not really. I'm just . . . I *think* a lot, and that must be the nanites, right? That they're working too hard or something?'

'Carl, that's why we have the group – because by talking out these things we find out that what we're feeling isn't so strange or uncommon, okay? I've had the same sensations, the same thoughts. You can't get better if you don't reach out to people, and I'm glad you called me about it. If you feel that there's something wrong, I want you to call the Pharmadene hotline and report it. They can check you out immediately. Understand?'

'Yeah.' He sounded better, a little. Calmer. 'Yeah, I forgot about the hotline. Sorry.'

'It's all right. You're anxious, and that's really pretty normal.' She laughed, a little sadly. 'As far as normal exists for us, anymore.'

'Okay. Thanks for saying that you've had these thoughts too. I thought . . . I thought I was out there in the dark, you know? On my own?'

'I know,' she said. 'If you need me, call back. I'll be here.'

He hung up, after a polite decompression moment of goodnight wishes, and Bryn closed the call and took a deep breath. It wasn't the first time she'd had the same conversation. All of them fell down the rabbit hole, sooner or later; not everybody was able to climb out.

When I get home, I'll get the group schedule, she promised herself. She knew how important it was for people to stick together, talk, connect.

Exactly what Pharmadene and the government *didn't* want them to do, of course. But screw that.

Bryn walked through the gardens, breathing in the roses and the rich, damp smell of earth, and was almost sorry when she reached the parking lot. Her car was parked next to two of the limousines, and she headed in that direction, half her mind on what she needed to do when she reached the estate. *Show Patrick the vids.* That was the first thing. He'd have some perspective on it, some insight she didn't. And she needed him to share this with her, help her process that helpless feeling of fear.

That was just about the time that she became aware that something was wrong out here in the darkness beyond the glow of the garden's lights.

Bryn felt that indefinable prickle at the back of her neck. *Ambush.* That was an instinct that never really went away, even after taking off the uniform – the feeling that a predator was watching you, waiting for a chance to strike.

She wished for a gun, but the fact was, she hadn't come entirely unarmed. As she walked on, Bryn fumbled in her purse as if searching for her keys and closed fingers around the solid weight of a collapsible riot baton that accounted for about half the weight of the bag. She thought about her cell phone, but she'd already dropped it back in its pocket, and even if she managed to dial 911, it wouldn't help; any possible fight would be over – in her favor, or against it – before help could arrive.

She felt a breath of air, something moving behind her, and lunged forward into a roll, yanking the baton out of her purse and flicking it out to full extension as she came back to her feet. The purse smacked to the pavement, and in the orange glow of sunset over the ocean, she saw two men dressed in plain clothes – jeans, work shirts, no identifying marks – who were wearing ski masks. They fanned out immediately, trying to work angles; she kicked the purse under the car to prevent it from fouling her footing and backed up between the car and the limousine on the other side.

She didn't speak.

Neither of them moved toward her yet. They were assessing her position, and finding it tactically sound. After a few seconds they exchanged a glance, and one of them reached down to his belt and tugged free a stun gun, the kind that shot out darts. She gasped and dropped flat, rolled under the limo and slapped her hands down to halt her momentum, then squirmed and rolled toward the tail of the long vehicle. She slithered out just as the man with the stun gun knelt down to peer underneath. He was temporarily distant from his friend, and she scrambled to her feet, lunged around between the cars, and hit him hard enough on the back of the head to knock him forehead first into the metal of the limo door. He left a sizable dent.

He dropped, and she kicked the stun gun under the vehicle.

The second attacker stared at her for a second, figured his chances of getting to the stun gun, and backed up instead. She held the baton ready. The guy she'd put down wasn't unconscious, just stunned. If the second one had a gun, the fight was over . . .

He didn't. He *did*, however, have a knife. It was a nice one, matte finish combat model, and he obviously knew a thing or two about how to use it.

Bryn felt a bit underdressed. And wished she hadn't gone with the heels for the office. Cargo pants and boots would have been . . . better. She considered for a second, then kicked off her shoes to stand barefooted, then backed away. He moved forward, taking the bait, and stepped over his supine, weakly moving friend. For just an instant, he was off balance and wrong-footed.

She instantly sprinted around the limo, up through

the gardens, and shattered the glass window inset in the front door.

Lights blazed on, and alarms began to shriek.

She stood there, balanced on the balls of her feet, as the knife man stumbled to a halt a few feet away. 'Five minutes or less response,' she said. 'You think you can get me, subdue me, get your friend, retrieve the stun gun and be out of here by then? Because I'm going to make it hard.'

Out on the road, a passing truck slowed down, drawn by the lights and sirens. Others would be calling in alarms.

And he knew it.

He pointed his knife at her in a *catch-you-later* motion, backpedaled, and scooped up his woozy friend. The friend had the car keys, which delayed them further.

They left the stun gun and ran for a nondescript black sedan parked out on the side of the road, almost hidden in the shadows of the hill.

Two and a half minutes, they were gone in a smoking shriek of tires.

Bryn kept the baton out. She was shaking too hard to put it away, and she wanted to sit down, badly. Instead, she stayed on guard, tense as a guitar string, until the first flashing lights appeared below, and sirens climbed up to meet her.

Then she sat down on one of the ornate decorative

cast iron benches, collapsed the baton, put it down beside her, and tried to draw in a breath that didn't shake. *They might have been robbers*, she told herself. *Or garden-variety perverts. Serial killers.* Any of that was preferable to what she was thinking they were really after. She couldn't stop the visions: being strapped down on a gurney, shot, shoveled into a furnace, waking up screaming as her flesh and muscle sizzled off of her bones, and screaming, and screaming . . .

'Ma'am?'

She'd somehow lost time, and the adrenaline that burst into her bloodstream made her shoot to her feet and simultaneously flick the baton out to its full, most dangerous reach before sanity kicked in, and she realized that she was planning to hit a *police officer* standing there with his hand on the butt of his pistol.

Bryn dropped the baton and raised her hands over her head. 'Sorry,' she said, or tried to say, just as the shouts of *down on the ground, down on the ground!* deafened her, and one of the cops grabbed her, shoved her face down, and held her there as he kicked the baton away.

Well, she'd earned that. And as the cuffs snapped on her wrists, she didn't struggle in any way.

In ten minutes, she told them her story, and in twenty, the police had found her purse and the stun gun both under the limo, just where she'd left them. They also found a dent in the limo's passenger door where one of her attackers had banged his forehead, and some blood drops. And her shoes.

It still took another hour for the necessary repetitive interviews and paperwork.

'Sorry about that,' said the patrolman as he removed the restraints from her wrists. 'Your security consultant is here to look at the damage to the building. We've verified your identity, Ms Davis. Next time, leave the baton on the ground when the police show up, okay? Wouldn't want any misunderstandings.'

Security consultant? She looked up, and saw Patrick McCallister standing near another of the cops, chatting as if he didn't have a care in the world. He smiled, traded a handshake with the man, clapped him on the back, and strolled their way. He stopped at the bottom of the steps, and said to the cop, 'Is Ms Davis free to leave now?'

'She'll need to come to the station and sign the reports.'

'Any injuries?' he asked – the cop, again, as if she wasn't even there.

'Not a scratch,' the cop said. 'Lucky lady. Two against one, both armed. Could have gone real bad for her.'

'Lucky,' Pat agreed without any expression at all, and for the first time looked at her directly. 'Very lucky.' He helped her to her feet. He'd brought her shoes over, and she stepped into them. Amazing, how much better she felt with footwear on – how much less vulnerable. 'I'll make sure she's available for any additional interviews you need. Oh, and there's a company on the way to replace the window, should be here any moment. Ms Davis's assistant director is on his way to supervise.'

Joe Fideli. Bryn could imagine how much fun that conversation had been around his home dinner table . . . *honey, sorry, I have to go back to the office, there's an alarm going off*. If his wife didn't believe by now that he was having an affair, they must have had the best marriage in the world.

The cops didn't speak to her again, or even look her way, now that she was someone else's responsibility; she was relatively uninteresting in the course of the investigation, which of course wouldn't go anywhere. They'd taken DNA samples from the blood drops, and maybe they'd get fingerprints from the stun gun, but it wouldn't go anywhere. These had been professionals.

And she had, indeed, been very lucky.

Patrick said nothing at all to her as he walked her over to his car. 'You drove?' she said. 'You're not supposed to be using that arm for a couple of days. We can take my car and I can—'

'Get in,' he said, and opened the passenger door. His eyes met hers, and she swallowed all objections, slid into the seat, and fastened her seat belt as he walked around the back.

Even when they were on the road, he maintained strict silence until she finally said, 'Who called you?'

'Joe,' he said. The word had an edge to it, like a thrown blade. 'He gets an alert from the alarm on his cell. He knew I could get here faster.'

Of course Joe got the alert; she knew that, she'd helped set up the system. Her brain felt slow just now, and bruised from all the day's stress, even though the nanites wouldn't *let* it bruise, would they? No damage. No damage to her at all, she walked away clean and unhurt.

Every time.

'Please pull over,' she said softly. Pat didn't respond, and suddenly she let it out in a full-throated, panicked scream. '*Pull over!*'

He steered to the shoulder of the road, and even before the tires had hissed to a stop she'd popped her seatbelt, thrown open her door and stumbled out into the cool early evening. The stars glittered overhead in an unusually clear sky, and she stared up at them as she trembled and gasped for breath, feeling – she didn't know *what* she was feeling, really, except it was overwhelming and painful, and it *wouldn't stop*.

Patrick's voice said from behind her, 'It's okay.' He wasn't angry anymore, he sounded concerned. 'Bryn, you're all right. Deep breaths. In through your nose, out through your mouth. Close your eyes.' He put his arms around her, using both of them, and after a second of leaning against him, concentrating on her breathing, she remembered one of them should have been in a sling and not being used like this. 'Relax. Relax. The fight's over now. Ease down.'

'Sorry,' she said faintly. 'I don't know what happened.'

'You were running on adrenaline even before this, and you overloaded.' His breath stirred her hair, and he kissed the side of her neck, very gently. 'I'm speaking from experience when I tell you that you'll be okay, but you can't run hot all the time. Gear down.'

Well, she *was* a machine, wasn't she? Run by machines, anyway. The black humor of that tickled the back of her throat, threatening a laugh she couldn't release because she knew it would sound like panic. Or screaming. Cars blurred by them on the road, blowing waves of cool air over them; Bryn's hair ruffled in the wind like silk, and she closed her eyes, finally, and let that rushing sensation take over. Patrick's body anchored her in place, and the wind stroked over her, soothed her, like the roar of the ocean.

It took long, slow minutes, before she was better – or better enough to go back to the car, get in, and keep control of the still-high flood of emotion on the drive home. She didn't quite freak out again when Pat asked, 'Can you tell me exactly what happened after you left the house?'

She swallowed, tasted something metallic and dry

in her throat, and wished she had water. Suddenly, she was burningly thirsty. 'I got the thumb drive decrypted. I went to work. I closed up the building. Two men tried to jump me as I walked to the car.' Stripped down to that, it didn't sound so bad, did it? 'I got away.'

'One had a knife, one had a stun gun, you had a baton,' Patrick said. 'Good thinking, breaking the window. Did you recognize them?'

'No.' She had, she realized, never seen their faces. 'They wore ski masks. But they were professionals at this kind of thing, seemed like.'

'Do you think they know you have the files from Graydon?'

That was a perfectly reasonable question, but Bryn shook her head. 'I don't see how they *could* know that. Pansy Taylor is the only one who knows, besides the two of us and Joe.' It went without saying that neither Joe nor Pansy were going to talk. 'Unless—' She had a sudden, blinding flash of the file that Zaragosa had given her at Pharmadene, with the tiny embedded tracking chip. 'Unless they LoJacked the drive.'

She looked sharply at Patrick, who glanced back with the same alarm. 'Do you have it?' he asked her.

'No,' she said. 'Pansy has it. She gave me an unencrypted copy on a second device. *Jesus.*'

He whispered something under his breath in a language she didn't even remotely recognize, and hit the hands-free call button on the car steering wheel. It took an agonizingly long moment for the call to go through, and of course, when it picked up, it was an automated message. Patrick waited it through impatiently, and as soon as the beep sounded, said, 'Manny, Pansy, if you haven't checked the thumb drive for trackers and bugs, do it now, right now. Call when you know. McCallister out.'

'You know, if I gave them something with a tracker in it—'

'Manny will freak the fuck out,' Patrick said grimly. 'And move. And it may be days before we hear from him.'

'If ever,' Bryn said. She felt a rising tide of panic, again. 'He'd know I didn't do it deliberately, won't he?'

Patrick visibly composed himself, and relaxed the tense muscles in his arms and back. 'He won't blame you,' he said. It sounded confident, but it was a lie, and Bryn knew it. 'Pansy will calm him down.'

'Patrick, if they came after me, they must have gone after them *first*.'

'Address,' he said, after a short, dark pause, and when she gave it, he headed in that direction.

Chapter Ten

The warehouse looked just the same, to Bryn's eyes, only now, at night, it was lit up like a spaceship. Manny must have paid a fortune not just in electricity, but in halogen bulbs. Patrick drove up to the gates and got out to show himself to the camera.

Nothing happened.

Bryn tuned the radio to the AM channel she'd used earlier, but there was nothing but static. No voice, even an unfriendly one, to indicate there was anyone at all inside the warehouse.

Patrick pressed the button on the control panel and said, 'Manny, I know you're in there. Let us in. Please.'

Nothing. Not a whisper. Bryn got out of the car, too. There was little traffic this time in the neighborhood, so it was quiet enough to hear the low-level buzz of the lighting.

'Those two couldn't have gotten in here, even if they did find the place,' Bryn said. 'It's Fort Knox.'

Patrick slammed his hand down on the control again. 'Manny! Answer the goddamn radio *now* or I'm calling the police and telling them there are shots fired and a hostage situation inside. *You* can try to explain it to them.'

The static went on, and on, for what seemed like eternity, and then the speaker clicked and Pansy's voice said, 'I'll meet you at the gate, Pat. Stay in the camera view.'

It took about ten minutes, and when Pansy came out, she was driving a big SUV, something with lots of power and thick, bullet-resistant glass – it looked like it was on loan from the Secret Service, or (more likely) a South American drug lord. Pansy was tiny in comparison when she hopped down from the cab and walked over. She was wearing a holster clipped to her blue jeans waistband, but it was empty. She held the matching semi-auto pistol down at her side – ready, but not threatening.

She looked, Bryn thought, incredibly tense.

Pansy said, 'Two men showed up at the gates after you left, Bryn. They drove around, cut the fence, and got as far as the elevator, but they couldn't hack the scanner. Gave it a damn good try, though. After they left, I looked at the thumb drive, and there was a tracking device built in – GPS enabled. We killed it, of course, but I've spent the last couple of hours trying to talk Manny down from running for Belize.'

'They came after me too,' Bryn said. 'But I didn't have the drive anymore.'

'Then they were surveilling you before you got here. Once they realized we were a hard target, I guess they went for you first.' Pansy sighed and holstered her weapon. 'These are not amateurs. If they're advance for some kind of serious clean-up crew, we're on the radar now, and they'll be back for you, and for me and Manny. I'm sorry, but we have to move. There's no choice.'

'Please don't,' Bryn said. 'I didn't mean for this to blow back on the two of you, you have to know that.'

'I know.' Pansy looked grim, but also grimly determined. 'Look, I like you. I trust you. But the fact is that *I* made the call to bring you here, let you in, and take something from *your* hands that compromised Manny, and that just doesn't fly. Just because he likes you doesn't mean he won't walk away. And just because I like you doesn't mean I won't let him.'

'Promise me you'll call when you're settled.'

Pansy shook her head slowly. 'I can't,' she said. '*Jesus*, Bryn, Manny's sliding over the edge with this thing. He's scared, and I agree. Seven people dead already, plus the three on the video . . . mercs sniffing around the perimeter . . . these are not people he wants to mess with. He loves the intellectual puzzle of working with you, but he's not going to take risks with our lives. Not for you.'

'Wait,' Patrick said, as she backed away from the still-locked gate toward her SUV. 'Six months ago, before he started modifying the formula itself, he had a separate drug developed to block Protocols in the nanites. Is it shelf stable?'

'As far as I know,' Pansy said. 'There's a box of it in the back.'

'Then get me the box, and the formula for that, until he feels safe enough to get back in touch,' Patrick said. 'It'll do for now. Please, Pansy. It's her life at risk too, and she *can't* run.'

She considered, and finally nodded. 'Stay here. I'll be back in five.'

Pansy climbed back in the SUV and headed toward the warehouse building at high speed, leaving the two of them bathed in the cold, white lights. Bryn shivered. If her two assailants wanted her dead, it'd be as easy as pie to take a shot out of the dark right now. Her and McCallister, both gone in a second.

But they didn't want me dead, she thought, and it came as a bit of a shock, somehow. She really hadn't thought about that at all until this moment. *They came with knives and stun guns as backup, but they started with bare hands*. Didn't they know she was Revived, and that bullets wouldn't do permanent damage anyway? Or was there some reason they didn't want to do anything fatal, even then?

No, the only logical answer was that they *didn't* know she was Revived. They just knew she'd handled the thumb drive, and they needed to know what she'd found. But they needed her alive to ask the questions.

They didn't need McCallister, though. And if they were a containment crew, they'd rather him dead than a witness. That made her chest tighten up until she felt she couldn't breathe. *Come on, Pansy. Hurry.* The longer they were exposed, the greater the danger to Patrick.

The black SUV came roaring back, almost on cue, and Pansy must have pressed a control on the way, because the gate suddenly activated and rattled back before her arrival. She braked, parked, and came out of the truck carrying a good-sized brown box, which she handed over to Bryn; it weighed about fifteen pounds, maybe twenty, and Bryn carried it to the back seat of Patrick's car.

'Here,' Pansy said, and handed McCallister a thumb drive – the silver one, Bryn thought, from Graydon. Then she handed him a second one, bright red. 'The red one has the Protocol-blocking formula on it. The silver one is the one Bryn brought us. We don't want anything to do with it. We've already wiped all the encrypted and decrypted files from our own system. We're keeping nothing.'

'Pansy,' he said. 'Don't let him run away from us. Not all the way. She needs him.'

'I'll try,' she said, and leaned forward to kiss him on the cheek. She hugged Bryn. 'Stay safe.'

'You too,' Bryn said. 'Both of you.'

The gate banged shut between them, and then Pansy

was gone, heading back for the warehouse where Manny would be breaking down the lab, packing it up, feverishly heading for a safe place far, far away.

It might be the last time she saw either of them, Bryn thought. And she'd brought it on herself, by involving them in the Graydon murders.

Patrick touched her shoulder. 'Let's go,' he said.

As they drove away, the security lights around the building clicked off, shrouding it all in darkness, and Bryn thought, *Goodbye*.

She hadn't really been prepared to feel so . . . lost.

Mr French was standing guard at the front door as Bryn came in, and he gave a happy bark and rushed for her ankles, sniffing with great interest to see where she'd been. Whatever he smelled, it made him growl softly, then sneeze, then sit back on his haunches and pant happily, looking at her with the unmistakable expectation that it was time to pay attention to him.

Maybe that was just what she needed. She crouched down to give him a loving scratch on the head and neck, and said, 'Stupid dog.' He slurped her hand, and she felt the pressure inside subside, just a little. There was something about his furry, unquestioning, adoring love that made her feel less . . . *alien*.

She looked up and found that Patrick was watching her. He looked concerned, but there was something unguarded about his smile. 'Do you want dinner?' he asked.

'Why, are you cooking?' That was a joke. Patrick, for all his many talents, was definitely *not* a chef.

'If you want to take a risk on my ability to heat up an MRE . . .'

'Not that hungry. But you want to talk about my friends in the ski masks, anyway.'

'I think it's a conversation that can't wait,' he agreed. 'I'm going to lock up these thumb drives. You said you had one with unencrypted data?'

Bryn had put her purse down to pet Mr French, and now she reached in left-handed, rooted around, and pulled out the drive. She handed it to him. 'It's video surveillance. You should know what's on it before you watch.'

'Did you know?' he asked, and searched her face for the answer. 'Then I'll watch it cold. Maybe I'll see something new. Fresh eyes.'

She almost warned him not to watch it before eating, but then the idea of watching it *after* dinner probably wasn't so great, either, so she held her tongue. Patrick was a big boy, he'd seen worse, almost certainly, and he didn't have her . . . emotional resonance to contend with.

He hesitated, though, and finally said, 'See you after I take a look. Will you be upstairs?'

'I need to change,' she said. 'And check on Annie. Patrick – thanks. Thanks for coming to get me. I needed . . . I needed you.' She stood up, and suddenly the space between them seemed to contract without either of them moving. It was the look in his eyes, and the sudden boil of emotion inside her.

And then Patrick took a step forward, touching-close, and murmured, 'Did you? Really?'

She only had to lean forward a little to touch her lips to his and say, 'Still do.' It wasn't a kiss, it was friction, her mouth moving against his. She expected him to lean in, press them close, but he didn't; it was on the trembling edge of happening, but he just held her there, suspended, not making a move. Her nerves woke up on fire, and she wondered if he knew just how incredibly sensual this felt.

She felt his mouth move. A smile. A wicked one.

'It's like braille,' he said, 'but with lips. I think I like it.'

Mr French interrupted them with a bark, and if dogs could frown, he did. Clearly, he was concerned with losing her attention, and Bryn stepped back. 'I need to change,' she said. 'I'll . . . see you soon.'

Patrick nodded, and watched her go.

Mr French bounded up the steps before her; her dog, Bryn thought, had learned the house faster than she had. It was a little disconcerting, actually. He ran straight to her room and inside, then back out. He dashed instead into Annie's room, next door, and as Bryn walked in, she found him sitting comfortably next to Liam's feet. Liam was still sitting in the armchair, still reading – but he wasn't the one Bryn focused on.

Because her sister was awake.

Bryn stopped dead in her tracks, feeling a rush of exalted relief that was quickly stopped by a more logical dread . . . until Annie turned her head and looked her way with a tired, faint smile. 'Hey,' she said. Her voice sounded rusty and rough. 'Thought I'd never see you again, sis.'

Bryn rushed forward and stopped a foot short of the bed as Liam cleared his throat. 'Carefully,' he said. 'She's better, but I felt it necessary to keep her restrained for now until we verify her Protocols are turned off.'

'He means,' Annie said, 'until he's sure I'm not going to go after you and your man with a butcher knife.' Her eyes filled up with sudden tears, and she pulled in a gasp. 'Oh God, I'm so sorry, Bryn. I would never have done that, *never*, but I just couldn't stop it—'

'I know,' Bryn said, and put a hand on her sister's cheek. She felt warm, soft, *alive*. 'It wasn't your fault, none of it. It never was. And we're fine. The important thing is to make sure *you're* fine.'

'I think I am,' Annie said, but she looked deeply uncertain. 'Maybe you should keep these things on for a while longer. I mean, I didn't *know*. I didn't *feel* that I was going to do anything, but I heard your friend leave the hall and it was like I couldn't stop myself. I got up, got the knife, and just – I was a *passenger*, Bryn. I couldn't *stop*.' She started breathing harder, and Bryn took her hand and held it. Annie squeezed hard. 'I hate this, I *hate it* – I just want it to go away. You know? All of it. I want to go home and I want to go back to my stupid bar job and . . . I want to *see Mom!*' That last came out as a wail, and Bryn felt her heart break, again. Annie's tears were overflowing now, running down into her tangled hair. She yanked against the restraints a little, but more in frustration than any desire to get free, Bryn thought. 'Can I see her? Can you ask her to come, at least? To take care of me?'

No, Bryn thought, appalled. The last thing she wanted was more of her family involved in this . . . horror that had taken her sister. And her. 'Maybe,' she lied. 'Calm down, Annie. What Liam's been giving you is making it better. You're in control now. You're back to being *you*.'

'Yeah?' Her sister's mouth set in a bitter little line, very *not* the Annie Bryn remembered. 'The loser sib who couldn't figure out how to balance a checkbook? Not much of an upgrade from crazy woman with a knife, is it?'

'Annie!'

'I know, self-pity isn't my most attractive look, right? But Jesus *Christ*, Bryn, I was *murdered*! And they . . . they . . .' Annie's gaze wandered, and Bryn saw the horror of the last few months come rushing back. '. . . did things to me.'

Liam was still in his chair, and Bryn sent him a quick look. He said, very quietly, 'Shall I go downstairs? Perhaps fix a small meal for us all?'

'Thank you,' she said. 'I think she needs something in her stomach, and I'm . . .' *starving,* she realized with a jolt of surprise '. . . ready for dinner too. Liam – thanks for staying with her. Keeping her safe.'

He favored them both with a warm smile as he stood. 'She's a lovely girl. And you, Annalie, were very wise in your choice of sisters, I think.'

After Liam was gone, Annie was quiet. Bryn stroked her hair gently, and finally said, 'If you want to talk about it, I'm here.'

'No,' Annie said, with unexpected force. 'No, I don't want to talk about it. I don't want to *remember*. So let's just . . . drop that, okay? Cut, print, move on. Dammit. Can you . . . uh . . . wipe my eyes or something? Damn, I think I need to pee, too. *Man.*'

For answer, Bryn yanked the Velcro off of her left wrist and put a tissue in her hand. Annie raised her arm and stared at it, as if not quite sure what it was (or, more likely, what it would *do*) then dabbed at her eyes with the tissue, blew her nose, and sighed. 'Oh God, it's ridiculous how good that feels. I didn't realize how tiring it was to be in the same position all the time.'

'Feel any impulse to throttle me with your free hand?' Bryn asked.

'Only a little,' Annie said, 'which, considering we're sisters, is probably normal.'

Probably. Bryn studied her for a few seconds longer, then undid the rest of the restraints. 'Hey!' Annie said, and sat up. 'Are you supposed to do that? I mean, *now*? Ow, I'm still wearing IVs. Can I take these out?'

'No,' Bryn said. 'But you can roll them with you to the bathroom, unless you have a real liking for bedpans.'

'Do you have to empty it when I'm done?'

'Not a chance, sweetie. I don't love you that much.'

Annie's smile was *almost* like her old one. 'You were in the running for best sister ever, but now you're back to, you know, just best in the room.'

'Except you?'

'So far, *you* haven't tried to stab me, so I think you're one up on me right now.' Annie swung her legs over the side of the bed and groaned. 'Ow. Sore. A little help?'

Bryn supported her and eased her to a standing position, and rolled the IV stand over so Annie could hold on to it. 'Better?'

'In one way. In another, now I *really* have to pee, now that it's actually possible to do it.'

'In there.' Bryn walked her to the bathroom door and shut it behind her. As she waited, she looked down at her suit – grimy now with her twisting and wriggling around on the pavement underneath the limo – and remembered that she'd been on her way to change, again. How many outfits had she ruined today?

Well, she couldn't change now until Liam came back to supervise Annie; she might trust her sister again, a little, but not enough to let her roam around the house without oversight. If her Protocols weren't completely deactivated, she might choose the moment Bryn was cleaning up to re-enact the shower scene from *Psycho*, and that wouldn't do anyone any good. Least of all the shower curtain.

Annie came out a few minutes later, looking almost herself again. She'd even taken a moment to brush her hair, which shone in bouncy, ridiculously shiny curls halfway to her waist. It still looked thinner than before, but it'd fill out. 'Okay, warden, I'm done.'

'Good. Back in bed.'

'Seriously?'

'Just for a few minutes,' Bryn said. 'I'll come back to get you.'

She fastened the Velcro around Annie's wrists, ankles, chest, waist and thigh, feeling stupid as she did so; Annie took it without any snarky commentary, which was nice, if unusual. 'I'm sorry,' Bryn said, smoothing the last fastener in place. 'I'll be back for you soon. Tomorrow, you won't need these at all.'

'No hurry,' Annie said. 'I'm not going anywhere.' She sighed, wriggled a bit, and closed her eyes. Mr French, who'd been following the two of them around with anxious concentration, trotted after Bryn as she went next door. After a moment of consideration, she locked the door, then started stripping off the old, stained clothes. *At this rate,* she thought, *I'll have to buy a whole new wardrobe every month.* Well, at least it wasn't a depressing idea, for a change. New clothes were always cheerful.

A fast, hot shower made her feel brand-new again, and Bryn toweled off and dressed from the skin up again – after consideration, she went for the best underwear she had, lacy and flirty, and over that, in compensation, a plain pair of jeans and matte jersey shirt. Comfortable. Not seductive. Overtly, anyway. Mr French decided not to follow her after that; he curled up in his dog bed and put his head down, evidently worn out by the day's trials. She shook her head and left him there as she checked on Annie.

She wasn't there.

Bryn did a fast, alarmed check of the room – no sign of Annie hiding in the closet with a butcher knife, or lurking in the bathroom, or under the bed.

Pat.

Bryn dashed back in her room, grabbed the handgun she kept in the nightstand, and raced out again. That got Mr French up and running at her heels; he seemed to think it was a fun chase game meant just for him, and he almost tripped her up as she took the steps at a terrifying pace . . .

. . . And almost ran straight into Patrick as he rounded the corner at the bottom. He took a step back, and she did too, almost knocking herself over as her heels encountered the stair riser. Pat's gaze fell to the gun in her hand. 'What's wrong?'

'I thought you—' Bryn took a deep breath and didn't try to holster the gun. 'Annie's not in her bed.'

'I let her loose,' Patrick said. 'And before you tell me I'm taking a risk, I tested her before I released her completely. She's doing fine, and Liam's keeping a sharp eye on her. I don't think she's liable to come after me at the table with a butter knife, but if she does, I assume you'll shoot.'

Relief made her weak at the knees for an instant, and then she felt her cheeks burn a little. Maddening, because she *hadn't* overreacted . . . not considering the circumstances.

'I watched the videos,' he said. That surprised her, and she realized with a shock that in the heat of dealing with Annie, she hadn't even *thought* about the videos. 'Two theories come to mind. First, someone is conducting a clean-up, officially sanctioned or not.'

'Which would explain why Graydon was on the list of vendors for Pharmadene, *after* the turnover in management.'

'Or, someone is abducting the Revived to find out exactly how they're still alive. Testing them.'

Bryn hadn't actually considered that. She'd been so focused on the method of their death that it hadn't dawned on her to think about what might have happened *before* . . . but it was possible. More than possible. *Someone* could have gotten wind of the existence, or possibility, of a drug-based immortality; they could have taken the logical step to find someone who was living proof and start experiments.

Which meant that when she'd seen Jason on the gurney being shot in the head and loaded into the furnace . . . that hadn't been the beginning of his suffering.

That might have been a merciful *end*.

Her brain raced ahead of her, imagining all the horrifying things that could be done to a body that wouldn't, and *couldn't* die – it made vivisection look sane and humane, and she tried to close the door on imagination, shut it off.

She'd go crazy if she spent much time in that dark, dark place.

'It could be something else,' Patrick said. He'd read her expression, she could tell from the sudden softness of his voice. 'Something we haven't considered yet. Let's keep from rushing to judgment, Bryn. This is going to take a little time.'

'Time to *what*?' she said. 'Track down two anonymous men in ski masks who are trying to abduct me?'

'No,' he replied, very calmly. '*Trap* two anonymous men in ski masks.'

Oh.

CHAPTER ELEVEN

Dinner seemed fine, although Bryn couldn't have said what it was exactly that she ate – chicken, she thought, with vegetables, all perfectly normal. Annalie, although pale and still nervous, was making an effort; she was all tinsel-bright smiles and eyes that were just a bit too wide, gestures too fast. Bryn watched her, waiting for any strange lapses, but she saw nothing but her sister, amped up a little too high. Liam didn't seem to be paying attention, but she knew he was; he was well within striking distance of Annie's fork, should she choose to go completely wrong, but her sister's Protocol order hadn't included the butler, just Patrick. And, of course, Bryn.

They were just finishing the dessert – a silky butterscotch pudding that was the first thing that actually made an impact on Bryn's senses – when a tone sounded from the kitchen. That, she recognized, was the security alert. Liam excused himself, then came back and said, 'Patrick, I believe you have guests. Again.'

'Wasn't expecting any.'

'These seem to be in a large vehicle, and they're wearing police-issue bulletproof vests. I'd guess that your FBI friends may be a bit unhappy.'

Bryn got up and went to the kitchen, where the surveillance monitors showed – just as described – a large tactical van, black and nondescript, with four men in helmets and flak vests standing around it.

Liam had forgotten to mention the semi-auto rifles they carried. Bryn tried the little joystick on the keyboard, and zoomed in.

FBI. It said so very clearly on their vests. And walking up in the center of them, also wearing a vest but no helmet, was Special Agent Riley Block.

She didn't look at *all* happy. That was extremely clear in the high-definition look she shot directly at the camera.

'Open the gates,' she said through the speaker, 'or I'm driving in over them. That would be awkward for you to explain to the neighbors.'

Not that explaining the presence of an armed tactical team was going to be any piece of cake, if said neighbors were taking a jog around the block, but Bryn shot a look at Patrick, who was standing behind her. He shrugged.

'Might as well,' he said. 'Knowing her, she'll start using the bullhorn in the next minute.'

What he didn't say was that this was an extremely vulnerable moment for them; if either or both of them disappeared into FBI custody, it might well be the last time they saw daylight, depending on what Riley knew, and how angry she was about it. But the alternatives were worse – shooting it out with the feds had never been much of an option.

Bryn pressed the gate release and disarmed the security system.

'What's going on?' Annalie asked from the doorway. She sounded scared. 'Is it . . . is it *them*?' She meant Jonathan Mercer and Fast Freddy, her captors.

'No, it's not,' Patrick said without turning. 'Mercer's not stupid enough to come here. It takes a federal employee for that.'

'Hey, play nice,' Bryn said. Patrick smiled grimly. 'Riley's probably angry over the fact I lied to her about Graydon. She'll have heard something else by now. What are we going to tell her?'

'The truth.'

'And the video?'

'We'll play it for her,' he said. 'Because I want to see her face when she gets a good look at what's going on. If she knows anything about those disappearances, it's going to be hard for her to hide it. If she doesn't know . . . that's instructive, too.'

The tactical van was rolling up the drive now, with the five agents riding the running boards. It was, Bryn thought, effective theater straight out of the Prohibition-era playbook. Riley knew perfectly well they weren't going to walk into a guns-blazing firefight, but she was making a point.

Loudly.

Liam headed for the front door, but Bryn cut him off. 'No,' she said. 'It's for me.'

'You want backup?' Patrick asked. She shook her head.

'Stay with Annie. I'll see if I can't make this go away without too much trouble.'

Patrick took Annie's arm and led her to the kitchen table, and as Bryn was leaving, he asked, 'Do you like hot chocolate?'

Bryn was sorry to have to go, if it meant missing out on the hot cocoa. But she firmly shut the kitchen door on the other three, and – Mr French tagging faithfully at her heels – went to the front door and swung it open just before Riley was about to deliver a wood-damaging knock with the blunt end of a very large flashlight.

Riley glared at her for a few seconds, then turned to her tactical team, waiting just behind her with weapons still hot. 'Stand down,' she ordered, and arched an eyebrow at Bryn. 'Unless you want to do it the hard way?'

Bryn silently stood aside to let her in. The team

commander followed her in and gestured for his other men to remain where they were. *Well,* Bryn thought, *at least we don't have to worry about my friends in the ski masks sneaking up on us just now.*

What she *did* have to worry about was the boiling fury kept barely under the surface in the FBI agent's body language.

'I suppose offering you coffee would be out of the question,' Bryn said, and got nothing, just a flat stare as she closed the door. 'Okay. Shoot. Metaphorically.'

'You lied to me,' Riley said, and every word was individually sharpened and polished to a high sheen, and flung at high speed. 'Do you really think your situation is *that* safe, Ms Davis? Do you think that because you're living here, you're no longer subject to the terms of the agreement you signed? Because lying to me is a very, very bad idea and will have serious, painful consequences, not just for you but for Mr McCallister as well, and any of his *associates* who want to earn themselves an accessory charge.'

Bryn hesitated for just long enough that it was clear she wasn't going to be bullied, then said, 'Let's discuss this somewhere more comfortable.' She turned and walked into Patrick's office-library. After a pause, Riley followed, trailing her somewhat unnecessary bodyguard. He, at least, seemed amused, and once they were in the library, took up an at-rest stance by the doors as Riley and Bryn crossed to the desk.

Bryn checked the computer quickly. Patrick had left the thumb drive plugged in, and she quickly copied the files over with a fast swipe of her fingertips on the pressure-sensitive trackpad.

'David,' Riley said, and knocked knuckles on the wood of the desk. 'Focus. What are you doing, checking Twitter? *You lied to me.*'

'About what?'

'I hope you're not stupid enough to think I'm kidding, because in about five seconds you're going to be in handcuffs, on your way to a location so secret that it'll take even McCallister ten years just to find it on a map.' Riley visibly controlled herself, and then said, in an artificially even voice, 'You said you didn't find anything at Graydon's offices. That was a lie. Go on, ask me how I know.'

'Manny Glickman,' Bryn said. 'He called and told you. But the question is, did he tell you what it was?'

'He said you brought it to him, and he refused to have anything to do with it.' Riley sat back, arms crossed, eyes half-hooded but bright with challenge.

Bryn said, 'I need to show you something.' She spun the monitor around and clicked PLAY.

Riley started to object – she clearly wanted to keep momentum in the meeting – but when the video began she stopped, frowning, then leaned forward. The frown deepened, and Bryn watched her closely.

She saw the almost imperceptible flinch as the shots were fired into Jason's head, and then the gradual dawning of horror as the furnace began doing its grim work. But Riley didn't ask for it to be turned off. She watched the whole thing, as if it was her sworn duty.

When it finally ended, Bryn said, 'I have two more. They're identical, except for the identities of the people being put in the furnaces. And from the length of time the screaming goes on, they're all Revived. Now. Let's start over. What do *you* know about this?'

Riley was silent for a few seconds, then said, 'The coveralls the workers were wearing had a logo on them. Was it Graydon doing the dirty work?'

'Cleaning up,' Bryn confirmed. 'Literally. And then they got the same treatment.' She smiled a little, but it wasn't from humor. 'The people in that office died from bullets in the head, then were burned when the bomb went off. I doubt that was any kind of an accident. I think it was done that way to send a message. Was that message from you, Riley?'

The bitter anger in the look she got spoke volumes. 'Do you really think I'd spend the last six months of my life playing grief counselor, nanny and Mother Teresa to a bunch of spoiled corporate ladder-climbers just to *shoot them and shove them in a furnace*? No, Bryn. It wasn't me.'

'Not even on executive orders?'

'It may have escaped you, so I'll spell it out slowly: I work in the FBI. That doesn't stand for Federal Bureau of *Incineration*.'

'Tell that to the employees of Pharmadene that didn't make it out of the Civic Theater when it blew up.' Riley shook her head, but Bryn didn't give her the chance to talk. 'You knew, and you let it happen, because it was one of those necessary evils. So is that what's going on here? Sanctioned murder, and a blind eye by your bosses? Because I swear to God, Riley, I will blow every whistle with every media outlet out there, including the *Daily Shopper*, if you don't make it *stop*!'

Riley sat back in the leather chair. 'If you threaten that kind of thing, you *know* I have to take you seriously. You don't want that, Bryn, you really don't. Because, for starters, you disappear into custody. You, your sister, McCallister, Joe, Liam, Manny Glickman, Pansy Taylor, maybe even Joe's wife and kids. It becomes a roll-up of everyone who has any personal knowledge of your status. Hell, even your staff at the funeral home. All confined to six-by-six cells. Do *not* mess with me. I don't play chicken. I wring necks.'

The threat wasn't anything Bryn hadn't expected, but it still chilled her, because the look in Riley's eyes was unyielding. She was right; the FBI couldn't take risks. Her job was to walk a delicate line between the care of the people who were – not by their own choice – addicted to Returné, and keep the secret from getting out. It wasn't by any stretch *easy*. And it required a certain level of unflinching, weirdly compassionate cruelty, too.

Mr French, lying at Bryn's feet, sensed the mood in the room get even darker, and raised his head to stare at Riley. He gave her a low, rumbling growl.

'These people couldn't just disappear,' Bryn said. 'They reported in daily for shots. If any of them missed two days in a row, the alarm must have sounded. You must have *known*, Riley.'

'What I know, and when I knew it, is none of your business.' Riley stood, grabbed the thumb drive from the laptop, and yanked it free. 'I won't ask if you kept copies; of course you did. But I'll just give you this one warning: *stop*. Agent Zaragosa asked you to do one thing: visit Graydon and see if it warranted a full investigation. You did. You found a massacre and a mystery. Your job's over. The rest, you leave to us. It's our job to protect you.'

'And you're doing such a great job.'

'Let me make it very, very clear,' Riley said. 'Go back to selling caskets to grieving relatives. Take care of your sister, I understand she's pretty fragile right now. And *let it go*. These killings died with Graydon. Understand?'

'Then who tried to abduct me tonight – Santa Claus?'

'We're *handling it*. And we have the resources to shut them down, so let us do our jobs. Stop playing Harriet the Spy, or your next room with a view looks out on Guantanamo Bay.'

Riley stood up and stalked for the door, and her tactical team leader opened it for her, then followed her out. There were no goodbyes. Bryn made sure they left, sealed the gates, turned on the security, locked the front door, and then went to the kitchen.

Liam was gone. It was just Patrick and Annie, and three empty mugs cooling on the table.

'Did you hear it?' she asked.

Patrick nodded. 'I thought you'd want us watching.' He pointed toward the security monitors, one of which now showed a view of the office. The camera was pointed toward the desk, and it would have shot over Bryn's shoulder, straight on Riley. 'In my opinion, she knew nothing about the murders. She knew *something*, but she had no idea those people had been killed. It came as a shock.'

'She's scared,' Bryn said. 'It's spinning out of control, and she knows it. No matter how many FBI agents she's running, it's not enough to keep everyone safe. She can't shadow everyone twenty-four seven, and even though she didn't say it, I think more have to be missing. It's bigger than just three people.'

Annalie looked from one of them to the other, and then asked, 'Um . . . sorry, what exactly does that mean? Isn't she in charge or something? How can she *not know*?'

'There's no such thing as being in charge of something like this. Someone up the chain of command could be lying to her, and she'd never know. That's what she's afraid of – that someone, somewhere within her organization has decided her operation is a threat to national security, and is mopping it up. FBI agents can disappear just as effectively as the Revived did.' He looked straight at Bryn and said, 'We can trust her, and take our chances that she can keep it together, or go around her. Either way, it's risky.'

'It's not a choice,' Bryn said. 'We have to take care of each other now.'

Annie tried a smile. 'Yay?'

Bryn grabbed her hand where it lay on the table, and squeezed it tight. 'Yay,' she said. 'We're going to be all right.'

She almost believed it herself.

Almost.

Riley's visit had taken any chance of romantic encounters with Patrick off the table, which was yet another thing to resent about her intrusion; Bryn spent the rest of the evening poring over paperwork, gathering names, files, everything she could on every single Revived individual she could – a task made some easier by Patrick's help, because he'd kept duplicates of a lot of the personnel records out of Pharmadene when he'd been employed by them. By two in the morning, they had at least a partial picture of the individuals the FBI had sworn to protect.

Failed to protect.

'It isn't good,' Patrick said, once he'd finished

compiling the information. 'Out of the fifty-two Revived we absolutely know survived out of Pharmadene, seven of them have dropped off the radar – no cell phone, home phone or credit card activity. It's been gradual, maybe one a week. They're just . . . going dark. Slipping away.'

'Is Jason one of them?'

'Yes.'

There were, Bryn estimated, about two hundred total Revived out there – counting her and Annie. If the proportions held true, at least fifteen more had dropped out of sight over the past three months. One after another, going out like light bulbs.

'Somebody's got access to the master lists from the FBI,' Bryn said. 'Or they've put things together with other insider information.'

'Not necessarily. If they're concentrating on Pharmadene employees, all they need is an old, publicly available organizational chart.' He pulled one up from when he was head of security and began marking off names. 'Right, the red X marks are those I know died or left Pharmadene before the drugs were administered.' That was about fifteen people. 'These are the confirmed dead from the explosion at the Civic Theater. Public records.' He used blue X marks for those. 'This is what we have left.'

It was about two hundred fifty names, but Bryn knew all those couldn't have survived the process of Revival;

even with reformulated drugs, the success rate wasn't perfect. No way to know which of those names had survived and which hadn't; Riley had that information, but she wouldn't share. Bryn looked over the names on the org chart, then focused on Jason Drake. Patrick drew a green circle around his name.

'He's at the top,' Bryn said.

'No, he's in the third tier,' Patrick said. 'A minor VP, not—'

'But he's at the top of those who *survived*. What if they're cherry-picking from the top? Those would be the ones most likely to have information about the drugs, right?'

'Maybe. But the science department employees would be a better bet.'

There were twelve apparent survivors under the Research and Development departmental structure – maybe ten who'd actually made it through Revival, Bryn estimated. 'Maybe they did both,' she said. 'Anyone in this department go dark recently?'

Patrick matched names to records, and circled two: Marjorie Dass and Chandra Patel. He brought up photographs. Dass was one of the women on the Graydon surveillance video – the first victim to burn. Patel wasn't, which put her on the list of missing, not dead. Not yet.

'We should focus our resources on Patel,' Patrick said. 'If she's our most recent abduction, and it seems she is, from the records, then that's the freshest trail . . . what is it?'

'Chandra,' Bryn said, and took in a deep breath. 'I know her. She's one of mine. She's in the support group. She and Jason got to be pretty close friends.' Her chest felt heavy under the press of anxiety, and she scribbled down a fast list of names and handed it to him. 'Check these names, it's the rest of the group I've spoken with.'

He compared the list to the list of those presumed missing.

One by one, he checked them off. Of the seven names they had, five were on her own list.

'They didn't start with the org chart,' she said. 'Oh God . . . they started with *me*. And I led them to the others.'

'We don't know that,' he said. 'It's easy to see a pattern where none exists, when you're looking at this kind of data. They could have just as easily started with Jason and had him list everyone whose name he knew. That would have had the same effect, Bryn.'

Maybe. But she couldn't escape the fact that if she hadn't opened those lines of communication, hadn't put these people in contact with each other to share their anguish and grief and fear, maybe this wouldn't have happened. Chandra was a slight, nervous young lady, very shy. She'd been scared to speak in front of others at first, but over the course of four weeks she'd seemed to really bloom. When she'd missed a couple of meetings, Bryn hadn't really thought much of it. She didn't expect people to come every time – only when they felt they needed help.

But they'd stopped because they'd been taken, and she hadn't wondered. Hadn't *tried*.

'Bryn!'

Patrick took hold of her shoulders, and she looked up at him with tears burning in her eyes. He couldn't understand how she felt, not fully. 'Chandra never hurt *anyone*, Patrick. She didn't work on Returné at all. She was making drugs for children's chemotherapy. She's *my age*, and first those bastards at Pharmadene put a bag over her head and brought her back as their slave, and then . . . then *this*? How is that fair?'

'It isn't,' he said. 'So let's focus. Let's find her. Let's find *them*.'

Bryn took a deep breath, nodded, and forced herself to think about the work, not the trauma, not the people she knew, liked, had shared coffee and tears with.

Chandra.

We'll get you back.

The morning came merciless and early, and Bryn was up before the sun and driving to the funeral home. Even then, she didn't beat Joe Fideli; when she pulled in and parked, his truck was already in the lot, and the lights of the business were on, windows glowing warm in the chill dawn.

The door was, as always, locked until opening time (and she could hardly even tell that new glass had been put in overnight) but the security was off, and as Bryn came in she smelled the sharp, welcoming aroma of brewing coffee. 'You,' she said when she entered the kitchen area, 'deserve a raise for that.'

Joe Fideli raised a cup to her, sipped, then put it down to pour her a mug of her own. She took it black, and would have mainlined it into a vein if she could have; the warmth spread through her aching muscles and helped steady her into something like normality.

'So,' Joe said, 'I heard you had adventures last night. Which seems a lot, on top of jumping out of a burning building.'

'How much did Patrick tell you?'

'He didn't,' Joe said. 'I gossiped with the cops who were still here on site. They said you'd been ambushed by two guys. Opinion was they were your garden-variety abducting serial killer types with a thing for hot blonde funeral directors.'

'*Excuse me?*'

'Which part of that did you object to? I hope not the hot blonde.'

'I think I should start with the cops thinking there's anything garden variety about serial killers.'

'Yeah, well, San Diego is prone to that sort of thing, in case you didn't know. We've had more sickos grow wild here than in Los Angeles. The police get a little jaded about it. Hell, the street talk is they just busted open a storage locker for one of those reality shows and found creepy photos from another Gacy or something. But anyway, the point is, you got jumped and stayed un-abducted, which, congratulations, by the way. How'd the broken window figure into it?'

She told him the whole thing, from the first moment of alarm to the arrival of police on the scene. One thing she loved about Joe – he was unflappable. He just sipped his coffee and nodded, as if *of course* it would have happened that way. 'They weren't garden variety,' he said. 'They sound like experienced professional murderers to me, not enthusiastic amateurs.'

'That makes it *so* much better.'

'Well, at least you rated someone getting paid to do you. That's a compliment, right?'

'Not really.'

Joe was quiet for a second, then said, in a different tone, 'And what else happened?'

She told him about the recordings, the disappearances, Riley's threats, everything. The only time she saw a reaction in him was when he heard Riley's threat to round up his family. Good thing he hadn't been there within grabbing distance of the agent's neck. It would have been over in seconds.

When he was done, though, he was back to his usual easy-going self. 'Eventful,' he said. 'So. I guess we're not backing off.'

'If you want to move Kylie and the kids . . .'

'To where, exactly?'

'There's room at the castle.' That was how the two of them always referred to the McCallister estate – half a joke, half-envy. 'The kids would love it.'

'If it comes to that, sure, but I'm not uprooting my family over it yet.'

'I just want them to be safe.'

'Kylie's all grown up, and you do *not* want to mess with her kids. That safe room in the back of my house has enough firepower to take down a medium-sized country, and she's checked out on every single piece of it. Relax. How do you want to go at this Chandra thing?'

'Patrick had a plan,' she said. 'You're not going to like it.'

'How do you know?'

'Because I don't like it. You still have some access to Pharmadene, don't you?' Joe had been an independent contractor for Patrick – someone nominally off the books, but he had a great deal of familiarity with the Pharmadene world, nevertheless.

'Not like I used to, but yeah, some. Friends on the inside, all that crap. Why, what do you need out of them?'

'Remember the trackers that Pharmadene put on their early Revival subjects? The ones that bind into bone? I need one.'

'Whoa, whoa, whoa, slow down. You want a tracker, I've got—'

'Nothing that can't be gotten rid of,' she interrupted. 'If they make me change clothes, drop my purse, I'll lose the chip. If you put it subcutaneously, they'll find it. These are pros, Joe, you said it yourself. They'll be looking for a trace. Anything that isn't deeply embedded, they'll find it fast.'

The Pharmadene tracking device was composed of nanites specially modified to lock to bone, link together, and broadcast. It was undetectable in terms of searches, and it broadcast on such a tight, specific wavelength that even a thorough scan probably wouldn't pick it up. Ingenious. Also, deadly to anyone who wasn't Revived . . . the nanites themselves created a toxic by-product that only someone who'd had a dose of Returné could survive.

'Okay,' Joe finally nodded. 'I get the tracker, you're marked so we can keep eyes on you. What then?'

'Then I wait,' she said, 'because they want me. They want to know what I know. They'll be coming for me, soon.'

'You're right. I really don't like any part of this at all.'

'Oh, that's not the part you won't like,' Bryn said, and smiled. 'It's the part where you have to lose a fight if you're around when they come for me.'

'Fuck. Bad enough I managed to actually get my ass

kicked by Fast Freddy Watson; this ain't doing anything for my image.' Joe tossed back the rest of his coffee. 'Whatever happened to the nice, calm death business where all we did was cuddle sad people and polish caskets? It used to be so . . . restful.'

'Glad you think so, because *you* get to deal with the gang funeral today. Watch out for drive-by tributes.' In truth, gang funerals were pretty much like any other kind, only quieter. The gangs never stinted on their memorial services – always top dollar. It had unnerved her how calm and watchful everyone had been at her first one, but to her surprise the gang members had been more polite than the average country club darling's friends, who were often drunk and weepy, not to mention entitled brats.

'You give me the best presents. Hey,' he said, as she refilled her cup, 'how much of a fight should I put up on your behalf, exactly?'

'Your call.' Her smile faded as she considered how long this might take. Days, maybe, before her attackers felt comfortable enough to come at her again – and she'd have to go down hard, to keep her credibility. This time, she felt, they wouldn't try such a straightforward abduction. It would be something else.

Something worse.

She hoped like hell she was wrong.

Chapter Twelve

The day dragged by, hour by stunningly normal hour. The sun shone nicely outside, the groundskeepers came and tended the grass, and around the city, as everywhere, people died. Most of those deaths were standard, peaceful, natural-causes events that were sad occasions, nothing horribly traumatic.

Bryn and Joe worked a service together that morning, from church to burial, and although she was alert for anything odd, she saw nothing.

At noon, Joe came in and gave her the usual shot, which burned. 'We've got another week's supply of Manny's latest batch,' he said. 'After that, we're back on Pharmadene standard formula plus the inhibitors. We've got enough of that to last maybe three months before we're out of the inhibitor.' She sat still until the worst of the shaking and pain rolled off, and saw he wasn't finished. He held up a second syringe. 'Tracker nanites. It's going to take about twenty-four hours for them to form the chains and start broadcasting. After that, you're golden. We can track you anywhere.'

She expected that to hurt, too, but it didn't. The shot did, but she'd gotten so used to the sensation of a needle that it hardly even registered anymore. *I have a solid career path as a junkie*, she thought, without much humor. She couldn't even get high; the nanites would burn it off within minutes.

Sucks to be me. But at least Patrick and Joe could keep an eye on her, virtually, once the trackers came online. There was probably even an app for it. Hell, she'd met a sniper in Iraq who'd had an app on his phone to calculate windage for distance shots. Amazing what they could do these days.

The afternoon was the gang funeral, which she'd assigned to Joe; Bryn stayed in the office, doing paperwork, then went downstairs to see if there was a backlog of work in the prep room. Their principal embalmer William was finishing the last stitches in the mouth of Mrs Gilbert. She'd passed in her eighties, and the infusions had given her back a faint flush of color through the crêpe-soft skin. She looked peaceful. 'Hey,' he said, and clipped the thread neatly. If you didn't know the thread was there, you'd never even suspect it. 'Want to put the caps in for me? It'd be a big help.'

She nodded, gloved and gowned up, and slipped

rounded plastic caps under Mrs Gilbert's eyelids. It was one of the few things that bothered her, this cosmetic touch that kept the face looking more like someone sleeping than deceased, as the eyes were the first thing to start drying and losing their firm shape. Bryn did it quickly, and tried not to think about it.

William added a few finishing touches, gently adjusting the skin on Mrs Gilbert's lips for best possible effect. 'I hear you added another green funeral option.'

'It's popular,' she said. 'No embalming, simple winding sheet, burial in a biodegradable coffin.'

'Ah, hell, no. I'm not rotting in some recycled cardboard crate, that's just not dignified. Just stick me in a wood chipper and blow me over the flower beds – does the same thing,' William said. 'Okay, Mrs Gilbert, you look fabulous. Time to put on your clothes.'

Together, they dressed the body, which was harder than it looked – living bodies cooperated, even unconscious, but the dead had no such consideration. Bryn was always struck, when it came to this, how careful William was, how gentle his touch. He treated the dead like his own – no hesitation, fear or callousness. It was one of the things she liked best about him. He took the time to get it exactly right, straightening the woman's dark-blue dress until it fell just so around her body.

'Did you have time to finish the reconstruction on the Lindells? The husband and wife?' Bryn asked, as he settled the sheet back over Mrs Gilbert.

'Yeah. It's not going to look as good as I'd like, but there's only so much you can do when the bone structure's broken like that. You can take a look if you want, they're in the cooler. Hey, I heard there was some kind of robbery last night. Broken window, right? Was anything taken?'

'They never got inside,' Bryn said. 'The cops were here in minutes. Nothing to worry about.'

'Good. I hate those assholes who come in to steal body parts and shit. Drunken jerks. My buddy took classes at the body farm on situational decomposition, and he said that kind of thing happened all the time out there. Had to have guards patrolling. Imagine that, armed guys to look after fields full of dead people. What's the world coming to, eh?' He rolled Mrs Gilbert back toward the large walk-in refrigerator. 'Would you get the door?'

'Sure.' She held it back for him, then went inside with him and inspected the reconstruction work on the Lindells. It was solid work, but there was no way it could look completely natural; still, she thought the kids would appreciate the opportunity to see their parents one more time. 'This looks good, William, thanks for the extra effort.'

'I think that's the last for today,' he said. 'The service for the Lindells is tomorrow afternoon, Mrs Gilbert is in the morning. I've got nothing much until they start bringing in today's customers – I heard there's four coming, so OT in the near future. Mind if I take an early day?'

'Not at all,' Bryn said. He smiled sunnily. 'Got plans?'

'Movies,' he said. 'And pizza with my buds. Maybe some beers, try to meet a girl. The usual. You know.'

She realized that she really, really didn't. Normal life had passed her by, at light speed; she'd cashiered out of the military and hadn't had time to form casual friendships before she'd taken the job at Fairview – and then her life had ended. Well, maybe not *ended*, but certainly morphed into something that was *not* normal even if it was sometimes amazing. When had she last had a simple, glorious evening of movies, pizza and beer with friends? Or even had one of those by herself?

William stripped off his lab gear and grabbed his motorcycle helmet – despite the statistics, he insisted on playing the odds – and was gone before she finished clipping all the paperwork together for the morning. She carried the packet upstairs and dropped it off with Lucy, then sat down at her desk to check her email.

Her phone rang, and she picked it up, only half-focused on it. 'Davis Funeral Home, Bryn Davis speaking.'

'Are you at your computer?' It was a female voice – brisk, unfamiliar, and cheerful.

'Excuse me?'

'Are you at your computer right now?'

'Yes, who is this?'

'Just bear with me. I want you to open your email.'

She just had. There were six new messages – two from Lucy about various office things, one from Gertrude Kleiman whose header was, surprisingly, I QUIT (and hallelujah about that one), two spam offers, and . . . one email with no sender name.

'You see the anonymous one with the subject line of PLAY ME?'

'Yes,' Bryn said. She pulled out her cell phone and began texting on it to McCallister. *Trace office phone call right now.*

'I sincerely urge you to click that file, Bryn.'

She switched her cell to silent mode and put it on the desk before her, then clicked the file attached to the email. She expected – braced herself for it – to see another of those creepy execution videos, but this was very different. It was taken with night vision, in the dark, and it was a close up on . . .

. . . On a child's face. A little boy with thick blonde hair and wide, scared eyes. A boy with a gag over his mouth.

The camera pulled back, showing Bryn that he was tied hand and foot, and sitting on a wooden box, in the dark.

'Oh God,' she said, stunned, and touched her fingers to her lips. 'What the hell – who are you?'

'Never mind me. That,' the voice said, 'is someone

you know – wait, the light should be coming on in just a second, you'll probably recognize him a little more clearly . . .'

She was right. There was a flare of light, the camera switched into full color mode, and now the little boy looked horribly familiar.

Bryn's chest ached as if she couldn't get a breath. 'Jeff,' she said. 'Jeff Fideli. Joe and Kylie's son.'

'A plus, Bryn, you're doing great. Now, this is what I need from you. You're going to take that cell phone you just put on the desk, open it up, and take out the SIM card. I'm not cruel, you don't have to destroy it and lose all your phone numbers, just put it in your office drawer. Then I want you to take your purse and walk straight for the exit. Don't talk to anyone. Don't stop for anything. Go straight out the door, get in your car, and meet me at Coffee Jack's. You know where that is, don't you? You're a regular there.'

'Yes, I know where it is,' she said. She was still staring at the screen, feeling numbed and frozen with terror. 'Let him go, he's just a *kid*!'

'We'll discuss those options once you come to the shop,' the woman said. 'But if you deviate from these instructions, or if you don't leave in the next fifteen seconds, this particular kid is deader than Dixie. Copy that?'

'Copy,' Bryn said, automatically slipping into the language of her military life. Fifteen seconds. She didn't have time to try to write a note, or give a signal, or do anything except leave all this on her screen . . .

. . . Except that, suddenly, her computer screen exploded into static, and then turned blue. The error box flashed, and the whole machine powered down.

'Sorry about the virus, hope you didn't have anything too valuable on that hard drive,' the voice said. 'You've now got about seven seconds. Better move.'

There was *no time* for a plan. She grabbed her purse and ran for the office door, then forced herself to slow to a walk down the hall. She passed Lucy's desk but didn't glance at her, didn't deviate at all as she went outside into the sunlight, through the gardens, out to the parking lot. Her fingers were shaking so badly it was hard to find the remote button to unlock her car, but she made it inside, and didn't hesitate there, either.

I have to think, she told herself as she drove. *I have to get word to Patrick and Joe.* Somehow, she knew, whoever had been talking to her would be watching her; she would have some way to see if Bryn tried to do anything counter to the instructions.

She simply couldn't take the risk of doing anything that might put Jeff in more danger, and she didn't have anything to tell them, except that Jeff had been abducted – which they'd know soon, if they didn't already. With time, they might be able to trace the email back, or analyze the video file, if it hadn't taken the email server down along with her hard drive, but if she screwed up *now*, it wouldn't matter. Jeff was a hostage for *her* good behavior.

She had to play it out. The problem was, her tracker nanites weren't fully attached; they wouldn't be active for hours yet.

And she'd just gone right off the reservation.

Bryn checked her rear-view mirror, in the forlorn hope that somehow, impossibly, she might have a tail, that Joe might have stuck with her at the office instead of doing his job at the funeral . . . or that Patrick might have somehow been close enough in the area to follow.

But the road was empty of traffic, and she kept hearing that cheerful, confident woman say, *deader than Dixie. Copy that?*

There wasn't any choice at all but to keep going.

She parked and lunged out of the car without bothering to lock it up, and felt a warm burst of relief when she saw that there was – as there often was – a San Diego police cruiser parked in the Coffee Jack's lot, and two uniformed officers standing in line at the counter. This might work out. This was *her* place, not the kidnapper's; she knew the people well. Dave the Doorman, for instance, he'd see her and know instantly that something was off. Maybe she could pass him a message as he held the door for her. Maybe . . .

. . . But she wasn't that lucky. Dave wasn't there. But then, she rarely came at this time of day. Maybe

Dave had someplace else he liked to haunt, a restaurant where he greeted another set of clientele by name and got his meals comped, as so often his coffee came free here for his good cheer.

There were six customers seated around tables in the interior of the shop, and two employees behind the counter. She didn't recognize either of them, but the shift would have changed from her usual morning crew. The warm smell wrapped around her like a fog – coffee, chocolate, steamed milk, cinnamon. Safety. Home. Familiar surroundings.

It shouldn't have felt so full of menace, so much like being trapped in a nightmare. She couldn't stop thinking about little Jeff, about the fragile courage on his small face. Bryn stared at the two police officers, willing them to turn and look at her, to see that something was wrong and approach her . . .

A hand fell on her shoulder. 'Bryn?'

It was *Carl*, her Pharmadene problem child, suddenly here and in the flesh. She blinked, and turned to face him. 'What . . . what are you—' It didn't matter. Didn't matter at all. 'I can't talk to you right now.' She had no patience with coddling him right now. He was an obstruction, not an opportunity. It'd take too long to try to make him understand enough to use him as a messenger.

Carl looked pale, shocky, hunched as if he'd been punched in the guts. 'Sit down for a second,' he said.

Bryn ignored him and looked around for the woman she was supposed to meet. No one presented themselves as a possibility.

Carl grabbed her arm, hard enough to bruise, and forced her to pay attention. 'Bryn! Sit *down*!'

She bent her knees and sank into the chair, staring now at him. 'What is this?'

He wet his lips. He looked terrible – really terrible. Gray, as if he was at least two doses down on Returné. 'It's not me,' he said. 'I'm not doing this. I'm a pawn – just like, a pawn . . . *no, sit down*! I don't have a choice.' He spoke in a terrified hiss, and held her wrist when she tried to get up. '*Sit!*'

She slowly lowered herself back to the chair. 'You're in this with her.'

'*No*,' he said. He didn't let go of her. His eyes were wild. 'Just wait. Wait.'

Suddenly, she knew what was happening. Carl was under orders.

Protocol orders. He didn't have a choice in what he was doing.

She didn't know what he was waiting for until the two cops, chatting and joking with the barista, claimed their coffees and headed out the door. Bryn tried to catch their eyes, and tensed to grab one, but Carl's desperation warned her that she'd better not try it.

Once the cruiser had pulled away into traffic, he let her go. 'Go get a drink,' he said. 'Go on. Get in line.'

'I don't want any goddamn *coffee*,' she hissed back. 'Where's Jeff? Where are they holding him?'

He stared back at her and didn't speak, just pointed at the counter. She grabbed her purse and walked to the counter. The register worker took her order and five dollars, and she moved to the other end, where the barista worked the machine and, in about a minute, put a cup up for her to take.

'You're Bryn, right?' he asked. 'Take it.'

The cup was empty.

She felt something blunt jammed low against her back, somewhere in the vicinity of her liver. 'Drop the purse,' a man's voice said – not Carl's this time. 'We're going to walk very quietly toward the bathroom hallway.'

Bryn stared at the barista, hoping desperately that he'd do something . . . but he stared back at her without any expression at all. She glanced over at the man working the register, the other new employee. Same blank indifference.

They knew. More than knew. They were part of the team.

'Do you want me to start shooting some of these nice people?' the voice whispered in her ear. 'Move it. Now.'

She did, but only to put a little distance between herself and the man herding her. She passed a woman seated next to the display of coffee makers, beans, and grinders. She was sipping and reading a folded newspaper, which she put down as Bryn made eye contact. *Help*, Bryn mouthed.

The woman raised her eyebrows, looked past her at her captor, and then turned casually toward the center of the room. 'Carl. Get up and lock the door and flip the sign. Do it now.'

No one in the coffee shop even *moved*, other than Carl, who looked deathly pale now, and very shaky. He did as directed. One of the other customers began pulling the shades down.

It wasn't just Carl. It wasn't just the baristas who were in on this.

It was all of them. The whole shop. *God.*

Her captor shoved her down into the chair opposite the woman. She was just . . . there. A soft, rounded face, dark hair, unexceptional but presentable. Even her clothing was nondescript. 'So. You're Bryn Davis,' she said. She reached down next to her and pulled a cell phone out of her purse, which she laid in the center of the table. 'Let's be clear. I know you can cause me trouble, and that's why we've gone to these lengths. But you *won't* cause any trouble, and this is why.' She took the phone and activated it, scrolled, and then faced it toward Bryn.

The same video setting as before – Jeff, sitting bound hand and foot on a box. Only now, his gag had been removed, and he was blinking into the camera's spotlight. His jaw was set in an expression that Bryn recognized as being straight from his dad. *Stubborn.* 'My dad's going to kill you,' he said to the videographer, in a remarkably matter-of-fact tone. 'But my mom's going to kill you *way more.*'

The video shut off, but that was all Bryn really needed to see. 'Fuck you,' Bryn said softly. 'Fuck you for using *kids.*'

'Not *just* kids. Oh, don't look at me like that, sweetie, I'll use anybody I need to use to finish the mission. Now. We're going to go into the bathroom, and I'm going to strip you naked and do the kind of search that requires rubber gloves inside of body cavities. Then you're going to put on the clothes I brought.'

She gritted her teeth until she saw stars. 'What happened to these people? The regulars in here?'

'They're safely sleeping it off in the storage room.' The woman's eyes weren't any remarkable color, just a plain dull brown, but the expression in them was extraordinary. 'Why, do you really care about them more than this precious little boy? That's just sad, and if you insist on asking me stupid questions we're going to have a problem that gets little Jeffy hurt.'

'No,' Bryn said tightly. 'No problem.'

She cast a filthy look at Carl as she got up, and he flinched. 'It's not my fault,' he blurted. 'I didn't have a choice.'

She did know, it just didn't make it any better. 'You

know they're not going to let either of us go now,' she said. 'You know that.'

He nodded, but she could tell he didn't actually believe it. He thought there would be a chance for escape, or mercy; he thought that he could clever his way out of it.

Bryn already knew. She'd seen it in the other woman's dark, chilling eyes.

Twenty-four hours until the nanites begin to broadcast our position.

That didn't matter. She needed to make sure Jeff was released unharmed. That was her primary, her *only* concern right now. Everything else – the pain that was sure to come, the eventual end of her life – all that had to be secondary.

She wouldn't let this happen.

Bryn glanced into the tote bag of clothes that the woman thrust into her hands. 'Not my color,' she said. 'But I'll make do.'

The woman's smile wasn't much warmer than her eyes. 'Move it.'

The strip search was humiliating and efficient. Bryn's clothes were bundled into a trash bag, and everything else – earrings, watch, necklace – went as well. The cavity search was unpleasant in every way possible, except that it was fast. It took a total of one minute to reduce Bryn to . . . nothing. No identity, nothing to call her own. Just a walking corpse.

Well, she thought, *that's not new, at least.* Odd how that could be comforting at a time like this.

After that, it was simple. She put on the plain pants and shirt, and her captor walked her out the back door to a brown SUV waiting there – not a flashy bulletproof model like the one Manny Glickman owned, but the kind thousands of soccer moms drove every day. There was even a baby-friendly sun screen on the rear window with SpongeBob featured on it.

Bryn took a seat on the passenger side, and belted in when ordered. Her captor wasn't alone; two other fake customers from the coffee shop got in the back. As the SUV pulled away, another took its place in the alley, and Bryn looked back to see Carl being loaded in with his own escorts.

'Eyes front,' said the woman. 'Hands on your lap. Don't bother trying the door; the child lock is enabled, so you can't open it yourself. Don't want you throwing yourself out at high speed from the vehicle.'

Too bad. Bryn had been considering the possibilities. 'What do I call you? Bitch?'

'Well, it has a ring to it, but you can call me Jane.'

'Jane Doe.'

'Something like that.' That seemed to entertain Jane a little, from the smile on her face. 'Don't worry. You'll get your questions answered when it's time.'

Bryn leaned forward, just a little, testing the limits of their patience as the SUV accelerated for the freeway entrance.

Something metallic flashed past her eyes, and as

she jerked instinctively back she felt the cold bite of something snugging tight against the fragile skin of her neck.

Jane sighed. 'Oh, Bryn, we discussed this. My friend John Smith in the back has this little thing called a commando saw – do you know what it is? Diamond-coated wire, can saw through wood, metal, bone, spinal cords . . . Really very easy to use. If you move again, he's going to start practicing his technique. Maybe he'll only saw through to your backbone and then let you heal. Or maybe he'll just take your fucking head off. I really don't know, how do you feel, John? Particularly into beheading?'

John didn't answer. He wasn't paid to banter, apparently, just to play lumberjack. Bryn stayed very, very still, hyperconscious of the cool, rough texture of the wire around her throat. 'Don't hit too many bumps,' she said. 'Or your detailer will be really unhappy.'

'Not my car, not my problem,' Jane said. 'Now shut up or I text my friend and little Jeffy gets a few bones broken for your attitude.'

Bitch, Bryn thought, but she couldn't do anything, anything at all, except sit quietly, and breathe.

CHAPTER THIRTEEN

The car had only traveled a few miles down the road before Jane said, 'Time for lights out for our guest. Mr Smith, if you please.'

For a heart-wrenching second, Bryn thought he was going to cut her head off, but instead, the wire noose's threat kept her pinned in place while he slipped a thick, blinding bag over her head. It was suffocatingly heavy, but by keeping calm she could draw in slow, thickened breaths.

The problem was *keeping calm*. She had this terror ingrained in her cells; she still woke up every night from a cold sweat, feeling that wet plastic bag molded to her skin like a cheap, oily shroud.

It's not the same, they're not trying to kill you, just keep you disoriented. She had to keep repeating that like a mantra, and when it failed, forced herself to count seconds for each slow breath. The inside of the bag started out dry and dusty, but quickly became hot and moist, and that added to the mounting tide of fear inside her. *Please not again, not like this again . . . not suffocating.*

They seemed to drive for hours after that, but Bryn had lost any sense of time. All she could do was . . . endure. Try to count her breaths.

Try to survive, one minute to the next.

'Out,' said a muffled voice, *finally*. The SUV had stopped, and her door had come open; she hadn't even noticed, immersed in fighting off her own demons. She pushed the seat belt release, stepped down out of the vehicle, and stumbled as her captor yanked her arm in a bruising grip. The noose tightened around her neck from behind. 'Remember your pretty diamond necklace. Don't go losing your head.'

Bad enough she was wearing her own personal guillotine, but stumbling along blind wasn't helping her feel more secure. One misstep, and even if it didn't actually cut her head off, the wire was thin and sharp enough to slice deep into veins and arteries. She was as careful as she could be, given his impatient shoving hand at her back.

Bryn could tell that they'd entered some kind of building by the blast of cool, dry air that washed over her skin, though her face remained hot and damp under the bag. The place was quiet, but over the harsh rush of her own breath she heard what sounded like someone crying weakly. Then the slow creak of wheels . . . a distant, sharp, angry cry . . . an old woman's voice saying, viciously, 'No, you can't have it, it's *mine*!'

There was carpet under her feet, thin and industrial. She heard a phone ringing shrilly off to her right, but it dopplered away as they moved on. More wheels passing them by – gurneys? Wheelchairs? And then the creak of a door. She and her leash-holder continued into what sounded like a small room, and the door slammed behind them.

The bag on her head suddenly tugged free, and she pulled in a deep, explosive breath, then coughed. Her tongue and lips tasted like dust and lint, and as she blinked and her eyes adjusted to the dim light, she saw that she was standing in a lifeless little room about twice the size of a prison cell, with a barred window up near the top of the far wall that let in a weak amount of light. The walls were a plain, though dingy, white, and marked with scuffs and scratches. One heavy gurney-style bed that looked at least two decades out of date. A cheap thrift store dresser with two drawers and a chipped corner. A metal prison-appropriate mirror bolted to the wall, over a stained porcelain sink. There was a toilet cubicle with no door.

Bryn swallowed hard and didn't move; there wasn't any point in trying anything, not yet.

Jane walked around from behind her and said, 'The door's locked, and if you don't do what I say, when I say it, little Jeff's going to have a very unpleasant assault-and-battery life experience. Do we understand each other?'

Bryn nodded as much as she could without damaging herself on the wire loop. Jane gave her a cool evaluating look, then nodded at Mr Smith behind her. He loosened the wire and slipped it over her head, and Bryn shuddered under the wave of relief that cascaded through her like glacier melt, but didn't try to run. She didn't doubt that Jane was capable of *anything*. 'What do you want?' she asked. Her voice sounded even and calm, which was something of a triumph.

'For now? Your unquestioning obedience,' Jane said. 'Here. Put this on.' She reached into a drawer, pulled out a hospital gown, the kind that tied in the back, and tossed it to Bryn. There was nowhere to go for privacy. Bryn turned her back to a wall, draped the gown over her clothes, and undressed beneath it. Even though they hadn't been her own clothes, and had fitted badly enough, they'd still been *something* connecting her to normal life. A hospital gown dehumanized her one step further. She tied the straps behind her as best she could, then waited.

'Good girl,' Jane said. 'Kick the clothes and shoes over. Then sit on the bed.'

Bryn followed every instruction to the letter. *Feet up. Lie down. Hands at your sides*. She wasn't surprised when they fastened the restraints on, and had a moment of flashback – these were the same restraints as Liam had used for Annalie, oddly enough. Ankles, wrists, chest, waist, thighs. She didn't resist. Houdini himself wouldn't have been able to wriggle out of this configuration, not without hidden tools and time.

Jane tested the straps, then nodded to Mr Smith. 'Good,' she said. 'Go on and make sure that idiot Carl's squared away. He's likely to throw some unfortunate fit.' He left. Like Jane, he was nondescript – an average-looking man, a little too heavy in the jaw, a little too small in the eyes to be considered handsome. Strong and well built, like Jane herself.

A cold, absolute professional.

Jane was watching her assess her opposition, with an amused smile lurking around her lips. 'You're not like Carl,' she said. 'You pick your shots, don't you?'

'Are we going to have girl talk now?' Bryn asked. 'Because I can't really braid your hair with my hands tied up like this.'

'You think you're funny, don't you?'

'Well, comparatively speaking, I'm probably the funniest in the room.'

'I think you'll find I'm a laugh riot when you get to know me. And you will, Bryn. Very well.' Jane met her eyes, and dialed a cell phone without looking at it. A pre-programmed number. 'The kid's served his purpose. Dump him.' Bryn gasped and lunged against the restraints as Jane hung up and gave her a slow, icy smile. 'Oh, relax. He's being left where he'll be found. You did a good job, so I don't feel the need to be . . . punitive. Unless the mouthy brat wanders out in traffic, he'll be home inside of an hour with a fun story to tell his friends at school.'

Bryn's heart was racing madly, her veins singing with the desire to *hurt* this bitch, but she forced a smile that probably held more than a trace of that black fury. 'I can't *wait* for you to meet his daddy, Jane.'

'Oh, I already have,' Jane said. 'Tall guy, six feet, bullet head? Wicked fast reflexes and charming as all get out. He'll remember me. He's got the scars.'

'Liar.' But Jane had shaken her confidence, because that *did* sound like Joe Fideli.

'Let's not start the name-calling. We've got loads of time before things get that catty. I'll tell you how this is going to go. This place . . .' Jane made a vague gesture at the room, the building in general '. . . is a black hole. People go in, they don't come out, and nobody bats an eye. Pretty genius, really. So you can forget about attracting someone's attention.'

'Not a prison, then,' Bryn said. 'A hospital. A mental hospital.'

'Oooh, close, but no. It's a locked facility. It's where they dump the severely impaired Alzheimer's patients, the ones without families, the ones who never get visited. No witnesses. And no one cares who comes in, since nobody ever leaves except in a body bag. Fucking creepy, if you ask me.' Jane sat back in her chair and crossed her arms. 'My point is this: you can scream and yell and curse as much as you want to. Doesn't matter. Somebody's always screaming in this ice-cold corner of hell. You won't sound any more delusional than the rest of the loonies.'

Bryn kept her mouth shut, grimly wishing she had a hand free so she could punch the bitch out. Just once. *Less than twenty-four hours*, she told herself. *You only have to make it less than a day. They'll find you. Find her, too. And when they do . . .*

That was a nice moment of warm, bloody fantasy, the idea of what Joe Fideli would do to the woman who'd kidnapped his son. If Patrick didn't take her apart first, of course.

'You're still wondering what I want from you,' Jane said. 'I can see it in your eyes, Bryn. The fact is, I'm going to ask you some questions. Now, you're probably thinking you won't answer. Word is you used to be a soldier. Maybe you think that makes you a badass, but baby, recruitment standards are so low they drag the ditches for volunteers these days; hell, half the gang members out there served their four years for free Uncle Sam-sponsored murder training. I wouldn't count on whatever backbone your cuddly little drill sergeant managed to beat into you lasting more than thirty minutes once we get down to it.'

She cocked her head, watching Bryn's face. 'Oh, and I also know all about your . . . what do you call it? *Healing*? That seems like an advantage until you begin to think it through and realize that all it *really* means is I don't have to hold back with you. I don't have to do some pansy flower waterboarding technique, I can actually *drown* you as many times as it takes. Or skin you. Or . . . wow, so many choices. I don't think I've ever really considered the possibilities.'

She shoved the chair back suddenly, and the noise of it made Bryn flinch, just a little. Jane stood up.

'So,' she said, looking down now, with a warm, genuine smile on her face. 'You just close your eyes and get some sleep, because when I come back, we're going to get things done, Bryn. Just see if we don't.'

She walked to the door, and Bryn didn't watch her go. She kept her gaze rigidly focused upward on the cracked ceiling. A spider had made a dusty web near the light fixture, and the silk billowed in the cold, dry breeze of the air conditioning. The spider herself was sitting right in the middle of the web, waiting. Just . . . waiting.

When she saw Jane leave in her peripheral vision, and heard the door slam and lock, Bryn finally closed her eyes.

Less than a day.

She could do this. She had to.

Jane was gone a long time, but there was no way to accurately gauge the clock. Bryn tried counting pulse beats for a while, but her attention wandered, drawn by distant querulous talking, or banging, or – shockingly loud – screaming. If there were nurses in this place, they didn't check on her, and Bryn wished rather pathetically that she'd taken the opportunity to use the toilet before letting them strap her down. Boredom was a strain, because there was nothing to stare at other than the single, fluttering spider's web, and the motionless arachnid. *Why there*, Bryn wondered? It didn't seem like a great hunting spot. But then, spiders were surprisingly smart for their size. The little creature probably knew something Bryn didn't.

She tried working the restraints, because it seemed like the prudent thing to do. After all, in any decent action movie, she'd find some weakness in the old bed, or a protruding screw, or *something* . . . but all she managed to do was chafe her skin raw, and introduce an annoying creak into the metal bed frame.

The light had faded outside, and the world outside the high glass slice of view seemed black – so black she couldn't even make out the entirely superfluous bars.

Nothing to do. Nothing to think. Nothing to plan.

Bryn wasn't good at waiting. The last time she'd been confined like this, she'd been in the white room, with that ominous drain in the middle of the floor and its easy-wash surfaces. Shambling from corner to corner, touching walls, counting steps while the nanites in her bloodstream degraded and turned toxic and her body began to turn on itself.

This was better, she told herself. A nice, comfy bed. And so far, she didn't need a shot.

That'll change, the cold, cynical part of her brain declared. *She'll hurt you, maybe kill you. You'll need that booster. And you won't get it. And we'll be right back in the white room, rotting, falling to pieces.*

No. She'd been in the white room for days, long days without treatment. Here, it would be over – one way or another – in less than twenty-four hours. She'd survive. Whatever Jane brought to the party, she'd survive. And Bryn was going to make it her personal mission from God to see that Jane got paid back, in full.

The spider moved, suddenly, skimming over the soft, strong field of its web and leaping on some tiny little creature with the bad sense to tangle itself up. Bryn was too far to see the details, but she could well imagine. Here she was, thinking she was the spider, when in fact, she was the fucking fly, trussed up in a tight cocoon for draining.

Jane was the spider.

And right on cue, Jane opened the door.

She was preceded by a metallic rattle of wheels, and a cheery, 'How you doing, Bryn? Hungry? I thought you might be. I brought you a little something.'

She was expecting – well, instruments of pain. Steel cutting tools, that kind of thing. But as Jane whipped the covering sheet off the tray, she saw . . . green Jell-O and a spoon.

'Wow,' she said. 'You're serious about your torture. *Green* Jell-O.'

'You're going to need your strength,' Jane said. She pulled up a chair and sat down, spooned up a bit of the gelatin, and guided it to Bryn's mouth. 'Here's the mama bird, feeding the baby bird . . . open wide . . .'

There was utterly no point in resisting; cooperating would at least get her a little something on her stomach, and it would be humiliating to spend the rest of her captivity smeared with fragments of the stuff. So Bryn opened her mouth, and Jane tipped the spoon. It went on like that, with Jane trying out bits of probably half-remembered cooing from her own mother. Choo-choo trains. Airplanes and airports. The glee Jane took in it was unholy, really, but as soon as the spoon clinked against an empty bowl, the fun was over. Jane put the bowl aside and shoved the cart out of the way with her foot, then sat back and crossed her legs.

She still had the spoon, and Bryn watched her turn it over and over nimbly in her fingers. 'So,' Jane said. 'Do you have any idea the damage a spoon can really do? Scoop things, obviously. It's best for eyes, but that's *so* obvious that it hardly even needs a remark. But it's also great for damage to the soft palate inside the mouth. If you're energetic, you can drive it all the way up into the brain and start scooping out things there, too.'

Bryn's mouth had suddenly gone very dry, but she forced herself to respond with a tight, sarcastic, 'Tease.'

Jane laughed. 'Oh, I like you. You really do think you're a hard ass, don't you? Been there, done that? Well, you haven't. Not like I have.' There was a flush in her cheeks, a sparkle in her eyes. Jane, Bryn realized with cold devastation, was a true sadist – and not the kind with a convenient safe word. She was a sociopath in the truest sense. 'I get paid for answers, and most people don't have the . . . resilience you do. So this is pretty interesting work for me. No taboos.'

'Just tell me what you want to know and we can get this over with,' Bryn said.

'What, *now*? I hope you're not going to let me down, Bryn, and get all girly on me. C'mon, woman up.' She gave Bryn's arm a friendly shake. 'I'll tell you what, I'll give you a sample question, and you can decide whether or not to answer it.' She paused – a dramatic pause – and then said, 'Boxers, briefs, or boxer briefs?'

'I don't wear any of them,' Bryn said.

'No, no, no, the question is, what does *Patrick McCallister* wear? Come on, Bryn. I know this is an easy one for you.'

Bryn smiled back at her, and it felt wild and fierce. 'Ask him yourself, bitch.'

'You think I have to ask?' Jane said. The smile disappeared, and what was left in her eyes was dark and endless. 'It's just a simple question, Bryn. C'mon, you can tell me. It's just us girls.' There was something behind all that, a trap Bryn didn't understand and didn't want to even try to guess. Something to do with Patrick.

And she wasn't going to go there.

'Fuck you,' Bryn said. '*Ask your question.*'

Jane tapped her lips with the rounded end of the

spoon, then said, 'What did you find at Graydon when you went into the building?'

'Dead people,' she said. 'Wrapped in plastic. And a bomb.'

'Oh, Bryn, I really was giving you a softball. Come on, now. We already know the answer. You're just being stubborn.'

Poor little fly, wrapped in your cocoon.

'A thumb drive,' Bryn said, because it was obvious by now that Jane *did* know. 'With encrypted data. We broke the encryption. It was three video files showing executions of Revived people.'

'Huh.' Jane's eyebrows rose, just a little. 'Truth. Interesting tactic. I'd appreciate you telling me just who helpfully decrypted that information for you – I always like to know who out there has special expertise, and I know my employers would really want to have a chat with them to find out the extent of what they know about all this. Trouble is, your friends who were in that warehouse seem to be a little difficult to find. Moved, left no forwarding address, that kind of thing. So how about parting with their names, for a start?'

Bryn shut her mouth. *Time to stop talking.* She'd wasted as much of the hour as she could, with the Jell-O and playing to Jane's catlike instincts, but she wouldn't give up Manny and Pansy. Not by name. These people might be able to find them, but she wasn't going to help. *Sorry, Manny. This is your worst nightmare, and I'm sorry I dragged you into it.*

Manny's extreme paranoia, in retrospect, didn't seem all that unreasonable after all. Not after meeting this woman.

'Oh,' Jane said happily, as Bryn turned her head and focused on the fluttering spiderweb on the ceiling, pressing her lips together. 'You really don't know how much this means to me. Thank you, Bryn. Thank you.'

The spoon touched her cheek and slid upward in a cool, sticky, damp trail, and Bryn shut her eyes.

It didn't help.

There were points where Bryn talked. Babbled, in fact, once her body had healed enough to allow words to come out. She confessed a few things – the fact that she had already figured out how many of the Revived were missing, the fact that she knew someone was experimenting on them. She gave the names of those who she'd identified. She even mentioned Fast Freddy Watson and Jonathan Mercer, just for the hell of it, but she didn't mention Annalie's name.

Jane probably knew it anyway.

Bryn didn't, out of sheer bloody fury, give up Manny and Pansy's names, though that was the most persistent question that was being asked of her. She didn't know anything *but* their names, and a couple of other locations where they'd been, but she wasn't about to let Jane have even that much of a chance at either of them. *I can take it*, she told herself. *It's just pain. Wounds heal. I can take it.* Jane couldn't scare her with permanent scarring, or even death; she needed her talking, so Mr Smith and his diamond-saw necklace weren't in the picture either.

In the end, she made up names for Manny and Pansy, cribbed from two of her least-favored fellow soldiers back in basic training. *Steve Hyatt and Terry Mueller.* Steve and Terry were bullies. They deserved it, if Jane came looking. Steve . . . Steve had grabbed her ass, threatened her, stolen from her. Terry, his girlfriend, had helped lure her into a dark room where Steve was waiting to get the drop on her. It hadn't happened, because Lieutenant . . . Lieutenant . . . *Bardley*, his name was *Bardley*, had walked in on them. Terry had sworn on the Bible that Bryn had come on to the two of them and it was all just some sick consensual game . . .

They deserved Jane, deserved it, *oh God can't think oh God oh God . . .*

Jane finally took a break; apparently, working with only a spoon was hard work. She left it lying bloody on the tray, with the dried bowl still sticky with Jell-O, and promised to come back with something sharper. Bryn lay trembling in the blood-soaked bed as gouged tissue healed, and thought, *I can't. I can't hold out for another* – how long would it be? Twelve hours? Eighteen? *God.* Jane wasn't even really interested in the answers to the questions yet. She hadn't, Bryn realized, really come down to business; she was still pleasuring herself.

The mattress under her body was cold with her blood, saturated and stinking of it. Her eyes were still shut, because she was afraid to open them, afraid she'd see darkness; Jane hadn't been kind to her there.

But she couldn't let the fear rule her, because once that started, it would never, ever stop. So Bryn forced herself to look.

Jane had turned on the lights at some point, and the harsh fluorescents were dizzying, throwing back red splashes on the walls, red beads and smears on her pale flesh. Overhead, the spiderweb still fluttered like a tattered flag.

I'm the spider. I'm the goddamn fucking spider. This is my web. See if it isn't.

She pulled at her restraints. The left wrist, the one that Jane had leaned over for hours, was looser than it had been because its Velcro closure had been rolled back a little from the friction – not much, but a little. Bryn grimly worked her hand back and forth, back and forth, and then steeled herself once she had braced at an awkward angle.

Then she threw her weight against it, violently, and snapped bones. She didn't try to smother the cry; as Jane had mentioned, no one cared. The bones compressed along the back of her hand now, shifting and grating as she pulled, and finally deformed enough that, in a white-hot burst of agony, she pulled free.

'Fuck,' she whispered, and took a few seconds to

just breathe before she raised her hand to her mouth, gripped her fingers one by one in her teeth, and pulled to put the bones back in line. She couldn't wait on the healing; it would take too long. She used her undamaged pinkie finger to reach out and hook under the edge of the rolling steel cart that held the Jell-O bowl . . .

. . . And the spoon.

It was an Olympic-level effort to reach for it, grasp it, and slip it under her hip, concealed in case Jane returned unexpectedly. Once Bryn had a weapon – and she'd never underestimate a spoon again – she began clumsily working on her other wrist restraint. It came loose after a torturous amount of effort. Her undamaged right hand was more than willing to take charge of the releasing of the chest, waist, thigh and ankle straps.

As she felt the icy-hot snap of the nanites knitting bones together, Bryn sat up. In the dull metal mirror she looked like something out of a horror movie – matted and soaked in gore, with drying blood running like terrifying clown make-up from her eyes. She bared her teeth. *Scary.* She didn't feel scary, though, she felt fragile, wounded, desperate and yet, at the same time, *angry.* A kind of fury she'd never felt before in her life.

In the drawer she found the bundled-up clothes she'd had on when she arrived, and she wiped most of the blood off her with the ruined hospital gown before pulling the pants and shirt on. Then she retrieved the spoon, used wadded-up old, thin pillow under the discarded bloody gown to at least hint at a body lying in the bed, refastened the restraints, and turned off the overhead lights. Before she did, though, she looked up at the spider's web, at the little hunter sitting in the center with infinite patience. At the lumpy mass of the insect she'd caught, hanging trembling in the corner. It was bigger than the spider. *Good for you*, Bryn thought. *Good for you. Wish me luck.*

She wedged herself into the narrow bathroom cubicle next to the door, and waited.

Jane didn't come back for so long that Bryn started to shiver; the chill was, she knew, a sign that the nanites were struggling to compensate for all the damage done. She needed a booster shot. The tiny machines were repairing tissue, organs, generating blood, but their power supplies were burning up fast. *Doesn't matter*, she thought. *You can wear Jane's skin as a coat if you get cold.* It was a macabre joke, but it made her feel better.

And she wasn't so sure she *did* mean it as a joke, after all. Something savage had been let loose in her, and she wasn't ready to cage it just yet.

It wasn't Jane who came back. It was Mr Smith, with his diamond saw looped casually in one hand. Whether Jane had tired of the game, or she'd just sent him to check, Bryn didn't know; it didn't matter. As the door swung shut behind him, Bryn lunged out of the dark, knocked him against the wall, and buried the spoon with brutal precision in his neck. It was blunt, but one thing Jane had taught her: apply enough force, and even a spoon could cut through flesh, and slice deep enough to cut through the thick rubbery surface of the carotid artery.

It was the second time today she'd been bathed in hot blood, but this time, at least it wasn't her own.

As his blood jetted out in panicked, high-pressure spurts, Bryn grabbed the commando saw, shoved him down, and knelt on his chest as she searched his pockets. He had a gun, too. She took it, checked the clip – full – and waited until the bleeding had faded to weak, barely perceptible wellings from his neck.

Then she got up and washed off in the bathroom as best she could. His leather jacket was bloody, but that sponged off; she put it on over her stained shirt, used a torn piece of his shirt to tie her hair back in a ponytail, and slipped out into the hallway.

It was never quiet here, and she tried to filter out the talking, arguing, crying or banging from other cells on the corridor. No sign of nurses or – if they existed – doctors. No sign of Jane, either. Bryn made sure her shoes were clean on the bottom and left no perceptible gory footprints, then put the gun in her pocket. She held it ready to fire through the leather, if necessary.

She walked as confidently as she could toward the exit.

The clock in the hallway read 3 *a.m.* Had it been that long? She'd been brought here around sunset. Her shot had been at noon, so fifteen hours had already passed. Nine to go before her tracking nanites came online. *Screw that.* She'd find a phone, or steal a car, walk into traffic – anything but stay here.

The door at the end of the hall claimed to be an exit, but it was keypad locked and alarmed. Opening that would draw instant attention, unless . . .

She heard a thin squeak of wheels behind her, and looked back to see a wheelchair slowly rounding the corner. The man in it was ancient, withered, and had a blank, vague terror in his eyes that struck a chord with her. She knew how that felt, now. At least hers could end, but his kind of torment wouldn't.

He came creaking down the hall, very slowly. No one was with him. No one was following him. He headed straight for Bryn like a tortoise-speed heat-seeking missile, a desperate kind of hunger in his face. When he reached her, he stretched his hand out to her and tried to speak.

She took his hand, very gently, and said, 'I'm sorry. I can't help you. But you can help me.'

He made a sound she didn't understand, and his claw-like fingers gripped hers with desperate strength. She managed to pull free, and pushed him to the door.

Then she opened it, ducked outside as the alarm began to sound its shrill noise, and left him with the wheelchair propped in the opening, as if he'd stuck trying to get out.

Then she ran.

Her hope was that they'd assume he'd somehow opened the door and not check further; Jane wouldn't be fooled long, but it might be a few minutes' grace before Mr Smith's body was discovered, and Bryn needed every second of distraction she could get.

Outside, she found a plain expanse of grass that really didn't qualify as a lawn; it was choked with weeds, its green color deceptively healthy. The exterior of the building was plain painted cinder block, functionally ugly. This particular building was cut off from the other, larger, more gracious facility; that part had an ornate garden behind it, with an ornamental gazebo and fountains. The more functional inmates of this prison stayed there, Bryn assumed; the ones who had family to visit them, and who for public relations purposes couldn't be penned up like convicts for the convenience of the staff. She had no idea if there was safety in that more graciously styled structure; could be that they had no idea what went on out here, in the internment camp, but she couldn't rely on that. On *anyone*.

The entire property – and it was large – was ringed by a high fence. There was a drive-through gate, but it, too, was locked up tight, and there were surveillance cameras watching. A few staff cars sat in the parking lot, but Bryn was fresh out of hot-wiring skills.

Phone. She needed a damn *phone*.

And the best place to find one would be inside the central building.

Bryn raced over the open area, trying to keep to the shadows as much as she could; the moonlight was traitorously bright out, but she made it to the garden and hid in the dark overhang of a still-blooming rose bush for a moment. Lights were on in the secured facility building, and she saw into the windows at the front; there were at least three or four burly, sour-looking nurses who were off to check the rooms. Someone would find Smith's body soon.

The patio doors off the garden were locked tight. No way inside. She followed the curve of the building around, testing windows, and finally found one that was open to admit a cool night breeze. She slid it up, careful of the noise, and cast a quick look inside to scout the footing. It was clear beneath, and she slithered over the sill and down to the carpet without much noise.

The old woman sleeping on the gurney – unrestrained, except for the metal railings – didn't stir. She looked as frail as a dandelion, but someone cared about her – there was a thick, hand-knitted afghan tucked around her, and a pillow nicer than anything available in the facility. Bryn scanned her bedside table, but found no trace of a cell phone or landline. She eased the door open. This facility had wider hallways, nicer carpet, big windows, and – unfortunately – more nurses. These were going door to door, methodically checking beds; when one went into a room, another came out, as if they'd planned it that way to cover any eventuality.

Bryn closed the door with a faint click and looked around. The bathroom wasn't big, and she had the distinct feeling they'd be looking inside it anyway as they searched. Likewise the narrow closet. She went back to the window and closed it, and heard footsteps approaching.

Time to decide.

She dropped to the carpet and rolled into the shadows cast by the dangling afghan on the far side of the gurney-bed. There was no way to get all the way underneath, so it was the best she could do. Her heart hammered as the attendant stepped inside, opened the bathroom, the closet, and came over to check the window.

He never glanced her way. The woman on the bed, as Bryn had guessed, would be of no real interest to him, and he'd be focused instead on the concealed places, not the open ones.

Bryn let out a slow breath as he finished his search, exited the room and shut the door behind him. She stood up and followed him, peeping out the narrow crack of wood to check the hallway. She waited until the staff had completely finished their search of the hall. One went back to the round nurses' station desks; the others moved on, presumably to the next set of rooms.

'Thanks,' Bryn whispered to the sleeping lady, and slipped out. She hugged the wall, watching the nurse at the station. This one was a woman, and she had her back turned as she spoke on the phone.

'No sign of anyone,' the nurse was saying. 'We're

clear in here. Blanton's checking the parking lot out front. The gates haven't opened, and we haven't had any motion detectors go off. Nothing on surveillance in the front. I think she must still be on your side.' That, at least, answered the question of whether or not the nurses in this building of the facility would be sympathetic. 'I'm telling you, we already checked the rooms. Every room. Either she's in your building or she's out on the grounds. Yeah, we're searching the garden. Keep your knickers on. She won't get far.'

The nurse hung up the phone, and Bryn backed up and into another room. This one held a sleeping man with an oxygen mask and an IV drip. Colorful, angular drawings were taped all over the walls – grandkids' or great-grandkids' projects, Bryn assumed. It was still a sterile, grim room, but it was trying to be cheerful.

There was a cell phone plugged in on the nightstand.

Bryn's heart leaped. She eased over to it and unplugged it, trying to move as quietly as possible. The thing was shut off, but once she'd touched the power button it gave out a nice, loud, musical tone she couldn't muffle.

The old man opened his eyes, removed his oxygen mask, and gazed at her blankly for a moment – and then he began yelling, shockingly loudly, '*Help! Help! Murder! She's taking my phone! Help, help!*'

Bryn cursed under her breath and headed toward the window, but it was latched tight, and the catch was stubborn. She finally racked it up with a shriek of metal just as the door opened, spilling light into the room. Even then, she would have kept going, except that Jane said, very softly, 'I'll kill the old man if you try it, Bryn.'

Bryn turned her head. Jane was standing by the old man's bedside; he'd stopped yelling, and was staring at her with mute terror, because she was holding a silenced semi-automatic pistol to his temple. Jane's face was pale and hard as bone, and the dark shadows pooled in her eyes. She looked . . . inhuman.

'I mean it,' she said. 'Try anything, and he dies, *then* I put a bullet in your brain. You can wake up. He won't. Either way, I shoot the holy fuck out of you before you can use that phone or make it off the grounds, so there's nothing to gain here. But by all means, go ahead. I'm sure it's a mercy killing, shooting this old fart.'

There wasn't any doubt at all that she meant every word of what she said.

Bryn shut her eyes for a second, then opened her fingers and let the cell phone drop to the floor. *Dammit, dammit, dammit . . .*

'Good choice,' Jane said. 'I'm really pretty upset about losing Mr Smith, but then again, nice use of the spoon. You're learning. Now, just hold still . . . if I do this right, it shouldn't really hurt much at all.'

Oh *hell*, no. Bryn let her knees go loose, dropped, rolled, and grabbed the phone in her left as she did. Her movement startled Jane into firing, but she missed, and Bryn shoved her right hand into her pocket, rose to her knees right in front of Jane, and fired, point-blank, through the leather of her jacket.

Three times.

Jane fired back, which was an impressive feat considering Bryn had scored three direct chest hits, but her bullet hit Bryn in the shoulder – not enough to slow her down. She felt it, but pushed the pain aside. Jane had taught her that, too – how to push the pain away.

Jane stumbled back against the wall, and the fury in her dark eyes was unmistakable. Her black shirt showed the bullet holes, and beneath, Bryn saw the flash of blood. Jane caught her balance and aimed, not for Bryn, but at the old man on the bed. She was going to kill him out of sheer spite.

Bryn took the gun out of her pocket, advanced, and fired twice into Jane's face.

The woman's trigger finger still convulsed, but the shot went wild, into the floor on the other side of the bed, and Jane went down hard.

Dead for sure.

Bryn wanted to keep on shooting her, just for the hell of it, but there wasn't time. She flipped open the cell – one of those easy-to-use kind for older people – and quickly dialed Patrick's number.

She was talking as soon as she heard the connection click in, even before his voice made it over the distance. 'It's Bryn. Don't ask any questions right now, just trace this phone and come heavy; I'm leaving it on and hiding it. I'll be around here somewhere. I have to find Carl and Chandra.' She didn't wait for him to respond, just opened a drawer and dropped the phone in. She *couldn't* talk to Pat just now; he'd infect her with his worry, he'd make her less focused on sheer survival. It had hurt to even hear his voice begin to say *hello*; the idea of having him say anything else, anything to comfort her, made her think she might break apart into tiny pieces.

The old man was still staring at her with blank terror. He was gasping for air. She reached over and fitted his oxygen mask over his mouth and nose and said, 'Sorry for all that, sir. You'll be okay.'

Then she pushed herself up, opened the window, and headed into the darkness. There was nothing here now for her except the certainty of being caught by the staff of the regular, presentable side of the business; rescue was coming, and they'd find Jane's body soon enough. Bryn didn't have a whole lot of time, and although hiding out was a good option, she knew Carl, at least, was still being held on the lockdown side of the complex where she'd been kept.

If it had been secure enough for the two of them, it was a good bet that any other Revived individuals they'd taken might be kept there as well . . . and there were some more still missing. Chandra Patel, for one. And Bryn owed it to Chandra, too, to try to get her out of this horror.

The gunshots had drawn attention all over the

nursing facility – lights blazing on, voices babbling – and as Bryn tried to make her way through the garden she had to keep to the ever-sparser shadows. She'd just made it past the gazebo when someone thought to turn on the full security lighting in the garden, which lit it up like a football field; Bryn sprinted for the edge of the bushes and out into the darkness beyond.

She didn't hear anyone yelling on her trail, so she headed straight for the cinder block building, slammed her back against the wall, and tried to *think*. She checked the clip, and controlled a burst of frustration – *should have picked up that bitch's gun too* – as she assembled a tactical plan. She'd have to go in through the front entrance, where two of the big male nurses were standing; either or both of them could be armed, and she didn't know for certain if they were guilty parties, or just innocent dupes. She'd rather have tried the rear exit, but the alarm had stopped sounding, which meant they'd closed the door. She didn't have superstrength or anything. Being hard to kill didn't qualify as much of a superpower.

If cockroaches were superheroes . . .

Someone spotted her shadow against the brick outside, and she heard a yell. A flashlight flared bright, and she moved for the reception area, fast, with the gun pointed at the two nurses. One raised his hands immediately. The other looked stunned.

'Open the door,' she ordered. No reactions. 'Hit the button and open the door! *You*!' She pointed at the one who hadn't raised his hands, and he reached beneath the counter.

She had just enough warning to dive out of the way as a shotgun blast tore through the cheap wood. The nurse yanked the gun free and fired again, nailing her left arm with pellets, but she shot back, two fast bullets to his chest, and he went over backward and took the shotgun with him.

She switched aim to the other nurse, still frozen with his hands in the air. 'Open it!' she screamed.

He slammed his fist down on a button, and she heard the harsh metallic buzzing as the lock clicked free.

Bryn hit it hip first, and cried out at the agony that zipped up her arm and across her body from the shotgun damage. Didn't matter. She had to duck to avoid a volley of shots from the other side. Another armed caregiver. That just didn't seem safe, somehow, having all these guns around the elderly. She didn't want to shoot back – too much risk of hitting a patient – but she didn't have much choice, and putting him down with a bullet in his side had the benefit of getting her a handful of room keys.

She found Carl in the third room, strapped to a gurney. He hadn't been tortured, or at least there was no evidence of blood, which was a mercy. No time to extract him, though. She left him and tried the other doors, looking for Chandra, and the other Revived she knew were in their hands.

She didn't find any of them, which meant either they'd never been here, or it was far too late.

She just barely had time to make it back to Carl's room before more gunfire sprayed her way, and stripped away his restraints fast. He was staring at her uncomprehendingly, and for a few panic-stricken seconds she thought they'd drugged him so thoroughly he wouldn't be able to move, but then he snapped out of it and said, 'Bryn? Oh my God, are you here to rescue me?'

She laughed. It rang hollow in the room, and had a bitter, wild edge. 'Sure,' she said. 'Why not? Get up, you ass, we have to get out of here.'

'I'm sorry about . . . you know,' he said, as he slid off the bed. They hadn't let him keep his own clothes, either; he was wearing – of all things – some dirty pair of denim overalls that sagged around him, and an equally dirty t-shirt.

'Selling me out?' she asked. 'They used your Protocol. You didn't have a choice. Never mind. Get down in that corner.' She shoved him toward it and backed to cover him, facing the door. She'd locked it, but she couldn't have taken the only set of keys, and even if by some miracle she had, these weren't the type to play a waiting game. 'Did you see Chandra in here?'

'I didn't see *anybody*,' he said, 'except that woman. Jane.'

'Jane's dead now.'

'Thank God.' His voice was trembling, on the edge of cracking. 'I'm sorry. I couldn't. I couldn't . . .'

Bryn couldn't really blame him; she'd been forced to cooperate, too. That didn't mean she had to *like* it. She checked the clip in her gun. Only three shots left, and she had the strong feeling that wouldn't go far. *Damn*, she was missing her riot baton. It made a great close-quarters weapon . . .

She spotted the aluminum cane in the corner a few seconds later, and laughed. It was the adjustable model – press in the round button, and the bottom section slid up and down. She slid it all the way out, weighed it, and then decided the top part of the cane was better weighted – more momentum from the heavy plastic grip.

She was back to being the spider, waiting for the fly . . . until the fly arrived.

The door banged open, and two tear gas grenades rolled inside. Bryn tried to kick them out again, but doubled over, coughing and choking on the fog, and through her tears she saw someone stride forward with a gas mask covering half her face.

Jane. There was no mistaking those eyes. Of course. How could it have never occurred to Bryn to think she was one of the Revived?

'Surprise,' Jane said, but it wasn't really. And then she kicked her in the head, several times, until Bryn went dark.

Chapter Fourteen

When Bryn woke up, fuzzy and sick, it all seemed that much worse. She'd wasted a lot of bullets on Jane, and it seemed pretty annoying to be kicked to death by her, afterward. But somehow, in the rear-view mirror, Bryn couldn't understand why she hadn't just assumed it from the beginning, that Jane was a Revival; half of those she'd met were clinging to sanity with both hands, and the other half had lost their shit entirely.

Jane was the same order of psychopath as Fast Freddy Watson . . . someone whose darker tendencies had been liberated by the drugs, who weren't afraid of death or pain or reprisals.

It wasn't good news, and the worst part of it came when Bryn realized just where she was . . .

Back in her original predicament.

Bryn's gaze focused up on the same grimy ceiling light,

the same cracked paint, the same fluttering spiderweb. The same spider sitting patiently in the center, waiting for a new, juicy snack to wander by.

She didn't bother trying her restraints, or even turning her head to see if Jane was there. She knew the woman would be.

'Who the hell thought it would be a good idea to Revive *you*?' she asked the ceiling, but she meant it for Jane, and turned to look at the woman's dim shape in the dark where it sat comfortably, legs crossed.

Jane shrugged and flipped a light switch, and Bryn winced. The damage from the tear gas had healed, but she still felt unusually sensitive to the brightness . . . but then, the nanites were overworked now, struggling to keep pace both with the body's natural self-destruction and that imposed on it from the outside. She could expect to be hurting soon – and for any further damage to be slow to heal.

'I'm useful,' Jane said. 'To the right people. Cheer up, Bryn. You can be useful too, if you work hard, study, eat your vegetables, and above all, stop fucking around with me.'

'Sorry,' Bryn said. 'That's just never going to happen. Maybe you'd better get your badass little spoon again. Or raise your game to a full-on spork.'

Jane leaned over her, and what was in her eyes was like looking through a peephole into the darkest, emptiest hell Bryn could ever imagine. 'You,' Jane said, 'are going to tell me anything and everything. You're going to beg me to ask you a question. You're going to want to tell me so bad you'd crawl over hot coals to lick my ass. Understand me, sweetie?' Her tone continued to be warm, sweet, bizarrely likable. 'You are *mine* for as long as I want to play with you. Nobody's coming to get you. Nobody's taking you away. There's no hiding.'

'Prove it,' Bryn said. She didn't blink. She'd let go of all that fear, all that pain, all that *anguish* that had been haunting her since she'd woken up screaming for the first time, with the taste of that plastic bag on her tongue. She had life, unlimited life, for as long as those nanites could scurry their little mechanical asses through her tissues and give it to her.

And she was going to use it to spit in Jane's face for as long as possible. If it was insanity, it tasted sweetly metallic, as if she was chewing tinfoil. She didn't care anymore. *Couldn't* care anymore.

I think I broke myself, she thought, and almost laughed.

Jane blinked first. Then she took a step back, cocked her head, and frowned, just a little. 'You're a weird little thing,' she said. 'I mean that completely as a compliment. But—Oh, dammit! Does this happen to you? You're getting really focused and there goes the cell . . .' Jane's phone, Bryn realized, was ringing. The ringtone was Britney Spears, 'Toxic'. If *that* wasn't appropriate . . .

'Yes?' Jane asked, and put the phone to her ear as she turned away. She strolled toward the door. Bryn focused up on the spiderweb, on the spider, on the cocooned future lunch. Maybe she wasn't the spider *or* the fly. Maybe she was the web. Sticky and impossible to tear apart, no matter how hard the struggle.

'Are you *kidding* me?' Jane said, lowering her voice to a hard whisper. '*No!* No, I'm telling you, this is the *one*, you do not want to waste this opportunity – trust me, we need—' She stopped talking and stood very still. 'All right. You're the boss.'

Those last words didn't sound like her at all. None of the cheer. None of the macabre joy. Just flat syllables. Jane hung up and dropped her phone back into her pocket, put her hands behind her back, and spun around to face Bryn with her face pulled into an utterly false smile.

'Aren't you just the luckiest damn girl in the world?' Jane asked. She was smiling with teeth, and it looked as if she wanted to bite chunks out of something. Maybe Bryn. 'I think maybe you are. *Sweetie*. Well, I have my orders. Let's get this fucking show on the fucking road.'

She lunged for the bed, and Bryn tensed all over to get ready for the pain. It didn't come. Jane stomped on something on the bottom of the gurney's rails, and Bryn felt the bed lurch as the brakes released.

Then Jane shoved the gurney out from the wall and steered it toward the door.

Bryn's breath rushed out, and she felt every muscle in her body tighten. *No, no, don't take me to the incinerator* . . . She knew what was coming, she'd seen it. But she wouldn't beg, not Jane. Never.

'Relax,' Jane said, and gave her a bright, delighted, upside-down smile. 'You look so tense, baby. We're just going for a little fresh air.' She opened the door and pushed Bryn's bed out into the hall, which still smelled of gun smoke and spilled blood. They'd be a while cleaning up the considerable property damage, which gave Bryn a bizarre sense of satisfaction. She'd hurt them. Not as much as they'd hurt her, but still. She hated to go down without a fight.

'Why are you doing this?' she asked breathlessly. 'What the hell broke you this bad?'

She surprised Jane, for once; the woman glanced down at her, and there was a momentary gleam in her eyes that wasn't driven by madness, chaos or bloodlust. It almost looked . . . human. 'It's never just one thing,' Jane said. 'It's like falling out of love. You look back and suddenly you don't know who that person was that fell in love with him, because it isn't you. You know what I'm talking about, Bryn. A year ago, who were you? Not who you are right now. And you'll keep changing, because out here on the fringes, there's no gravity left to hold you down.'

One of the nurses was dead, and two were wounded; she saw the sheeted body, and one on a gurney while the other was being bandaged. The survivors glared. Not in the Revival club, Bryn thought. Not important enough to whatever this bizarre cause might be.

Jane kept pushing her right through the door at the end of the hallway, out into the night air. There was a thin, tentative blush of dawn on the horizon. 'I found the old man's cell phone, by the way,' Jane said. 'In the drawer. Still on.'

'Good for you.'

'If you think they're going to come running to find you, they won't,' she said. 'I had a guy drive it south of the border. Ought to be deep in Cartel Land by now. With any luck, your white knights will go riding into a bunch of machetes and get mailed back in wet little pieces.'

'Don't pretend like you're not fucked,' Bryn said, very pleasantly. 'The signal got out, and they will have traced it, because those phones like that? The ones for old people? They make them very easy to locate. In case someone falls and can't get up.'

Jane looked pinched around the mouth this time, and pushed the bed faster. 'You think they'll come rushing into some old folks' home, guns blazing? Don't be stupid. By this time, there's no trace of you in the main building to find. They'll think it was a decoy.'

'It's hard to cover up the damage back there. All those bullet holes. All that blood.'

'That's why, in fifteen minutes, a fire is going to

gut the inside,' Jane said. 'Terrible tragedy, all those
innocent people caught like that. Three of our staff are
going to die trying to save them.'

'Three? I only killed one.'

'Well, you wounded two, and I don't want to explain
it to the cops. Much easier if they die selfless heroes. Do
you know what the word verisimilitude means?'

'You're hard on your minions.'

'Oh, baby, you watch too many bad movies, and I
don't have minions. I have *co-workers*. Being paid by
the same company doesn't make us family, and they'd
shiv me in the back for an extra dollar an hour. Just like
in any other business.'

Bryn realized they weren't heading for the main
building – or for any building, come to that. They were
heading for the square, blocky shape of an ambulance
that sat flashing its lights in the parking lot – probably
a very common sight here. No one would remark on it
at all, even if anyone noticed. A uniformed paramedic
in a ball cap was standing at the rear of the vehicle, and
as Jane wheeled her gurney up, he nodded and took
control to load Bryn inside. He locked her wheels down
into braces on the floor, then jumped down to talk with
Jane in a low voice.

Jane climbed inside and leaned over to look
into Bryn's face. 'This is where we say our sad little
goodbye. It's been fun, Bryn. Don't blame yourself for
how this turned out; sometimes you're the windshield,

and sometimes, you're the bug.' She squeezed Bryn's shoulder and winked. 'I just got my new assignment. I'll be paying a visit to the Fideli family. Just in case little Jeffy remembers something he shouldn't.'

Bryn lunged against her straps. 'You *fucking bitch*!'

'Oh, sure, look who's talking. If you ask me nicely, I'll go easy with the kids. They won't feel a thing. Can't promise the same thing for the parents, though, since I owe you one. Here's something on account.'

She tapped Bryn on the forehead, hard, and gave her that eerily warm smile again, then reached over to a gurney lying across from Bryn's and tugged the sheet loose as she climbed out of the ambulance.

Bryn hadn't really registered the fact that there was someone lying across from her until that moment when the sheet was pulled off the body.

It was Carl. And Carl was really, sincerely dead. His head had been severed, not very neatly, and the gurney was soaked in fresh red blood. The ambulance reeked with it, Bryn realized. The loose head had been tucked beneath his left arm, to keep it from rolling free, and Jane had positioned it for maximum effect, facing directly toward Bryn. Gravity had opened his mouth, and made it seem as if he'd never stopped screaming.

My fault, she thought. She'd thought it unlikely she could feel shock again, but it swept over her in a cold, numbing wave. *This one's my fault*. She'd left Jane out there alive and free to go after innocents. Carl had died horribly. A whole hallway full of confused old people would burn to cover up her disappearance.

Now maybe the whole Fideli family was going to pay for her mistake, too.

God, she had to kill that bitch *for ever*.

But she couldn't get out of the goddamn restraints.

The ambulance took off and drove for about five minutes before slowing down, and Bryn thought, *they're not bothering to dismember us very far from the crime scene*; it showed a kind of stunning, unsettling arrogance that made her worry that Jane not only could keep her promises, but might outdo them. Carl had gone down screaming, but Bryn decided she wouldn't; if anything, when her head came off, she'd go down biting. Maybe she could take a piece off of her killer, at least.

The ambulance came to a stop, and for a moment she thought Carl's head would roll off the gurney, but it stayed in place. That was a strange relief that evaporated as she heard the engine shut off, the driver's door open, and footsteps move around to the doors.

Get ready, she told herself. But how did you get ready for this final moment when all hope was gone? It seemed crazy and absurd that she'd survived Jane only to die like this, for no good purpose.

The doors opened, and the paramedic climbed in. He pulled off his cap and crouched down next to Bryn, and she was treated to a big, toothy smile . . .

. . . From *Fast Freddy Watson*. The man they'd fought at the marina. The one who'd killed, and then kidnapped, her sister Annalie.

Her own *original murderer*.

'Hey, Bryn,' he said. 'What's shakin', bacon?' He flipped open a long-bladed knife, hesitated for a few seconds with his gaze on her face, and then neatly began slitting open her Velcro restraints. 'Welcome to your rescue party.'

She sat up fast, as he methodically finished with the last of the straps, ready to defend herself if he decided to go psycho on her – but after Jane, Freddy seemed weirdly quite normal. Her scale of crazy had definitely undergone some vast expansion.

He cast a look at Carl and said, 'Guess we'll be leaving him.' He patted Carl's bloodless cheek. 'Sorry, buddy. Sucks for you, I know.'

With that, Freddy folded his knife and jumped down from the back, and Bryn followed, feeling shaky with a toxic mix of adrenaline, relief, uncertainty, and decaying nanites. The ambulance was parked on a small side road off the main one leading down the hill; they were surrounded on three sides by swelling dark hills.

And they weren't alone. A blue sedan idled nearby, and Freddy walked over to it and opened the back door. When she hesitated, he said, 'The ambulance is stolen. If you go joyriding it around for long, especially with your headless friend in the back, you'll be having some fun with the local yokels real soon. C'mon, Bryn. Could have hurt you already if I was going to do it – oh, and if I leave you here, Jane'll find you soon. You don't want that. Trust me.'

She really didn't. After another second or two, she slid into the back seat of the sedan. Freddy shut the door and got into the passenger seat.

The man in the front seat said, 'Hello, Bryn,' and she realized that it was no surprise, really.

Jonathan Mercer was driving the car. Fast Freddy's boss . . .

. . . And the inventor of Returné.

'I came to save your life,' he said. 'How am I doing so far?'

'Great,' Bryn said. She lunged forward over the seat, put him in a headlock, and said, 'Give me your cell phone or I'll break your fucking neck, you psycho.'

He choked, flailed, and pointed wildly at Fast Freddy . . . who dug a phone from his pocket and held it out. Bryn let go of Mercer's chicken-thin throat, took the phone, and sank back against the cushions as she dialed with lightning-fast fingers.

Patrick answered on the first ring this time.

'It's Bryn,' she said. 'I'm out. They're coming for Joe and his family. Get everyone safe, right now. Don't worry about me.'

'Does Mercer have you?' Patrick answered. She could hear the tension in his voice.

'Did you *hear me*? Kylie and the kids—'

'Are safe,' Joe said, clicking in on another line. 'Liam's okay, too. So's your dog, in case you're wondering, although he's getting a little pissed at you for all the inconvenient abductions. It's hell on his routine. Does Mercer have you?'

This was so confusing it made her head hurt. 'Is he *supposed* to have me?'

'Yes,' said Patrick. 'It was the best way we could get you out of there safely. They were looking for us. Not for someone we'd shoot on sight.'

She was feeling a little out of her depth, suddenly. Back was front. White was black. And Jonathan Mercer and Fast Freddy, apparently, were *allies*. 'How the hell . . . ?'

'Long story,' Fast Freddy said, and plucked the phone out of her hand. 'No time. We're coming in,' he said into it, and hung up the call. 'You can chat all you want later, but right now, we need to *go*. When Jane gets where she's heading and figures out it's a trap, she's going to come looking for us, and I really don't want to be found.'

Mercer turned around and glared at Bryn. 'It probably goes without saying, but try grabbing me again and you'll end up headless in a ditch. Got it?'

Bryn glared back at him in the rear-view mirror, and didn't make any promises.

'Seat belt,' he said. 'And shut up. You too, Freddy.'

It was a silent drive.

It was a long drive, as they veered north-east from San Diego, and out into the desert landscape . . . not much traffic in the predawn hours, especially as the car headed into what wasn't much more than wilderness. Bryn watched the sky turn from black to cobalt blue to lapis as the sunrise drove away the night. Now that she had time to think without the masking veil of adrenaline clouding everything, she couldn't believe she was still alive – well, still *functioning*.

She'd met a true, nearly soulless psycho killer, and walked away. *For now*, some part of her whispered. *And you'll never really leave that room, in a whole lot of ways that matter*. She could feel it, the damage Jane had done to her – not physically, that would heal, but in other, subtler, more awful ways. The idea of being touched by anyone made her feel sick and light-headed. She could feel her body trying to process out the stress in random twitches and shakes, but they were like the lightest possible surface tremors, and deep inside, tectonic plates were shifting, crashing, reforming. The damage had to go somewhere, and it turned inward.

She thought that was what Jane had been trying to tell her, there at the end. *It changes you.*

Bryn had a new, desperate fear that it *would* change her, rip her apart and cobble her back together into something that was only human on the outside, like Jane – something that had lost all sense of what it meant to love and be loved in return. Something that only understood pain. Because right now, that was all she could see, smell, hear, touch, taste, *be*. Psychic, raw pain.

Bryn leaned her forehead against the cool window glass and stared blindly out at the dawn. Mercer and Fast Freddy tried to talk to her, but she ignored them; eventually, Freddy settled on an oldies rock station on the radio, and that was oddly soothing. She might feel like an alien in a human suit just now, but the Rolling Stones were always relevant.

The car passed a billboard reading SALTON SEA RECREATION AREA. It was an ancient, decaying, leprously peeling artifact of a far different era: 1950s' hopeful families, finned cars, and a would-be resort that now existed only in faded postcards . . . and ruins.

Bryn leaned forward, but not enough to put a headlock on Mercer. Yet. 'Where are we going?' She'd expected to head back to the estate, or failing that, some locked-down location in the city. Instead, they were heading out to the literal middle of nowhere.

'Bombay Beach,' Mercer said.

'Isn't that abandoned?'

'For years now, except for addicts and thrill-seekers,' he said. 'You know, you haven't asked anything yet. Not even why I'm suddenly your best friend, coming to your rescue.'

'I don't figure you'll tell me the truth,' she said.

'Oh, Bryn, after all I've done for you? That hurts.'

'I don't think you've earned any trust points. You sent my own sister to try to *kill me*.'

'Granted, but things have changed. It's not a fight for market share for my product, it's survival. Jane's employers are taking away *my* customers, not just targeting your Pharmadene drones on the government dole. I *need* my customers.' Jonathan Mercer had, she'd heard, started out as an idealistic scientist, but something about Returné had broken him, too – not in the literal sense, because he wasn't on the drug (and was still alive) but because he'd lost that rosy glow of belief. He'd been betrayed by his own, and his response had been to betray them back, over and over.

The only thing that really mattered to him now was money, lots of it, acquired as fast as possible. He was the one who'd started illegally running Returné in a blackmail scheme with Lincoln Fairview, Bryn's former boss; indirectly, he was responsible for Bryn's murder and rebirth.

And directly responsible for Annie's.

Mercer stared at her in the rear view. Pharmadene's brand of psychotic idealism meant using the drug to turn all of the *best people* – in their opinion, of course – into the Revived, living for ever, and owing their very existence to the great corporate god. The only good thing that Bryn could say about Mercer was that he wasn't a kingmaker; he didn't try to judge who should get the drug and who shouldn't. He believed that if you could pay, you should play.

It wasn't egalitarian, except in the very commercial sense, but at least it had been better than Pharmadene's new world order plans.

Mercer had gotten tired of her silence. 'The point is, I have no quarrel with you personally, Bryn. Nor with Mr McCallister. My fight with the government's control of my business will have to wait for a better time, because they have absolutely no clue about what they're facing.'

'Do you?' Bryn asked.

'Oh yes,' Mercer said. 'Quite a bit of one, and trust me when I tell you that however afraid you are right now, you are not afraid enough.' He glanced over at Freddy. 'We've arrived. Make the call.'

Freddy pulled out a cell phone and dialed, and just said, 'Ready,' before hanging up again.

'This seems very spy-friendly,' Bryn said. 'Please tell me if I've joined the Impossible Mission Force.'

'I think you did that the day you died,' Mercer said – and sadly, she thought, he was probably right. 'You're looking quite gray, you know. If you want a shot, then be quiet and do as you're told. If all works well, you should have most of your answers in under an hour. I don't think you'll enjoy them, but you will have them.'

They passed Salton City, which was about the only claim in the whole area to civilization; the Salton Sea

Recreation Area had been a half-assed attempt to create a tourist trap by sheer force of will, on an inland saltwater lake that was in the process of ecological crash. The creators had envisioned a California version of Las Vegas, only without (presumably) as much gambling.

What was left of that utter failure was sun-baked, dry and defeated; the boarded-up, crumbling motels looked post-apocalyptic, and the few stores and restaurants struggling to stay open seemed like places to avoid, not frequent.

And that was the thriving part of the area. Bombay Beach was much, much worse.

The sedan slowed down as they entered the real devastation. Most of the eyesores around Salton City had been quietly bulldozed, but here, in Bombay Beach, they *were* the landscape. If anyone still lingered here, it was because there was no way out for them. Where there were actual houses, they had been left to the elements, windows broken out and ragged, sun-rotted curtains flapping in the breeze. The departing owners must not have made much of an effort to take their furniture, because many pieces lay broken and dismembered. A disemboweled sofa with chunky sixties-style lines bled tattered foam where it lay half-on, half-off a sagging porch.

They kept going, past row after row of utter destruction and neglect. No sign of people, just circling, wheeling birds over the flat, harsh lake. The white spots she'd initially taken for foam on the water's surface were, in fact, dead fish. Hence, the greedy birds.

It was, beyond any doubt, the most blighted and depressing area Bryn could imagine that hadn't been bombed out of existence.

Mercer slowed the sedan, finally, as a chain link fence appeared ahead. It was ancient, but still upright and doing its job – odd that it hadn't been ripped apart by vandals, as so many others had been. Behind it lay a large, square cinder block building that looked beaten, but not quite as broken as the others.

Mercer parked. Freddy got out of the car and slid back a section of the fence that had been cut loose from the post; Mercer scraped through with only a minor loss of paint, and Freddy restored the fence and twisted some kind of fastener back in place to hold it. *That* was why vandals hadn't bothered to rip it down . . . they didn't need to do so. Easy access.

They parked in front of the building. It had a single, closed door, and a faded, illegible sign that Bryn couldn't make out. She thought it looked like the ghost of a sailboat, and water, but this place was like a real-world Rorschach test – you could impose your own meaning on anything you saw here.

'Out,' Freddy said, and opened her car door. She didn't like it, suddenly, didn't like *this* . . . it was rarely good news to be driven to the middle of abandoned nowhere and marched out of a car. But in truth, if Mercer had wanted her dead, he could have let her go to the incinerator and not put forth the effort.

So she went – although she remained acutely aware of Fast Freddy's knife, and where he kept it. In a crisis, she'd go for that.

She also didn't let anyone touch her. Not at all.

Mercer walked right up to the door and knocked. Three strong, steady bangs of his knuckles, then three more, as if it was some kind of signal. Bryn listened. There was no sound out here at all except the unearthly crying of the gulls diving on the fish, and the rattle of wind. The smell of the place struck her hard – a hard-to-stomach aroma of pure, rotten death. *Recreation area my ass*. The only recreation still thriving out here was conducted in the dark, fueled by booze, drugs, and violence.

The door opened on shadows, and Fast Freddy tried to push her inside; that was a mistake. As he reached for her, Bryn stepped into the gesture, grabbed his arm, and twisted it behind him, then frogmarched him over the threshold as a human shield. 'Touch me again,' she whispered in his ear, 'and I'll cut things off you, asshole.'

He laughed. *Laughed*. 'I forgot,' he said. 'You've met Jane.'

She twisted harder, and got a wince out of him. 'What do you mean by that? You think I'm *her*?'

'I think nobody is the same after they meet Jane,' Freddy said, and for once, there wasn't any mockery in his voice. 'I damn sure wasn't.'

Mercer entered behind her, and Bryn backed to the side, taking Freddy with her; she didn't want Mercer at her back any more than she did anyone else just now. He didn't comment, not even to ask her to let go of his sidekick; he just shut and locked the door.

A rank of lights flickered on overhead – old fixtures, dirty bulbs, it was amazing any of it still worked. The room itself was just a rectangular box that vaulted up into a curved concrete roof spiderwebbed with cracks and peeling turquoise paint.

There were two people standing in the center of the room, and both of them were armed.

One of them was Liam. It was very odd seeing him here, dressed in his sweater vest and dress pants under Kevlar, with what looked like a.380 semi-automatic pistol in his hand – what was even odder was that he looked completely comfortable with it, especially as he aimed it two-handed, with impeccable form, at Mercer's head. 'Please don't move,' he said. 'This might not damage your friend, but I understand it would greatly hamper your future plans.'

Mercer, looking amused, shrugged and raised his hands. 'And here I thought we were all friends.' He glanced at Bryn. 'You can let him go now. You're safe.'

She released Fast Freddy, because the other armed

person was Pat McCallister. No comfortable sweater, no dress pants, he was dressed for war and death, and he looked *very* intimidating. His dark, very cold stare fixed on Fast Freddy as Bryn let go of him. 'Hands,' he said. 'Up on your head. Down on your knees.'

'Do it, Freddy,' Mercer said. 'Let's not start off our collaboration with so much drama. Please have your man stop posturing. You can't afford to kill me, McCallister. You need what I know.'

'Not as much as I'd like to blow your brain stem out the back of your skull for all the misery you've caused,' Pat said. 'Don't underestimate how much I hate you, Mercer.'

Mercer made it look like the prisoner-of-war pose was his own idea, even as Pat slammed him face down to the concrete, zip-tied his hands and ankles, and flipped him over on his back to search him. He came up with two guns, which he added to his own arsenal, and then repeated the process with Fast Freddy. He didn't miss the knife.

Only after the two men were down and helpless did he nod to Liam, who relaxed and stepped back.

And *then* he finally looked at Bryn.

She didn't remember him moving, but suddenly he was there, within touching distance, arms open for her, and McCallister was the only safe place she could imagine left in the world. The only solace.

But she flinched when he reached out. It was sheer

gut reaction, utterly beyond her control; she saw the flicker of shock in his face, and then the understanding, which was worse. He didn't try to embrace her.

Instead, he slowly, carefully put his hands on either side of her face. They felt sunshine-warm. So did his voice. 'I'm sorry,' he said. It was little more than a whisper, and his eyes were fierce and desperate. 'I'm sorry I couldn't come for you myself. It was safer this way. We didn't have the firepower to take that place, Bryn. The only thing we could do was trust that Mercer could pull this off. I hated leaving you there even an extra second, believe me.'

'I know,' she said, and wrapped one hand around his wrist. His pulse was tapping hard against her fingers. 'It's okay. Everything's okay now.' She was lying – to him, to herself – but she couldn't say anything else. Nothing else would help that anxious, tense look on his face. 'Where's Joe?'

'With his family. I wouldn't ask him to leave them now, not after—'

'After Jeff went missing,' Bryn said, and felt a horrible surge of fear. 'He's all right, isn't he? They let him go? He wasn't hurt, was he?' That was the one rock to which she'd clung through all that horror with Jane – that at least she'd saved Jeff. If she hadn't . . . if she hadn't, the tide would rush her over the cliff.

'He's fine. Scared as hell, like his mom. Kylie was going out of her mind, and Joe—' McCallister cut himself off, and shook his head. 'I can't let him put them at risk anymore. Or himself. Joe's out of this, he has to be.'

'Yes,' she said. 'I don't want him hurt either.' She took a deep breath and said, 'I also don't want *you* putting yourself at risk. Or Liam. This isn't about you, it's about me, and Annie. About the Revived. You're just going to get hurt, Pat. These people . . . they're not like Pharmadene, as bad as that was. They're something else. Something far worse.'

'She's right,' Mercer called from where he was on the floor. 'You have no idea how much worse this really is. *I'm* nothing. *Pharmadene* is nothing. Widen your scope of disaster, McCallister.'

Patrick stepped away from Bryn and walked to Mercer. He put a booted foot on the man's chest, and said, 'What do you know?'

'More than you.' Mercer gave him a chilling smile. 'If you want a *clue*, then I'll give you one for free. The nursing home where they were holding your girl is just a start. Just a tiny little air bubble on the tip of the iceberg, if you will. But to give you an idea of scale, they've killed at least fifty people there. Old, sick people. Who misses them? Who cares, when they've got nobody left? It's inevitable progress, they're dying anyway. But they're still useful for one thing.'

'Test subjects,' Bryn guessed.

'Oh no,' he said. '*Incubators*. In a way, you really

have to admire their ruthless efficiency, don't you? And all I had to use were chimpanzees.'

Pat's expression had gone just a little bit unhinged, and he pressed down hard with his heel, driving the breath out of Mercer's chest with a pained gust. 'Start making sense while you still can.'

Mercer made some wheezing attempts, and Pat finally eased up on the pressure to let him draw in a whooping gasp. 'Can't tell you here,' he said, and coughed. 'No time. We need to get out of here and find a safe haven before her tracker starts sending a signal.' He read the frown on their faces, and shook his head. 'Idiots. Of *course* they know about the trackers. They know about the nanites, and the frequencies they broadcast. And they'll be *listening*.' He jerked his chin at Bryn. 'You've got about two hours before that happens, at the most. It'll start out as a weak, intermittent signal, so maybe three hours for them to get a firm lock. But she's a beacon, and she'll pull them straight at us.'

'Pat?' Bryn asked anxiously. 'Is he right? Can they track me?'

'It's possible,' he finally said. 'And it's possible this piece of shit is lying to make us go where he wants.'

'Listen, GI Jarhead, if you *want* to reacquaint yourself with the lovely Jane, just go ahead and—'

Patrick went utterly, completely still, and then he put his full weight on the boot on Mercer's chest and barked, '*What did you just say?*'

'Pat! Pat, you'll kill him!' Bryn blurted. From the sharp cry Mercer let out, a rib had already snapped. And Patrick clearly didn't care. '*Pat!*'

Even Liam was looking alarmed, and moving toward his boss with the clear intent of pulling him off – until Pat sent him a look that stopped him cold in his tracks. 'Mercer,' Pat said. 'I'm only going to say it one more time, and then I will stomp on your chest as many times as it takes to splinter your breastbone and get your complete fucking attention. *What did you say?*'

'Jane,' Mercer wheezed. He'd gone gray with pain, and a good deal of actual fear. 'They have Jane working for them. She's one of them.'

Patrick took his foot off of Mercer and took two long steps back, as if he didn't trust himself not to follow through, regardless. There was something black and totally out of control inside him, something that shocked Bryn down to the core; she'd known he was capable of violence, but this was beyond all that.

This was feral.

'Pat?' she asked. He looked up at her, then down, as if he couldn't hold her stare. 'Pat, who's Jane?'

'My wife,' he said. 'Jane was my wife.'

CHAPTER FIFTEEN

My wife.

Jane.

My wife.

It kept running through Bryn's head like white noise, and she just couldn't comprehend it. He didn't have a wife. He *couldn't* have a wife, because he'd never, ever talked about it. And if he ever had married someone, it certainly, absolutely could not be *Jane*.

That was utterly impossible. He was a good man, a decent man, and Jane . . . Jane was everything foul in the world. A walking toxic spill.

'That's not true,' Bryn said aloud. 'Pat – that's just not *true*.' She stared at him, but he'd veered away as if he didn't dare come close to her now, either. He stalked toward the corner, boots scraping on the dusty concrete, fists clenched.

Lying on the ground, Mercer laughed, but it dissolved

into painful coughing. He rolled on his side and spit up blood. 'Ask him,' he said, and grinned with bloody teeth. 'In case you think I'm making it up, her full name is Jane Desmond Franklin.'

'She's dead,' Patrick flung back without turning.

'Well, I think we could all agree, there's dead and then there's really, sincerely *dead*. And Jane's the former, not the latter. By the way, congratulations on your taste in women, you do run to type, my man. Bryn's got that same crazy, strong energy, doesn't she? Doesn't give up. Just like . . . Jane. You know, before.'

Patrick turned and went for him, and if Liam hadn't gotten in his way and deflected the rush, Bryn was utterly sure that Mercer would have been bleeding out his life on the concrete. She couldn't move. She felt as if she'd been nailed in place, then frozen solid.

Liam shoved Patrick back with surprising strength and shouted, 'Don't play his game!' Patrick subsided, breathing hard, eyes fixed on Mercer's laughing face. Liam swung around on Mercer himself. 'Jane cannot be alive.'

'Ask Bryn about her.'

'Bryn—' Liam glanced at her, and his eyes widened. 'Bryn?'

Something inside her had just . . . shut down, so her voice came out flat and mechanical as she said, 'There was a woman. She said her name was Jane. She's the one who was in charge, who took Jeff, who got me.' *Who took me apart. Jane. Jane Jane Jane. Spider to my fly.*

'It's the same woman,' Mercer said. 'Freddy saw her.'

'I did one better than that,' Freddy said. 'Check my cell phone. Coat pocket.'

Liam knelt beside him and got the phone out. He turned it on and rose to his feet, staring at the screen in disbelief.

Patrick came to join him, took the phone out of his unresisting hand, and what was in his face as he gazed at the picture wasn't disbelief at all. It was the face of a man gazing into his own burning and inevitable hell.

He turned off the phone and dropped it on the ground, and paced away, head down.

'She can't be,' Bryn said. 'She can't be your *wife*.' In no universe did that make any sense at all. Tectonic plates shifted inside, broke open, and lava scorched her soul to ashes. 'Patrick, *tell me she isn't your wife*.'

Patrick didn't speak. Didn't even look her way. It was as if he was trapped in a black, black box somewhere far from here.

It was Liam who said, in a very shaken tone, 'She was, once. They were married when both were in the military, then divorced. She was killed in action.'

'They *said* she was killed in action,' Mercer said. He sounded smug now, and oddly delighted. 'I had her file, you know. She went from black ops to so deep under cover even *you* weren't read in, Patrick. And she wanted it that way. When she came to us as part of the military program, we were explicitly told you were not to have any information. But then, the restraining order you had against her was something of a clue you might not want further contact.'

Patrick stopped walking, but he didn't turn in their direction. His head stayed down. 'Military program,' he repeated. His voice was soft, but it echoed through the concrete room. 'There was no military program. It was terminated before the test subjects arrived.'

'So the records state,' Mercer said. 'I only had a couple of successes out of it in any case. And I don't really consider Jane *successful*. She was described to me as a diamond in the rough, and I think that was very accurate; the problem with diamonds is that they shatter if cut the wrong way. And Jane shattered. She just . . . enjoyed it.'

'She was insane long before that,' Liam said flatly.

Fast Freddy laughed. 'You know, there's a rule that says don't stick your dick in crazy. Should have remembered that one, *Patrick*.'

Patrick made a sound that Bryn had never heard before – warning, threat, an animal fury that raised the hair on her neck and chill bumps on her arms. He turned, and there was a shine in his eyes that made even Fast Freddy's smile vanish. 'You don't know what happened to her,' he almost whispered. 'So shut your mouth before I rip your jaw off.' Whatever history there was between him and Jane was . . . monumental, Bryn realized. Fear, anger, loathing, a complicated kind of pity, horror, maybe even a little damaged and fragile love.

No. No, you can't. You can't feel anything for her. What she did to me . . . Jane had been the one to inflict the damage, to drink up Bryn's pain and blood and tears, but it was *Patrick* who cut her now, to the core.

His feelings for Jane, *about* Jane, were a kind of betrayal she'd never been prepared to feel.

Patrick's wife. Jane.

It changed everything, tainted everything. If he'd hated the woman, if he'd just purely *loathed* her, it might have been okay; Bryn could have learned to live with that. But it had been that tiny little flash of compassion, of regret, that had destroyed her.

And now he looked at Bryn, and she looked at him, and she didn't understand him at all, not at *all*. He was a man who'd romanced *Jane*. Who'd kissed *Jane*. Who'd dreamed of a family with *Jane*.

It didn't even matter if it had ended in bitterness, divorce, anger. He'd loved her, once, and that made Bryn want to die.

'We have to go,' she said. Her voice still had that eerie sound, flat and mechanical, unfeeling, as if the nanites were talking for her. 'If they can track me, we can't hide here. We need to go somewhere safe.'

Liam looked hugely relieved at that, pitifully grateful that they didn't have to discuss *Jane*. 'The mansion is strong, but not defensible against a genuine assault. This place, on the other hand—'

'No,' Patrick said. His voice was rough and low, but

under control again. He blinked, and that animal shine left his eyes. 'Can't stay here. She came here once. She'd know its weak spots.' *She* meant *Jane*. Now that his anger had passed, he had that stricken look again, as if he was afraid he'd gone mad.

She was wondering if *she'd* gone mad. If all this was some dream she'd escaped into, to evade the reality of Jane and her cutting smiles. Maybe none of this was really happening. That would, in fact, be better. It'd mean that she didn't have to live in a world where Jane Desmond Franklin had been married to the man she loved.

Patrick finally snapped out of it long enough to say, 'Everyone in the van on the east side. We'll leave Mercer's car behind.'

'Everyone? Including these two?' Liam looked down at Freddy and Mercer, who were struggling against their bonds.

'I'm not leaving anyone for Jane. Not even them.' Patrick, to prove it, grabbed Fast Freddy under the shoulders and dead-dragged him to a door Bryn hadn't even noticed – it was small, inset, and he had to hunch to get through it as he shoved it open with Freddy's shirt collar crushed in one fist.

Liam grabbed Mercer and towed him toward the same exit.

Bryn didn't move for a moment. *I could just run*, she thought. *I could just run and get away from all this . . .*

But she needed the shots, didn't she? In the end, it

always came down to that, to one more day of survival. She didn't want to be in the same vehicle with Patrick right now, she didn't want to know how all this shook out. She didn't want to hear about his life with Jane.

She wanted it to not be true, at all.

Liam paused in the doorway and looked back at her, and said, 'You can't stay, Bryn. Come on. Hurry.'

'Who is he, Liam? Really?' It burst out of her in a rush, and she wished she could take it back, because the fact was, she really didn't even want to know. She already knew too much.

Liam shook his head. 'Not the time. Come on. Now, Bryn; we have to clear the estate as well. Your sister's still there.'

That got her moving, finally; the idea that she'd let anything happen to Annalie was unthinkable. She'd done enough to her sister already – and once again, she'd plunged her into something uncontrollable, and dangerous. *Mr French.* She thought about her dog, too; she couldn't leave him behind. Jane would love to find something Bryn loved, just so she could take it apart.

She took a step, and – to her surprise – stumbled. Her thigh muscles felt weak, and trembled unsteadily as she righted herself. Her arms were tingling, too. Bryn knew this feeling, all too well; she felt chilled now, too, as the nanites exhausted their power and stopped their very necessary repairs to the ongoing destruction. Death couldn't be stopped, only delayed, and she could feel it creeping through her body like shadows.

Liam knew it, too, she saw it in his face. 'I'll give you the injection in the van,' he said. 'Hurry.'

She stopped and said, 'No.' Even Mercer, being dragged, looked taken by surprise. 'Give me a shot right now. I'm taking Mercer's car. *I'll* get Annie.'

'And go where?' Liam asked. 'If the people who held you have the tracking frequencies—'

'Then I'll lead them someplace they can't go,' Bryn said. 'Right to the gates of Pharmadene.' It was the only logical choice; if she couldn't hide, she could make it next to impossible for Jane and her bosses to get their hands on her, and Annalie. Let Patrick and Liam find their own hole to crawl in. *He lied to me, he should have told me about Jane, about his wife . . .*

She didn't say it, but she didn't have to; Liam knew. He opened a pocket in his vest, took out a syringe, and crossed to deliver the injection.

She hardly felt it at all. Her scale of pain had widened quite a bit.

When it was done, Liam smoothed his hand gently over the injection site, a gesture of comfort, and even that made her flinch. 'I'm sorry,' he said. 'Be careful. I'll tell him . . . something.'

'He should have told me something, too,' Bryn said. 'Liam – thank you. For everything.'

Then she turned and walked away.

* * *

The one shot that Liam had given her helped her maintain, but healing was, at this moment, beyond her reach. Bryn drove fast and recklessly, and swore under her breath at her lack of a cell phone to call ahead to Annie. *She'll be all right.*

She'd better be all right, or I'll kill Jane for that, too. Over and over and over.

Upon her tire-screeching arrival, the mansion looked the same as it ever had – gates shut and locked, everything right and proper. The gardeners were finishing for the day, and rolling the plastic bins down toward the pickup point on the street; they waved to her as she drove in. All very normal.

Except her skin still looked gray and slack over her muscles, and she could feel the *wrongness* inside her. The big industrial refrigerator in the kitchen held the lockbox with the last of Manny's special formula shots; she'd grab those, inject two, and take the rest with her. And the box of inhibitors; she and Annalie would need those, if they were to rely on the Pharmadene formula of Returné. The idea of being under the control of those built-in Protocols didn't sound like something Bryn could handle. Not now.

Her self-control was like a thin, fragile crust over a vast abyss of betrayal; she tried not to think of what was going to happen when she finally broke through it and fell into that boiling cauldron of emotion. She'd loved Patrick, *really* loved him, and the damage he'd done to her was as great, in its own way, as Jane had managed.

Bryn parked Mercer's sedan and ran up front steps – or tried. Her legs felt clumsy, as if the nerves were only making partial contact with the muscles. It took three tries to fit her key into the locks on the door. She heard Mr French barking on the other side.

As she stepped in, his glad rush toward her skidded to a stop, and he backed up a couple of tentative steps with a whine of puzzled distrust.

'Oh, sweetie,' Bryn said. 'It's okay. I'm still me.'

Mr French took another step back, still whining. From the library doorway, one of the house's Rottweilers – Maxine, Liam's favorite – advanced stiff-legged and growling.

'Annie!' Bryn yelled. 'Annie, get down here!'

'Bryn?' Her sister's voice echoed faintly from somewhere upstairs. 'Oh thank God, I was so worried, Patrick was going out of his mind . . .' She appeared at the railing on the second floor and paused, eyes going wide. 'What—?'

Maxine was steadily advancing on Bryn, who stood very still, trying not to look like any more of a threat than she already did. The Rottweiler was normally very sweet, but she was in guard mode now, and Bryn no longer smelled like someone who belonged here.

She smelled like *danger*.

'Call her off,' Bryn said. 'Hurry.'

Mr French had backed all the way to the stairs, clearly torn by confusion – he *wanted* to protect her, but his instincts were all in conflict with his senses. Maxine wasn't conflicted at all. She just wanted Bryn *gone*.

Annalie hurried breathlessly down the stairs. 'Maxine!' She clapped her hands sharply. The Rottie didn't even glance her way. Liam was her master, and the others were just tolerated guests. 'Maxine, *stop*!'

She grabbed the dog by her collar just as Maxine's growl dipped down to a truly menacing range. Maxine, surprised, tried to lunge forward, but Annalie held on and dragged her back over the slick marble floor, into the library, and blocked her way out until she could slide the door shut and trap the dog inside. Maxine wasn't one for barking, but she did then, deep-throated and vicious sounds of alarm. The scrabble of her claws against the wood made Bryn wince. 'Jesus!' Annie said, and backed away from the door, then turned to look at her. 'Oh. Oh God.'

'I need shots,' Bryn said. Her throat felt horribly dry, and her voice sounded thin. This was happening much faster than she was used to, but then, she'd been through a lot; the stabilizing influence of the single shot Liam had given her was wearing off incredibly fast. 'Mr French—'

He was huddling against Annie's leg. Her sister knelt and petted him, then picked him up. Mr French didn't generally like being carried, but he didn't resist this time.

And he never stopped watching Bryn with that dark, confused, betrayed stare.

'Come on,' Annie said. 'Let's get you fixed up.' She sounded less bothered than Bryn would have thought, but then again, Annie had been through six months with Mercer and Fast Freddy. 'Where *were* you?'

'At a nursing home.'

'I'm serious.'

'So am I,' Bryn said. She followed Annie into the back kitchen, spotlessly clean as always. 'I can't believe they left you alone here.'

'Well, there wasn't much choice, apparently. Liam said he couldn't let Patrick run off by himself, and Joe—' Annie pulled the lockbox from the refrigerator and put it on the table, then frowned. 'I don't know the combination.'

Bryn punched it in, opened the box, and uncapped one of the syringes before rolling up her sleeve and plunging the needle home. The burn of the nanites was especially tough this time, and she sank down into one of the dining chairs until the pain subsided enough to breathe. 'What about Joe?' She uncapped a second shot and rammed that one home as well. She just managed not to convulse this time, or scream. When the pounding faded from her ears, Annie was talking.

'. . . kids,' she said. 'I don't know where they went, but he was definite that he'd be back once they were safe, but I haven't seen him or heard from him. It's been . . . quiet.' Annie blinked, and Bryn saw tears shining on her cheeks before she hastily wiped them off with the back of one hand. 'Why is this happening to us? Is it me? Are these people after me?'

'No, not . . . it's not you, Annie.' She managed to get that out, somehow, even though the agony burning through her from head to toe was so great she thought her flesh might start to smolder. Then it started to fade, thankfully. Bryn felt a rush of warmth instead, the billions of tiny machines rushing through her body, searching for all of the million things to put right again. *It's going to be okay*, she told herself. 'Pack a bag. We have to go in about five minutes.'

'Go? Go where?'

'The place I used to work. Pharmadene.'

'But . . . you said that was the *last* place I should ever go!'

'I know. But things have changed. It's the only place we'll be safe. They can protect us there.'

'I don't know, maybe . . . maybe you should talk to Liam. Or Patrick. Here, I can call—'

Bryn grabbed her sister's arm and forced it down to the table, and took the phone out of her hand. 'No,' she said. 'No calling. No discussion. Go pack, *now*. In five minutes, meet me at the car.'

Annie stared at her, frowning, and pulled her arm free to rub it resentfully. 'I hope you know what the hell you're doing,' she said. 'Jesus, Bryn. What's eating you?'

Fear, Bryn thought. *Reality*. 'Just do it.'

Her sister left, taking Mr French with her. Bryn

cleared the used hypos and put them into the biohazard container near the trash can, then went upstairs herself to grab a few things. She didn't bother with anything she could replace – just the necessary overnight accessories and a couple of changes of clothing. A zip-up pair of low boots that provided both comfort and traction. She looked around the room a little blindly, but everything else was just noise now, just distractions she couldn't afford in this moment.

She took the bag downstairs and put it in the trunk.

Maxine had gone quiet behind the library door. Bryn checked her own skin; it still had a gray cast to it, but didn't look quite so off as it had. 'Max?' she said, and tapped on the wood. 'Maxine?' She got a low growl in response. Taking Maxine out of here would be difficult at best, and being trapped in a car with an angry, suspicious Rottweiler didn't seem like a very good plan. But the dogs didn't deserve what was likely to come calling here. If she wouldn't leave Mr French, she couldn't leave the other dogs, either.

So she got the rest of them rounded up – the greyhounds, the pug, and the other Rottie, who was much less suspicious – and put them in the back seat of the car together. Annie came back with her bag, and Mr French tagged at her heels; he sniffed at Bryn suspiciously, then barked and seemed comfortable enough to settle in near her again, though he didn't beg for a petting.

When Annie let her out, Maxine kept her distance,

too, but she didn't growl or attack. Still, there was something in the Rottweiler's steady attention that kept Bryn on her guard. 'Put her in a crate,' she said. There were travel crates, folding ones, stacked in the utility room off the kitchen, and Annie put one together and got Maxine inside; she and Bryn managed to fit the crate into the back of the car, barely. It was an uncomfortable fit with all the other dogs, even with the pug and Mr French up front – one on Annie's lap, one at her feet on the passenger side.

But it wouldn't be a long trip.

Bryn headed for Pharmadene.

'What *happened* to you?' Annie demanded as Bryn drove. Bryn didn't reply; her attention was focused around them, looking for any signs that Jane might have locked on already to her location. She was hyperaware now of the danger, and the ticking clock. 'Hey! Bryn, you're scaring me! Where's Patrick? And Liam? They went to meet you – are they okay? What *happened*?'

Annie wasn't going to shut up until she got some kind of answer, even a half-assed one, so Bryn finally said, 'I met them. Everything's fine. This is part of the plan. I can't tell you the details right now.'

'Oh,' Annie said, and sat back, crossing her arms. She got that thundercloud frown on her pretty face. 'I see. So you don't trust me. *Still*.'

'Jesus, Annie, why does everything have to be about

you?' For a wild, bitter moment, Bryn almost regretted making the trip to get her sister, but then she felt a surge of shame. 'I'm sorry. I didn't mean to snap at you, but . . . things are bad right now.'

Annie's frown faded, and she said, much more gently, 'Is that why Patrick's not here with you? Has something happened?'

'No.' *Yes.* 'Patrick's fine. Everybody's fine, we just . . . need to split up right now. For safety.' *Because I might kill him if I hear him say Jane's name again.* 'It'll be okay. We'll be safe here. The FBI will protect us.'

'Okay.' Annie didn't seem too convinced, but she contented herself with calming the excited, agitated pug wiggling around in her lap. Mr French was maintaining a dignified sitting position at her feet, leaning on her leg. The greyhounds and free Rottweiler prowled restlessly in the back, as nervous as Bryn herself felt.

She phoned Zaragosa when she made the turn-off for the Pharmadene front gates, and got his well-dressed assistant. 'This is Bryn Davis,' she said. 'I need to talk to your boss. Right now.'

'I'm sorry, Mr Zaragosa is in a meeting,' the assistant said. She could almost see his expression of total indifference. 'I can have him return your call, but he has a full calendar—'

'Tell Zaragosa that I am half a mile from the facility, and I'm coming in the front gate. It's his choice how that happens. I've got my sister with me—'

'Tell him about the dogs,' Annie whispered.

Bryn ignored her. '—and we need admittance to the grounds and a pass to get inside. It's important.'

'I'm sorry, but I was told your employment with Pharmadene had ended. That means you'll need to make an appointment to visit Mr Zaragosa, and your sister needs to undergo all the usual background checks—'

'*Jeremy.* You're not listening. Closed or open, I am *coming in the gate*. Make that happen so nobody has to get hurt in the process. And tell Zaragosa that people will probably be tracking me to your front door. Bad people who aren't going to be nearly as concerned about the well-being of your people as I am. Understood?'

'Hold,' he said, and she heard the soft, New Age music start playing. Bryn fought the urge to curse him, and didn't let up on the gas as she took the curves heading up the hill to where the Pharmadene property began.

'Bryn?' Annie said. The gates were in sight. Bryn didn't slow. 'Um, Bryn? Those are *closed*. And there's a guard.'

The hold music went off. 'Mr Zaragosa wants to speak with you, but you're going to have to wait.'

'Tell him I am one minute from crashing into his gate at seventy miles an hour. See if he can make a hole in his schedule for that.'

This time, she got hold *without* music. Annie, who was sitting tensely now, arms protectively around Mr French, said, 'Bryn, *slow down*.'

'I can't,' she said. 'We're playing chicken, Annie. The

first one who blinks, loses, and we can't be left out here. We're dead if they don't let us inside.'

'But—'

Mr Zaragosa's voice came on the line. 'Bryn, you can't just—'

'Thirty seconds from the front gates,' she said. 'It's going to take at least ten seconds for them to roll back. Your choice, but you've got a max of fifteen seconds to get it done once I stop talking.'

He only wasted one second in silence, then said, 'Gate's opening.'

'Not yet it isn't.'

'Jeremy's calling the guard. Slow down, Bryn. I swear, we're working on it.'

'Work faster.' Instincts were trying to pull her foot off the gas, but she fought them and kept going. She needed to see the guard making the effort, or it would be for nothing.

The guard ducked back into the shack and picked up the phone.

They were less than fifteen seconds from hitting the gates. 'Bryn!' Annie shouted, and Mr French barked, responding to the alarm in her voice. The greyhounds were moving agitatedly in the back seat, worried by the tension thickening the air.

I'm going to kill us all.

The guard hit the controls, and the gates began to roll back. Bryn hit the brakes, slowing fast, but even then, the front right bumper of the car caught the metal and crumpled. The car scraped through, but only just, and then the guard reversed the course of the gates behind them to wheel them shut as Bryn brought the vehicle to a skidding stop.

And then, of course, heavily armed guards surrounded the car as it came to a stop – a battalion of them, looked like. Bryn dropped the phone, killed the engine, and held up both hands. Annie looked frozen in place. 'Pretend like you just got busted by the cops,' Bryn said. 'Do exactly what they say. Don't argue, don't resist.'

Annie tentatively raised her hands, too. The dogs were all barking excitedly, except for the pug, who was now cowering on the floor between Annie's feet and next to Mr French. He just looked like he wanted some peace and quiet.

Bryn's and Annie's doors were pulled open at the same time, and Bryn popped her seat belt so the guard who reached in could pull her free without effort and send her face down to the pavement. Annie hit the ground on the other side of the car. Mr French bailed out and started trying to bite the guard holding Bryn, but he was kicked aside.

'Run!' she screamed at Mr French. He took a step back from her, looking confused. 'Run, you stupid dog!'

He wouldn't have, Bryn thought, but then one of the guards tried to grab him, and that sent him fleeing.

Chasing something was what the greyhounds did for

a living, so they jumped out of the open car door and took off in graceful leaps after him, followed by the pug. The Rottweiler followed, leaving Maxine still in the cage. She was snarling and fighting to get out.

The fleeing dogs ran for the parkland and woods beyond the building. Someone fired a shot, but it missed.

'Don't hurt them!' Bryn turned her head to yell. 'You sons of bitches!'

'No need for that,' said a voice from somewhere over her head, and she looked up to see the CEO of Pharmadene walking quickly toward them, trailed by his assistant Jeremy and a couple of others. 'Nobody will hurt the dogs.' He looked at the guard who had her down on the ground. 'Let her stand up.'

The guard held to the letter of the order, but he slipped handcuffs on her just to be safe. Zaragosa didn't object. He looked tired, Bryn thought, and careworn. Presiding over this place, keeping all these secrets, probably wasn't a restful occupation.

'Now,' he said. 'You want to tell me what's so critical you had to pull a stunt like that just to see me?'

'Sir, we should get this car out of here. It wasn't scanned properly,' a man at his side said – from his badge, he was some kind of high-level security officer by the name of Robinson. 'Should I kill this dog?'

'No need,' he said, and gestured to Jeremy. 'Let the dog go. Outside the gates.' He gave Bryn an apologetic half-smile. 'I love dogs. I'd have it brought inside but we really don't have any facilities for animals, other than in the labs. I assume you don't want it there.'

'*Hell* no,' Bryn said. The idea of seeing the dogs, especially *her* dog, in those cages made her shudder. She watched Jeremy pick up Maxine's crate by the handle and hold it at arm's length while the dog barked and snarled, and walk it toward the fences where the other dogs had disappeared. 'He should watch out. She's in a bad mood.'

'Mine isn't doing too well either, so why don't you tell me what you want, Bryn?'

'Do you really want to talk about this now? Right here?' Bryn asked. 'Because I can promise you, there will be something I say that all these people aren't cleared to hear.'

Zaragosa considered her for a long second, then nodded and turned to Robinson. 'Search and clear them, then bring them down to the conference room. C-17. I want badges on both of them, and two escorts each. Armed.'

That seemed extreme, but Bryn could see his point; she and Annie had just obtained access, by threat, to what should have been a highly secure government facility. If he was taking them inside, he'd do it cautiously. That was only good sense.

Of course, the safest thing to do would have been to shoot them in the heads and drag them back outside the fences to recover, but luckily, Zaragosa wasn't *quite* as cold-blooded as Bryn herself was.

Not yet, anyway.

She and Annie didn't resist the searches, although Annie made some smartly worded comments about hands in places she hadn't invited them to go; Bryn, who'd recently undergone a cavity search by Patrick McCallister's *wife*, didn't much care. She listened to the lectures on security procedures, indicated her agreement, and got escorted to the elevator along with Annie and four armed personnel.

She expected to go up to the executive offices.

Instead, the elevator went *down*. Instead of showing the spacious atrium view, suddenly the glass walls were full of views of concrete. Bryn felt claustrophobia setting in, and a scraping sense of worry. 'I thought we were going to a conference room,' she said. Robinson was one of the four security personnel, and he sent her a sideways glance.

'You are,' he said. 'C-17. It's below ground.'

It was part of the lab complex. As the doors opened on thick glass, white walls, familiar awful *white walls*, Bryn felt the worry turn to a sickening flood of dread and panic, but she breathed in slowly and tried to keep it at bay.

They walked *right past* the white room with the drain, the one where she'd been confined to rot. It was sparkling clean. If anyone had died there, had their decayed flesh scrubbed off the tiles and washed away, there was no sign of it.

This was *not right*. Bryn felt it stinging all over her,

and the sharp, bitter taste of fear filled her mouth like acid. 'I want to talk to Riley Block,' she said, and resisted a little when they tried to hurry her along. 'Get her!'

Robinson said, 'No can do. Agent Block has been reassigned to another project.'

'*Reassigned*?' Bryn repeated. 'When? By whose order?' There was no way that would happen, unless Riley herself had requested it, or something spectacularly bad had blown up in her face, politically speaking – bad enough to need a scapegoat at the highest levels. Riley might hate the assignment at Pharmadene, but she'd never walk away from it – and the government wouldn't let her, because they didn't need more eyes on those top-secret files than was strictly necessary. Riley was read in. She'd stay.

'Sorry, don't know the details, lady. Above my pay grade,' Robinson said, and led them past doors marked with lurid biohazard stickers, secured with keypads and scanners. Nothing was marked, except with numbers. He paused at C-17, which didn't have any warnings on it, and keyed in a code to open the door, then ushered Bryn and Annie inside.

This isn't right, Bryn thought. *Not right at all.* She had a terrible, sickening sense of having made the worst choice of her life . . . and it was too late, way too late, to change it.

It was, to Bryn's huge relief, a conference room, after all; she'd been half-expecting some kind of vivisection lab with autopsy tables. *Or that furnace, that horrible furnace.*

This wasn't the showroom conference room, either; it held a battered long table, some less-than-new chairs, and whiteboard walls with dry-erase markers scattered randomly over every surface. Some of what had been scribbled there remained ghostly on the surface, even after cleaning. Formulas. Equations. Molecular drawings.

Zaragosa, already seated at the table, nodded to Robinson and said, 'You stay, Pete. Bryn and . . . Annalie, right? Please sit down. The rest of you, outside.' Meaning that the three extra security guards were firepower, but not cleared all the way for the kind of conversation they were about to have. Robinson obviously was.

Without asking, Robinson took the handcuffs off of Bryn, and then Annie, and fetched them each a sealed bottle of water from a built-in fridge. He tossed one to Zaragosa as well, who thanked him and cracked the seal to drink, as if he knew they'd want some reassurance that it wasn't drugged.

It wouldn't have mattered, frankly; she didn't waste a second in unscrewing the top anyway. Bryn was shocked at how good the water tasted. She hadn't realized how thirsty she'd been.

Annie didn't drink. She looked wary, pale, and terrified, and Bryn reached over and took her hand, drawing a startled flinch. 'Hey,' she said. 'It's okay.

We're okay.' She turned her attention to Zaragosa. 'I'm going to confess up front that I used you. I needed to get us somewhere safe, somewhere the people who were just holding me *can't* reach. The only place I know is here, inside Pharmadene.'

'You're talking about the same ones who slaughtered those people at Graydon,' Zaragosa said. 'The ones who've been picking off our Revived employees, one by one.'

'You knew about that?'

'Yes. Riley kept me informed of the disappearances, and the developments at Graydon.'

Don't trust Riley, he'd written on the back of his business card, yet he'd trusted her himself. Odd. 'How many of your people have gone missing?' she asked.

'Twenty-three that Riley was able to discover,' he said. 'It's possible a few of those have run away instead of being taken, but if so, they've figured out how to beat the tracking nanites. Like you did, when you first escaped.'

'I didn't beat the trackers. I had them scraped off my bones. It wasn't pleasant.'

'Evidently, they've grown back,' Zaragosa said. 'Mr Robinson says you're broadcasting a signal, loud and clear.'

'That's part of why I came here,' Bryn said. 'Because I'm being tracked, and I can't afford to lead the people who are following me anywhere else. You've got a hardened facility, you've got armed guards and security countermeasures, with the strength of the government behind you. Anywhere else would be vulnerable . . . where's Riley Block?' It was a strange segue, but Bryn couldn't keep her mind off the agent's absence. It bothered her, deeply.

Zaragosa shrugged. 'Agent Block was reassigned by her own request.'

'Agent Block *asked* to be reassigned when there were people she was in charge of protecting who'd gone missing? She never struck me as the type to break down and walk away from people in trouble. People she *knew*.'

'I only knew her professionally, not personally; I can't tell you what was going on in her head,' he replied. 'Only that the paperwork crossed my desk, I signed, and she left. It was the best thing, really. She wasn't entirely trustworthy. Let's get back to the issue at hand – what happened to you, exactly?'

Too much to tell you, Bryn thought, but she condensed it down, describing the failed attempt to abduct her at her funeral home, and then the successful coercive operation that had taken her to the nursing home. She skipped Jane altogether because even thinking about the woman made her also think of Patrick, and that was like putting her hand on a hot stove. *Operative* was a much less painful way to describe the woman. *An operative questioned me at length.*

'A nursing home,' Zaragosa repeated, when she was done. 'You're sure about this?'

'Completely. I can tell you approximately where it is. I wasn't driven far before I was released from the restraints in the ambulance, so there can't be that many possibilities. I'll know it on sight.'

Annie hadn't heard any of this, Bryn realized; now, she had tears in her eyes, and grabbed for Bryn's hand on the table. 'I'm sorry,' she whispered. 'We were so afraid for you, but I didn't know you'd be—'

'I'm all right,' Bryn said, and smiled. 'Look, no scars.'

Zaragosa gestured to Robinson, who leaned over; whatever passed between them was said in a whisper, and then Robinson rose and walked out of the room. The door clicked shut behind him. 'You're sure you could recognize the location,' Zaragosa said.

'If you've got a laptop with Google Earth I can show you the place right now. It's vital you get a strike team out there and take the people that run it into custody before they have time to destroy more evidence. There was something terrible going on out there. The people, the actual patients, they're in danger just by being around the staff. Trust me, nobody has their best interests at heart in there.'

'Robinson's fetching help now,' Zaragosa said, and leaned forward, hands clasped on top of the table. 'You said you were kept in a building that was separated from the main one. Do you have any idea what they were doing there?'

'Only vaguely,' Bryn said. 'The patients kept there

were in end-stage dementia, according to what they told me. They were using them as some kind of test subjects. No . . .' Bryn thought back, and frowned. The temperature of the room seemed to drop a few degrees. '*Incubators.*'

Zaragosa looked grim, and nodded. He sat back, folded his arms, and looked down, clearly deep in thought. 'That's very troubling,' he said. 'You heard them say that. That exact term.'

No, she'd heard that part from Jonathan Mercer, but she couldn't disclose that; the FBI had always made Mercer their primary target, and just now, she couldn't afford them splitting their focus. Jane and her crew were the first-order danger, not Mercer. 'Yes,' she said. 'I did.'

'Incubators for *what*, exactly?'

'That I don't know, but it doesn't sound good, does it?'

'No,' he agreed. 'Not at all.' There was a buzzing sound, and the locked conference door swung open. Robinson was back, and he'd brought a small laptop, which he put down on the table in front of Bryn. She navigated the map to the area she wanted, then zoomed in and switched to the street view. It took her all of three minutes to find the right place.

'There,' she said. She zoomed in on the sign in front. 'Arcadia Nursing and Rehabilitation. A division of the Fountain Group.'

Robinson nodded, closed the laptop, and stood up. Zaragosa motioned him out the door. 'What do you know about the Fountain Group?' he asked Bryn.

'Nothing. It's probably some kind of holding company, that's all I can guess. Why? Do you think they knew what was going on there?'

'If their patients are disappearing, then I'd assume someone knows; it's unlikely all this would happen without significant funding and approval from higher up.' He seemed deeply troubled now, and tired. Zaragosa scrubbed his hands with his face, as if trying to will himself awake, and Bryn realized that he looked as if he'd not been home in days – a wilted suit, a fresh shirt that looked as if it had been taken out of the package, crease lines intact, and a wicked growth of beard that wouldn't have been out of place on a street light-hugging drunk. Maybe Riley *had* broken under the strain. Bryn wouldn't have blamed her, really; the trauma and emotion of any of these jobs was brutal, and so was the toll they took. 'Please wait here, ladies. I'll be back in a moment.'

Zaragosa stood and walked to the door. Annie said, 'Um, if we're taking a bathroom break I could sure use one myself . . .' Her voice trailed off, because Zaragosa had kept on going, and the door clicked shut behind him. 'Wow. Rude. Is this guy some kind of friend of yours?'

'Not really. I don't think he's rude, just got a lot on his mind. He's in charge of this place. It's a lot to manage, and I just dropped some significant info on him he needs to look into.'

'Well, I think he's rude.' Annie went to the door and pulled the handle. It didn't open. 'Huh. Did he press a secret button or something? Because it's locked.' Bryn came to her side and tried it, which made Annie give her a roll of the eyes. 'Wow. Yeah, I tried that. Like I said. Locked. There must be some sort of trick to it . . .'

But there wasn't. It was a simple lever system – push down, and the door was supposed to open. Only it didn't.

Bryn looked around the room with its clean floor and whiteboard walls, and started feeling that bad, old claustrophobic impulse click in again. Another white room at Pharmadene. *Bad, very bad. Get out.* That was her panic talking; they were safe in the heart of a very strong facility, and nobody meant them harm. If Jane or her employers wanted to get to them here, they'd have a pitched battle on their hands, one that would draw public attention. Not even Jane would want that.

Bryn knocked on the door. 'Hey! Bathroom break?' No one answered. She tried the speakerphone on the counter, and when the reception desk picked up, she said, 'We've been accidentally locked in conference room C-17, and we need someone to open the door.'

'Of course,' the woman said, in a soothing, calm voice. 'Let me page someone for you. You're wearing Escorted Visitor badges, correct?'

'Yes.'

'Well, that's why the door won't open, then. Your encoded escorts aren't with you at the moment, so you're on lockdown until they return for you. I'm very sorry for the inconvenience, but I'm sure it will only be a few moments.'

Right on cue, Bryn heard the door lock buzz behind them, and smiled in relief at Annie. 'Thanks, they're here,' she said, and hung up the phone as she turned. 'So, can we have a bathroom . . .' Her voice died, locked tight in her throat.

Because *Jane Desmond Franklin* walked into the room, and behind her came Mr Robinson, and his armed security guards. Jane had on basic black that mimicked fatigues, and she'd tied her hair back in a sloppy bun, but it was definitely her.

She can't be here. She can't.

Jane smiled in slow delight at the look on Bryn's face. 'Awww,' she said. 'That's really adorable. You just don't get it, do you, sweetie? Frying pan, fire? Escaping *into* prison? I have to hand it to you, it would have been a really good strategy, except for, you know, being entirely wrong.' She turned her gaze on Annalie, and the smile widened. 'And who's your little friend? Oh, that's right. *Annalie*. Your sister. Nice to meet you, Annie.'

'Uh . . .' Annie shot a look at Bryn, and was evidently unnerved and confused by her stillness. 'Hi, I guess?'

'Sit down,' Jane said to both of them. 'You aren't going anywhere until I let you.'

'Where's Zaragosa?' Bryn asked. She licked suddenly dry lips. *No, no, this can't be happening, he's FBI, this is a government-run facility . . .*

Yeah, and you should always trust the government, right? She could almost hear Joe Fideli's lightly sarcastic response in her head. *They're always so damn trustworthy.*

'Mr Zaragosa has delegated responsibility for this particular operation to me,' Jane said. 'You won't be seeing him again, which is probably a blessing, right? Boring man. Accountant, you know, all about the numbers. The funny thing is, nobody blames the accountants; they seem so unthreatening. But I guarantee you accountants have killed more people in this world than soldiers.' She read the sudden wild impulse to fight in Bryn's shift of body weight, and shifted her own to match, going from languid to feral in a second. 'Don't.' It was a blunt, cold word. No smile this time, no *sweetie*. 'You're both Revived, and so am I. You might be able to take me, Bryn, I'll give you credit for your ferocity, if not your skills. But the fact is you can't take me *and* make it out the door before one of my friends here shoots you dead. So let's not play. If I was you, I'd bide my time, wait it out.'

That, Bryn thought, was good advice, even coming from Jane. She eased up, took a slow breath, and glanced at Annie. Her sister was milky-pale, and very confused. 'Bryn? You know her?'

'Oh, we're almost related,' Jane assured her, and draped herself over a handy chair like a sun-drowsy lioness. 'I'm Patrick's wife.'

'Ex,' Bryn said. Just for the hell of it. That earned her a flicker of a cold glance.

Annie's face was so blank that it strongly resembled the whiteboard. 'That's impossible,' she said. 'You mean *Patrick* Patrick?'

'No, I mean the other one. *Yes,* dear, *that* Patrick. Under whose roof you've been living these past couple of days. The one who's fucking your sister.' Jane outright laughed at the expression on Bryn's face. 'Do you really think I don't keep track of who's around him? That last was just a guess, by the way, but it was pretty safe. I knew you were playing house together, and since you aren't five I'd assume you were getting busy. Trust me. I know he's hard to resist.'

Annie's mouth opened, then snapped shut. Bryn thought about trying to rip Jane's throat out, again, but the same logic that had held her still thirty seconds before still held true. Jane *wanted* her to attack, was prodding her to do it like a picador with a bull. She wanted Bryn angry enough to ignore opportunities, and she was waving the red flag of Patrick to do it.

You have to be smarter.

'What's this about? The nursing home? No, I'll bet it

was something else,' Bryn said. 'Zaragosa got nervous once I talked about incubators. He was asking questions to find out how much I knew, and once I knew those things, it was obvious I knew too much. Right?'

'Oh, don't beat yourself up. He was going to kill you anyway, whatever you did or didn't know; fact is, he called me at Arcadia and told me to just get rid of you. *I* was all for keeping you alive until we knew everything you knew. It's Zaragosa who wanted you sent straight to the oven.'

'It's been Pharmadene all along,' Bryn said. She felt a little numb, and bizarrely unsurprised. 'Graydon was your janitorial staff. You've been eliminating the Revived. But if that's true, why send me to them at all? Zaragosa could have killed that—'

'Riley was the one who made the connection,' Jane said. 'And she made it public above his pay grade. So Zaragosa had to be seen to take action. He figured by using you we could send you into a trap, get you blown to bits, and take care of two birds with one stone. Like I said, he's an accountant. All about saving resources. And it isn't Pharmadene, sweetie. Pharmadene doesn't exist anymore, except as a name on a letterhead. The government controls it, you're absolutely right about that, but you know what the government is particularly good at doing?'

'Screwing up?' Annie said.

'Huh,' Jane said, and gave Annalie a longer, more

thoughtful look. 'That's a valid point. But no. They like to give work to *contractors*. The FBI is overworked and underpaid, and they've got terrorists to chase, not to mention interstate bank robbers and kidnappers and serial killers.'

'So they outsourced,' Bryn said. 'Outsourced *what*, exactly?'

Jane put a finger to her lips, crossing an impish smile. 'That would be telling,' she said. 'Would you like to guess?'

'The incubation?'

'Nice, for shooting blind.'

'Why did he make me point out the facility?'

'Killing time,' Jane shrugged. 'I was late getting here. And I guess he just wanted to confirm that you really did know where you were kept. Last nail in your coffin, Bryn. By the way, FG runs about a thousand other medically related businesses, but their real business happens to be in bioweapons research and development. Who told you about the incubation process?'

The question was slipped in smoothly, in the same lazy tone, but Bryn's nerves were raw and razor sharp. She didn't answer. She and Jane continued to exchange stares for so long that Bryn lost count of her heartbeats, and then Jane finally shrugged.

'Doesn't really matter,' she said. 'You have a pretty limited circle of friends, Bryn. We roll them up, we get everyone who might know. Sorry, Annie, but that includes family, too. You're just along for the ride. Sucks, I know.' Jane looked over her shoulder to Robinson. 'Pete, do we have a twenty on Patrick?'

'Not at present,' he said. 'I have a team at the estate, but nobody's home. She even brought the dogs with her, which means McCallister and the butler aren't planning to come back.'

'Do you know where they are, Bryn?'

'Not a clue,' she said. 'And he's not a butler.'

'Amusing that you think that matters, Bryn. All right. This has been really nice, and Annie, lovely to meet you, but I've got to get back to work tracking down all the cockroaches running from the light. Tedious.' Jane rose and went to the door, opened it, and said, 'In case you're wondering, the oven you saw on the surveillance? That's here. It's where they dispose of live Revivals they're done using. Sorry I can't watch, but I'll be sure to run the tape later.'

The door slammed shut behind her with a boom, and Bryn and Annie were left with Robinson and his guards. The man had a blank, soulless look in his eyes. There was no point in appealing to his humanity, Bryn realized; he didn't see either one of them as remotely like him.

'Let's go,' he said. 'Now.'

CHAPTER SIXTEEN

There was a time for fighting for their lives, and it came as they stepped outside the conference room.

Annie had been the first one out, and her flinch and attempt to pull free of the guard holding her was Bryn's first clue that something was wrong – *more* wrong. Then she caught a glimpse of the two medical gurneys lined up in the hallway, complete with restraints, and experienced a horrible flashback of being strapped down, Jane, the spoon, the surveillance video of Jason screaming in the incinerator's flames . . .

And Bryn snapped. Hard and clean.

Her elbow caught the first guard right where it should – squarely in the nose, shattering it and sending him reeling back off balance. Bryn spun and followed with a sharp heel-of-the-hand blow that drove the broken bone up into his brain.

His eyes rolled up to show whites, and he dropped. Dead, or so badly disabled it wouldn't matter in terms of the fight. Bryn went down with him, which led to a confusion of people tripping over their bodies as she wrestled the gun out of his limp, warm hand.

She rolled, sending another guard reeling for balance, and while he was gaining it she shot him three times. The bullets entered under his chin and exited through the top of his skull in a bright-red mist.

Two down, but her window of opportunity had snapped shut. These weren't mall cops; they were highly trained security personnel, most likely with military backgrounds themselves. As she reached to retrieve the second guard's gun, she took fire from the third, the one holding Annie as a shield.

The bullets hit her in the side, the back, and the shoulder – not the head, which would have stopped her. The damage was probably fatal, but not immediately so, and she didn't fucking care. At all. Bryn's legs went numb, but she twisted around and aimed left-handed.

The agent was almost completely covered up by her sister, and he fired again, missing Bryn's head by inches.

'Annie, *drop!*' she yelled, and shifted her aim to Robinson, who was in the process of drawing his sidearm. She killed him with three shots to the face, counting on the fact that it would take Annie a second to process her instructions, and sure enough, her sister had just decided to release her knees and drop when Bryn guided the muzzle back.

The agent was pulled inevitably forward to hold on to Annie – off balance and with too many things on his mind. He fired, but missed, and then his hostage's head dipped, and Bryn had a good, hard target.

She fired three more shots, and he fell backwards, dragging Annie with him. She fought free of his limp arms, grabbed his gun, and stumbled over to Bryn. 'Get up!' Annie screamed, and dragged at her elbow. 'God, Bryn, get up!'

'Can't,' Bryn said. She felt terribly calm just now. 'One of the bullets hit my spine, it'll take time to repair. Go, Annie.'

'Go *where*?' Her sister was crying, on the verge of hysteria. 'Bryn, *get up*!'

'Try to get to the loading docks, that's probably the best chance of an open exit.' There, on the opposite side of the hall, was the locked door with the ominous BIOHAZARD sticker. 'Drag Robinson down there. Hurry!'

Annie grabbed the fallen agent by the collar and dragged him over the guards' bodies, then down the hall. There were alarms sounding, and it was a matter of seconds before this would all be for nothing.

'Use his palm on the scanner!' she said. 'Then swipe his card!'

Annie did it, but she had to swipe twice before the lock clicked open. She grabbed it and swung it open, propped Robinson's body against it, and came back to grab Bryn under the arms and drag her in that direction. Then she kicked the dead agent out of the way and slammed the door shut. 'They can get in,' she said. 'And we kind of left a trail.' Of blood. Bryn's blood.

'I know that,' Bryn said. They were in an airlock with thick glass inset into the next door, and another scanner and – this time – a numeric keypad. Beyond that glass was another room.

It looked like a hospital ward. Gurneys, each docked at a medical monitoring station with read-outs.

Hundreds of gurneys, all full. Most of them were occupied by elderly people, but there were a few younger ones . . . and Bryn recognized two of the faces.

Riley Block and Chandra Patel. Hooked up to machines, lying as still and silent as all the others in that room. There were two people awake, wearing negative-pressure biohazard suits, checking machines and making notes on clipboards.

Bryn raised her gun and fired into the glass, one pull after another. The first two only cracked the surface; the fourth punched straight through, and the fifth broke half of the glass free of the mounting.

A new alarm started sounding. The two Pharmadene employees inside the room turned to stare in confusion, but Bryn wasn't worried about them; they were lab dweebs, unarmed and about as dangerous as the Pillsbury Doughboy in those inflated suits.

Annie didn't need prompting on this one; she reached

through the broken glass and turned the inner handle on the door, and silicone seals broke with a sound that made Bryn think of lips smacking, as if the room itself was consuming people. Annie dragged Bryn inside and slammed the inner door again, not that it would help, and propped her up against the wall.

Bryn's body tingled and zinged as the nanites zipped around frantically trying to repair her damage. She could feel one of the bullets, the one in her shoulder, being pushed slowly back out through the wound track. Nauseating. 'Unhook Riley and Chandra,' she said. 'Get them out of there.'

She pointed, and Annie rushed to do it, and pulled the central line free from Riley's bone-pale arm. There was a gout of blood, and then . . .

. . . Then, it almost instantly healed before Annie could even press her fingers over the spot.

'What . . . ?' Annie said, and looked to Bryn for some kind of explanation. 'Okay, that's weird, right? Even you don't heal that fast . . .'

Riley Block sat up with an indrawn gasp, and *screamed*. That was a very familiar sound, a lost and awful wail that trailed off into confusion, and then Riley opened her eyes.

Even from the distance of several feet away, Bryn could see how wrong those eyes were. They were almost . . . metallic, though after a few blinks the color changed and grew darker.

But there was something eerily reflective about them, still.

'Get Chandra. The next bed over,' Bryn said, and Annie went to the next bed where the small woman lay. She pulled out the IV, with the same instant-healing result.

Chandra's shriek was unearthly, and familiar.

'Riley?' Bryn said, and the woman's head turned toward the sound of her voice. The focus of those eyes woke something primitive inside Bryn, something that recognized a dangerous predator, and she went very, very still in the hopes it would go away. She couldn't speak. Couldn't even try to move, although now she felt a jolt of agony in her lower back that mean the spinal column was trying to reconnect severed nerves. Spinal cord damage took almost as long as brain injuries to heal; she'd be effectively paralyzed for fifteen minutes or more, depending on the extent of the carnage back there.

Now Chandra was sitting up in the bed next to her, graceful and feline. She swung her legs off the bed and stood up. She was naked beneath the sheet, and didn't seem to notice or care.

'Get out of here,' Riley whispered. 'Hurry, Bryn. Go.' She tried to get up, but it seemed she wasn't as well off as Chandra; she almost fell as she stood up.

Chandra walked straight to Bryn with calm, firm, unhurried strides. That darkly metallic shine was in her eyes, and it was more pronounced than it had been in

Riley's. Bryn wanted, very badly, to curl up into a ball and hide her eyes, and she didn't even know why. *Don't. Don't do it.* Her instincts were whispering, not screaming, as if they were afraid to be heard. *Don't let her touch you . . .*

When Bryn tried to pull herself back, Chandra simply closed the distance and grabbed her arm.

'No!' Riley shouted, and lunged forward, but she went down, hard. 'No, don't—'

A shattering wave of heat cascaded into Bryn, agony that started exactly where Chandra's skin touched hers, and she couldn't keep back a raw, thin scream. Annie pointed her stolen gun at Chandra, but that was useless and she knew it; she didn't even try to fire.

This is impossible, Bryn was thinking. It felt as if Chandra's very touch was injecting waves of nanites into her. The same burn she was used to feeling, but bigger, stronger, *more*. She could almost see the thin silver threads of transference between their two bodies, but it had to be imagination, *had* to be, she couldn't see something that small . . .

And then the heat, the agony, turned into waves of blessed cool *bliss* as the nanites traveled through her veins, her nerves, soothed every injury, every pain, like the golden touch of God Himself.

Chandra let go of her arm, and her suddenly blank eyes rolled up into her head to show the whites . . . and she collapsed in a heap on the floor.

Bryn blinked in confusion. Everything looked so

bright, so very *bright* and sharp and clear. She felt as if she focused, she could see, and see, and see, all the way down to the very tiniest particle. The excitement of that was so heady that she felt she might laugh. *I'm high*, she thought. *Higher than a fucking kite.* Nothing scared her. Nothing mattered – not the horrified look on Annie's face, or the fact that the door to the lab was being opened by their enemies, and they were all seconds away from being taken prisoner or shot to temporary death.

And then she saw Jane.

Patrick's wife.

That mattered.

Jane opened the inner door, careless of cuts from the glass, and stepped inside. She was armed with a P90, but she didn't point the lethal little machine gun; it hung on the strap around her chest. She wasn't smiling this time; Bryn had seen her look insane, and hungry, and delighted, and vicious, but this was a whole new expression.

She was *afraid*.

'Damn. You spoiled the harvesting,' Jane said. 'Someone's going to be *very* upset with you, Bryn. You took nanites that weren't meant for you, and we can't get them back now until the new colony matures.' She stepped back behind a couple of the guards. 'Concentrated fire on all of them, on my mark.'

Riley stood up, as she finally got her balance. So did Bryn, in an absolutely effortless motion like levitation – she didn't even feel her muscles working at all. Annie was staring at the two of them, then at Jane and the guards behind her, and she clearly had no idea what to do now.

But Bryn did. And as she exchanged a glance with Riley, she knew the agent knew it, too. 'Is Chandra dead?' Bryn asked.

'No,' Riley said. 'Just traumatized. She'll be all right in about an hour.' It was an hour they didn't have. 'I'm sorry she infected you, but her nanites were ready to be harvested. It's not a choice. It's a compulsion, to pass them on. Like the hunger.'

Bryn's feel-good wave crested and began to fall, it left her with a healed, finely calibrated body. She even felt that she could *think* faster. Possibly even react faster. It was her body, but . . . perfected.

'Don't be sorry,' she said. 'Whatever she did to me, it feels great.'

'For now,' Riley said. 'We'll discuss downsides later. For now . . .' she shot a glance at Jane, and the armed men who'd filled the rank behind her '. . . that's the only exit.'

Bryn bared her teeth in a grin. 'Then let's take it.'

Jane said, 'Mark,' and the two guards started shooting.

Bryn didn't even see Riley *move*, but suddenly she had closed the distance, and she was holding both of the guards' necks in her hands and *squeezing*. Bones snapped with a gruesome popping sound, and the two mens' bodies jerked, danced, and went limp except for residual tremors.

Dead.

By that time, Bryn – without even consciously willing it – had crossed the room and grabbed another one. She was aware he was shooting into her, but it didn't hurt, and it didn't even figure into her calculations. She was razor-sharp aware of the terror in his face, though.

That made her happy, for the approximately five seconds he was alive to actually feel the fear. It didn't occur to her then that she'd killed him with her bare hands, with *one blow*, until she was dropping the next one, and then the next. She was aware she was bleeding, but it was minor leaks, quickly closing up.

One of them fired straight into her face, and that stung; it took a second for the darkness to clear from her eyes, but then she was ripping his arm away at the elbow, and the blood, the *blood* was so red and clear and amazing that she involuntarily raised her fingers to her lips and tasted it.

Iron and fear.

Jane was gone. She'd run. And the guards were dead in pieces.

And Riley was *eating one*. She had an arm, raw and bloody, and she was chewing on it. That should have shocked Bryn, but it didn't, it seemed . . . right.

And the blood in Bryn's mouth, the blood she'd licked from her fingers, tasted *so good*. She reached down for one of the pieces of meat, not even thinking that it was part of a *person*, because the desire to refuel was so . . . so . . .

Someone was screaming.

Annie.

Bryn jolted back to herself with a shock. Annalie was huddled against the wall, hiding her face, still screaming like a little child. When Bryn touched her shoulder, Annie flinched and scuttled away, still screaming. The stark horror in her made Bryn freeze in place.

Riley dropped the arm she was holding. She didn't look surprised, or particularly shocked. She walked to a tray that held towels and took one that she used to wipe the blood from her hands and mouth, then brought a clean one over to Bryn. 'Here,' she said, and pressed it in her hands. 'Wipe your face, you're scaring your sister.'

'What—?' Bryn stared blankly at the towel, then raised it to her face and swiped it over her mouth. It came away red. Bloody. She felt a little surge of repulsion, and cleaned up in earnest, scrubbing her hands, her neck, her face until the skin tingled.

There was a taste in her mouth, iron and fear, and it horrified her that she still liked it. Didn't want to consider the consequences of that at all. 'What happened?' she asked, and didn't really want to know, she realized. 'Riley, *what did she do to me?*'

'Put you one up on the food chain,' Riley said. 'Let's go.'

The hallway outside the lab was deserted except for the bodies of the agents Bryn had killed before . . . *before.* She felt as if someone had drawn a dividing line across her life. Someone had, of course, the first time she'd died and been Revived, but this felt like an even bigger break. She didn't know what was ahead, but she knew it was *different*. 'What about Chandra?' she asked.

Riley shook her head. 'We can't carry her,' she said. 'She'll be too weak to move for a while. We have to leave her.'

The entire lab floor was locked down; every door was sealed shut. Riley finally recognized that she was naked, and stripped pants and a shirt from a fallen guard; she didn't bother with shoes. She did, however, pick up a gun – another P90 like the one Jane had been wearing. Someone had used it, Bryn thought; she could see the heat rising from the barrel. Maybe it was one of the bullets that Jane had left littering the floor behind her.

Whatever Chandra's invasive touch had done to her, injuries were processing much faster than before. She didn't even bleed much.

'They'll pump in gas,' Riley said. 'Try to suffocate us and keep us down until they can move us to the incinerators.' She checked the clip in the gun. 'It works. They managed to take down two others that way. We need to get off this level.'

'What did she do to me?'

Riley didn't even glance her way. 'I think our best bet is the elevator shaft. We can pry the doors and climb, but we need to start now. They'll be pumping the inert gas in soon, if they haven't already.'

She was right, Bryn realized; there was a breeze coming from the air vents, and a slightly sweet smell to it. Annalie seemed especially vulnerable to it, because she slowed down as they headed for the elevators; Bryn had to pull her along in a stumble, and then carry her.

As Riley pried open the doors, she said, 'It wasn't Chandra's fault. It was the nanites; they were ready for harvesting. Normally the docs come in and draw them off in a syringe when they mature, but they're programmed for self-transfer if the host is awake and mobile. They transfer the excess supply to the nearest identified ally.' The elevator shaft was empty, the car somewhere up above and likely locked down. Riley took a breath and jumped. She grabbed the cables and looked up. 'Let's go,' she said. 'Can you handle her weight?'

'Yes,' Bryn said. She wasn't sure – Annie wasn't exactly skin and bones – but Bryn 2.0 felt capable enough. Riley was climbing the steel cables bare-handed, which should have been impossible; since it wasn't, Bryn jumped and grabbed on. Annie's weight overbalanced her and almost sent her tumbling down the open shaft, but she clung to the cables with sudden, panicked strength, and began to inch her way up.

It wasn't hard. It hurt, but it wasn't hard at all.

Above her, Riley jumped like a cat and landed on the tiny metal ledge with her hands outstretched to either side to lock herself into the narrow space. She balanced herself and began to pry the doors apart.

They were waiting on the other side, and as the metal doors screeched apart, Bryn saw the hail of bullets hit Riley, punch through her body, and tear open bloody holes in their wake . . .

But the holes didn't bleed more than a few drops, and Riley lunged forward.

Bryn kept climbing, careful of her balance, and once she'd gotten to the opening, she swung around the cable, building momentum, and jumped as she held Annie tight against her shoulder.

She landed on bodies. It was a good thing Annie was still out, because it was gruesome. Riley was the only one still standing, and she looked . . . feral. There was a silvery, reflective shine deep in her eyes, and as Bryn watched, she lifted a raggedly severed arm and . . .

. . . And ate until the shine went away. Then she dropped the gnawed flesh, wiped her mouth on her shirt sleeve, and looked away. 'It's not a choice,' she said. It was the second time she'd mentioned that, Bryn thought. 'The nanites need energy. They take it how they can get it, it's part of the programming, and protein is what they crave.'

She was right, horribly and awfully right. Bryn should have found the heap of dismembered limbs sickening, but when her stomach complained, it was rumbling, not heaving. *Dear God, no, no let me not be hungry . . .*

She licked her lips and tasted blood. It was delicious.

'Keep moving,' Riley said.

This level was empty, too, but Bryn thought that there must have been personnel still alive and sealed up behind doors, because there was no attempt to gas them. Annalie woke up – groggy and confused, which was good because it meant maybe she wouldn't remember what had happened before so clearly. The stairs that Riley headed for were locked up, but that didn't seem to pose a problem anymore, to Upgraded Riley. She just smashed the locks, picked out the pieces, and led the way up.

They met Jane halfway to the next level. She was standing on the landing. 'You know I can't let you leave,' she said. She must have been afraid, Bryn thought, but there was nothing of that on her face, or in her body language. She just looked . . . hard, and uncompromising. 'Sorry.'

'*You* did this,' Riley said. 'We're just the lab rats. You're the ones who conducted the experiments. Can't blame us if it goes wrong.'

'You're not stupid, Riley, and you're not vicious. You know what happens if you get outside the Pharmadene building; you know the risk of vector infection. The government knows, too. If you make it even one floor closer to the world, they'll vaporize this place with a nuclear strike, because that's the *only way*. And I wouldn't bet that you and Bryn can survive that. You'll be taking most of San Diego with you in the process. Innocent lives.'

'Well, on the upside, we'd be taking *you*,' Bryn said. 'What do you mean, vector infection?'

Jane actually smiled a little. 'Those nanites inside you are self-replicating. That was what Fountain Group was tasked to create – self-replicating, self-powering nano-soldiers that don't need injections, and can convert others as they go. The only thing they haven't mastered yet is how to program them accurately for combat situations, but you know what? You're doing just fine without it.'

'You called it *harvest*,' Bryn said. 'You were using those people in the lab as incubators for the nanites, and harvesting the crops.'

'I told them that if they made them touch-transfer enabled it would be a mistake,' Jane said. 'But too late now. The rat's out of the cage, and all that crap. You can't leave here, Bryn, because you're a walking colony that's going to replicate, and when that happens, you'll pass it on. Vector infection. It's not even a choice.'

'It can only pass to someone without a live immune system,' Riley said. 'Don't let her spook you. You can't infect the living, only someone already Revived.'

'You sure about that?' Jane asked. 'Because I'm not. And the consequences are a global plague the likes of which only Revelations predicted. So you're not leaving. Are you?'

Bryn was dizzy with the imagined horror of it. Chandra hadn't been able to control the impulse to transfer the nanites, and the *hunger* . . . 'Self-powering,' Bryn whispered. 'The hunger. We'll eat anything, won't we? Even other people.' She wanted to be sick, but her body refused to allow it. No, the *nanites* refused. They were in charge now.

'Protein,' Jane said. 'Think about it. In battle, there's always a source of protein around. Living or dead. It's just good strategy.'

Bryn leaned against the stairwell wall, suddenly faint. She collapsed to a sitting position on the stairs.

'Don't give up,' Riley said. 'Bryn, *don't give up.*'

'Let Annie go,' Bryn said. 'She's not infected. Let her go, and I'll stay. I swear.'

'Oh, sweetie,' Jane said softly. She had a remorseless look in her eyes that was almost, almost sad. 'It isn't even vaguely a possibility that we're negotiating here.' A door opened above her on the landing, and she glanced up, but not with any surprise; she was clearly expecting reinforcements. 'See? You've got zero shot here, ladies. Absolutely ice-cold zero.'

'I'd recalculate that if I were you,' said Patrick McCallister, as he leaned over the railing and pointed a P90 directly at Jane's forehead. 'Hello, Jane.'

'Hello, Pat,' she said. Other than a flicker of her eyelids, and a slight tightening of muscles, her self-control was impressive. 'How'd you get in?'

'I had help,' he said. 'On your knees, Jane. Face the wall, hands up and flat, you know the drill.'

'You're a fool if you think you can take them out of here. Oh, it *can* be done, but you have got to ask yourself, Pat – *should* it be done? Because what you're taking out of here isn't your sweet little not-quite-dead girlfriend. This thing inside her skin, it's not really human anymore. And it's weaponized.'

Patrick's face tightened, and he failed to hide his fury; it shone in his eyes, impossible to miss. 'Not going to say it again. Knees. Wall. Hands.'

Jane shrugged and followed his orders, and that was when Bryn realized that McCallister wasn't alone. Joe Fideli was at his back, and Liam, and – dear God – *Manny Glickman*, wearing body armor and carrying a truly badass machine pistol. Pansy Taylor was with him.

'Joe,' Patrick said. 'Secure that bitch.'

'Securing the bitch, aye. Hey, how ya doing, Jane?' Joe jumped down onto the landing, pulled Jane's right arm behind her, snapped on cuffs, and then the left. He made sure they were tight, then zip-tied her ankles. 'I thought you were dead.'

'I was,' Jane said. 'And you're going to wish you were, too. Especially if you don't *listen*.'

'Knew I forgot something,' Joe said, and pulled a strip of duct tape from a row of them stuck to his pants. He put it over Jane's mouth. '*Now* you're secure.' He wasn't taking chances. He searched her and removed anything that could have possibly constituted a weapon, or a lock-pick, and propped her into the corner. She was trying to yell through the gag, and her eyes glittered furiously.

'You shouldn't be here,' Bryn said. She felt horribly numb now, and resigned. 'None of you should have come.'

Joe turned to Bryn and gave her the warmest, most heartbreaking smile she'd ever seen. 'Hey,' he said. 'Come on, cheer up. This is a rescue, not a wake.'

Riley put her hand on Bryn's shoulder and said, 'If we stay here, they'll burn us. There's no question about it. Annie, too.'

'And if we go?' Bryn raised her head and stared into Riley's face, saw the flash of silver in her eyes. Knew it was in her own. 'My *God*, Riley. Look at what we *are*.'

'We're what they made us,' Riley said. 'And we'll have to deal with that. But *we will*.'

'No,' Bryn said. 'I can't. I won't take the risk.' She pulled in a deep breath. 'Patrick. Jane's right. You can't take us out of here. We're infected.'

'I know,' Patrick said. 'Manny figured out the incubations, and what they were planning to produce. We'll take precautions, but I'm not letting you stay here and burn, Bryn. I can't.'

'You can't trust me. And I can't trust you,' she said, and met his eyes. She saw him flinch, and knew he was having the same reaction she'd felt on recognizing Riley's change. 'Go. Take Annie and *go*.'

'Shit,' Riley said. 'You mean that, don't you?' She looked past Bryn, and her eyes widened. 'Annie, *don't*!'

It was a bluff, and it worked, because for a split

second Bryn took her attention off of the threat in front of her, and looked toward her sister . . . who looked utterly shocked, and was definitely not attacking her.

Dammit.

Even her nanite-fueled reaction time wasn't enough to stop Riley from crushing her neck.

Bryn came back to life strapped down to a gurney – not with Velcro, but with heavy-duty leather and chains that probably would have held a ship's anchor, much less a somewhat woozy woman. Without leverage, there was no way to break free.

She was in the back of a van, and the van was moving.

Patrick McCallister was sitting next to her, staring down at her face. Annie and Riley were next to him, and Joe Fideli. She didn't see Liam, Manny or Pansy; she guessed they were up front in the cab of the truck.

'How?' she asked. 'How did you get us out?'

'I had help,' he said. 'The FBI wanted in; they knew something had gone wrong in there. I just tagged along. They were looking for a missing agent who'd tipped them to problems.' He glanced aside at Riley. 'I let them know she was probably still inside and in grave danger.' He looked grim and tense, and didn't quite meet Bryn's gaze. 'I knew you were headed to Pharmadene, and once we understood that Riley had gone missing, we knew that was no longer safe. Mercer talked about the new generation of nanites they were brewing; that was enough for the FBI to make the decision to move on them.'

Then how . . . ? 'They don't know about me and Riley,' Bryn said. 'You didn't tell them about us. About the nanites we're carrying and incubating.'

'I couldn't,' Patrick said. A muscle jumped in his jaw, and he tried to relax it. 'Riley says you won't be contagious, either of you, for about at least thirty days. It takes that long for the new generation being built inside you to mature.'

'Riley lies. You should remember that.'

'Sitting right here,' Riley murmured, but she didn't dispute it.

'I did remember,' he said. 'Manny pulled files from the servers, and she's telling the truth. We've got about thirty days to stop you and Riley from replicating. If we don't make it, Manny says he can still safely remove the excess nanites to storage and start over.'

Bryn realized she was crying – slow, inevitable tears of fury and failure. 'Her head was strapped down in place. She couldn't even shake it. 'You cannot take this risk. You *have* to turn us over. *God*, Patrick, we *eat people* and we can't be *stopped*. Did Riley tell you that? *Did she?*'

He didn't say anything to that. None of them did until finally Joe said, 'If it comes to burning you down, I won't let him get in the way, Bryn. But it ain't gonna come to that.'

'Trust me,' McCallister said, and took her hand. 'Please.'

'You should have told me about Jane,' she said. The

pain she was feeling inside was nothing the nanites could fix. 'God, Patrick, why didn't you tell me?'

'I would have, but it's not a pretty time of my life. I wanted . . . I wanted you to think better of me, just for a while. And I had no idea she was alive.' He shook his head. 'Doesn't matter. What matters is that I love you. And I'm not letting it end like this. We *will* stop this.'

It's too late, she thought. She could feel the nanites inside her, building their own future generations and destroying her life in the process. What if Jane was right? What if the nanites *could* infect regular, living people? What would stop them?

You will, she told herself. *And Riley. And Patrick. And Joe. And even Annie and Manny and Pansy. We will stop them.*

Patrick was holding her hand, and after the instinctive flinch of horror that she might somehow transfer her doom to him, she was grateful for that. For the warmth, and the silent promises. She knew he hadn't lied to her about Jane; he would have told her. And she knew he didn't love Jane.

We will stop this. We have to.

She opened her eyes and met Patrick's steady, warm gaze. She didn't need to say what she was thinking. He knew. His fingers brushed the hair back from her forehead, and he pressed a gentle kiss there in a bloom of warmth. 'We will,' he said.

It was a promise she would have to trust.

TRACK LIST

As always, I love my music, so I'm sharing my track list with you! Please check out these great artists and if you enjoy them, give them money, 'cause that's how they keep on making more.

'Rags and Bones'	Thea Gilmore
'This Night'	Black Lab
'The Chain'	Three Days Grace
'Into Pieces'	State Line Empire
'Sonata Rabidus'	Modus Operandi
'My Body is a Cage'	Peter Gabriel
'Lies'	McFly
'Guns'	Lovehammers
'Start Shootin''	Little People
'Violins and Violence'	Knives at Noon
'Days Are Forgotten'	Kasabian
'Rising River'	Id Guinness
'Red Rocking Chair'	Rani Arbo & Daisy Mayhem
'When Daylight Dies'	Heaven Below
'Bleed Me Dry'	The Murder of My Sweet
'Mumbai's the Word'	Michael Giacchino

Acknowledgements

So many lovely people have been enthusiastic and supportive, but I have to give a special shout-out to Sarah Weiss, whose eleventh-hour text messages were absolutely wonderful. Thanks for the candles, Sarah, particularly the one for Our Lady of Deadlines. I'm burning it at both ends!

And to my family and friends who suffered through the dreaded Deadline During Christmas again. Thanks for sticking with me. Again.

If you enjoyed *Two Weeks' Notice,* read on to find out about other books by Rachel Caine . . .

To discover more great fiction and
to place an order visit our website at
www.allisonandbusby.com
or call us on
020 7580 1080

Also by Rachel Caine

The Weather Warden series

The Wardens Association has been around pretty much forever. Some Wardens control fire, others control earth, water, or wind – and the most powerful can control more than one element. Without Wardens, Mother Nature would wipe humanity off the face of the earth. Joanne Baldwin – fashion addict and professional, if unwilling, hero – is part of the thin, well-dressed line protecting the innocent.